Markinfield Addey

Life and Imprisonment of Jefferson Davis

together with The life and military career of Stonewall Jackson, from authentic

sources

Markinfield Addey

Life and Imprisonment of Jefferson Davis
together with The life and military career of Stonewall Jackson, from authentic sources

ISBN/EAN: 9783337091927

Printed in Europe, USA, Canada, Australia, Japan

Cover: Foto ©Raphael Reischuk / pixelio.de

More available books at **www.hansebooks.com**

LIFE AND IMPRISONMENT

OF

JEFFERSON DAVIS,

TOGETHER WITH THE

LIFE AND MILITARY CAREER

OF

STONEWALL JACKSON,

FROM AUTHENTIC SOURCES.

WITH PORTRAITS OF JEFF. DAVIS, STONEWALL
JACKSON AND GEN. R. E. LEE.

———⟶•⟵———

NEW YORK:

M. DOOLADY, PUBLISHER,

448 BROOME STREET.

1866.

LIFE OF JEFFERSON DAVIS.

CHAPTER I.

Parentage and birth—His father a soldier in the American war of Independence—Removes to Kentucky, where Jefferson Davis is born—His father
again removes to Mississippi—Jefferson graduates at West Point—Enters
the army—Black Hawk war—Marries and becomes a planter—Enters
Congress—Distinguished in the Mexican War—Elected to the United
States Senate.

SAMUEL DAVIS, the father of Jefferson Davis, was a soldier in
the American War of Independence, serving as a cavalry officer
in the local forces of the State of Georgia. From Georgia he
removed to Christian County, (now Todd Co.,) Kentucky, where
the Confederate leader was born, June 3, 1808. Soon after the
birth of his son, Samuel Davis removed to the State of Mississippi,
then only a territory of the United States, where he settled near
Woodville, in Wilkinson County.

By a singular coincidence, the same State in which Jefferson
Davis was born (Kentucky), a little more than half a year afterwards, witnessed the nativity of Abraham Lincoln. It would
seem as if even now was foreshadowed the divergence which
marked the future careers of these men. Only a very few years of
the childhood of each was passed in this Border State, when their

parents, again seized with the prevalent migratory passion of the country, removed to regions not more diametrically opposed in geographical than in social position.   Thomas Lincoln sought the wilds of free Indiana ; Samuel Davis elected to cast his destiny and that of his posterity in the slave-holding territory of Mississippi. Those anthropologists who hold man to be a natural cosmopolite, *may* be right in the physical aspect of the question, but socially and religiously, he is, alas, a denizen, imbibing and assimilating the ideas of his locality as he does its fruits !   Let the partizan, of whatever creed, who reads these lines, here pause and contradict history by sending Thomas Lincoln to Mississippi and Samuel Davis to Indiana !

After receiving a good academic education, Jefferson was sent to Transylvania College, Kentucky, where he remained until 1824, when he was appointed by President Monroe a cadet in the celebrated military school of the United States at West Point.   He graduated with honor in 1828, at twenty years of age.   He was soon after appointed brevet second lieutenant in the United States army, and at his own request, at once assigned to active service in a regiment commanded by Colonel Zachary Taylor.   He continued in the United States army for seven years, and served as an infantry and staff officer in the Black Hawk war of 1831–2 with distinction.   Mr. Davis's gallantry and skill were rewarded with a commission as first lieutenant of dragoons, in which capacity he was employed in 1834 in various expeditions against the Comanches, Pawnees, and other hostile Indian tribes.

After seven years of active service, Lieutenant Davis, in 1835, resigned his commission in the army.   Three years before his resignation he had married (clandestinely) a daughter of General Zachary Taylor, afterwards President of the United States.   He now retired to private life, and became a cotton planter in the State of Mississippi.   For several years he only varied the monotony of his retirement with such legal and political studies as fitted him for the very prominent political positions he afterwards occupied.   It was not until 1843 that he began to take an active part in public affairs.   He was from the first identified with the Democratic party, and, in 1844, was chosen one of the presidential electors of Mississippi, and in that capacity he cast the vote of his constituents for Mr. Polk, who was duly elected President.

In November, 1845, Mr. Davis was elected a member of the House of Representatives, where he soon proved himself an active, energetic, and able supporter of the measures of his party.   He participated actively in the discussions of the session on the tariff, the Oregon question, and more particularly upon the questions connected with the prosecution of the Mexican war, and upon the constitutional principles involved in the organization of State militia when called into the service of the United States.

Still imbued with the old attachment of his youth for military life, he could not resist an active participation in the Mexican war ; and being informed while in Congress, that the first regiment of Mississippi volunteers had elected him its colonel, he promptly resigned his seat and hastened to place himself at its head.   Overtaking his command at New Orleans on its way to the seat of war, he led it to reinforce the army of General Taylor on the Rio Grande.

Colonel Davis took an active part in the storming of Monterey,

September, 1846, and was one of the commissioners for arranging the terms of the capitulation of that city. In the beginning of the next year, February 23, 1847, was fought the fiercely contested battle of Buena Vista. In this engagement, he acquitted himself with great distinction. His regiment, attacked by an immensely superior force, for a long time maintained their ground wholly unsupported, while Colonel Davis himself, although severely wounded, remained in the saddle until the close of the action.

Of his conduct in that action it has been said that "Jefferson Davis at the head of the 'Mississippi rifles' had ventured to do that of which there is perhaps but one other example in the military history of modern times. During the invasion of the Crimea, at the battle of Inkerman, in one of those desperate charges, there was a British officer who ventured to receive the charge of the enemy without the precaution of having his men formed in a hollow square. They were drawn up in two lines, meeting at a point like an open fan, and received the charge of the Russians at the muzzles of their guns and repelled it. Sir Colin Campbell for this feat of arms, among others, was selected as the man to retrieve the fallen fortunes of England in India. He did, however, only what Jefferson Davis had previously done in Mexico, who in that trying hour, when with one last desperate effort to break the lines of the American army, the cavalry of Mexico was concentrated in one charge against the American line—then, I say, Jefferson Davis commanded his men to form in two lines extended as I have shown, and receive that charge of the Mexican horse with a plunging fire from the right and left from the Mississippi rifles, which repelled, and repelled for the last time, the charge of the hosts of Mexico."*

For his extraordinary gallantry in this engagement he was deservedly complimented by the commander-in-chief in his despatch of the 6th of March following.

The term of the mere handful that remained of the first Mississippi volunteers expired in July, 1847, and Mr. Davis was ordered home. He soon after received a high testimonial of the appreciation of his services at Washington, in the offer by President Polk of a commission as brigadier-general of volunteers. But Mr. Davis belonged even at that period of his political career to the extreme wing of the State-rights Democracy. At the session of Congress which immediately preceded the commencement of hostilities, he had taken a decided stand against the power of the general government to organize and officer the militia of the States even when engaged in the service of the general government. He could not therefore consistently accept an office in the State troops at the hands of the Federal executive, and refused the offer. This incident, though trivial enough in itself, is worth noticing, as at once illustrating the personal character and political principles of the late Confederate chief. The question had been decided against him by the vote of Congress, including a large portion of his own party, and the right of appointment was sanctioned, and on this occasion exercised by the now chief of that party. Yet such was the firmness or obstinacy of Mr. Davis, and such his estimate of the dignity and prerogatives of the separate State governments, that he rejected on this occasion the de-

*Lecture delivered February 11, 1858, Boston, by Hon. Caleb Cushing.

cisions of both. In August, 1847, he was appointed by the governor of Mississippi to fill a vacancy in the United States Senate, and at the ensuing session of the State legislature, January 11, 1848, was unanimously elected to the same office for the residue of the term, which expired March 4th, 1851.

CHAPTER II.

Repudiation.

WHILE Mr. Davis, in 1849, was filling the term of his special appointment as United States Senator from Mississippi, an old controversy was revived in regard to what is known as the Mississippi Repudiation. It was begun by the publication in the " Washington Union" of a letter from Mr. Davis, in which he endeavored to prove that the accusations against his State imputing a disregard of its honest obligations in the premises, were unfounded. To this letter a reply appeared in the money article of the London " Times," of 13th of July, 1849, followed soon after by a rejoinder from Mr. Davis. In July, 1863, the prominent position filled by the President of the Southern Confederacy again occasioned the revival of the subject, which was treated at great length in a letter of the Hon. Robert J. Walker, since published in book form. The gist of the whole question may be stated thus :

In 1838, the Legislature of Mississippi pledged the faith of the State to the payment of certain bonds issued by the Union Bank of Mississippi, at the same time subscribing on behalf of the State for the greater part of the stock issued. The bank failed about two years afterwards, and the Legislature, in pursuance of the recommendation of the Governor, declined the payment of the bonds, mainly on the ground that the preceding Legislature, in contracting the obligation, exceeded its authority, and that the obligation was, therefore, void.

The Constitution of Mississippi provides that—

" No law shall be passed to raise a loan of money upon the credit of the State for the payment or redemption of any loan or debt, unless such law be proposed in the Senate or House of Representatives, and be agreed to by a majority of the members of each house . . . and be referred to the succeeding Legislature . . . and unless a majority of each branch of (such succeeding) Legislature . . . shall agree to and pass such law."

The law which authorized the issuance of the bonds in question, was enacted in strict compliance with the requirements of the Constitution, but after its passage by the second Legislature, that Legislature passed a *second* act which materially modified the first by making the State itself the chief stockholder in the bank, and thus converting the State into the principal debtor instead of a mere surety as the first act contemplated. This second, or supplementary act was not, in accordance with the requirements of the Constitution, submitted to any succeeding Legislature, and hence was void ; nor was its unconstitutionality at all cured by the declaration of that Legislature that it was constitutional.

It was asserted on the other side that as Mississippi actually received the money, this constituted a ratification of the agency of the Legislature. But to this Mr. Davis replies that the

State did *not* receive the money, it having been all paid over to the Union Bank and disposed of by that corporation ; and to the objection that the State was the largest stockholder in that bank, his rejoinder was, that the law making the State a stockholder was the very portion of the enactment which lacked a second legislative sanction, and was therefore void. That a great part of the money passed by way of loan into the hands of citizens of the State was true, and upon those individuals rested a clear obligation to the amount received. In reply to the objection that the constitutionality of the legislative act had been determined in favor of the creditors by the judicial tribunals created by the Constitution to decide such questions, it was answered that this was true, but that the Constitution never intended that the judiciary should dictate to the Legislature the passage of certain laws, it being designed to create in that department merely a check analogous to the executive veto upon unauthorized acts of power by the law-making body. That the Legislature, therefore, might well differ with the courts upon the constitutionality of the late act contracting the debt in question, and could certainly refuse to impose the taxation necessary for its payment.

Mr. Davis, during his present imprisonment at Fortress Monroe, in speaking to his physician, Dr. Craven, on this subject, declared that the stories in circulation that he had effected the repudiation of the Mississippi bonds were utterly false :

"There is no truth in the report," he said. "The event referred to occurred before I had any connection with politics—

my first entrance into which was in 1843 ; nor was I at any time a disciple of the doctrine of repudiation. Nor did Mississippi ever refuse to acknowledge as a debt more than one class of bonds—those of the Union State Bank only.

" To show how absurd the accusation is," continued Mr. Davis, " although so widely believed that no denial can affect its currency, take the following facts : I left Mississippi when a boy to go to college ; thence went to West Point ; thence to the army. In 1835, I resigned, settled in a very retired place in the State, and was wholly unknown, except as remembered in the neighborhood where I had been raised. At the time when the Union Bank Bonds of Mississippi were issued, sold and repudiated—as I believe, justly—because their issue was in violation of the State Constitution—I endeavored to have them paid by voluntary contributions ; and subsequently I sent agents to England to negotiate for this purpose."

CHAPTER III.

State of parties—Mr. Davis's position—Division in the ranks of the Democratic party—Debate on the Missouri Compromise—Mr. Davis defeated in election for governor of Mississippi.

IT has been said, that Mr. Davis was a Democrat in his political principles. But in that ever-widening divergence of opinion which finally ushered in the open rupture of the party, the general term, Democracy, after a time ceased to clearly define the tone and actual positions of men and parties. At least this was the case with the great and all-absorbing question of slavery restriction. The Missouri Compromise of 1820, which prohibited the extension of slavery to any of the public territories of the United States north of 36° 30', was, like every compromise, ever adopted on that, or perhaps any other question, totally lacking in the very necessary quality of explicitness. While slavery was prohibited north of the line, a cautious silence is preserved in regard to the domain on the south side, and a wide margin was left for future cavil. It so happened, however, that for thirty years every new State which applied for admission into the Union, from the south side of the line, elected a slave constitution, and no occasion arose for a conflicting construction of the Missouri Compromise during that time. Indeed, so insignificant was the extent of the public domain in that direction, that the question of the extension or non-extension of slavery thereto ..

was a matter of no practical importance, and would doubtless have been yielded by the North.

On the other hand, so immense was the territory to the north-west wholly devoted by the terms of the Missouri Compromise to free labor, that there could be no doubt, that when formed into States, it would give to the North the three-fourths majority requisite to change the constitution itself, and thus abolish slavery in the States where it already existed. It was this event, anticipated and feared by far-seeing statesmen like Mr. Calhoun, which first turned the attention of the Southern people to the acquisition of new territory in the South-west, wherewith to preserve the equilibrium between the Free and Slave States.

With this view, Texas was annexed. But Texas was already a Slave State, and although opposition, and most strenuous opposition,* was made to the annexation itself, no question could arise as to slavery extension. But the immense territories of Arizona and New Mexico, acquired during the Mexican war, aroused afresh the fierce controversy which had slumbered so long. Even before the end of the war Mr. Wilmot introduced his famous proviso for the prohibition of slavery throughout all that vast region. The agitation culminated before the approaching Presidential election of 1848, and by that time the seeds were sown of that division in the ranks of the Democratic party which wrought its dissolution ten years later. The question which had been discreetly ignored by the Missouri compromise, was forced upon the country by the very magnitude of the stake at

---

* Many leading Abolitionists, as Mr. John Quincy Adams, pronounced the acquisition of Texas a good cause for dissolution of the Union.

issue. " The immense territory of the South-west must not, shall not be devoted to slavery," said the Abolitionists. " We fought for and paid for these common lands as well as yourselves," said the South, " and insist on the right to occupy them, and carry with us all of our property of every kind, and in the exercise of this right claim the protection of Congress." " You are both wrong," said the Douglass Democrats ; " Congress has not the power either to protect or prohibit slavery in the territories ; the question must be left to the people of the territories themselves."

The Presidential election of 1848 resulted in the choice of the Whig candidate, General Zachary Taylor. General Taylor received a strong support in the South, for which he was indebted to the fact of being a large slaveholder. Mr. Davis was better acquainted with the genuine sentiments of his father-in-law on the subject of slavery-extension, and illustrated the unbending strength of his convictions by throwing the whole weight of his influence against his election.

The first act of the new President convinced the South that interest is not always to be relied on as a test of principle. The slaveholding President hurried on, by every means in his power, the admission of California as a Free State, thus presenting to the South their first instalment of that compensating balance of power which they expected to derive from their Mexican acquisitions. It is necessary to hasten over the events which followed. To allay the dangerous excitement which succeeded the admission of California, Mr. Clay brought forward in 1850 his famous compromise. Occupying the middle ground, one acceptable to the bulk of the people, it was adopted by Congress, and became,—the basis of fresh disputes. In common with the Democracy who advocated Congressional protection in the territories, Mr. Davis promptly placed himself in opposition to the measure. The concluding remarks of one of his speeches during the Congress of 1850, clearly defines the position assumed at this period by his party :—

" But, sir, we are called upon to receive this as a measure of compromise—as a measure in which we of the minority are to receive something. A measure of compromise ! I look upon it as but a modest mode of taking that the claim to which has been more boldly asserted by others ; and, that I may be understood upon this question, and that my position may go forth to the country in the same columns that convey the sentiments of the Senator from Kentucky, I here assert, that never will I take less than the Missouri Compromise line extending to the Pacific Ocean, with the specific recognition of the right to hold slaves in the territory below that line ; and that, before such territories are admitted into the Union as States, slaves may be taken there from any of the United States, at the option of the owners. I can never consent to give additional power to a majority to commit further aggressions upon the minority in this Union ; and I will never consent to any proposition which will have such a tendency, without a full guarantee or counteracting measure as connected with it."

The debates on the Compromise Resolutions of Mr. Clay, occurred in January, 1850. In March of the same year, Mr.

Davis, in a debate with Mr. Cass of Michigan, expressed his views as to the Missouri Compromise.

"MR. CASS.—I wished to ask the honorable Senator from Mississippi if he could vote for the Missouri Compromise?"

"MR. DAVIS.—I will answer the Senator from Michigan with great pleasure. I have stated on several occasions that I would take the Missouri Compromise. This I have said deliberately and decidedly on several occasions, and explained at some length in a recent speech on the resolutions of the Senator from Kentucky. I have stated that I considered it an ultimatum, less than I believed to be the rights of the South, but which I would now accept, to stop the agitation which now disturbs and endangers the Union."

"MR. CASS.—As I had a conversation with the Senator on this subject in the morning, I supposed he understood the precise object I had in view. As this, however, appears not to be the case, I will ask him if he would accept the Missouri Compromise as it was reported by the statute providing for the admission of Missouri into the Union."

"MR. DAVIS.—I understood the Senator, in a conversation this morning, to make that inquiry. I then told him I would not. I now answer before the Senate, No. To meet this inquiry, I waited in the Senate chamber expecting that he would, at the expiration of the morning hour, address the Senate ; but as he did not, I left here to answer the summons to see a sick friend. I returned in a few minutes, as I was informed, after the Senator from Michigan commenced his address, and learned that he had signified a wish to ask me a question. It seemed to me proper to remind him, at the close of his remarks, of the wish he had announced. I now answer his question in its modified form. I would not take the terms of the Missouri act, but would accept its spirit if presented in terms expressible to this case. When I spoke of the Missouri Compromise, I spoke of it as an arrangement by which the territory was divided between the slaveholding and the non-slaveholding interests ; I spoke in reference to the result—the intent of that compromise—which gave to each a portion. I have always been ready to rebuke that mean spirit that would evade its true meaning by a delusive adherence to its words.

" I would not take the Compromise in the terms by which it was applied to the remaining part of the territory acquired under the name of Louisiana. I would not take it as applied to Texas, when that state was admitted into the Union, because the circumstances of both were different from those of the Mexican territory ; but I would take it if more applicable to the existing case, and extended to the Pacific. I considered that when the Senate had yesterday voted to receive petitions and to refer them to committees to consider upon the power of this government over slavery in the territories, over slavery in the District of Columbia, and over the future admission of slave states, we had taken one great step in advance, and one which should awaken the apprehension of the South ; and when in close connection with this action of the Senate, followed the remark of the honorable Senator from Michigan, that the Missouri Compromise could not be extended to the recent acquisitions from Mexico, I looked upon it as a conjunction in our political firmament, which boded one of those likely to be destroyed by the joint attraction of these planets. It was therefore that I spoke of the declaration as a thing to be noted—marked as the foreshadow of an event. If we are not to have non-intervention, the right to go into these territories and there claim whatever may be decided to be ours by the decree of nature—if we are to be debarred from acquiring by emigration, by enterprise, by adventure, by toil and labor equally with others from the common domain of the Union—if we are to be forbidden to use the commons belonging to the common field, of which we are joint owners—if, in addition to all this, we are told that no division can be made—that all of that of which we own in common must finally become the exclusive property of the other partners—in truth, sir, we are rapidly approaching that state of things contemplated by the Senator from South Carolina (Mr. Calhoun,) when, without an amendment of the constitution, the rights of the minority will be held at the mercy of the majority. Give us our rights under the Constitution—the Constitution fairly construed—and we are content to take our chance, as our fathers did, for the maintenance of position and the Union. We are content to hold on to the old compact and, as we believe in the merits of our own institutions, we are willing to trust to time and fair opportunity for the working out of our own salvation. If we are to be excluded by Congressional Legislation from joint possession on the one hand, and denied every compromise which, by division, would give us a share, on the other—neither permitted to an equality of possession as a right, nor a divided occupation as a settlement, between proprietors—I ask what is the hope which remains to those who are already in a minority in this confederacy? What do we gain by having a written constitution, if sectional pride or sectional hate can hurt it, or passion, or interest, or caprice may dictate? What do we gain by having a government based upon this written constitution, if, in truth, the rights of the minority are held in abeyance to the will of a majority."

The Compromise was effected. The South yielding to the urgent appeals made to her in behalf of the Union, and influenced by the conspicuous talents of another of the Senators, Mr. Clay, gave her reluctant consent to the measure. In the various State elections of 1850, for Governors, Congressmen, &c., the question was put to the people whether they were ready to secede from the Union upon the failure to procure Congressional protection for slavery in the territories. In every State except South Carolina the decision was in the negative. In Mississippi the question came up in the elections for Governor, Mr. Davis being the secession, and Henry S. Foote the Union candidate. Mr. Davis was rejected, but his opponent was elected by a majority of a little over nine hundred votes. It is cited as an instance of the personal popularity of Mr. Davis in his own State, that while he was defeated by fewer than a thousand votes, the majority in favor of the Union Convention two months before was seven thousand.

The South, in accepting the Compromise of Mr. Clay, declared that it was the last concession they could make to the North, and that they would resist any further aggression on their rights, even to the extremity of the dissolution of the Union. But this declaration was derided in the North, and the anti-slavery sentiment became bolder with success, as had been predicted by Mr. Calhoun, Mr. Davis, and the other opponents of compromise, and now aspired to the complete overthrow of the peculiar institution that had distinguished the people of the South from those of the North.

CHAPTER IV.

Mr. Pierce's Administration—Mr. Davis is made Secretary of War—Kansas-
Nebraska Struggle—Lecompton Constitution—Dred Scott—Secession re-
solved upon—Mr. Lincoln Elected—Secession—Mr. Davis's Adieu to the
Senate.

IN the meantime, Mr. Davis continued to occupy the position
of United States Senator. On the elevation of Mr. Pierce to
the Presidency, in 1852, he was made a member of the Cabinet
in the capacity of Secretary of War—a post for which his peculiarly administrative talents well fitted him.

Many measures of importance were introduced by him into his
department. Among these were, the revision of the army regu-
lations for the better observance of discipline; the increase of
the medical corps ; the introduction of camels ; the introduction
of the light infantry or rifled system of tactics ; rifled muskets
and the minie ball ; the increase of the army, and the explora-
tion of the western frontier.

Closely occupied during Mr. Pierce's administration in the
routine of office, Mr. Davis is not particularly identified with any
of the political events which occurred from 1852 to 1856. Nevertheless, in order to preserve somewhat the connectedness of the
previous and subsequent events of Mr. Davis's career, it is essential to devote a passing notice to that great struggle for terri-

torial dominion which seemed even more than the events of 1850 to threaten a great catastrophe.

In 1850, the question was upon the extension of slavery to the south of 36° 30′. The contest which succeeded related to territory north of that line.

In 1853, a bill was introduced for the organization of Kansas into a territorial government preparatory to admission into the Union. Kansas lies north of the latitude of 36° 30′, and consequently was not included in the terms of the last compromise, but *was* comprehended by the Missouri Compromise. The Committee on Territories in the Senate reported the bill for the organization of the territory, and this bill declared that the Missouri Compromise was superseded by the compromise measures of 1850. It held that the Missouri Compromise act being " inconsistent with the principles of non-intervention by Congress with slavery in the States and Territories, as recognized by the legislation of 1850, commonly called the Compromise Measures, is hereby declared inoperative and void; it being the true intent and meaning of this act not to legislate slavery into any territory or State, nor to exclude it therefrom, but to leave the people thereof perfectly free to form and regulate their domestic institutions in their own way, subject only to the Constitution of the United States." After a lengthened contest, the resolutions were carried, the Missouri restriction repealed, and all the territories thrown open to the competition of slavery and freedom. Now came the struggle for Kansas. Thr North, enraged at the repeal of the Missouri Compromise, made desperate efforts by means of Emigrant Societies, by violent appeals from her pulpits, by incendiary harangues at public assemblies, by fierce appeals through the press to stimulate emigration to Kansas and secure her organization as a Free State.

A convention was held at Lecompton, and a form of constitution adopted. With this constitution Kansas proceeded to apply for admission into the Union; but the constitution containing a clause establishing slavery in the State, the application was rejected upon the ground of alleged illegality in the proceedings. It was declared that the Constitution had not been submitted to the people for their approval, and hence did not represent the true sentiments of the community. The constitution, as a whole, it is true, had not been submitted, but the convention, however, had taken care to submit to the popular vote for ratification or rejection the clause respecting slavery. It was also asserted that even this clause had not been submitted to the entire people of the State, some thirteen counties out of the forty-four not having registered their votes, and hence were not represented in the popular result. But it was shown that of these thirteen counties, four had refused to register their votes or to take any action on the subject, being principally settled by free-state men, who refused to recognize all legal authority in the State ; and that the neglect in the remaining nine occurred on account of their being so thinly settled, as shown in the later election held by the abolition convention, when they polled but ninety votes ; hence it was claimed that the opposition of the people of these counties to the measure could not have effected the result. But the application for admission was rejected, principally on account of the opposition of Mr. Douglas, who, startled at the intense unpopularity which his efforts for the repeal of the Missouri Compromise had created for him in the North, was endeavoring to recover lost ground in that section, by measures that he supposed would conciliate the prejudices of the North. A large number of Democrats sided with Mr. Douglas, and the party became hopelessly divided into what were called the "Lecompton" and the "Anti-Lecompton" factions Meanwhile, the Free-State men met in convention at Topeka, framed a constitution, submitted it for popular approval, none but Free-State men appearing at the polls ; and, declaring this instrument to have received the sanction of the people, they presented themselves at the door of Congress, claiming admission. A long, bitter struggle ensued ; and in this Kansas controversy we see the immediate forerunner of the intestine war between the two sections of the Union.

About this time the famous Dred Scott decision by the Supreme Court was obtained, which established the proposition that the Legislature of a Territory had no authority to exclude slavery from its limits.

This decision aroused the North anew ; and the ultra wing of the Democratic party accepting it as a cardinal principle, while the Douglas division of the party maintained the theory of the right of the people of a territory to retain or exclude slavery at their option, without the intervention of the general government, the split in the party became radical and permanent.

Mr. Davis was, meanwhile (1857), re-elected to the Senate. He entered zealously into the exciting Kansas struggle, identifying himself as usual with the extreme constitutional wing of his party.

The organization of the Republican party, their nomination in the presidential election of 1860 of a distinctively sectional candidate on a distinctively sectional and anti-slavery platform, was, in the judgment of Mr. Davis, in the event of its success, sufficient cause for the withdrawal of the South from a union with a people who were determined to disregard the obligations and to overrule the limitations imposed by the compact on which that Union was based.   Mr. Davis energetically advocated the right, and asserted, under such a contingency, the necessity of the dissolution.   In the Democratic nominating convention in Mississippi, July 5, 1859, Mr. Davis said that—

" The success of such a party would, indeed, produce an ' irrepressible conflict.'   To you would be presented the question, Will you allow the constitutional Union to be changed into the despotism of a majority ?   Will you become the subjects of a hostile government ?   Or will you, outside of the Union, assert the equality, the liberty and sovereignty to which you were born ? For myself, I say—as I said on a former occasion—in the contingency of the election of a President on the platform of Mr. Seward's Rochester speech, let the Union be dissolved.   Let the great, but not the greatest, evil come ; for—as did the great and good Calhoun, from whom is drawn that expression of value—I love and venerate the union of these States, but I love liberty and Mississippi more."

At the last session of Congress, in February, 1860, Mr. Davis introduced a series of resolutions into the Senate, embodying the principles of the constitutional pro-slavery party, as set forth in the Dred Scott decision. They propounded the sovereignty of the separate States ; asserted that negro slavery formed an essential part of the political institutions of various members of the Union ; that the union of the States rested on equality of rights ; that it was the duty of Congress to provide for the protection of slave property in the territories ; and that the inhabitants of a territory, when forming a State constitution, and not *before*, may provide for the continuance or abolition of slavery.

At the Democratic presidential convention at Charleston, in the opening of the same year, Mr. Davis's Senate Resolutions were brought up and offered for acceptance as the official assertion of the principles of the party. But the Douglas Democrats were in great force at the convention, and determined not only on the nomination of their favorite as the presidential candidate, but on the official incorporation into the platform of the party of that distinctive principle in reference to slavery in the territories first promulgated by Mr. Douglas, and commonly described as " Squatter Sovereignty." But, after a session of three weeks, the convention broke up, unable to agree either upon a platform or a candidate, and adjourned to meet at Baltimore in June. The re-assembling of the convention resulted in a final and embittered separation of opposing delegations. The Southern representatives were determined to accept no less than an enunciation of principles corresponding with Mr. Davis's Senate Resolutions, and the Northern delegation, already yielding to the force of fanatical opinions in the North, equally resolute upon the nomination of Mr. Douglas and the acceptance of his peculiar views, separate conventions were held by the two fragments, and two separate candidates, Mr. Douglas and Mr. Breckenridge, were put in nomination against Mr. Lincoln, whose election as President was the result.

During the canvass, the North had been distinctly warned by the conservative parties, that the election of Lincoln by a strictly sectional vote, would be taken as a declaration of war against the South. The election of a President on strictly geographical grounds, an avowed hostility to an entire section of the country, with the confessed purpose of admitting the government in the interest and in accordance with the views of a majority in utter disregard of the constitutional rights of the minority, were considered and asserted to be sufficient grounds for the withdrawal of the aggrieved States from the copartnership. Hence, when the result became known, the South did not hesitate. South Carolina took the lead, and in convention on the 18th of December, formally announced her connection with the States of the Union terminated and dissolved. On the 9th of January, 1861, the State of Mississippi followed the example of the " Palmetto State;" Alabama and Florida on the 11th of the same month, Georgia on the 20th, Louisiana on the 26th, and Texas on the 1st of February, successively withdrew ; and, solemnly declaring their connection with the states under the former compact of union annulled and terminated. Secession was a completed fact—and for more than four years these States in conjunction with North Carolina, Virginia, Tennessee and Arkansas, maintained their separate and seceded condition ; how eventually conquered by the armies of the North, all the world knows.

In a few days after the withdrawal of Mississippi from the Union,

January 11th, Mr. Davis announced the secession of the State which he represented, and took a formal leave of the Senate. He preceded his withdrawal with an address, through which runs a vein of dignified moderation, not unmixed with a subdued sadness. He said :—

" I rise, Mr. President, for the purpose of announcing to the Senate that I have satisfactory evidence that the State of Mississippi, by a solemn ordinance of her people in convention assembled, has declared her separation from the United States. Under these circumstances, of course, my functions are terminated here. It has seemed to me proper, however, that I should appear in the Senate to announce the fact to my associates, and I will say but very little more. The occasion does not invite me to go into argument ; and my physical condition would not permit me to do so if it were otherwise ; and yet it seems to become me to say something on the part of the State I here represent, on an occasion so solemn as this.

" It is known to Senators who have served with me here, that I have for many years advocated, as an essential attribute of State sovereignty, the right of a State to secede from the Union. Therefore, if I had not believed there was justifiable cause ; if I had thought that Mississippi was acting without sufficient provocation, or without an existing necessity, I should still, under my theory of the Government, because of my allegiance to the State of which I am a citizen, have been bound by her action. I, however, may be permitted to say that I do think that she has justifiable cause, and I approve of her act. I conferred with her people before that act was taken, counselled them then that if the state of things which they apprehended, should exist when the Convention met, they should take the action which they have now adopted.

"I hope none who hear me will confound this expression of mine with the advocacy of the right of a State to remain in the Union, and to disregard its constitutional obligations by the nullification of the law. Such is not my theory. Nullification and secession, so often confounded, are indeed antagonistic principles. Nullification is a remedy which it is sought to apply within the Union, and against the agent of the States. It is only to be justified when the agent has violated his constitutional obligation, and a State, assuming to judge for itself, denies the right of the agent thus to act, and appeals to the other States of the Union for a decision; but when the States themselves, and when the people of the States, have so acted as to convince us that they will not regard our constitutional rights, then, and then for the first time, arises the doctrine of secession in its practical application.

"A great man who now reposes with his fathers, and who has been often arraigned for a want of fealty to the Union, advocated the doctrine of nullification, because it preserved the Union. It was because of his deep-seated attachment to the Union, his determination to find some remedy for existing ills short of a severance of the ties which bound South Carolina to the other states, that Mr. Calhoun advocated the doctrine of nullification, which he proclaimed to be peaceful, to be within the limits of State power—not to disturb the Union, but only to be a means of bringing the agent before the tribunal of the States for their judgment.

"Secession belongs to a different class of remedies. It is to be justified upon the basis that the States are sovereign. There was a time when none denied it. I hope the time may come again, when a better comprehension of the theory of our Government, and the inalienable rights of the people of the States, will prevent any one from denying that each State is a sovereign, and thus may reclaim the grants which it has made to any agent whomsoever.

" I therefore say I concur in the action of the people of Mississippi, believing it to be necessary and proper, and should have been bound by their action, if my belief had been otherwise ; and this brings me to the important point which I wish on this last occasion to present to the Senate. It is by this confounding of nullification and secession that the name of a great man, whose ashes now mingle with his mother earth, has been invoked to justify coercion against a seceded State. The phrase ' to execute the laws,' was an expression which General Jackson applied to the case of a State refusing to obey the laws, while yet a member of the Union. That is not the case which is now presented. The laws are to be executed over the United States, and upon the people of the United States. They have no relation to any foreign country. It is a perversion of terms, at least it is a great misapprehension of the case, which cites that expression for application to a State which has withdrawn from the Union. You may make war on a foreign State. If it be the purpose of gentlemen, they may make war against a State which has withdrawn from the Union ; but there are no laws of the United States to be executed within the limits of a seceded State. A State finding herself in the condition in which Mississippi has judged she is, in which her safety requires that she should provide for the maintenance of her rights out of the Union, surrenders all the benefits, (and they are known to be many), deprives herself of the advantages (they are known to be great), severs all the ties of affection (and they are close and enduring), which have bound her to the Union ; and, thus divesting herself of every benefit, taking upon herself every burden, she claims to be exempt from any power to execute the laws of the United States within her limits.

"I well remember an occasion when Massachusetts was arraigned before the bar of the Senate, and when then the doctrine of coercion was rife, and to be applied against her, because of the rescue of a fugitive slave in Boston. My opinion then was the same that it is now. Not in a spirit of egotism, but to show that I am not influenced in my own opinion because the case is my own, I refer to that time and that occasion as containing the opinion which I then entertained, and on which my present conduct is based. I then said, if Massachusetts, following her through a stated line of conduct, chooses to take the last step which separates her from the Union, it is her right to go, and I will neither vote one dollar nor one man to coerce her back ; but will say to her, God speed, in memory of the kind associations which once existed between her and the other States.

" It has been a conviction of pressing necessity, it has been a belief that we are to be deprived in the Union of the rights which our fathers bequeathed to us, which has brought Mississippi into her present decision. She has heard proclaimed the theory that all men are created free and equal, and this made the basis of an attack upon her social institutions ; and the sacred Declaration of Independence has been invoked to maintain the position of the equality of the races. That Declaration of Independence is to be construed by the circumstance and purposes for which it was made. The communities were declaring their independence ; the people of those communities were asserting that no man was born —to use the language of Mr. Jefferson—booted and spurred to ride over the rest of mankind ; that men were created equal—meaning the men of the political community ; and that there was no divine right to rule ; that no man inherited the right to govern ; that there were no classes by which power and place descended to families, but that all stations were equally within the grasp of each member of the body politic. These were the great principles they announced ; these were the purposes for which they made their declaration ; these were the ends to which their enunciation was directed. They have no reference to the slave ; else, how happened it that among the items of arraignment made against George III. was, that he endeavored to do just what the North has been endeavoring of late to do—to stir up insurrection among our slaves ? Had the Declaration announced that the negroes were free and equal, how was the Prince to be arraigned for stirring up insurrection among them ? And how was this to be enumerated among the high crimes which caused the colonies to sever their connection with the mother country ? When our Constitution was formed, the same idea was rendered more palpable ; for

2*

there we find provision made for that very class of persons as property : they were not put upon the footing of equality with white men—not even upon that of paupers and convicts ; but, so far as representation was concerned, were discriminated against as a lower caste, only to be represented in the numerical proportion of three-fifths.

" Then, Senators, we recur to the compact which binds us together—we recur to the principles upon which our Government was founded ; and when you deny them, and when you deny to us the right to withdraw from a Government which, thus perverted, threatens to be destructive of our rights, we but tread in the path of our fathers when we proclaim our independence, and take the hazard. This is done, not in hostility to others, not to injure any section of the country, not even for own pecuniary benefit, but from the high and solemn motive of defending and protecting the rights we inherited, and which it is our sacred duty to transmit unshorn to our children.

" I find in myself, perhaps, a type of the general feeling of my constituents towards yours. I am sure I feel no hostility to you, Senators from the North. I am sure there is not one of you, whatever sharp discussion there may have been between us, to whom I cannot now say, in the presence of my God, I wish you well ; and such, I am sure, is the feeling of the people whom I represent towards those whom you represent. I therefore feel that I but express their desire when I say I hope, and they hope, for peaceful relations with you, though we must part. They may be mutually beneficial to us in the future, as they have been in the past, if you so will it. The reverse may bring disaster on every portion of the country ; and if you will have it thus, we will invoke the God of our fathers, who delivered them from the power of the lion, to protect us from the ravages of the bear ; and thus, putting our trust in God, and in our own firm hearts and strong arms, we will vindicate the right as best we may.

" In the course of my service here, associated at different times with a great variety of senators, I see now around me some with whom I have served long. There may have been points of collision ; but whatever of offense there has been to me, I leave here : I carry with me no hostile remembrance. Whatever offense I have given which has not been redressed, or for which satisfaction has not been demanded, I have, Senators, in this hour of our parting, to offer you my apology for any pain which, in heat of discussion, I have inflicted. I go hence unencumbered of the remembrance of any injury received, and having discharged the duty of making the only reparation in my power for any injury offered.

" Mr. President and Senators, having made the announcement which the occasion seemed to me to require, it only remains for me to bid you a final adieu."

CHAPTER V.

Confederate Congress at Montgomery—Inauguration of Mr. Davis as Provisional President—Commissioners to Europe—Fort Sumter—Mr. Lincoln's call—Confederate Finances—Mr. Davis at Bull Run—Mr. Davis re-elected for six years—Mason and Slidell.

THREE weeks after Mr. Davis's withdrawal from Congress, on the 4th of February, 1861, the delegates to the Confederate Congress assembled at Montgomery, Alabama. Their first act was the formation of a provisional constitution to continue in operation for one year. Under this constitution, Mr. Davis was elected President, and Alexander H. Stevens of Georgia, was elected Vice-President. The inauguration took place on the 18th of February.

The new government being organized, and provision made for collecting revenue and the formation of an army of 100,000 men, its attention was next directed to anticipated foreign relations. Early in the month of March, commissioners were sent to the leading powers of Europe and to Washington.

The commissioners to Washington were refused all official intercourse by Mr. Seward, yet they held an informal communication with the Secretary through John A. Campbell, one of the justices of the Supreme Court of the United States. The burden of this irregular correspondence between the Confederate commissioners and Mr. Seward related to the affair of Fort Sumter, which was one of the two Federal strongholds which the Southerners failed to peacefully occupy. The commissioners demanded its surrender, which was refused ; but President Lincoln gave an assurance that he would give notice of his intention should he determine to provision the fort. He gave the notice accordingly, and the attempt to supply the garrison was the immediate occasion of the attack which followed. Fort Sumter was bombarded on the 12th of April, 1861. It was the first act of the war.

In his message of April 29, Mr. Davis, after mentioning the fact of the refusal by Mr. Lincoln to grant an audience to the Confederate Commissioners, proceeds thus :—

"During the interval, the Commissioners had consented to waive all questions of form, with the firm resolve to avoid war, if possible. They went so far even as to hold, during that long period, unofficial intercourse through an intermediary, whose high position and character inspired the hope of success, and through whom constant assurances were received from the Government of the United States of its peaceful intentions—of its determination to evacuate Fort Sumter ; and, further, that no measure would be introduced changing the existing status prejudical to the Confederate States ; that in the event of any change in regard to Fort Pickens, notice would be given to the Commissioners.

" The crooked paths of diplomacy can scarcely furnish an example so wanting in courtesy, in candor, in directness, as was the course of the United States Government towards our Commissioners in Washington. For proof of this, I refer to the annexed

documents, taken in connection with further facts, which I now
proceed to relate :—

"Early in April, the attention of the whole country was attracted to extraordinary preparations for an extensive military and
naval expedition in New York and other Northern ports. These
preparations commenced in secrecy, for an expedition whose destination was concealed, and only became known when nearly completed ; and on the 5th, 6th and 7th of April, transports and
vessels of war with troops, munitions, and military supplies, sailed
from Northern ports, bound southward.

"Alarmed by so extraordinary a demonstration, the Commissioners requested the delivery of an answer to their official communication of the 12th of March ; and the reply dated on the
15th of the previous month, from which it appears that during
the whole interval, whilst the Commissioners were receiving assurances calculated to inspire hope of the success of their mission, the
Secretary of State and the President of the United States had
already determined to hold no intercourse with them whatever ;
to refuse even to listen to any proposals they had to make, and
had profited by the delay created by their own assurances, in
order to prepare secretly the means for effective hostile operations.

"That these assurances were given has been virtually confessed
by the Government of the United States, by its act of sending a
messenger to Charleston to give notice of its purpose to use force
if opposed in its intention of supplying Fort Sumter.

"No more striking proof of the absence of good faith in the
conduct of the Government of the United States towards the

Confederacy can be required, than is contained in the circumstances which accompanied this notice.

" According to the usual course of navigation, the vessels composing the expedition, and designed for the relief of Fort Sumter, might be looked for in Charleston harbor on the 9th of April. Yet our Commissioners in Washington were detained under assurances that notice should be given of any military movement. The notice was not addressed to them, but a messenger was sent to Charleston to give notice to the Governor of South Carolina, and the notice was so given at a late hour on the 8th of April, the eve of the very day on which the fleet might be expected to arrive.

" That this manœuvre failed in its purpose, was not the fault of those who controlled it. A heavy tempest delayed the arrival of the expedition, and gave time to the commander of our forces at Charleston to ask and receive instructions of the Government. Even then, under all the provocation incident to the contemptuous refusal to listen to our Commissioners, and the treacherous course of the Government of the United States, I was sincerely anxious to avoid the effusion of blood, and directed a proposal to be made to the commander of Fort Sumter, who had avowed himself to be nearly out of provisions, that we would abstain from directing our fire at Fort Sumter if he would promise not to open fire on our forces unless first attacked. This proposal was refused. The conclusion was, that the design of the United States was to place the besieging force at Charleston between the simultaneous fire of the fleet and fort. The fort should, of course, be at once reduced. This order was executed by General Beauregard with skill and success."

Three days after the bombardment of Sumter, Mr. Lincoln issued his memorable call for seventy-five thousand troops, and in a few weeks more all the Border States save Kentucky, Missouri and Maryland had passed ordinances of secession.

Meantime, on the 17th of April, a proclamation was issued by Mr. Davis offering letters of marque to all persons who might desire to engage in privateering. Volunteering, too, proceeded rapidly and with enthusiasm. The military force now in the field was 35,000 men. Of this number about 19,000 were at Charleston, Pensacola and Mobile. The remainder were on the route to Virginia.

The plan of the war was controlled and decided by circumstances. It would have been absurd for an agricultural people to enter upon a war of invasion within three months after their organization as a nation, and that, too, against a commercial and manufacturing people, greatly superior in numbers and wealth. Peace or defensive warfare were the only alternatives of the Confederate State. Without the means wherewith to clothe, equip, or move an army, unless imported from abroad—accustomed to depend upon their very enemies for everything, save food, they could not undertake a war of invasion with any hopes of success. Yet there was a large party opposed to the administration, who, to the last, advocated that policy, and chiefly to their clamors were owing the disastrous offensive movements attempted at a later period of the war.

Another consequence of their isolated position and purely agricultural resources, was the lack of money. Cotton had always been the only resource of the people, and that, owing to the blockade, soon failed the Government. Loans were resorted to, but the people could only lend cotton, and very soon had little of that commodity to lend. There were two methods of supplying its wants open to the Treasury—one was taxation in kind, the other, an indefinite issue of Treasury notes and Government bonds. By the former mode the army might at least have been supplied with clothing and provisions, without a resort to credit ; but it was not adopted till the currency had already been ruined by inflation. Accordingly, Treasury notes were issued, which, like the money generated by all civil commotions, even when successful, speedily depreciated.

Many efforts were made to sustain the credit of the Government ; some bank directors placed the whole means of the corporations they controlled at the disposal of Government, thenceforth issuing only Confederate notes, and the State Legislatures authorized executors, trustees and guardians, to invest the whole of the funds controlled by them in Government securities. The history of the French assignats, and the American revolutionary paper of eighty years previous, might have shown the futility of these efforts. But the mass of mankind can only be taught by personal experience. By the end of 1861, the currency had already depreciated thirty per cent.

One of the means resorted to for the purpose of replenishing the Treasury was the sequestration of the property of "alien enemies ;" that is, of Northern citizens. It was estimated that the amount of indebtedness from Southern to Northern citizens was two hundred millions of dollars. On the 21st of May the Confederate Congress passed an act prohibiting the payment by

individuals of any portion of this debt. Process of garnish-
ment was also authorized, to reach debts in the hands of attor-
neys for collection. But these measures ceased as the first bit-
terness of the struggle wore away.

Dr. Craven, in his interesting work, "The Prison Life of Jefferson Davis," relates an interesting conversation held with Mr.
Davis on the subject of the failure of the Confederate currency :
"Being interested," says Dr. Craven, "by what Mr. Davis had
said of the failure of the Confederate currency, and of some
scheme by which it might have been prevented, I expressed my
curiosity, and ventured to request some explanation, as there
appeared to me no manner in which Confederate paper could
have been sustained at par.

"Mr. Davis replied, that one rule of his life was, never to express regret for the inevitable : to let the dead bury its dead in
regard to all political hopes that were not realized. Fire is not
quenched with tow, nor the past to be remedied by lamentations.
It would, however, have been possible, in his judgment, to have
kept the currency of his people good for gold, or very nearly so,
during the entire struggle ; and, had this been done, the contrast, if nothing else, would have reduced United States securities to zero, and so terminated the contest. The plan urged
upon Mr. Memminger was as follows—a plan Mr. Davis privately
approved, but had not time to study and take the responsibility
of directing, until too late :

"At the time of secession there were not less than three million bales of cotton in the South—plantation bales of 400 pounds

weight each. These the Secretary of the Treasury recommended
to buy from the planters, who were then willing, and even eager
to sell to the Government at ten cents per pound of Confederate
currency. These three million bales were to be rushed off to
Europe before the blockade was of any efficiency, and there held
for one or two years, until the price reached not less than seventy
or eighty cents per pound—and we all know it reached much
higher during the war. This would have given a cash basis in
Europe of not less than a thousand million dollars in gold, and
all securities drawn against this balance in bank would maintain
par value. Such a sum would have more than sufficed all the
needs of the Confederacy during the war; would have sufficed,
with economic management, for a war of twice the actual duration; and this evidence of Southern prosperity and stability
could not but have acted powerfully on the minds, the securities
and the avarice of the New-England rulers of the North. He
was far from reproaching Mr. Memminger. The situation was
new. No one could have foreseen the course of events. When
too late the wisdom of the proposed measure was realized, but
the inevitable ' too late' was interposed. The blockade had become too stringent, for one reason, and the planters had lost
their pristine confidence in Confederate currency. When we
might have put silver in the purse, we did not put it there. When
we had only silver on the tongue, our promises were forced to
become excessive."

On the 21st of May, the Confederate Congress permanently
adjourned to Richmond, foreseeing that Virginia would be the

most important theatre of the approaching conflict. At that time it was estimated that the organized forces of the Southrons amounted to about one hundred thousand men. Of these, sixty thousand were concentrated in Virginia, at Manassas Junction. On the 22d of July, the battle of Bull Run was fought at that point, and resulted, as is well-known, in the disastrous defeat of the Federal forces.

On the day after the battle, the following despatch from Mr. Davis was read in the Southern Congress :

"MANASSAS JUNCTION, Sunday Night.

"The night has closed upon a hard-fought field. Our forces were victorious. The enemy were routed, and precipitately fled, abandoning a large amount of arms, knapsacks and baggage. The ground was strewn for miles with those killed, and the farm-houses and grounds around were filled with the wounded. Pursuit was continued along several routes towards Leesburg and Centreville until darkness covered the fugitives. We have captured many field-batteries and stands of arms, and one of the United-States flags. Many prisoners have been taken. Too high praise cannot be bestowed, whether for the skill of the principal officers, or the gallantry of all our troops. The battle was mainly fought on our left. Our force was 15,000 ; that of the enemy was estimated at 35,000.

"JEFFERSON DAVIS."

Mr. Davis rightly attached immense importance to the result of this first battle of the war. He had made great preparations to ensure success, and was himself present upon the field.

Its most beneficial results to the Confederacy was the immense impetus which it gave to recruiting. Under the intense and wide-spread enthusiasm awakened by it, the army quickly swelled in numbers from one hundred thousand to two hundred and ninety thousand men. Forward movements were made, and in the elation which followed the battle, the advocates of an "On to Washington" policy increased. The flag of the "Stars and Bars" was, indeed, flaunted from the summit of Munsen's Hill, where the inhabitants of the city of Washington could see its proud folds waving. The rapid increase of the Federal forces, however, determined the administration against offensive movements.

Moreover, a change was made in the war policy of the United States, which promised to give full occupation to the Confederate troops in other fields than those of Virginia. Notwithstanding the attempted neutrality of Kentucky, troops were organized by the Confederate authorities, and sent into that State ; while in Missouri, although rather left to her own resources by the insurrectionary government, the most active military operations took place. The military genius of the Southern Commanding General, Price, enabled him to sustain himself, and carry on an active campaign with almost no assistance from the Government.

At the expiration of his provisional authority, Mr. Davis again became a candidate for the Presidency. The election under the permanent Constitution was held on the 6th of November, and resulted in the choice of Mr. Davis for President, and Mr. Stephens for Vice President.

The presidential message was transmitted to Congress in a few days after the re-election. So much as embraces a condensed *resumé* of the progress of events up to its date may be given here :—

    " *To the Congress of the Confederate States :*—

    "The few weeks which have elapsed since your adjournment have brought us so near the close of the year, that we are now able to sum up its general results. The retrospect is such as should.fill the hearts of our people with gratitude to Providence for his kind interposition in their behalf. Abundant yields have rewarded the labor of the agriculturist, whilst the manufacturing interest of the Confederate States was never so prosperous as now. The necessities of the times have called into existence new branches of manufactures, and given a fresh impulse to the activity of those heretofore in operation. The means of the Confederate States for manufacturing the necessaries and comforts of life within themselves increase as the conflict continues, and we are gladly becoming independent of the rest of the world for the supply of such military stores and munitions as are indispensable for war.

    "The operations of the army, soon to be partially interrupted by the approaching winter, have afforded a protection to the country, and shed a lustre upon its arms, through the trying vicissitudes of more than one arduous campaign, which entitle our brave volunteers to our praise and our gratitude.

    "From its commencement up to the present period, the war has been enlarging its proportions and extending its boundaries, so as to include new fields. The conflict now extends from the shores of the Chesapeake to the confines of Missouri and Arizona ; yet sudden calls from the remotest points for military aid have been met with promptness enough, not only to avert disaster in the face of superior numbers, but also to roll back the tide of invasion from the border.

" When the war commenced, the enemy were possessed of certain strategic points and strong places within the Confederate States. They greatly exceeded us in numbers, in available resources, and in the supplies necessary for war. Military establishments had been long organized, and were complete ; the navy, and, for the most part, the army, once common to both, were in their possession. To meet all this, we had to create, not only an army in the face of war itself, but also military establishments necessary to equip and place it in the field. It ought, indeed, to be a subject of gratulation that the spirit of the volunteers and the patriotism of the people have enabled us, under Providence, to grapple successfully with these difficulties.

" A succession of glorious victories at Bethel, Bull Run, Manassas, Springfield, Lexington, Leesburg, and Belmont, has checked the wicked invasion which greed of gain and the unhallowed lust of power brought upon our soil, and has proved that numbers cease to avail when directed against a people fighting for the sacred right of self-government and the privileges of freemen. After seven months of war, the enemy have not only failed to extend their occupancy of our soil, but new States and Territories have been added to our Confederacy ; while, instead of their threatened march of unchecked conquest, they have been driven, at more than one point, to assume the defensive ; and, upon a fair comparison between the two belligerents, as to men, military means, and financial condition, the Confederate States are relatively much stronger now than when the struggle commenced.

"Since your adjournment, the people of Missouri have conducted the war, in the face of almost unparalleled difficulties, with a spirit and success alike worthy of themselves and of the great cause in which they are struggling. Since that time, Kentucky too has become the theatre of active hostilities. The Federal forces have not only refused to acknowledge her right to be neutral, and have insisted upon making her a party to the war, but have invaded her for the purpose of attacking the Confederate States. Outrages of the most despotic character have been perpetrated upon her people ; some of her most eminent citizens have been seized, and borne away to languish in foreign prisons, without knowing who were their accusers, or the specific charges made against them ; while others have been forced to abandon their homes, their families, and property, and seek a refuge in distant lands.

" Finding that the Confederate States were about to be invaded through Kentucky, and that her people, after being deceived into a mistaken security, were unarmed, and in danger of being subjugated by the Federal forces, our armies were marched into that State to repel the enemy, and prevent their occupation of certain strategetic points, which would have given them great advantages in the contest—a step which was justified, not only by the necessities of self-defense on the part of the Confederate States, but also by a desire to aid the people of Kentucky. It was never intended by the Confederate Government to conquer or coerce the people of that State ; but, on the contrary, it was declared by our Generals that they would withdraw their troops if the Federal Government would do likewise. Proclamation was also made of the desire to respect the neutrality of Kentucky, and the intention to abide by the wishes of her people as soon as they were free to express their opinions.

"These declarations were approved by me, and I should regard it as one of the best effects of the march of our troops into Kentucky if it should end in giving to her people liberty of choice, and a free opportunity to decide their own destiny according to their own will."

The year 1861 closed with a blow to the hopes of the Confederate States from a quarter where much that was favorable had been anticipated. The main hopes for the speedy success of their cause entertained by both the Government and people was founded upon the confident expectation of interference by England and France. The complication arising out of the capture of Mason and Slidell on the 8th of November, it was hoped, would ripen into open hostility on the part of England. It was believed throughout the Southern States that the long-expected crisis had now arrived. England had demanded the surrender of the prisoners, and it was believed, from the tone of the Northern press, that the demand would be refused. All eyes were turned with intense interest to the American Secretary of State. Despite the immense popular pressure brought to bear upon him by the peace party North, Mr. Seward, casting aside the technical doubts and difficulties which, strangely enough, seem to have beset his view of the law of the case, decided to surrender the prisoners. Thus at once were dashed to the ground the hopes of intervention which had been conceived by the Confederates.

CHAPTER VI.

Dearth of Arms—Reverses—Fort Donelson—Evacuation of Bowling Green and Nashville—Mr. Davis recasts military system—Reverses continue— New Orleans and Memphis fall—Affairs in Virginia.

THE worst result to the South of the neutrality of Europe was felt in a deficiency of arms and munitions. Disappointed in their expectations of supplies from foreign markets, the Confederate authorities turned their attention to their manufacture. In default of muskets and rifles, old shot-guns were brought up and dirks and pikes for a while supplied the place of bayonets.

They were fated to experience, in the outset of the campaign of 1862, several reverses in the field. In the latter part of February, the Federal army of the West obtained their first important successes. Forts Donelson and Henry were captured, Bowling Green evacuated, and Nashville surrendered. The Confederate line of defense in the West, indeed, was swept away, and the heart of the South-Western States menaced.

The imminent dangers threatened by these reverses only infused redoubled energy into Mr. Davis's Administration. The army was placed upon a different footing. Nearly all the troops, anticipating a short war, had enlisted for a year; many for six months only. Mr. Davis had, from the first, been opposed to short enlistments. He had served in the Mexican war, where he had witnessed its bad effects. "I deem it proper," he said in his message of February, "to advert to the fact, that the process of furloughs and re-enlistments in progress for the last month had so far disorganized and weakened our forces, as seriously to impair our activity for successful defense ; but I heartily congratulate you that this evil which I had foreseen, but was powerless to prevent, may now be said to be substantially at an end, and that we shall not again during the war be exposed to seeing our strength diminished by this frightful cause of disaster —short enlistments."

There was another fault in the manner of raising armies in the South ; it depended on voluntary enlistment. This might suffice for a short war, but for prolonged effort it could not be relied upon. It moreover had the effect of throwing the burden of the war upon the patriotic, leaving the lukewarm, the selfish, and the mercenary to escape the dangers and inconveniences of active services. Mr. Davis, therefore, transmitted to Congress the following message :—

" *To the Senate and House of Representatives of the Confederate States :*

" The operation of the various laws now in force for raising armies has exhibited the necessity for reform. The frequent changes and amendments which have been made have rendered the system so complicated as to make it often quite difficult to determine what the law really is, and to what extent prior amendments are modified by more recent legislation.

" There is also embarrassment from conflict between State and

Confederate legislation. I am happy to assure you of the entire harmony of purpose and cordiality of feeling which has continued to exist between myself and the executives of the several States ; and it is to this cause that our success in keeping adequate forces in the field is to be attributed.

"These reasons would suffice for inviting your earnest attention to the necessity of some simple and general system for exercising the power of raising armies, which is vested in Congress by the Constitution.

"But there is another and more important consideration. The vast preparations made by the enemy for a combined assault at numerous points on our frontier and seaboard have produced results that might have been expected. They have animated the people with a spirit of resistance so general, so resolute, and so self-sacrificing, that it requires rather to be regulated than to be stimulated. The right of the State to demand, and the duty of each citizen to render military service, need only to be stated to be admitted. It is not, however, a wise or judicious policy to place in active service that portion of the force of the people which experience has shown to be necessary as a reserve. Youths under the age of eighteen years require further instruction ; men of mature experience are needed for maintaining order and good government at home, and in supervising preparations for rendering efficient the armies in the field. These two classes constitute the proper reserve for home defense, ready to be called out in case of any emergency, and to be kept in the field only while the emergency exists.

"But in order to maintain this reserve intact, it is necessary that in a great war like that in which we are now engaged, all persons of intermediate ages not legally exempt for good cause, should pay their debt of military service to the country, that the burdens should not fall exclusively on the most ardent and patriotic. I therefore recommend the passage of a law declaring that all persons residing within the Confederate States between the ages of eighteen and thirty-five years, and rightfully subject to military duty, shall be held to be in the military service of the Confederate States, and that some plain and simple method be adopted for their prompt enrolment and organization, repealing all of the legislation heretofore enacted which would conflict with the system proposed.

'JEFFERSON DAVIS.

In accordance with the recommendations of this message, an act was passed on the 16th of April, which provided for the enrolment of all persons liable to military duty between the ages of eighteen and forty-five.

The Confederate line of defense in the west, was, in consequence of the late reverses, greatly contracted. It now extended from Memphis, in the west, through Grand Junction, Corinth, and Chattanooga, along the northern borders of Alabama and Mississippi. Despite the serious check received by the Federal forces at Shiloh, they slowly continued to gain ground in this quarter. Corinth was occupied in April, as were the towns of Huntsville and Florence, in North Alabama. In the south-west, still more important successes were achieved by the Union forces in the capture of New Orleans on the 1st of May, and that of Memphis on the 6th of June following. In Missouri, too, the Confederates were equally unfortunate, being entirely driven from that State.

In Virginia the Confederates were more successful. In a series of great battles, of which the most noted were those of Martinsburg, Seven Pines, and Fredericksburg, the Confederates were entitled to the claim of brilliant victory. But at last nothing decisive resulted from any of these bloody struggles, while the terrible expenditure of strength and resources which they cost the rebellion told heavily against it in the future. Already the drain had begun to deplete the country of its young men, and it was found necessary to extend the age of liability to conscription. Accordingly, Mr. Davis, in his Message of the 15th of August, called the attention of Congress to this subject :

" The report of the Secretary of War, which is submitted, contains numerous suggestions for the legislation deemed desirable in order to add to the efficiency of the service. I invite your favorable consideration especially to those recommendations which are intended to secure the proper execution of the conscript law, and the consolidation of companies, battalions, and regiments, when so reduced in strength as to impair that uniformity of organization which is necessary in the army, while an undue burden is imposed on the Treasury. The necessity for some legislation for controlling military transportation on the railroads, and improving their present defective condition, forces itself upon the attention of the Government, and I trust that you will be able to devise satisfactory measures for attaining this purpose. The legislation on the subject of general officers involves the service in some difficulties, which are pointed out by the Secretary, and for which the remedy suggested by him seems appropriate.

"In connection with this subject, I am of opinion that prudence dictates some provision for the increase of the army, in the event of emergencies not now anticipated. The very large increase of force recently called into the field by the President of the United States, may render it necessary hereafter to extend the provisions of the conscript law, so as to embrace persons between the age of thirty-five and forty-five years. The vigor and efficiency of our present forces, their condition, and the skill and ability which distinguish their leaders, inspire the belief that no further enrolment will be necessary; but a wise foresight requires that if a necessity should be suddenly developed during the recess of Congress, requiring increased forces for our defense, means should exist for calling such forces into the field, without awaiting the reassembling of the legislative department of the Government."

Meanwhile, the currency continued to depreciate alarmingly. The price of the necessaries of life, partly in consequence of this depreciation, became enormous, and at one period there was great fear lest there should be an almost total failure in the supply of salt. A special Act of Congress exempted from military service those who were engaged in its manufacture; the earthen floors of old smoke-houses were filtered with water, and boiled down; and farmers hundreds of miles in the interior drove their wagons to the coast, and supplied themselves and their neighbors with the precious commodity; yet, despite these efforts, salt reached, in many localities, the fabulous price of fifty dollars per bushel.

On the whole, the events of the year 1862 augured unfavorably for the final success of the war for the Southern cause. The Confederate territory was constantly growing smaller, the number of able-bodied men was being fatally reduced, while the depreciation of the currency was approaching the verge beyond which it would be worthless; yet the tone of Mr. Davis's administration was as bold and defiant as ever

CHAPTER VII.

Emancipation Proclamation—Pres. Davis's Message on the subject—Vicksburg—Gettysburg—Chickamauga—The Currency—Military Events of 1864—Failure of Sherman's First Expedition—General Banks's Disaster—Spottsylvania, Wilderness—Georgia hesitates—Atlanta Falls. Re-election of Mr. Lincoln—Sherman's Second Campaign—Final Catastrophe—Particulars of Davis's Flight from Richmond.

THE gloomy aspect of affairs in the Confederate States was heightened by the new policy adopted by Mr. Lincoln for the future conduct of the war. On the 1st of January, 1863, was issued the famous Emancipation Proclamation, declaring the immediate enfranchisement of all slaves in the rebellious States, which was thus adverted to in Mr. Davis's Message of January, 1863 :—

" The public journals of the North have been received, containing a proclamation dated on the first day of the present month, signed by the President of the United States, in which he orders and declares all slaves within ten of the States of the Confederacy to be free, except such as are found within certain districts now occupied in part by the armed forces of the enemy. We may well leave it to the instincts of that common humanity which a beneficent Creator has implanted in the breasts of our fellow men of all countries to pass judgment on a measure by which several millions of human beings of an inferior race—peaceful and contented laborers in their sphere—are doomed to extermination, while at the same time they are encouraged to a general assassination of their masters by the insidious recommendation ' to abstain from violence unless in necessary self-defense.' Our own detestation of those who have attempted the most execrable measure recorded in the history of guilty man, is tempered by profound contempt for the impotent rage which it discloses. So far as regards the action of this Government on such criminals as may attempt its execution, I confine myself to informing you that I shall—unless in your wisdom you deem some other course more expedient—deliver to the several State authorities all commissioned officers of the United States that may hereafter be captured by our forces in any of the States embraced in the proclamation, that they may be dealt with in accordance with the laws of those States providing for the punishment of criminals engaged in exciting servile insurrection. The enlisted soldiers I shall continue to treat as unwilling instruments in the commission of these crimes, and shall direct their discharge and return to their homes on the proper and usual parole."

The elation of the Confederates, caused by the splendid victory of Chancellorsville, was converted into gloom by the loss of one of their greatest generals—Stonewall Jackson ; and the terrible reverses which soon followed entirely disheartened them. The news of the defeat at Gettysburg and the fall of Vicksburg was received at Richmond on the same day. Vicksburg was occupied on the 4th of July, and the fall of Port Hudson, which speedily followed, completed that series of operations which at last opened the navigation of the Mississippi, and completely severed the Confederacy in half. In the West, affairs were not much brighter, for, although the tide of reverses seemed to be turned by the battle of Chickamauga in September, yet, before the close of the year, the total defeat suffered by the Confederates in the battle of Missionary Ridge, again overspread the Confederacy with gloom.

The distrust in its eventual success, excited by the disasters in the field, aggravated the already desperate condition of the currency, which, long before the termination of the year, represented only one-twentieth part of its nominal value. The odium which a few months before deterred creditors from refusing it in payment of debts was fast subsiding, and the time was evidently approaching when it would be worthless for this purpose. The planters themselves, who were most interested in sustaining it, received it in purchase of grain with evident reluctance, and only under the temptation of the most exorbitant prices.

Indeed, the currency at the close of 1863 was despaired of in every quarter save one. The Administration still refused to admit the possibility of its becoming utterly valueless, and continued to urge upon Congress fresh devices for its appreciation and restoration to par value. In his message of December, 1863, Mr. Davis proposed to remedy the financial disorders by heavy taxation, and by a system of compulsory funding. His scheme was adopted in its general features by the next Congress. A load of taxation was at once thrown upon the people, such as has never been known, even in the Old World ; while, in accordance with the recommendation of forced funding, holders of Treasury notes were required to invest them in Government securities during stated periods, under the penalty of repudiation. The result of these vigorous, but obviously desperate measures, was, that whereas, just before their passage, gold commanded a premium of twenty to one, in a few weeks after brokers refused even thirty dollars in Treasury notes for one in specie.

The military events of the year 1864 were, up to the 1st of September, on the whole greatly favorable to the Confederates. The failure of General Sherman's expedition into Mississippi, the disastrous Louisiana campaign of General Banks, the severe Federal reverses in Florida, and the repeated and bloody repulse of General Grant at Spottsylvania, the Wilderness, and before Petersburg, infused new hopes and renewed vigor into the Confederate cause. Strong indications of a disposition to make separate terms with the United States had been manifested in Georgia, insomuch that Mr Davis deemed his personal interposition necessary to prevent the defection of that State. Whether his eloquent and fervid appeals alone would have sufficed to retain Georgia in the Confederacy under less favorable auspices than those which now for a moment cheered the drooping spirits of the Southrons, is doubtful. But, in addition to the encouragement derived from the repeated repulses of the Federal troops, in Virginia, a peace party was rapidly growing up in the Northern States, and in exact proportion to its increase was the wane of the corresponding sentiment South. The horrible and seemingly fruitless carnage attending the recent operations of the Army of the Potomac, in connection with the other Federal reverses just reverted to, had revived the hopes of the Democratic party North, and encouraged them to attempt the defeat of Mr. Lincoln in the coming Presidential election. General McClellan was accordingly nominated on the 29th of August as the opposing candidate, and entered upon the campaign with fair prospects of success. In just three days after his nomination, Atlanta was occupied by General Sherman, and his hopes were nipped in the bud..

Mr. Lincoln was re-elected on the 8th of November. On the 16th, General Sherman commenced the memorable campaign which was soon to change the whole aspect of the war.

From the commencement of the march through Georgia, a steady train of reverses befell the fast declining cause of the Confederacy, which was unrelieved by a single favorable event. The capture of Savannah speedily followed the fall of Atlanta, and the serious defeats at Winchester, and the repulse of Hood at Franklin, intervened. Then came the loss of Fort Morgan, at Mobile, the capitulation of Wilmington, while the seizure of Branchville and Columbia, South Carolina, led to the abandonment of Charleston. This event was soon succeeded by the last battles before Richmond, the retreat of the Southerners, and finally, on the 9th of April, 1865, the surrender of General Lee and his whole forces.

The fall of the Confederacy was so sudden and complete as to take every one by surprise, except perhaps the Confederate leaders themselves. Mr. Davis had made desperate efforts in the latter part of 1864 to infuse some of his own indomitable fortitude into the people, and hurrying through the chief cities left to the narrowing limits of the Confederacy, made stirring appeals to the bravery and patriotism of their inhabitants. Even his iron firmness showed symptoms of sinking under the events which followed his return to Richmond. His message to the Congress of 1864-65 lacked the tone of self-possession and unwavering confidence which had hitherto characterized his communications to that body. Speaking of General Sherman's campaign and the concurrent disasters in other quarters, he said :—" Recent military operations of the enemy have been successful in the capture of some of our seaports, in interrupting some of our lines of communication, and in devastating large districts of our country. . . . The capital of the Confederate States is now threatened and is in greater danger than it has heretofore been during the war." He also indicated unmistakably his opinion of the serious nature of the crisis by urging the employment of negro soldiers.

Foreseeing, as Mr. Davis evidently must have done, the possibility if not probability of the early fall of Richmond, it is somewhat singular that he should not sooner have taken measures for the removal of the State archives from that city. It was not, however, till the memorable 2nd of April that he decided to leave Richmond. The departure of Mr. Davis was coeval with the fall of the Confederacy. The events that followed his departure are drawn from Mr. Davis's own account as related in Dr. Craven's book, to which previous reference has been made.

" On leaving Richmond he went first to Danville, because it was intended that Lee should have moved in that direction, falling back to make a junction with Johnson's force in the direction of Roanoke River. Grant, however, pressed forward so rapidly, and swung so far around, that Lee was obliged to retreat in the direction of Lynchburgh with his main force, while his vanguard, which arrived at Danville, insisted on falling back and making the rallying-point at Charlotte in North Carolina.

"In Danville Mr. Davis learned of Lee's surrender. Immediately started for Goldsboro', where he met and had a consultation with Gen. Johnson, thence going on South. At Lexington he received a dispatch from Johnson requesting that the Secretary of War (Gen. Breckinridge) should repair to his headquarters near Raleigh—Gen. Sherman having submitted a proposition for laying down arms which was too comprehensive in its scope for any mere military commander to decide upon. Breckinridge and Postmaster-General Reagan immediately started for Johnson's camp, where Sherman submitted the terms of surrender on which an armistice was declared—the same terms subsequently disapproved by the authorities at Washington.

" One of the features of the proposition submitted by Gen. Sherman was a declaration of amnesty to all persons, both civil and military. Notice being called to the fact particularly, Sherman said, ' I mean just that ;' and gave as his reason that it was the only way to have perfect peace. He had previously offered to furnish a vessel to take away any such persons as Mr. Davis might select, to be freighted with whatever personal property they might want to take with them, and to go wherever it pleased.

" Gen. Johnson told Sherman that it was worse than useless to carry such a proposition as the last to him. Breckinridge also informed Gen. Sherman that his proposition contemplated the adjustment of certain matters which even Mr, Davis was not empowered to control. The terms were accepted, however, with the understanding that they should be liberally construed on both sides, and fulfilled in good faith—General Breckinridge adding that certain parts of the terms would require to be submitted to the various State governments of the Confederacy for ratification.

"These terms of agreement between Johnson and Sherman were subsequently disapproved by the authorities at Washington, and the armistice ordered to cease after a certain time. Mr. Davis waited in Charlotte until the day and hour when the armistice ended; then mounted his horse, and, with some cavalry of Duke's brigade (formerly Morgan's), again started southward, passing through South Carolina to Washington, in Georgia. At an encampment on the road, he thinks, the cavalry of his escort probably heard of the final surrender of General Johnson, though he himself did not until much later. Being in the advance, he rode on, supposing that the escort was coming after.

" As with his party he approached the town of Washington, he was informed that a regiment, supposed to belong to the army of General Thomas, was moving on the place to capture it, in violation, as he thought, of General Sherman's terms. On this he sent back word to the General commanding the cavalry escort to move up and cover the town—an order which probably never reached its destination—at least the cavalry never came; nor did he see them again, nor any of them. Thinking they were coming, however, and not apprehending any molestation from the Federal troops, even if occupying the same town, he entered Washington, and remained there over night—no troops of the

United States appearing. Here he heard of his wife and family, not having seen them since they had left Richmond, more than a month before his own departure. They had just left the town before his arrival, moving South in company with his private secretary, Colonel Harrison, of whose fidelity he spoke in warm terms, and accompanied by a small party of paroled men, who, seeing them unprotected, had volunteered to be their escort to Florida, from whence the family, not Mr. Davis himself, intended to take ship to Cuba.

Mr. Davis regarded the section of country he was now in as covered by Sherman's armistice, and had no thought that any expedition could or would be sent for his own capture, or for any other warlike purposes. He believed the terms of Johnson's capitulation still in force over all the country east of the Chattahoochie, which had been embraced in Johnson's immediate command ; citing as an evidence of this, that while he was in Washington, General Upton, of the Federal service, with a few members of his staff, passed unattended over the railroad, a few miles from the place, *en route* for Augusta, to receive the muster-rolls of the discharged troops, and take charge of the immense military stores there that fell into General Sherman's hands by the surrender. General Upton was not interfered with, the country being considered at peace, though nothing could have been easier than his capture, had Mr. Davis been so inclined.

" At this very time, however, a division of cavalry had been sent into this district, which had been declared at peace and promised exemption from the dangers and burdens of any further military operations within its limits, for the purpose of capturing himself and party; and this he could not but regard as a breach of faith on the part of those who directed or permitted it to be done, though he did not wish to place himself in the condition of one who had accepted the terms of Johnson's capitulation, or taken advantage of the amnesty which Sherman had offered. But the district in which he then found himself had been promised exemption from further incursions, and he did not think himself justly liable to capture while within its limits—though he expected to have to take the chances of arrest when once across the Chattahoochie.

"Hearing that a skirmish-line, or patrol, had been extended across the country from Macon to Atlanta, and thence to Chattanooga, he thought best to go below this line, hoping to join the forces of his relative, Lieutenant-General Dick Taylor, after crossing the Chattahoochie. He would then cross the Mississippi, joining Taylor's forces to those of Kirby Smith—of whom he spoke with marked acerbity—and would have continued the fight so long as he could find any Confederate force to strike with him. This, not in any hope of final success, but to secure for the South some better terms than surrender at discretion. 'To this complexion,' said Mr. Davis, 'had the repudiation of General Sherman's terms, and the surrenders of Lee and Johnson, brought the Southern cause.'

"Mr. Davis left Washington accompanied by Postmaster-General Reagan, three aides, and an escort of ten mounted men with one pack-mule. Riding along, they heard distressing reports of bands of marauders going about the country stealing horses and whatever else might tempt their cupidity—these rumors finally maturing into information which caused him to change his course and follow on to overtake the train containing his wife and family, for whose safety he began to feel apprehensions.

"This object he achieved after riding seventy miles, without halt, in a single day, joining Mrs. Davis just at daylight, and in time to prevent a party he had passed on the road from stealing her two fine carriage-horses, which formed a particular attraction for their greed. 'I have heard,' he added, 'since my imprisonment, that it was supposed there was a large amount of specie in the train. Such was not the fact, Mrs. Davis carrying with her no money that was not personal property, and but very little of that.'

"Having joined his family, he travelled with them for several days, in consequence of finding the region infested with deserters and robbers engaged in plundering whatever was defenseless, his intention being to quit his wife whenever she had reached a safe portion of the country, and to bear west across the Chattahoochie. The very evening before his arrest he was to have carried out this arrangement, believing Mrs. Davis to be now safe ; but was prevented by a report brought in through one of his aides, that a party of guerillas, or highwaymen, was coming that night to seize the horses and mules of his wife's train. It was on this report he decided to remain another night.

"Towards morning, he had just fallen into the deep sleep of exhaustion, when his wife's faithful negro servant, Robert, came to him, announcing that there was firing up the road. He started up, dressed himself and went out. It was just at grey dawn, and by the imperfect light he saw a party approaching the camp.

They were recognized as Federal cavalry, by the way in which they deployed to surround the train, and he stepped back into the tent, to warn his wife that the enemy were at hand.

"Their tent was prominent, being isolated from the other tents of the trains ; and as he was quitting it to find his horse, several of the cavalry rode up, directing him to halt and surrender. To this he gave a defiant answer. Then one whom he supposed to be an officer asked, had he any arms, to which Mr. Davis replied : 'If I had, you would not be alive to ask that question.' His pistols had been left in the holsters, as it had been his intention, the evening before, to start whenever the camp was settled; but horse, saddle and holsters were now in the enemy's possession, and he was completely unarmed.

"Colonel Pritchard, commanding the Federal cavalry, came up soon, to whom Mr. Davis said : 'I suppose, sir, your orders are accomplished in arresting me. You can have no wish to interfere with women and children ; and I beg they may be permitted to pursue their journey.' The Colonel replied, that his orders were to take every one found in my company back to Macon, and he would have to do so, though grieved to inconvenience the ladies. Mr. Davis said his wife's party was composed of paroled men, who had committed no act of war since their release, and begged they might be permitted to go to their homes ; but the Colonel, under his orders, did not feel at liberty to grant this request. They were all taken to Macon, therefore, reaching it in four days, and from thence were carried by rail to Augusta—Mr. Davis thanking Major-General J. H. Wilson for having treated him with all the courtesy possible to the situation.

" The party transferred to Augusta consisted of Reagan, Alexander H. Stevens, Clement C. Clay, two of his own aides and private secretary, Mrs. Clay, his wife and four children, four servants and three paroled men, who had generously offered their protection to Mrs. Davis during her journey. Breckinridge had been with the cavalry brigade, which had been the escort of Mr. Davis, and did not come up at Washington. He and Secretary Benjamin had started for Florida, expecting to escape thence to the West Indies. There was no specie nor public treasure in the train—nothing but his private funds, and of them very little. Some wagons had been furnished by the Quartermaster at Washington, Georgia, for the transportation of his family and the paroled men who formed their escort, and that was the only train. Mr. Davis had not seen his family for some months before, and first rejoined them when he rode to their defense from Washington."

CHAPTER VIII.

Mr. Davis at Fortress Monroe—Outrages upon the ex-President—Account of his being Shackled.

It was on the 19th day of May, 1865, that the propeller *William P. Clyde* dropped anchor in Hampton Roads, having on board as prisoners, Jefferson Davis, late President of the late Confederacy, and his family ; Alexander H. Stephens, Vice-President ; John H. Reagan, late Postmaster-General ; Clement C. Clay, and several more State prisoners belonging to the Confederacy.

Preparations had been going on in Fortress Monroe for some days for the reception of the distinguished prisoners. On the morning of the 21st of May, Mr. Stephens, Mr. Reagan, and others of the prisoners, were removed to the gunboat *Maumee*, which then steamed for Fort Warren, in Boston harbor, and on the afternoon of the same day, the arrangements being completed, Messrs. Davis and Clay were removed to their quarters in Fortress Monroe.

The parting between Mr. Davis and his wife, four children, and the other members of his family and household who were on board the *Clyde*, was extremely affecting—the ladies sobbing passionately as the two prisoners, Messrs. Clay and Davis, were handed over the ship's side and into the boat, which was in waiting for them.

" The procession into the fort," says Dr. Craven, "was simple though momentous, and was under the immediate inspection of Major-General Halleck and the Hon. Charles A. Dana, then Assistant Secretary of War ; Colonel Pritchard, of the Michigan cavalry, who immediately effected the capture, being the officer in command of the guard from the vessel to the fort. First came Major-General Miles, holding the arm of Mr. Davis, who was dressed in a suit of plain Confederate grey, with a grey slouched hat—always thin, and now looking much wasted and very haggard. Immediately after these came Colonel Pritchard, accompanying Mr. Clay, with a guard of soldiers in their rear. Thus they passed through files of men in blue from the Engineer's Landing to the Water Battery Postern ; and on arriving at the casemate which had been fitted up into cells for their incarceration, Mr. Davis was shown into casemate No. 2, and Clay into No. 4, guards of soldiers being stationed in the cells numbered 1, 3, and 5, upon each side of them. They entered ; the heavy doors clanged behind them, and in that clang was rung the final knell of the terrible, but now extinct, rebellion. Here, indeed, is a fall, my countrymen. Another and most striking illustration of the mutability of human greatness.

" Being ushered into his inner cell by General Miles, and the two doors leading thereinto from the guard-room being fastened, Mr. Davis, after surveying the premises for some moments, and looking out through the embrasure with such thoughts passing over his lined and expressive face as may be imagined, suddenly seated himself in a chair, placing both hands on his knees, and asked one of the soldiers pacing up and down within his cell, this significant question : ' Which way does the embrasure face ?'

" The soldier was silent.

" Mr. Davis, raising his voice a little, repeated the inquiry.

" But again dead silence, or only the measured footfalls of the two pacing sentries within, and the fainter echoes of the four without.

" Addressing the other soldier, as if the first had been deaf and had not heard him, the prisoner again repeated his inquiry

" But the second soldier remained silent as the first, a slight twitching of his eyes only intimating that he had heard the question, but was forbidden to speak.

" ' Well,' said Mr. Davis, throwing his hands up, and breaking into a bitter laugh, ' I wish my men could have been taught your discipline !' and then, rising from his chair, he commenced pacing back and forth before the embrasure, now looking at the silent sentry across the moat, and anon at the two silently pacing soldiers who were his companions in the casemate.

" What caused his bitter laugh—for even in his best days his temper was of the saturnine and atrabilious type, seldom capable of being moved beyond a smile ? Was he thinking of those days under President Pierce, in which on his approach the cannon of the fortress thundered their hoarse salute to the all-powerful Secretary of War—the fort's gates leaping open, its soldiers presenting arms, and the whole place under his command ? Or those later days under Mr. Buchanan, when, as the most powerful member of the Military Committee of the Senate, similar honors were paid on his arrival at every national work ?

4

" And was not his question significant—'Which way does this
embrasure face ?' Was it north, south, east, or west ? In the
hurry and agitation of being conducted in, he had lost his reckon-
ing of the compass, though well-acquainted with the localities ;
and his first question was in effect : ' Does my vision in its reach
go southward to the empire I have lost, or North to the loyal
enemies who have subdued my people ?'—for it is always as
' his people' that Mr. Davis refers to the Southern States.

" His sole reading-matter, a Bible and prayer-book ; his only
companions, those two silent guards ; and his only food, the ordinary rations of bread and beef served out to the soldiers of the
garrison—thus passed the first day and night of the ex-President's
confinement."

But on the morning of the 23d of May a bitter trial and humil-
ation was in store for the proud spirit—a humiliation severer
than has ever in modern times been inflicted upon one whose
career has been so eminent. The particulars of the outrage of
shackling the Confederate ex-president are recorded by Dr. Craven in his interesting work on the " Prison-Life of Jefferson
Davis," and cannot fail to excite the deepest indignation and
shame in every reader who has the reputation and fairfame
of his country at heart. There is no motive that can be assigned
for the infamous act, but the bitter and infuriated malice of the
Government—a motive that sought during the entire war to cast
every obloquy upon the character of the great Southern Chief,
that without evidence and in face of all probability accused him
in the face of the world as an assassin and murderer, that hoped to

overwhelm him in ridicule and humiliation by a trumped up story
of his attempt to escape disguised as a woman, and which was
sought to brand him with a felon's shame by degrading him with
a felon's shackles. The outrage deserves the scorn and indignation of the world, and should stamp those who ordered, and
those who consented to the act with everlasting infamy. Where
was the honor and dignity of the officer-in-command who consented to descend from his high position to that of a common
jailor ?. He should have resigned at once, rather than have executed the order. Did the officers of our army possess that spirit
and that sense of honor that traditionally belongs to the soldier
and the officer, the Government would have found it impossible
to have carried out their design—the entire rank would have
resigned rather than have disgraced their epaulettes by such a
foul and dastardly piece of business. When Napoleon was carried to St. Helena, the English officer-in-command demanded his
sword worn merely as an ornamental side-arm, and all Europe rang
with the insult and outrage. Napoleon, indeed, refused to surrender
it, and he was allowed to wear it, the English government, sensible
of the indignity thus offered their illustrious prisoner, and of the
feeling that the outrage excited in Europe, ordered the officer-in-
command to withdraw his demand. How different the conduct
of our own government toward a prisoner scarcely less eminent
than the great Corsican ! How can we but feel that the act
of our government is a blot upon our civilization, a stain and a
shame upon our fair name, exhibiting us low in civilization, without dignity, and animated by petty animosities and spites ! Here
was a man who a few short weeks before was the acknowledged

ruler of six millions of people; with immense armies at his command; with Cabinet officers, embassadors, and a staff of devoted adherents; filling a foremost place in history, the world ringing with his deeds and in sympathy with his hopes; he who has founded an empire, and maintained it through a war more formidable than any of modern times—a man thus eminent and conspicuous, cast into a dungeon and shackled like any common felon! There is indeed little in history to parallel it, and the indignity intended as a humiliation to Jefferson Davis, has reacted and become our own burning shame.

"It was," says Dr. Craven, "while all the swarming camps of the armies of the Potomac—over two hundred thousand bronzed and laureled veterans—were preparing for the Grand Review of the next morning, in which, passing in endless succession before the mansion of the President, the conquering military power of the nation was to lay down its arms at the feet of the civil authority, that the following scene was enacted at Fort Monroe:

"Captain Jerome E. Titlow, of the Third Pennsylvania Artillery, entered the prisoner's cell, followed by the blacksmith of the fort and his assistant, the latter carrying in his hands some heavy and harshly-rattling shackles. As they entered, Mr. Davis was reclining on his bed, feverish and weary after a sleepless night, the food placed near to him the preceding day still lying untouched on its tin plate near his bedside

"'Well?' said Mr. Davis, as they entered, slightly raising his head.

"'I have an unpleasant duty to perform, sir,' said Captain Titlow ; and, as he spoke, the senior blacksmith took the shackles from his assistant.

"Davis leaped instantly from his recumbent attitude, a flush passing over his face for a moment, and then his countenance growing livid and rigid as death.

"He gasped for breath, clutching his throat with the thin fingers of his right hand, and then recovering himself slowly, while his wasted figure towered up to its full height—now appearing to swell with indignation and then to shrink with terror, as he glanced from the captain's face to the shackles—he said slowly and with a laboring chest :

"'My God !' You cannot have been sent to iron me ?"

"'Such are my orders, sir,' replied the officer, beckoning the blacksmith to approach, who stepped forward, unlocking the padlock and preparing the fetters to do their office. These fetters were of heavy iron, probably five-eighths of an inch in thickness, and connected together by a chain of like weight. I believe they are now in the possession of Major-General Miles, and will form an interesting relic.

"'This is too monstrous,' groaned the prisoner, glaring hurriedly round the room, as if for some weapon or means of self-destruction. 'I demand, Captain, that you let me see the commanding officer. Can he pretend that such shackles are required to secure the safe custody of a weak old man, so guarded, and in such a fort as this ?'

"'It could serve no purpose,' replied Captain Titlow; 'his orders are from Washington, as mine are from him.'

"'But he can telegraph,' interposed Mr. Davis eagerly ; 'there must be some mistake. No such outrage as you threaten me with, is on record in the history of nations. Beg him to telegraph, and delay until he answers.'

" ' My orders are peremptory,' said the officer, ' and admit of no delay. For your own sake, let me advise you to submit with patience. As a soldier, Mr. Davis, you know I must execute orders.'

" ' These are not orders for a soldier,' shouted the prisoner, los. ing all control of himself. ' They are orders for a jailor—for a hangman, which no soldier wearing a sword should accept ! I tell you the world will ring with this disgrace. The war is over ; the South is conquered ; I have no longer any country but America, and it is for the honor of America, as for my own honor and life, that I plead against this degradation. Kill me ! kill me !' he cried, passionately, throwing his arms wide open and exposing his breast, "rather than inflict on me, and on my people through me, this insult worse than death.'

" ' Do your duty, blacksmith,' said the officer, walking towards the embrasure as if not caring to witness the performance. ' It only gives increased pain on all sides to protract this interview.'

" At these words the blacksmith advanced with the shackles, and seeing that the prisoner had one foot upon the chair near his bedside, his right hand resting on the back of it, the brawny mechanic made an attempt to slip one of the shackles over the ankle so raised ; but, as if with the vehemence and strength which frenzy can impart, even to the weakest invalid, Mr. Davis suddenly seized his assailant and hurled him half-way across the room.

"On this Captain Titlow turned, and seeing that Davis had backed against the wall for further resistance, began to remonstrate, pointing out in brief, clear language, that this course was madness, and that orders must be enforced at any cost. 'Why compel me,' he said, 'to add the further indignity of personal violence to the necessity of your being ironed?'

"'I am a prisoner of war,' fiercely retorted Davis; 'I have been a soldier in the armies of America, and know how to die. Only kill me, and my last breath shall be a blessing on your head. But while I have life and strength to resist, for myself and for my people, this thing shall not be done.'

"Hereupon Captain Titlow called in a sergeant and file of soldiers from the next room, and the sergeant advanced to seize the prisoner. Immediately Mr. Davis flew on him, seized his musket and attempted to wrench it from his grasp.

"Of course such a scene could have but one issue. There was a short, passionate scuffle. In a moment Davis was flung upon his bed, and before his four powerful assailants removed their hands from him, the blacksmith and his assistant had done their work—one securing the rivet on the right ankle, while the other turned the key in the padlock on the left.

"This done, Mr. Davis lay for a moment as if in stupor. Then slowly raising himself and turning round, he dropped his shackled feet to the floor. The harsh clank of the striking chain seems first to have recalled him to his situation, and dropping his face into his hands, he burst into a passionate flood of sobbing, rocking to and fro, and muttering at brief intervals: 'Oh! the shame! the shame!'

" It may be here stated, though out of its due order—that we may get rid in haste of an unpleasant subject—that Mr. Davis some two months later, when frequent visits had made him more free of converse, gave me a curious explanation of the last feature in this incident.

"He had been speaking of suicide, and denouncing it as the worst form of cowardice and folly. 'Life is not like a commission that we can resign when disgusted with the service. Taking it by your own hand is a confession of judgment to all that your worst enemies can allege. It has often flashed across me as a tempting remedy for neuralgic torture ; but, thank God ! I never sought my own death but once, and then when completely frenzied and not master of my actions. When they came to iron me that day, as a last resource of desperation, I seized a soldier's musket and attempted to wrench it from his grasp, hoping that in the scuffle and surprise, some one of his comrades would shoot or bayonet me !' "

CHAPTER IX.

Health of the Ex-president—His Cruel Treatment—Sovereignty of the States—
Conversations with Dr. Craven—His Improved Treatment—Approaching
Trial.

THE health of Mr. Davis was now failing rapidly. Suffering
greatly from neuralgic disorders and other various affections,
greatly reduced in system, without appetite, unable on account
of his shackles to take exercise, supplied with coarse rations and
refused even a knife and fork, without books, pen, paper or
even a pencil, incessantly watched by two sentinels, who night
and day passed his cell ; thus depriving him of even so poor a
boon as solitude and silence, the health of the unfortunate prisoner
failed rapidly, and would soon have succumbed entirely to the inhuman treatment to which he was subjected, had not Dr. Craven
actively interested himself in his behalf and procured the removal
of the shackles, and some changes in his rations. But still the
prisoner was a great sufferer ; his nights were sleepless ; he was
without appetite ; the incessant pacing, night and day, of his
ever-present guards, acted acutely upon his nervous system and
tormented him almost into insanity.

Referring once to the severity of his treatment, Mr. Davis said
to Dr. Craven : " Humanity supposes every man innocent until
the reverse shall be proven ; and the laws guarantee certain

privileges to persons held for trial. To hold me here for trial, under all the rigors of a condemned convict, is not warranted by law—is revolting to the spirit of justice. In the political history of the world, there is no parallel to my treatment.. England and the despotic governments of Europe have beheaded men accused of treason ; but even after their conviction no such efforts as in my case have been made to degrade them. Apart, however, from my personal treatment, let us see how this matter stands :

" If the real purpose in the matter be to test the question of secession by trying certain persons connected therewith for treason, from what class or classes should the persons so selected be drawn ?

" From those who called the State Conventions, or from those who, in their respective conventions, passed the ordinance of secession ? Or, from the authors of the doctrine of State rights ? Or, from those citizens who, being absent from their States, were unconnected with the event, but on its occurrence returned to their homes to share the fortunes of their States as a duty of primal allegiance ? Or from those officers of the State, who being absent on public service, were called home by the ordinance, and returning joined their fellow-citizens in State service, and followed the course due to that relation ?

" To the last class I belong, who am the object of greatest rigor. This can only be explained on the supposition that, having been most honored, I, therefore, excite most revengeful feelings—for how else can it be accounted for ?

" I did not wish for war, but peace ; therefore sent Commissioners to negotiate before war commenced ; and subsequently strove my uttermost to soften the rigors of war ; in every pause of conflict seeking, if possible, to treat for peace. Numbers of those already practically pardoned are those who, at the beginning, urged that the black flag should be hoisted, and the struggle made one of desperation.

"Believing the States to be each sovereign, and their union voluntary, I had learned from the Fathers of the Constitution that a State could change its form of government, abolishing all which had previously existed ; and my only crime has been obedience to this conscientious conviction. Was not this the universal doctrine of the dominant Democratic party in the North previous to secession ? Did not many of the opponents of that party, in the same section, share and avow that faith ? They preached and professed to believe. We believed, and preached, and practised.

"If this theory be now adjudged erroneous, the history of the States, from their colonial organization to the present moment, should be re-written, and the facts suppressed which may mislead others in a like manner to a like conclusion.

But if—as I suppose—the purpose be to test the question of secession by a judicial decision, why begin by oppressing the chief subject of the experiment ? Why, in the name of fairness and a decent respect for the opinions of mankind, deprive him of the means needful to a preparation of his defense ; and load him with indignities which must deprive his mind of its due equilibrium ? It ill comports with the dignity of a great nation to evince fear of giving to a single captive enemy all the advantages possible for an exposition of his side of the question. A question settled by violence, or in disregard of law, must remain unsettled for ever.

"Believing all good government to rest on truth, it is the resulting belief that injustice to any individual is a public injury, which can only find compensation in the reaction which brings retributive justice upon the oppressors. It has been the continually growing danger of the North, that in attempting to crush the liberties of my people, you would raise a Frankenstein of tyranny that would not down at your bidding. Sydney, and Russell, and Vane, and Peters, suffered; but in their death Liberty received blessings their lives might never have conferred.

"If the doctrine of State Sovereignty be a dangerous heresy, the genius of America would indicate another remedy than the sacrifice of one of its believers. Wickliffe died, but Huss took up his teachings; and when the dust of this martyr was sprinkled on the Rhine, some essence of it was infused in the cup which Luther drank.

"The road to grants of power is known and open; and thus all questions of reserved rights on which men of highest distinction may differ, and have differed, can be settled by fair adjudication; and thus only can they be finally set at rest.

At another time, Mr. Davis remarked that it was "contrary to reason, and the law of nations, to treat as a rebellion, or lawless riot, a movement which had been the deliberate action of an entire people through their duly organized State governments. To talk of treason in the case of the South, was to oppose an arbitrary epithet against the authority of all writers on international law. Vattel deduces from his study of all former precedent—and all subsequent international jurists have agreed with him—that when a nation separates into two parts, each claiming independence, and both, or either, setting up a new government, their quarrel, should it come to trial by arms or by diplomacy, shall be regarded and settled precisely as though it were a difference between two separate nations, which the divided sections, *de facto*, have become. Each must observe the laws of war in the treatment of captives taken in battle, and such negotiations as may from time to time arise shall be conducted as between independent and sovereign powers. Mere riots, or conspiracies for lawless objects, in which only limited fractions of a people are irregularly engaged, may be properly treated as treason, and punished as the public good may require ; but Edmund Burke had exhausted argument on the subject in his memorable phrase, applied to the first American movement for independence : 'I know not how an indictment against a whole people shall be framed.'

"But for Mr. Lincoln's untimely death, Mr. Davis thought there could have been no question raised upon the subject. That event—more a calamity to the South than North, in the time and manner of its transpiring—had inflamed popular passions to the highest pitch, and made the people of the section which had lost their chief now seek as an equivalent the life of the chief of the section conquered. This was an impulse of passion, not a conclusion which judgment or justice could support. Mr. Lincoln, through his entire administration, had acknowledged the South as a belligerent nationality, exchanging prisoners of war, establishing truces, and sometimes sending, sometimes receiving, propositions for peace. On the last of these occasions, accompanied by the chief member of his cabinet, he had personally met the Commissioners appointed by the Southern States to negotiate, going half-way to meet them not far from where Mr. Davis now stood ; and the negotiations of Gen. Grant with Gen. Lee, just preceding the latter's surrender, most distinctly and clearly pointed to the promise of a general amnesty ; Gen. Grant, in his final letter, expressing the hope that, with Lee's surrender, 'all difficulties between the sections might be settled without the loss of another life,' or words to that effect."

Following Dr. Craven, we find that the health of Mr. Davis grew sensibly worse. Step by step, the kind-hearted physician obtained an amelioration of the condition of the eminent prisoner ; but the severity of the treatment he had experienced in the early part of his confinement, still told greatly on his health—and it can readily be appreciated how any confinement to a man in his physical and mental condition, must have resulted unfavorably to his health. Proceeding to follow Dr. Craven, we extract passages from several interesting conversations had with the prisoner ; and we also quote from the worthy Doctor's diary, a few references to the physical condition and suffering of his illustrious patient :

" *June 8th.*—Was called to the prisoner, whom I had not seen for a week. Found Mr. Davis relapsing, and very despondent. Complained again of intolerable pains in his head. Was distracted night and day by the unceasing tread of the two sentinels in his room, and the murmur or gabble of the guards in the outside cell.

He said his casemate was well-formed for a torture-room of the inquisition. Its arched roof made it a perfect whispering gallery, in which all sounds were jumbled and repeated. The torment of his head was so dreadful, he feared he must lose his mind. Already his memory, vision, and hearing, were impaired. He had but the remains of one eye left, and the glaring, whitewashed walls were rapidly destroying this. He pointed to a crevice in the wall where his bed had been, explaining that he had changed to the other side, to avoid its mephitic vapors.

" Of the trial he had been led to expect, had heard nothing. This looked as if the indictment were to be suppressed, and the action of a Military Commission substituted. If so, they might do with him as they pleased, for he would not plead, but leave his cause to the justice of the future. As to taking his life, that would be the greatest boon they could confer on him, though for the sake of his family, he might regret the manner of its taking."

" Mr. Davis remarked that when his tray of breakfast had been brought in that morning, he overheard some soldiers in the guard-room outside commenting on the food given our prisoners during the late war. To hold him responsible for this was worse than absurd—criminally false. For the last two years of the war, Lee's army had never more than half, and was oftener on quarter rations of rusty bacon and corn. It was yet worse with other Southern armies when operating in a country which had been campaigned over any time. Sherman, with a front of thirty or forty miles, breaking into a new country, found no trouble in procuring food ; but had he halted anywhere, even for a single week, must have starved. Marching every day, his men ate out a new section, and left behind them a starving wilderness.

" Colonel Northrop, his Commissary-General, had many difficulties to contend with ; and, not least, the incessant hostility of certain opponents of his administration, who, by striking at Northrop, really meant to strike at him. Even General ——, otherwise so moderate and conservative, was finally induced to join this injurious clamor. There was food in the Confederacy, but no means for its collection, the holders hiding it after the currency had become depreciated ; and, if collected, then came the difficulty of its transportation. Their railroads were over-taxed, and the rolling-stock soon gave out. They could not feed their own troops ; and prisoners of war in all countries and ages have had cause of complaint. Some of his people confined in the West and at Lookout Point, had been nearly starved at certain times, though he well knew, or well believed, full prison-rations had been ordered and paid for in these cases.

" Herd men together in idleness within an inclosure, their arms taken from them, their organization lost, without employment for their time, and you will find it difficult to keep them in good health. They were ordered to receive precisely the same rations given to the troops guarding them ; but dishonest Commissaries and Provost-Marshals were not confined to any people. Doubtless the prisoners on both sides often suffered, that the officers having charge of them might grow rich ; but wherever such dishonesty could be brought home, prompt punishment followed. General Winder and Colonel Northrop did the best they could, he believed ; but both were poorly obeyed or seconded by their sub-ordinates. To hold him responsible for such unauthorized priva-tions, was both cruel and absurd. He issued order after order on the subject, and, conscious of the extreme difficulty of feeding the prisoners, made the most liberal offers for exchange—almost willing to accept any terms that would release his people from their burden. Non-exchange, however, was the policy adopted by the Federal Government—just as Austria, in her late campaigns against Frederick the Great, refused to exchange ; her calculation being, that as her population was five times more numerous than Prussia's, the refusal to exchange would be a wise measure. That it may have been prudent, though inhuman, situated as the South was, he was not prepared to deny ; but protested against being held responsible for evils which no power of his could avert, and to escape from which almost any concessions had been offered."

" *Sunday, July 11th.*—Was sent for by Mr. Davis. Found prisoner very desponding, the failure of his sight troubling him, and his nights almost without sleep. His present treatment was killing him by inches, and he wished shorter work could be made of his torment. He had hoped long since for a trial, which should be public, and therefore with some semblance of fairness ; but hope deferred was making his heart sick. The odious, malig-nant and absurd insinuation that he was connected in some man-ner with the great crime and folly of Mr. Lincoln's assassination, was his chief personal motive for so earnestly desiring an early opportunity of vindication. But apart from this, as he was evidently made the representative in whose person the action of the seceding States was to be argued and decided, he yet more strongly desired for this reason to be heard in behalf of the defeated, but to him still sacred cause. The defeat he accepted, as a man has to accept all necessities of accomplished fact ; but to vindicate the theory and justice of his cause, showing by the authority of the Constitution and the Fathers of the Country, that his people had only asserted a right—had committed no crime— this was the last remaining labor which life could impose on him · as a public duty."

" Of Stonewall Jackson, Mr. Davis spoke with the utmost tenderness, and some touch of reverential feeling, bearing witness to his earnest and pathetic piety, his singleness of aim, his immense energy as an executive officer, and the loyalty of his nature, making obedience the first of all duties. ' He rose every morning at three,' said Mr. Davis ; ' performed his devotions for half an hour, and then went booming along at the head of his command, which came to be called "Jackson's foot cavalry," from the velocity of their movements. He had the faculty, or rather gift, of exciting and holding the love and confidence of his men to an unbounded degree, even though the character of his campaigning imposed on them more hardships than on any other troops in the service. Good soldiers care not for their individual sacrifices when adequate results can be shown ; and these General Jackson never lacked. Hard fighting, hard marching, hard fare, the strictest discipline—all these men will bear, if visibly approaching the gaol of their hopes. They want to get done with the war,

back to their homes and families ; and their instinct soon teaches
them which commander is pursuing the right means to accomplish
these results. Jackson was a singularly ungainly man on horseback, and had many peculiarities of temper, amounting to violent
idiosyncrasies ; but everything in his nature, though here and
there uncouth, was noble. Even in the heat of action, and when
most exposed, he might be seen throwing up his hands in prayer.
For glory he lived long enough,' continued Mr. Davis, with much
emotion ; ' and if this result had to come, it was the Divine mercy
that removed him. He fell like the eagle, his own feather on the
shaft that was dripping with his life-blood. In his death the
Confederacy lost an eye and arm, our only consolation being that
the final summons could have reached no soldier more prepared to
accept it joyfully. Jackson was not of a sanguine turn, always
privately anticipating the worst, that the better might be more
welcome.' "

"Mr. Davis expressed some anxiety as to his present illness.
He was not one of those who, when in trouble, wished to die.
Great invalids seldom had this wish, save when protracted sufferings had weakened the brain. Suicides were commonly of the
robuster class—men who had never been brought close to death
nor thought much about it seriously. A good old Bishop once
remarked, that ' dying was the last thing a man should think
about,' and the mixture of wisdom and quaint humor in the phrase
had impressed Mr. Davis. Even to Christians, with the hope of
an immortal future for the soul, the idea of physical annihilation—
of parting forever from the tenement of flesh in which we have

had so many joys and sorrows—was one full of awe, if not terror.
What it must be to the unbeliever, who entertained absolute and
total annihilation as his prospect, he could not conceive. Never
again to hear of wife or children—to take the great leap
into black vacuity, with no hope of meeting in a brighter and
happier life the loved ones left behind, the loved ones gone
before !

"He had more reasons than other men, and now more than
ever, to wish for some prolongation of life, as also to welcome
death. His intolerable sufferings and wretched state argued for
the grave as a place of rest. His duties to the cause he had
represented, and his family, made him long to be continued on the
footstool, in whatever pain or misery, at least until by the ordeal
of a trial he could convince the world he was not the monster his
enemies would make him appear, and that no willful departures
from the humanities of war had stained the escutcheon of his
people. Errors, like all other men, he had committed ; but
stretched now on a bed from which he might never rise, and looking with the eyes of faith which no walls could bar, up to the
throne of Divine mercy, it was his comfort that no such crimes as
men laid to his charge reproached him in the whispers of his conscience.

"'They charge me with crime, Doctor, but God knows my inno-
cence. I indorse no measure that was not justified by the laws of
war. Failure is all forms of guilt in one to men who occupied my
position. Should I die, repeat this for the sake of my people, my
dear wife, and poor darling children. Tell the world I only loved
America, and that in following my State I was only carrying out

doctrines received from reverenced lips in my early youth, and adopted by my judgment as the convictions of riper years.' "

" Had General Albert Sidney Johnston lived, Mr. Davis was of opinion, our success down the Mississippi would have been fatally checked at Corinth. This officer best realized his ideal of a perfect commander—large in view, discreet in council, silent as to his own plans, observant and penetrative of the enemy's, sudden and impetuous in action, but of a nerve and balance of judgment which no heat of danger or complexity of manœuvre could upset or bewilder. All that Napolean said of Dessaix and Kleber, save the slovenly habits of one of them, might be combined and truthfully said of Albert Sidney Johnston. Johnston had been opposed to locating the Confederate Capital at Richmond, alleging that it would involve fighting on the exterior of our circle, in lieu of the centre : and that as the struggle would finally be for whatever point was the capital, it was ill-advised to go so far north, thus shortening the enemy's line of transportation and supply. ' Whatever value this criticism may have had in a military point of view,' added Mr. Davis, ' there were political necessities connected with Virginia which left no choice in the matter. It was a bold courting of the issue, clearly planting our standard in front of the enemy's line and across his path. Such reflections are of no use now,' concluded Mr. Davis, ' and the Spaniards tell us when a sorrow is asleep not to waken it.'

" Recurring to the management of the negroes by professed philanthropic civilians of the North, Mr. Davis said that all the best men of both sections were in the armies, and that these civilian camp-followers partook in their nature of the buzzards who were the camp-followers of the air.   He said they reminded him of an anecdote told in Mississippi relative to a professed religionist of very avaricious temper, which ran as follows :

"Driving to church one Sunday, the pious old gentleman saw a sheep foundered in a quagmire on one side of the road, and called John, his coachman, to halt and extricate the animal—he might be of value.   John halted, entered the quagmire, endeavored to pull out the sheep ; but found that fright, cold, damp and exposure had so sickened the poor brute that its wool came out in fistfuls whenever pulled.   With this dolorous news John returned to the carriage.

"'Indeed, John.   Is it good wool—valuable ?'

"'Fust class.   Right smart good, Massa.   Couldn't be better.'

"'It's a pity to lose the wool, John.   Yon'd better go see ; is it loose everywhere ?   Perhaps his sickness only makes it loose in parts.'

"John returned to the sheep, pulled all the wool, collected it in his arms, and returned to the carriage.

"'It be's all done gone off, Massa.   Every hair on him was just a fallin' when I picked 'um up.'

"'Well, throw it in here, John,' replied the master, lifting up the curtain of his wagon.   'Throw it in here, and now drive to church as fast as you can ; I'm afraid we shall be late.'

"'But de poor sheep, massa,' pleaded the sable driver.   'Shan't dis chile go fotch him ?'

"'Oh, never mind him,' returned the philanthropist, measuring the wool with his eye.   'Even if you dragged him out, he could never recover, and his flesh would be good for nothing to the butchers.'

"'So the sheep, stripped of his only covering, was left to die in the swamp,' concluded Mr. Davis; 'and such will be the fate of the poor negroes entrusted to the philanthropic but avaricious Pharisees who now profess to hold them in special care.'"

"*September 6th.*—Called upon Mr. Davis once or twice, I remember, between the interval of my last date and this, but have lost notes. Called to-day, accompanied by Captain Titlow, Third Pennsylvania Artillery, officer-of-the-day, and found prisoner in a more comfortable state of mind and body than he had enjoyed for some days. Healthy granulations forming in the carbuncle.

"Mr. Davis said the clamor about 'treason' in our Northern newspapers was only an evidence how little our editors were qualified by education for their positions. None seemed to remember that treason to a State was possible, no less than to the United States: and between the horns of this dilemma there could be little choice. In the North, where the doctrine of State sovereignty was little preached or practised, this difficulty might not seem so great; but in the South a man had presented the unpleasant alternatives of being guilty of treason to his State when it went out of the Union, by remaining, what was called 'loyal' to the Federal Government, or being guilty of treason to the General Government by remaining faithful to his State. These terms appeared to have little significance at the North, but were full of potency in the South, and had to be regarded in every political calculation."

Dr. Craven's Record of the Prison-Life of Mr. Davis continues until November, 1865, when his earnest efforts in behalf of his prisoner, so far excited the ire of the powers that be, that he was at first forbidden to hold any intercourse with the prisoner, and afterwards removed entirely.

But the treatment of Mr. Davis is now essentially changed. He has been removed to better quarters, is now supplied with adequate food, is allowed books, his family are permitted to see him, his friends have access to him ; and his position in all things is now more nearly worthy the dignity of a great country, and suitable to his rank as an eminent state prisoner, and not a convicted felon.

He and the country now await with interest his approaching trial. Thanks to the firmness of the President, the efforts of certain of the Radicals to bring him to a mock trial before a Military Commission, in which the result would be only a foregone conclusion, has been thwarted, and he will undergo a constitutional trial before the highest tribunal in the country. It is feared, however, by some, that that trial will never come off, but by one pretext or another, will be postponed from time to time, until the prisoner, harassed by hope deferred, and carried into a fatal illness by his confinement, will die. A fair, searching, exhaustive trial, in which the doctrine of State sovereignty shall receive a ventilation and logical assertion it has never yet received, in which the limitations and conditions of the Government, under the Constitution, shall be examined by an acumen and learning never yet brought to bear upon the subject, would be a trial, not of Jefferson Davis, but of the Republican party and its acts ; and this trial the leaders and controllers of that party dare not meet. They may feel some assurance in the fact, that a conspicuous member of their party will preside at the trial; but the doctrine of State sovereignty, if once authoritatively asserted by the Supreme Court, would extenuate, if it did not justify Secession, would render the present attitude of the party toward the Southern States untenable—would thwart and check their scheme for centralization—would establish the unconstitutionality of many of their laws affecting the status of the citizens of the several States—would overthrow their whole theory of the Union, their platforms, their logic, and their ambitions, and re-assert the ancient Jeffersonian land-marks and principles. Will they dare stand this test? They *may*, relying on the partizan proclivities of the Chief-Justice ; but men who have studied the Constitution of the United States, and comprehend its real significance and meaning, need fear to see that doctrine of State sovereignty under which the seceding States acted, brought to the tribunals of the Court, need fear for a moment the triumphant issue of the attempt to try JEFFERSON DAVIS for treason.

5

APPENDIX.

LETTER.

RICHMOND, *July 6th*, 1861.

To ABRAHAM LINCOLN, *President, and Commander-in-Chief of the Army and Navy of the United States :—*

SIR,—Having learned that the schooner *Savannah*, a private armed vessel in the service, and sailing under a commission issued by the authority of the Confederate States of America, had been captured by one of the vessels forming the blockading squadron off Charleston harbor, I directed a proposition to be made to the officer commanding that squadron, for an exchange of the officers and crew of the *Savannah* for prisoners of war held by this Government " according to number and rank." To this proposition, made on the 19th ult., Capt. Mercer, the officer-in-command of the blockading squadron, made answer on the same day that " the prisoners (referred to) are not on board of any of the vessels under my command."

It now appears by statements made without contradiction in newspapers published in New York, that the prisoners above-mentioned were conveyed to that city, and have there been treated, not as prisoners of war, but as criminals ; that they have been put in irons, confined in jail, brought before the Courts of Justice on charges of piracy and treason, and it is even rumored that they have been actually convicted of the offenses charged, for no other reason than that they bore arms in defense of the rights of this Government, and under the authority of its commission.

I could not, without grave discourtesy, have made the newspaper statements above referred to the subject of this communication, if the threat of treating as pirates the citizens of this Confederacy, armed for service on the high seas, had not been contained in your proclamation of the — April last. That proclamation, however, seems to afford a sufficient justification for considering these published statements as not devoid of probability.

It is the desire of this Government so to conduct the war now existing, as to mitigate its horrors as far as may be possible ; and, with this intent, its treatment of the prisoners captured by its forces has been marked by the greatest humanity and leniency consistent with public obligation : some have been permitted to return home on parole, others to remain at large under similar condition within this Confederacy, and all have been furnished with rations for their subsistence, such as are allowed to our own troops. It is only since the news has been received of the treatment of the prisoners taken on the *Savannah*, that I have been compelled to withdraw these indulgences, and to hold the prisoners taken by us in strict confinement.

A just regard to humanity and to the honor of this Government now requires me to state explicitly that, painful as will be the necessity, this Government will deal out to the prisoners held by it the same treatment and the same fate as shall be experienced by those captured on the *Savannah*, and if driven to the terrible necessity of retaliation by your execution of any of the officers or crew of the *Savannah*, that retaliation will be extended so far as shall be requisite to secure the abandonment of a practice unknown to the warfare of civilized man ; and so barbarous as to disgrace the nation which shall be guilty of inaugurating it.

With this view, and because it may not have reached you, I now renew the proposition made to the commander of the blockading squadron, to exchange for the prisoners taken on the *Savannah*, an equal number of those now held by us according to rank. I am yours, etc.,

JEFFERSON DAVIS,
President, and Commander-in-Chief of the Army and Navy
of the Confederate States.

MESSAGE.

DELIVERED AT RICHMOND, JULY 20

Gentlemen of the Congress of the Confederate States of America :

My message addressed to you at the commencement of the last session, contained such full information of the state of the Confederacy, as to render it unnecessary that I should now do more than call your attention to such important facts as have occurred during the recess, and the matters connected with the public defense.

In this war, rapine is the rule ; private houses, in beautiful _ rural retreats, are bombarded and burnt ; grain crops in the field are consumed by the torch, and, when the torch is not convenient, careful labor is bestowed to render complete the destruction of every article of use or ornament remaining in private dwellings after their inhabitants have fled from the outrages of brute soldiery. In 1781, Great Britain, when invading the revolted colonies, took possession of every district and county near Fortress Monroe, now occupied by the troops of the United States. The houses then inhabited by the people, after being respected and protected by avowed invaders, are now pillaged and destroyed by men who pretend that Virginians are their fellow-citizens. Mankind will shudder at the tales of the outrages committed on defenseless families by soldiers of the United States, now invading our homes ; yet these outrages are prompted by inflamed passions and the madness of intoxication. But who shall depict the horror they entertain for the cool and deliberate malignancy which, under the pretext of suppressing insurrection (said by themselves to be upheld by a minority only of our people), makes special war on the sick, including children and women, by carefully-devised measures to prevent them from obtaining the medicines necessary for their cure. The sacred claims of humanity, respected even during the fury of actual battle, by careful diversion of attack from hospitals containing wounded enemies, are outraged in cold blood by a Government and people that pretend to desire a continuance of fraternal connections. All these outrages must remain unavenged by the universal reprehension of mankind. In all cases where the actual perpetrators of the wrongs escape capture, they admit of no retaliation. The humanity of our people would shrink instinctively from the bare idea of urging a like war upon the sick, the women, and the children of an enemy. But there are other savage practices which have been resorted to by the Government of the United States, which do admit of repression by retaliation, and I have been driven to the necessity of enforcing the repression. The prisoners of war taken by the enemy on board the armed schooner " Savannah," sailing under our commission, were, as I was credibly advised, treated like common felons, put in irons, confined in a jail usually appropriated to criminals of the worst dye, and threatened with punishment as such. I had made application for the exchange of these prisoners to the commanding officer of the enemy's squadron off Charleston, but that officer had already sent the prisoners to New York when application was made. I therefore deemed it my duty to renew the proposal for the exchange to the constitutional commander-in-chief of the army and navy of the United States, the only officer having control of the prisoners. To this end, I dispatched an officer to him under a flag of truce, and, in making the proposal, I informed President Lincoln of my resolute purpose to check all barbarities on prisoners of war by such severity of retaliation on prisoners held by us as should secure the abandonment of the practice. This communication was received and read by an officer-in-command of the United States forces, and a message was brought from him by the bearer of my communication, that a reply would be returned by President Lincoln as soon as possible. I earnestly hope this promised reply (which has not yet been received) will convey the assurance that prisoners of war will be treated, in this unhappy contest, with that regard for humanity, which has made such conspicuous progress in the conduct of modern warfare. As measures of precaution, however, and until this promised reply is received, I still retain in close custody some officers captured from the enemy, whom it had been my pleasure previously to set at large on parole, and whose fate must necessarily depend on that of prisoners held by the enemy. I append a copy of my communication to the President and commander-in-chief of the army and navy of the United States, and of the report of the officer charged to deliver my communication. There are some other passages in the remarkable paper to which I have directed your attention, having reference to the peculiar relations which exist between this Government and the States usually termed Border Slave States, which cannot properly be withheld from notice. The hearts of our people are animated by sentiments toward the inhabitants of these States, which found expression in your enactment refusing to consider them enemies, or authorize hostilities against them. That a very large portion of the people of these States regard us as brethren ; that, if unrestrained by the actual presence of large armies, subversion of civil authority, and declaration of martial law, some of them, at least, would joyfully unite with us; that they are, with almost entire unanimity, opposed to the prosecution of the war waged against us, are facts of which daily-recurring events fully warrant the assertion that the President of the United States refuses to recognize in these, our late sister States, the right of refraining from attack upon us, and justifies his refusal by the assertion that the States have no other power than that reserved to them in the Union by the Constitution. Now, one of them having ever been a State of the Union, this view of the constitutional relations between the States and the General Government is a fitting introduction to another assertion of the message, that the executive possesses power of suspending the writ of habeas corpus, and of delegating that power to military commanders at their discretion.

ADDRESS TO THE PEOPLE OF THE CONFEDERATE STATES.

EXECUTIVE OFFICE, RICHMOND, *April* 10, 1863.

IN compliance with the request of Congress, contained in the resolutions passed on the fourth day of the present month, I invoke your attention to the present condition and future prospects of our country, and to the duties which patriotism imposes on us all during this great struggle for our homes and our liberties. These resolutions are in the following language :

[Here follow the resolutions passed by the Confederate Congress, requesting Mr. Davis to issue an address.]

Fully concurring in the views thus expressed by Congress, I confidently appeal to your love of country for aid in carrying into effect the recommendations of your Senators and Representatives.

We have reached the close of the second year of the war, and may point with just pride to the history of our young Confederacy. Alone, unaided, we have met and overthrown the most formidable combinations of naval and military armaments that the lust of conquest ever gathered together for the conquest of a free people.

We began this struggle without a single gun afloat, while the resources of our enemy enabled them to gather fleets which, according to their official list, published in August last, consisted of four hundred and thirty-seven vessels, measuring eight hundred and forty thousand and eighty-six tons, and carrying three thousand and twenty-six guns ; yet we have captured, sunk, or destroyed a number of these vessels, including two large frigates and one steam sloop-of-war, while four of their captured steam gun-boats are now in our possession, adding to the strength of our little navy, which is rapidly gaining in numbers and efficiency.

To oppose invading forces composed of levies which have already exceeded thirteen hundred thousand men, we had no resources but the unconquerable valor of a people determined to be free ; and we were so destitute of military supplies that tens of thousands of our citizens were reluctantly refused admission into the service from our inability to furnish them arms, while for many months the continuation of some of our strongholds owed their safety chiefly to a careful concealment of the fact that we were without a supply of powder for our cannon.

Your devotion and patriotism have triumphed over all these obstacles, and calling into existence the munitions of war, the clothing and the subsistence, which have enabled our soldiers to illustrate their valor on numerous battle-fields, and to inflict crushing defeats on successive armies, each of which our arrogant foe fondly imagined to be invincible.

The contrast between our past and present condition is well calculated to inspire full confidence in the triumph of our arms. At no previous period of the war have our forces been so numerous, so well organized, and so thoroughly disciplined, armed and equipped, as at present. The season of high-water, on which our enemies relied to enable their fleets of gunboats to penetrate into our country and devastate our homes, is fast passing away ; yet our strongholds on the Mississippi still bid defiance to the foe, and months of costly preparation for their reduction have been spent in vain. Disaster has been the result of their every effort to turn or storm Vicksburg and Port Hudson, as well as every attack on our batteries on the Red River, the Tallahatchie, and other navigable streams. Within a few weeks the falling waters and the increasing heats of summer will complete their discomfiture, and compel their baffled and defeated forces to the abandonment of expeditions on which was based their chief hope of success in effecting our subjugation.

We must not forget, however, that the war is not yet ended, and that we are still confronted by powerful armies and threatened by numerous fleets, and that the Government that controls those fleets and armies is driven to the most desperate efforts to effect the unholy purposes in which it has thus far been defeated. It will use its utmost energy to avert this impending doom, so fully merited by the atrocities it has committed, the savage barbarities which it has encouraged, and the crowning attempt to excite a servile population to the massacre of our wives, our daughters, and our helpless children.

With such a contest before us, there is but one danger which the government of your choice regards with apprehension ; and to avert this danger it appeals to the never-failing patriotism and spirit which you have exhibited since the beginning of the war.

The very unfavorable season, the protracted droughts of last year, reduced the harvests on which we depend far below an average yield, and the deficiency was, unfortunately, still more marked in the northern part of our Confederacy, where supplies were specially needed for the army. If, through a confidence in an early peace, which may prove delusive, our fields should now be devoted to the production of cotton and tobacco, instead of grain and live stock, and other articles necessary for the subsistence of the people and army, the consequences may prove serious, if not disastrous, especially should this present season prove as unfavorable as the last. Your country, therefore, appeals to you to lay aside all thought of gain, and to devote yourselves to securing your liberties, without which these gains would be valueless.

It is true that the wheat harvest in the more Southern States, which will be gathered next month, promises an abundant yield ; but even if this promise be fulfilled, the difficulties of transportation, enhanced as it has been by an unusually rainy winter, will cause embarrassments in military operations, and sufferings among the people, should the crops in the middle and northern portions of the Confederacy prove deficient. But no uneasiness may be felt in regard to a mere supply of bread for men. It is for the large amount of corn and forage required in the raising of live stock, and the supplies of the animals used for military operations, too bulky for distant transportation ; and in them the deficiency of the last harvest was mostly felt. Let your fields be devoted exclusively to the production of corn, oats, beans, peas, potatos, and other food for man and beast. Let corn be sowed broadcast, for fodder, in immediate proximity to railroads, rivers and canals ;

and let all your efforts be directed to the prompt supply of these articles in the districts where our armies are operating. You will thus add greatly to their efficiency, and furnish the means without which it is impracticable to make those prompt and active movements which have hitherto stricken terror into our enemies, and secured our most brilliant triumphs.

Having thus placed before you, my countrymen, the reasons for the call made on you for aid in supplying the wants of the coming year, I add a few words of appeal in behalf of the brave soldiers now confronting your enemies, and to whom your government is unable to furnish all the comforts they so richly merit. The supply of meal for the army is deficient. This deficiency is only temporary, for measures have been adopted which will, it is believed, soon enable us to restore the full rations ; but that ration is now reduced at times to one-half the usual quantity in some of our armies. It is known that the supply of meat throughout the country is sufficient for the support of all ; but the distances are so great, the condition of the roads has been so bad during the five months of winter weather through which we have just passed, and the attempt of groveling speculators to forestal the market and make money out of the life-blood of our defenders, have so much influenced the withdrawal from sale of the surplus in hands of the producers, that the Government has been unable to gather full supplies.

The Secretary of War has prepared a plan, which is appended to this address, by the aid of which, or some similar means to be adopted by yourselves, you can assist the officers of the Government in the purchase of the corn, the bacon, the pork, and the beef known to exist in large quantities in different parts of the country. Even if the surplus be less than believed, is it not a bitter and humiliating reflection that those who remain at home, secure from hardship, and protected from danger, should be in the enjoyment of abundance, and that their slaves also should have a full supply of food, while their sons, brothers, husbands and fathers, are stinted in the rations on which their health and efficiency depend?

Entertaining no fear that you will either misconstrue the motives of this address, or fail to respond to the call of patriotism, I have placed the facts fully and frankly before you. Let us all unite in the performance of our duty, each in his sphere, and with concerted, persistent, and well-directed effort, there seems little reason to doubt that, under the blessings of Him to whom we look for guidance, and who has been to us our shield and strength, we shall maintain the sovereignty and independence of the Confederate States, and transmit to our posterity the heritage bequeathed to us by our fathers.

JEFFERSON DAVIS.

SPEECH

BEFORE THE LEGISLATURE OF MISSISSIPPI, DECEMBER 26.

Friends and Fellow-Citizens, Gentlemen of the House of Representatives and Senate of the State of Mississippi :

After an absence of nearly two years I again find myself among those who, from the days of my childhood, have ever been the trusted objects of my affections, those for whose good I have ever striven, and whose interests I have sometimes hoped I may have contributed to subserve. Whatever fortunes I may have achieved in life have been gained as a representative of Mississippi, and before all, I have labored for the advancement of her glory and honor. I now, for the first time in my career, find myself the representative of a wider circle of interest ; but a circle in which the interests of Mississippi are still embraced. Two years ago, nearly, I left you to assume the duties which had devolved on me as the representative of the new Confederacy. The responsibilities of this position have occupied all my time, and have left me no opportunity for mingling with my friends in Mississippi, or for sharing in the dangers which have menaced them. But, wherever duty may have called me, my heart has been with you, and the success of the cause in which we are all engaged has been first in my thoughts and prayers. I thought, when I left Mississippi, that the service to which I was called would prove to be but temporary. The last time I had the honor of addressing you from this stand I was influenced by that idea. I then imagined that it might be my fortune again to lead Mississippians in the field, and to be with them where danger was to be braved and glory won. I thought to find that place which I believed to be suited to my capacity—that of an officer in service of the State of Mississippi. For, although in the discharge of my duties as President of the Confederate States, I had determined to make no distinction between the various parts of the country—to know no separate State—yet my heart has always beat more warmly for Mississippi, and I have looked on Mississippi soldiers with a pride and emotion such as no others inspired. But it was decided differently. I was called to another sphere of action. How, in that sphere, I have discharged the duties and obligations imposed on me, it does not become me to constitute myself the judge. It is for others to decide that question. But, speaking to you with that frankness and that confidence with which I have always spoken to you, and which partakes of the nature of thinking aloud, I can say, with my hand upon my heart, that whatever I have done, has been done with the sincere purpose of promoting the noble cause in which we are engaged. The period which elapsed since I left you is short ; for the time, which may appear long in the life of man, is short in the history of a nation. And in that short period remarkable changes have been wrought in all the circumstances by which we are surrounded. At the time of which I speak, the question presented to our people was : "Will there be war ?" This was the subject of universal speculation. We had chosen to exercise an indisputable right—the right to separate from those with whom we conceived association to be no longer possible, and to establish a government of our own.

I was among those who, from the beginning, predicted war, as the consequences of secession, although I must admit that the contest has assumed proportions more gigantic than I had anticipated. I predicted war, not because our right to secede and to form a government of our own was not indisputable and clearly defined in the spirit of that declaration which rests the right to govern on the consent of the governed, but saw that the wickedness of the North would precipitate a war upon us. Those who supposed that the exercise of this right of separation could not produce war, have had cause to be convinced that they had credited their recent associates of the North with a moderation, a sagacity, a morality they did not possess. You have been involved in a war waged for the gratification of the lust of power and aggrandizement, for your conquest and your subjugation, with a malignant ferocity, and with a disregard and a contempt of the usages of civilization, entirely unequaled in history. Such, I have ever warned you, were the characteristics of the Northern people—of those with whom our ancestors entered into a Union of consent, and with whom they formed a constitutional compact. And yet, such was the attachment of our people for that Union, such their devotion to it, that those who desired preparation to be made for the inevitable conflict, were denounced as men who wished to destroy the Union. After what has happened during the last two years, my only wonder is, that we consented to live for so long a time in association with such miscreants, and have loved so much a government rotten to the core. Were it ever to be proposed again to enter into a Union with such a people, I could no more consent to do it than to trust myself in a den of thieves.

You in Mississippi have but little experienced as yet the horrors of the war. You have seen but little of the savage manner in which it is waged by your barbarous enemies. It has been my fortune to witness it in all its terrors; in a part of the country where old men have been torn from their homes, carried into captivity, and immured in distant dungeons, and where delicate women have been insulted by a brutal soldiery, and forced even to cook for the dirty Federal invaders; where property has been wantonly destroyed, the country ravaged, and every outrage committed. And it is with these people that our fathers formed a union and a solemn contract. There is indeed a difference between the two peoples. Let no man hug the delusion that there can be renewed association between them. Our enemies are a traditionless and homeless race ; from the time of Cromwell to the present moment, they have been disturbers of the peace of the world. Gathered together by Cromwell from the bogs and fens of the North of Ireland and of England, they commenced by disturbing the peace of their own country ; they disturbed Holland, to which they fled, and they disturbed England on their return. They persecuted Catholics in England, and they hung Quakers and witches in America.

Having been hurried into a war with a people so devoid of every mark of civilization, you have no doubt wondered that I have not carried out the policy, which I had intended should be our policy—of fighting our battles on the fields of the enemy, instead of suffering him to fight them on ours. This was not the result of my will, but the power of the enemy. They had at their command all the accumulated wealth of seventy years—the military stores which had been laid up during that time. They had grown rich from the taxes wrung from you for the establishing and supporting their manufacturing institutions. We have entered upon a conflict with a nation contiguous to us in territory, and vastly superior to us in numbers. In the face of these facts, the wonder is not that we have done little, but that we have done so much. In the first year of the war, our forces were sent into the field poorly armed, and were far inferior in number to the enemy.

We were compelled even to arm ourselves by the capture of weapons taken from the foe on the battle-field. Thus in every battle we exchanged our arms for those of the invaders. At the end of twelve months of the war, it was still necessary for us to adopt some expedient to enable us to maintain our ground. The only expedient remaining to us was to call on those brave men who had entered the service of the country at the beginning of the war, supposing that the conflict was to last but a short time, and that they would not be long absent from their homes. The only expedient, I say, was to call on these gallant men ; to ask them to maintain their position in front of the enemy, and to surrender for a time their hopes of soon returning to their families and friends. And nobly did they respond to the call. They answered that they were willing to stay ; that they were willing to maintain their position, and to breast the tide of invasion. But it was not just that they should stand alone. They asked that the men who had stayed at home—who had thus far been sluggards in the cause—should be forced likewise to meet the enemy.

From this resulted the law of Congress, which is known as the Conscription Act, which declared all men, from the age of eighteen to the age of thirty-five, to be liable to enrolment in the Confederate service. I regret that there has been some prejudice excited against the act, and that it has been subjected to harsher criticism than it deserves. And here I may say that an erroneous impression appears to prevail in regard to this act. It is no disgrace to be brought into the army by conscription. There is no more reason to expect from the citizen voluntary service in the army than to expect voluntary labor on the public roads, or the voluntary payment of taxes. But these things we do not expect. We assess the property of the citizen—we appoint tax-gatherers: why should we not likewise distribute equally the labor, and enforce equally the obligation of defending the country from its enemies? I repeat that it is no disgrace to any one to be conscripted, but it is a glory for those who do not wait for the conscription. Thus resulted the Conscription Act; and thence arose the necessity for the Conscription Act. The necessity was met; but when it was found that under these acts enough men were not drawn into the ranks of the army to fulfill the purposes intended, it became necessary to pass another Conscription Act, and another Conscription Act. It is only of this latter that I desire to speak. Its policy was to leave at home those men needed to conduct the administration, and those who might be required to support and maintain the industry of the country—in other words, to exempt from military service those whose labor, employed in other avocations, might be more profitable to the country and to the Government than in the ranks of the army.

I am told that this act has excited some discontentment, and that it has provoked censure, far more severe, I believe, than it deserves. It has been said that it exempts the rich from military service, and forces the poor to fight the battles of the country. The poor do, indeed, fight the battles of the country. It is the poor who save nations and make revolutions. But is it true that in this war, the men of property have shrunk from the ordeal of the battle-field? Look through the army; cast your eyes upon the maimed heroes of the war whom you meet in your streets and in the hospitals; remember the martyrs of the conflict; and I am sure you will find among them more than a fair proportion drawn from the ranks of men of property. The object of that portion of the act which exempts those having charge of twenty or more negroes, was not to draw any distinction of classes, but simply to provide a force, in the nature of a police force, sufficient to keep our negroes in control. This was the sole object of the clause. Had it been otherwise, it would never have received my signature. As I have already said, we have no cause to complain of the rich. All our people have done well, and, while the poor have nobly discharged their duties, most of the wealthiest and most distinguished families of the South have representatives in the ranks. I take, as an example, the case of one of your own representatives in Congress, who was nominated for Congress and elected ; but still did a sentinel's duty until Congress met. Nor is this a solitary instance, for men of largest fortune in Mississippi are now serving in the ranks.

Permit me now to say that I have seen with peculiar pleasure the recommendation of your Governor in his Message, to make some provision for the families of the absent soldiers of Mississippi. Let this provision be made for the objects of his affection and his solicitude, and the soldier engaged in fighting the battles of his country will no longer be disturbed in his slumber by dreams of an unprotected and neglected family at home. Let him know that his mother Mississippi has spread her protecting mantle over those he loves, and he will be ready to fight your battles, to protect your honor, and in your cause to die. There is another one of the Governor's propositions to which I wish to allude. I mean the proposition to call upon those citizens who are not subject to the Confederate conscription law, and to form them into a reserve corps for the purpose of aiding in the defense of the State. Men who are exempted by law from the performance of any duty, do not generally feel the obligation to perform that duty unless called upon by the law. But I am confident that the men of Mississippi have only to know that their soil is invaded, their cities menaced, to rush to meet the enemy, even if they serve only for thirty days. I see no reason why the State may not, in an exigency like that which now presses on her, call on our reserved forces, and organize them for service. Such troops could be of material benefit, by serving in intrenchments, and thus relieving the veteran and disciplined soldiers for the duties of the field, where discipline is so much needed. At the end of a short term of service they could return to their homes and to their ordinary avocations, resuming those duties necessary to the public prosperity.

In the course of this war our eyes have been often turned abroad. We have expected sometimes recognition and sometimes intervention at the hands of foreign nations, and we had a right to expect it. Never before in the history of the world had a people so long a time maintained their ground, and showed themselves capable of maintaining their national existence, without securing the recognition of commercial nations. I know not why this has been so, but this I say, "Put not your trust in princes," and rest not your hopes on foreign nations. This war is ours : we must fight it out ourselves ; and I feel some pride in knowing that so far we have done it without the good-will of anybody. It is true that there are now symptoms of a change in public opinion abroad. They give us their admiration—they sometimes even say to us God-speed—and in the remarkable book written by Mr. Spence, the question of secession has been discussed with more of ability than it ever has been even in this country. Yet England still holds back, but France, the ally of other days, seems disposed to hold out to us the hand of fellowship. And when France holds out to us her hand, right willingly will we grasp it.

During the last year, the war has been characterized by varied fortunes. New Orleans fell—a sad blow it was to the valley of the Mississippi, and as unexpected to me as to any one. Memphis also fell; and besides these we have lost various points on the Atlantic coast. The invading armies have pressed upon us at some points; at others they have been driven back; but take a view of our condition now, and compare it with what it was a year ago—look at the enemy's position as it then was and as it now is; consider their immense power, vast numbers, and great resources; look at all these things, and you will be convinced that our condition now will compare favorably with what it was then. Armies are not composed of numbers alone. Officers and men are both to be disciplined and instructed. When the war first began the teacher and the taught were in the condition of the blind leading the blind; now all this is changed for the better. Our troops have become disciplined and instructed. They have stripped the gun-boat of its terrors; they have beaten superior numbers in the field; they have discovered that with their short-range weapons they can close upon the long-range of the enemy and capture them. Thus in all respects, moral as well as physical, we are better prepared than we were a year ago.

ADDRESS

TO THE SOLDIERS OF THE CONFEDERATE STATES.

AFTER more than two years of a warfare scarcely equaled in the number, magnitude, and fearful carnage of its battles—a warfare in which your courage and fortitude have illustrated your country, and attracted not only gratitude at home, but admiration abroad—your enemies continue a struggle in which our final triumph must be inevitable. Unduly elated with their recent successes, they imagine that temporary reverses can quell your spirit or shake your determination, and they are now gathering heavy masses for a general invasion, in the vain hope that by a desperate effort success may at length be reached.

You know too well, my countrymen, what they mean by success. Their malignant rage aims at nothing less than the extermination of yourselves, your wives and children. They seek to destroy what they cannot plunder. They propose as the spoils of victory that your homes shall be partitioned among the wretches whose atrocious cruelties have stamped infamy on their government. They design to incite servile insurrection, and light the fires of incendiarism whenever they can reach your homes, and they debauch the inferior race, hitherto docile and contented, by promising indulgence of the vilest passions as the price of treachery. Conscious of their inability to prevail by legitimate warfare, not daring to make peace lest they should be hurled from their seats of power, the men who now rule in Washington refuse even to confer on the subject of putting an end to outrages which disgrace our age, or to listen to a suggestion for conducting the war according to the usages of civilization.

Fellow-citizens, no alternative is left you but victory, or subjugation, slavery, and the utter ruin of yourselves, your families, and your country. The victory is within your reach. You need but stretch forth your hands to grasp it. For this and all that is necessary is that those who are called to the field by every motive that can move the human heart, should promptly repair to the post of duty, should stand by their comrades now in front of the foe, and thus so strengthen the armies of the Confederacy as to insure success. The men now absent from their posts would, if present in the field, suffice to create numerical equality between our force and that of the invaders—and when, with any approach to such equality, have we failed to be victorious? I believe that but few of those absent are actuated by unwillingness to serve their country ; but that many have found it difficult to resist the temptation of a visit to their homes, and the loved ones from whom they have been so long separated ; that others have left for temporary attention to their affairs, with the intention of returning, and then have shrunk from the consequences of their violation of duty ; that others again have left their posts from mere restlessness and desire of change, each quieting the upbraidings of his conscience by persuading himself that his individual services could have no influence on the general result.

These and other causes (although far less disgraceful than the desire to avoid danger, or to escape from the sacrifices required by

6

patriotism) are, nevertheless, grievous faults, and place the cause of our beloved country, and of everything we hold dear, in imminent peril. I repeat that the men who now owe duty to their country, who have been called out and have not yet reported for duty, or who have absented themselves from their posts, are sufficient in number to secure us victory in the struggle now impending.

I call on you, then, my countrymen, to hasten to your camps, in obedience to the dictates of honor and of duty, and summon those who have absented themselves without leave, who have remained absent beyond the period allowed by their furloughs, to repair without delay to their respective commands ; and I do hereby declare that I grant a general pardon and amnesty to all officers and men within the Confederacy, now absent without leave, who shall, with the least possible delay, return to their proper posts of duty ; but no excuse will be received for any delay beyond twenty days after the first publication of this proclamation in the State in which the absentee may be at the date of the publication. This amnesty and pardon shall extend to all who have been accused, or who have been convicted and are undergoing sentence for absence without leave or desertion, excepting only those who have been twice convicted of desertion.

Finally, I conjure my countrywomen, the wives, mothers, sisters, and daughters of the Confederacy—to use their all-powerful influence in aid of this call, to add one crowning sacrifice to those which their patriotism has so freely and constantly afforded on their country's altar, and to take care that none who owe service in the field shall be sheltered at home from the disgrace of having deserted their duty to their families, to their country, and to their God.

Given under my hand, and the Seal of the Confederate States, at Richmond, this first day of August, in the (SEAL.) year of our Lord one thousand eight hundred and sixty-three.

JEFFERSON DAVIS.

By the President :

J. P. BENJAMIN,
Secretary of State.

ACCOUNT OF THE ESCAPE FROM RICHMOND

AND

SUBSEQUENT CAPTURE OF JEFFERSON DAVIS.

BY ONE OF HIS STAFF.

"Mr. Davis went, as usual, to St. Paul's Episcopal Church, where political and Christian hopes were, once a week, blended for his edification. He looked careworn, yet contrived to tinge his concern with a briskness which warded off suspicion. A certain ominous telegram that he received in the early part of the morning was, however, a tormenting demon, manifestly too much for the perfect quiet which would be needed in the house of prayer and praise.

"While heaven was being assailed for favor and protection in every church of Richmond, Colonel Taylor Wood hastened to the door of St. Paul's, and despatched the sexton to Mr. Davis's pew. Only a few words were whispered softly in the ears of the Confederate President—a few words which told him another despatch had come, and that he was immediately wanted. It was enough. The concourse of worshipers within St. Paul's read the whisper by the action of Mr. Davis, who instantly left the Church. No telegram ever flashed through the electric wires more swiftly than this unspoken intelligence shot from eye to eye of that dismayed congregation. Had an unseen hand written the coming doom on the wall in letters of fire, the effect could not have been more appalling or more instantaneous.

"Orders were issued, about two o'clock, to the principal military and civil officials to have all the government archives not yet removed, and which it was possible to remove, ready by seven o'clock ; what could not be easily transported were to be destroyed. Orders were also given to these same personages to meet Mr. Davis at the Danville depot by eight o'clock.

"All the way to the rendezvous assigned for the flying 'Presidential party' was blocked by panting fugitives, or by groups of wonder-gapers. At last the Danville depot is reached through a crush of eager men scrambling for admission to the platform. Two militia regiments had parties on duty. None were admitted to the 'Presidential train' except a specified few. Other trains had gone, others were to go. The crowd must push aside. Provost-Marshal Carrington, with a select guard, saw that no one entered unless duly authorized. He called for each cabinet officer to designate his special few. It was done amidst fierce confusion.

"By eight o'clock all intended for this train were seated and ready to go. Several other trains were in course of preparation. But it was ten o'clock before the Davis train moved. The delay begat a variety of surmises. Some held that Lee had won a great victory, and that the necessity for going had passed away. Others imagined that the Southern army was unable to defend the road, and that the necessity for staying was imperative. Meanwhile, the militia, who were doing guard duty, began gradually to 'go home ;' and before we left, not half the number were at their posts ; meanwhile, also, pillage and riot had begun in the city, of

which we were blissfully ignorant; meanwhile, too, a guard of
two hundred picked men entered a car ready for them between
the engine and the Davis carriage ; finally, General Breckinridge
arrived with news for the Davis party that Lee could not save
the city, but that the road was clear, and likely to remain so until
this precious freight was out of immediate danger.

"Then Mr. Davis and his party tightened their spurs to their
heels (horses were in a car for the Cabinet and staff), saw to their
small arms, leaned back on their seats, and the signal puff was
given. And then and there began the flight—there, at ten
o'clock on the night of April 2, 1865—there, amid a turmoil
seldom equaled, and thence through scenes and incidents as
varied and harassing as any in history.

"Burkesville, which we reached shortly after daybreak, was
the first place at which any of our distinguished men got off the
train—it was also the first place we had a clear-eyed view of
since the night before. I am particular in mentioning this, for
there was something ominous in that first place and first view.
It was a wreck—a woful ruin—one of the saddest havoc-sights
Mr. Davis had yet seen. Raiders had torn it to pieces, and the
pleasant, bustling little junction of other days was only visible
in its vestiges. Mr. Davis got out and walked a few minutes on
the platform. Owing to his unsightly spectacles he was not at
once recognized by the people who were even thus early at the
station. Judge Reagan was also there. As soon as the few
stragglers at the station knew that the train contained their President, they sought him, crowded around him, kindly and res-
pectfully spoke in smothered tones, and looked most sorrowful.

"About forty miles beyond the junction we came up with two trains which had stopped. Both contained minor officials and convalescent soldiers, and both had gone off the track. The foremost train had one of its cars broken, five lives being the cost of the accident. Everything appeared burdened with a portent of evil, thus far. The five victims of this accident were laid out near a grove as we came up. They were wounded soldiers from Alabama—gallant men who had dragged their lives most gloriously from the battle-field, to have them most ingloriously sacrificed by incompetent or reckless railway officials. There they lay, all their aspirations for the home to which they hoped themselves bound, sunk forever within the confines of one common, coffinless grave preparing for them. There was no need to give sadder zest to the sadness we all felt ; but this calamity upon which we so unexpectedly trod, left us

'Stunned by death's twice mortal mace.'

"Mr Davis got out to inquire into the circumstances of the disaster ; all the others got out too ; but no one except myself went over to where the 'nameless heroes lay,' in a most melancholy row—a neighboring farmer keeping the flies from their ghastly faces, and two negroes digging a long hole in which what was left of the luckless soldiers was to be deposited.

"'Taking this sort of interruption as an omen, I don't relish it,' said Benjamin, when his companions were once more seated.

"'Yet it is preferable to the kind we expected,' remarked a Major Wheeler immediately behind him, who had a holy horror of Sheridan.

"'Not preferable,' cried Lubbock, sharply ; 'some may distrust their personal safety, but we are enough to whip a whole brigade of raiders. Give me an interruption from living Yankees, whom I can slay, but no interruption like this.'

"'It was to be,' whined one of the preachers, emphatically.

"Mr. Davis said not a word, sighed, and leaned back to peer vacantly at dim distance.

"Approaching Danville, the question, 'Whither are we going?' came up for consideration. To leave Richmond by the safest route, and get clear of Grant, was the only object in view at starting. Now that Richmond was abandoned to Grant, and the escaped Government free from immediate danger, its destination was not easily determined. Danville was supposed to be too small for a temporary capital, and the good points of all other eligible cities were discussed generally and warmly. At length Mr. Davis put a stop to the matter by saying that he would not leave Virginia until Lee was whipped out of it.

"'Then you can make up your mind to a long residence,' said Mr. Bruce, of Kentucky, confidently.

"'A day or two more will decide that,' was the wary remark of Mr. Benjamin.

"The course finally determined on was this: the War and Navy Departments were to remain intact at Danville. As the State Department had nobody but Mr. Benjamin, and his assistant, Mr. Washington, there was no trouble about that. As the Navy Department had only Mr. Mallory and three others, there was no trouble about that. As the Department of Justice had only Mr. George Davis himself, there was no trouble about that. The

War Department had General Cooper and a host of clerks ; that was the only trouble left. By sending all the Quartermaster's and Commissary General's clerks on to Charlotte, the difficulty was brought to a practicable bearing. This settled, the new condition of the Government was fixed, and Danville was, for the time being, to be its focus.

"At the depot in Danville, a crowd, but not a great one, awaited us. All was silence and sadness. Mr. Davis divested himself of spurs, spectacles, and other similar appurtenances. So did all those who with him had prepared themselves for an attack and a different sort of flight across the country. He walked out to the platform, accompanied by Colonels Johnston, Lubbock and Ives. After him went his Cabinet, followed by Generals Cooper, Terry and Stuart. Colonel Harrison, Mr. Davis's private secretary, remained to see to the presidential baggage. On the platform were gentlemen representing the city of Danville, to offer its hospitalities to the capitalless President and his fleeing followers. Major Sunderland, one of the most eminent citizens of Danville, was present to invite Mr. Davis and Mr. Mallory to the most palatial residence in the place. The Mayor (Walker) was indefatigable in his attentions to all others. He was chief of a committee having charge of the hospitalities, and his committee did all that men could do to uphold old Virginia's claim to genial generosity. Every private house in the city was thrown open to all in our train ; not a being along with us was unprovided with a home ten minutes after the arrival of the train.

" But, aside from this, what a sad plight we were in ! Not a word of encouragement from Lee—not a word at all, in fact.

" Next morning, the street and depot news was slightly more definite.

"Mr. Davis was up very early, and out on the portico of his Danville residence, anxiously awaiting the arrival of a despatch or a courier. None, however, came, and both Lee and Breckinridge were pronounced remiss. He issued a proclamation to reassure the public, and to persuade them that it was for the special accommodation of Lee's new tactics—field tactics as opposed to entrenched positions—that Richmond was abandoned. The proclamation was very spirited, and breathed defiance to the last.

" Having nothing else to do, and confident that 'no news was good news,' Mr. Davis resolved on establishing his capital. An executive office was rented, and the President's aids set to work opening and referring letters. General Cooper started a war department, and Mr. Mallory an office for the navy. Judge Reagan seized the Masonic Hall for a post-office department, and had chiefs of bureaus to go on with public business. Captain Lee— the General's brother—went through the usual red tapeism of an order and detail office for the navy, and found himself soon as busy as ever he was in Richmond. Attorney-General Davis and Mr. Benjamin rested—law and foreign affairs were in abeyance.

"The 6th, 7th and 8th of April came and went, yet not a word from Lee. Most ominous silence ! In vain rumorists got up pleasing fictions ; to no purpose were sweeping theories devised ; apprehension laid hold of every one, and some misfortune was expected. Mr. Davis evinced uneasiness, but no alarm. He was exemplary in his patience. It was that sort of patience which may be called carnage in repose.

" Late on Saturday evening, the 8th, a handsome story crept out and bloomed all over the city. A despatch was said to be received—indeed, Captain Lee, the General's brother, told me it was received—and it read thus :—

" 'We have squarely beaten the Yanks in two days' fight. Lee is all right, and his army well in hand.

" ' Breckinridge.'

" This sent a thrill through the city, and when Sunday came, with fine, clear weather, the new capital looked happy, halcyon.

" Everything looked prosperous on Monday morning, the 10th—everything but the weather, and that was lowering. About the usual breakfast time, however, people's faces wore a sombre appearance. The brilliant news bubble which gaily floated all day before was burst, and no news was still the answer to all inquiries about Lee. The effect was worse than if the fiction had not been invented. Toward mid-day the anxious crowds in the vicinity of the hotel, or loitering around the improvised department offices, or lounging at the railroad depôt, began to be more than lugubrious. The railroad track at Burkesville was at last known to be torn up ; the telegraph wires in that locality were known to be cut ; the Federal army was known to be between us and Lee. Alas for the hopes of Danville, and the defensive efforts of Brigadier-General and Admiral Semmes ! Information of all this was too positive and too perplexing. Early in the afternoon it took a shape which scattered to the winds the fond speculations of Sunday. On every countenance you read panic. News, aye, positive, distinct, and direct news had at last arrived from Lee.

"But, heavens! what news it was. The consternation in Richmond at the evacuation was as nothing when compared with the dismay depicted on every face in Danville as soon as that news leaked out. Lee had been whipped. Well, he can recover from the blow. But Lee had surrendered. Impossible! What, Lee surrender! Robert E. Lee do any such thing! The very thought seemed absurd. Yet the fact was so; and slowly and reluctantly it had to be credited. Gloom the densest was abroad, and in harmony with its horrors the sky poured out its torrents, making Danville the most miserable and muddy place I ever tried to drag my feet through.

"Orders were given for the evacuation of Danville at five o'clock on the evening of Sunday, the 10th of April. Mr. Davis was at the depôt by half-past five o'clock. Mr. Trenholm, who was very ill, was carried there in an ambulance. Mr. Mallory rode about the city, issuing orders and doing hard work, to secure the transportation of all that was most valuable belonging to the navy. At the depôt, amid a crush little inferior to that in Richmond eight days before, Judge Reagan sat moodily on a trunk. Near him was Mr. Benjamin, couched on some soft baggage, and the Attorney-General seated on a valise. Confusion was supreme, and it was half an hour before there was order enough to enable the President's train to receive its evacuating freight. At length the turmoil was over, and Mr. Davis, accompanied by the same party as when leaving Richmond (with the exception of Colonel Ives, who remained in Danville), started off for Greensboro in North Carolina.

"The news, which was long looked for, and so unwelcome when

it came, stunned all. Its effect on most of the old citizens of Richmond was to deter them from going further; and thus the second stage of the evacuation had fewer to follow the fortunes of Davis than had the first.

" Our progress was the progress of ill news speeding apace. As the tidings of the evacuation of Richmond had not preceded but accompanied us, so intelligence of Lee's surrender was borne along by our presence. No one in Greensboro even suspected it. We arrived early in the day. Both Johnston and Beauregard— the latter first, he being in command there—were soon with Mr. Davis. The interview was short, and evidently only a preparatory one.

" In Greensboro, as in Danville, the naval store was well stocked. Fortunately it was ; for in Greensboro, as not in Danville, the people were inhospitable. The home of the flying President was a railroad car. Not a soul offered the slightest courtesy. Mr. Trenholm alone, being very ill, was tendered the shelter of a house, and he was taken to Governor Morehead's. All the others, cabinet and staff, roomed and mealed in the cars. Mr. Davis was persuaded to adopt a compromise—to sleep at a little house in which the wife and family of Colonel Taylor Wood had for some weeks been staying, and to spend the rest of his time with his companions in the cars.

" It would have been ludicrous, if it were less provocative of painful reflections, to think that the whole rebel government was cooped in those miserable cars.

" General Breckinridge joined us at Greensboro, and brought all the details of Lee's surrender. Soon after his arrival, he and

Mr. Davis, and Generals Johnston and Beauregard, had a prolonged consultation.

"It was held on the slope of a little hill, just off the railway track. The little hill was itself historic. It was there that Nat Greene, of revolutionary fame, held his council of war the night before the battle of Guildford Court-House. It was there that on the day after Green's defeat, Lord Rowen had his headquarters. It was near to there that the churlish Quaker refused Greene the hospitality of his house, saying, 'Get thee hence, wicked man; I have nought to do with such as thee.' It was there that Greensboro first laid its claim to the cold unconcern which marked its conduct toward the tottering fortunes of the Confederate chiefs. It was there these chiefs were now grouped—Davis, Breckinridge, Beauregard, and Johnston—forming one picture; Benjamin, Mallory, Reagan, and George Davis, another.

"Although the collapse of the Confederacy was evident to every one, since the surrender of Lee's army, the completeness of that sudden and astounding collapse was not thoroughly manifest until after this interview on the little historic hill beside the railroad at Greensboro. The indecision and vacillation of the 'constitutional advisers' of Jefferson Davis were distressing. Neither he nor they seemed to know what next should be attempted, or what they should do even with themselves. They were utterly powerless, and evinced an absolute incapacity to deal with the dangers which encircled them as individuals.

"On Good Friday orders were given to evacuate Greensboro. As the railroad was cut at Jamestown, twelve miles from Greensboro, the very morning of our arrival at the latter place, it was decided that the 'Presidential party' must take to horses and wagons.

"Thanks to the indefatigable efforts of Mr. Mallory, three ambulances were obtained. General Cooper, seeing the cramped accommodation, grew vehemently angry, and declared he would not go further. Mr. Mallory, who was on horseback, soon succeeded in soothing the enraged soldier, and he found himself at last seated by Mr. Benjamin in a wretched ambulance. Reagan, Mallory, and Breckinridge, with the members of his staff, etc., accompanied Mr. Davis on horseback.

"I said it was raining, pouring. A bleaker evening's ride, under circumstances, too, sadly in keeping with the drenching character of the weather and the miry quality of the roads, no equestrian party ever took. We camped in a wood near Jamestown, and had a soaking soldier's night of it. Next morning, for potent reasons, Breckinridge, accompanied by Reagan, returned to Greensboro. What Johnston might choose to agree on, in his convention with Sherman, was a matter which needed looking into. The terms first submitted were Breckinridge's. These were rejected. They were the only terms Johnston was authorized to make, so far as Mr. Davis could give him authority. The compromise terms afterwards allowed by Breckinridge were not approved at Washington, and after waiting two days in the neighbourhood of the negotiations, Breckinridge consented to permit General Johnston to do the best he could.

"The first positive information received in Charlotte as to Johnston's surrender came in the form of a telegram to his wife, then staying there. It advised her to remain in Charlotte, and he, paroled, would soon join her.

"I should mention that General Breckinridge telegraphed, among other things, to Charlotte the mere fact that President Lincoln was killed. The circumstances were not known until our arrival. Except some thoughtless enthusiast, no one heard the particulars and was unshocked. Mr. Davis said nothing in my hearing in the least like the remarks that have been ascribed to him. He made an inquiry similar to that of Benjamin, and looked rather than spoke his horror when the facts were put before him. 'It is awful,' was all I heard him say.

"Next day, accompanied by a cavalry escort of about two thousand men, Jefferson Davis, cabinet, and staff, evacuated Charlotte, somewhat undetermined as to a future course. There had been some semblance of a capital, some show of governmental routine, some pretense of the power he was elected to wield, up to this ; but now all that was vanished, and thenceforth the Confederate President was a fugitive, with hardly the shadow of authority. He looked sad, and, indeed, hopeless. Never a word escaped him which betrayed the faintest yielding.

"Much has been said, and more supposed, in regard to the treasure he was carrying off in his train. The Confederate treasure was never with him or his train. It was the Richmond Bank specie that was fastened to his train at any time—its custodians deeming that course the safest. The Confederate specie was usually far away from him. It left Charlotte in charge of the midshipmen before he arrived there. What became of it finally I know not, although I know that a portion of it was used to pay off certain troops, and others at various points, from Charlotte to Washington, in Georgia.

"As Mr. Davis practically ceased to be a President from that day he evacuated Charlotte, and his course, after that, was an incessant flight, I can quickly tell all I have to add. From Charlotte the Presidential party, attended by a more imposing escort than yet honored its progress, went to the Catawba river. It was like the sun setting—this array—the expiring glories of a four-years' gallantly-maintained power. George Davis had resigned the Attorney-Generalship of Charlotte. Mr. Trenholm resigned the Treasury-Secretaryship on the banks of the Catawba. Not only had the 'Presidential party' become smaller by degrees, but the high officials had begun to dwindle away, and the whole party was at length reduced to scanty numbers, though its escort was still large. Judge Reagan was appointed Acting-Secretary of the Treasury at the Catawba, about the last executive deed of the flying President.

"Delays were now not thought of, and on toward Abbeville, *via* Yorkville, the party struck, taking full soldiers' allowance of turmoil, and camping all the journey. Only intent on pushing to certain points on the Florida coast, onward it went. Rumors of Stoneman, rumors of Wilson, rumors even of the ubiquitous Sheridan, occasionally sharpened the excitement. The escort, for the sake of expedition, was shorn of its bulky proportions, and by the time we reached Washington in Georgia, there were only enough to make a fair fight with a respectable raiding party.

"It was manifest at Washington that the disintegration which had been apparent, more or less, from the outset among the Presidential followers had culminated. It was equally clear that Mr. Davis had little to expect from the people. Except at Charlotte, and there only qualifiedly, he experienced little like cordiality since leaving Virginia. North Carolina was positively cold or lukewarm. South Carolina displayed no marked indications of sympathy; and now in Georgia, and near to the home of Alexander H. Stephens, what could he expect?

"His companions all saw how it was, if not how it was so soon going to be. The personal safety of each became a question, and each was urged to secure it as he best could. Acting on the suggestion, Mr. Mallory quietly left his horses in charge of a friend, and boldly ventured himself in a railroad train to Barnett Station, thence on to Atlanta, where the Federals were in force. That far he was accompanied by Louis Wigfall, the quondam General and Texas Senator. From Atlanta the Confederate Navy Secretary took the West Point train and successfully reached Lagrange, where his family were, and where he was captured.

"Mr. Benjamin disappeared before Washington, no one knew how or where. Thus, the Confederate President had left him only one cabinet officer, and that one the Postmaster General.

"At last he got information that his own wife and family were in danger from the assaults of military marauders. Mrs. Davis, with her three children, accompanied by her sister, Miss Howell, had a wagon train of her own about twenty or thirty miles from her husband's party. She was very anxious to go her own way and be no embarrassment to him. She felt equal to the task of protecting herself from reckless Confederates, and felt sure of avoiding Federals. But no sooner did he ascertain that she was in danger, that two gangs had concocted a scheme to seize all her trunks, under the impression that she carried the rebel gold, than he resolved, at all hazards, to go to her rescue. It was a fond husband's, a fond father's infatuation. No remonstrance availed. He set out and rode eighteen miles to meet the object of his love and solicitude. He met them, and the first to rebuke him for his excess of fondness was the anxious wife and mother. A tent or two was already pitched, and he, weary to exhaustion, went to sleep, intending to retrace his steps before morning. Had he not gone to assure himself of his wife's safety, and had he not been excessively fatigued while there, Colonel Pritchard would be without the honor of capturing him, for nothing was easier than his escape, as Breckenridge, and Wood, and the writer of this know, and by meeting no interruption, themselves have proved. Their immunity might have been his.

"But Davis ran his risks and took his chances, fully conscious of imminent danger, yet powerless, from physical weariness, to do all he designed doing against the danger. When the musketry firing was heard in the morning at 'dim grey dawn,' it was supposed to be between the rebel marauders and Mrs. Davis's few camp defenders. Under this impression he hurriedly put on his boots and prepared to go out for the purpose of interposing, saying :—

"'They will at least as yet respect me.'

"As he got to the tent door thus hastily equipped, and with this good intention of preventing an effusion of blood, by an appeal in the name of a fading but not wholly faded authority, ho saw a few cavalry ride up the road, and deploy in front.

" ' Ha, Federals !' was his exclamation.

" ' Then you are captured,' cried Mrs. Davis, with emotion.

" In a moment she caught an idea—a woman's idea, and as quickly as women in an emergency execute their designs, it was done. He slept in a wrapper—a loose one. It was yet around him. This she fastened ere he was aware of it, and then bidding him adieu, urged him to go to the spring, a short distance off, where his horses and arms were. Strange as it may seem, there was not even a pistol in the tent. Davis felt that his only course was to reach his horse and arms, and complied. As he was leaving the door, followed by a servant with a water bucket, Miss Howell *flung a shawl over his head*. There was no time to remove it without exposure and embarrassment, and as he had not far to go, he ran the chance exactly as it was devised for him. In these two articles consisted the woman's attire of which so much nonsense has been spoken and written, and under these circumstances and in this way was Jefferson Davis going forth to perfect his escape. No bonnet, no gown, no petticoats, no crinoline ; nothing of all these ; and what there was happened to be excusable under ordinary circumstances, and perfectly natural as things were.

" But it was too late for any effort to reach his horses, and the Confederate President was at last a prisoner in the hands of the United States."

CONTENTS.

CHAPTER I.

FIRST STEPS TO FAME.

An Anxious Visitor—Obstacles overcome—The Journey of Life commenced—A Dreary March — Perseverance rewarded — Our Hero's Birth and Parentage—His Early Life—He becomes a Student at West-Point—Slow at Study—Futile Attempt to play the Flute—Specimens of Eccentricities—He Graduates—Class-Mates—Enters the Army—Proceeds to Mexico — Promoted for his Bravery—Instances of Gallantry—Retires from the Army—Becomes Professor of Mathematics at Lexington, Va.—Escapes Assassination—Married —Becomes a Widower—Married a Second Time—Religious Teachings and Counsel, ... 11

CHAPTER II.

THE UPPER POTOMAC.

Jackson resigns his Professorship and joins the Confederate Army —Becomes a Colonel—Joins Johnston's Forces on the Upper Potomac—Rebel Evacuation of Harper's Ferry—Scenes of Devastation —Encounter with Patterson at Falling Waters — Jackson's First Display of Strategetic Ability—Johnston eludes Patterson and joins Beauregard—Jackson made a Brigadier-General, ... 27

CHAPTER III.

THE BATTLE OF BULL RUN.

Jackson's Position at the Opening of the Battle—His Timely Appearance upon the Principal Scene—Origin of the Sobriquet "Stonewall"—Description of the Main Battle-Ground—Desperate Position of the Confederates—Terrible Conflicts between the Opposing Forces —Gallantry of Jackson's Brigade—The Federals finally repulsed—They become Panic-Stricken—Reasons why they were not pursued by the Rebels—Beauregard's Official Remarks on Jackson's Heroism —His Appearance on the Field of Battle, ... 31

CHAPTER IV.

WINTER CAMPAIGN ON THE UPPER POTOMAC.

Lull in Military Proceedings—Jackson placed in Command on the Upper Potomac—March to Hancock—Severity of the Weather and Suffering of the Troops—Skirmish at Bath—Engagement at Hancock—Results of the Expedition—Jackson's Energy as a Commander —His Endurance of Fatigue—Illustrations of his Piety, . . . 41

CHAPTER V.

THE BATTLE OF WINCHESTER.

Jackson retires from the Upper Potomac—Skirmish at Blue's Gap— Encounter at Blooming Gap—Death of General Lander—Harper's Ferry reöccupied by the Federals—Advance of General Banks to Winchester—Skirmishes before the Battle—Country around Winchester — Opening of the Engagement — Terrific Conflict near a Stone Wall — The Confederates finally repulsed — Numbers and Losses of the Combatants, ... 49

CHAPTER VI.

CAMPAIGN IN THE VALLEY OF THE SHENANDOAH—RETREAT OF GENERAL BANKS.

Retreat of Jackson up the Valley—Federal Plans to capture him— Battle of McDowell—Compels Banks to retreat—Battle of Front Royal—Alarm of General Banks at Strasburgh—He commences a . rapid Retreat—Disasters by the Way—Exciting Scenes in Winchester —Second Battle of Winchester—Safe Arrival of the Federals in Maryland—Estimate of Losses, ... 62

CHAPTER VII.

VALLEY OF THE SHENANDOAH—FEDERAL PURSUIT OF JACKSON.

Excitement in the North—Federal Plan to capture Jackson—Attack on Harper's Ferry—Front Royal recovered—Fremont and Shields pursue Jackson—Death of General Ashby—Battle of Cross Keys—Port Republic—Jackson escapes his Pursuers—Discomforts of Fremont's March—The Valley Devastated—Jackson's Devotional Habits, . 80

CHAPTER VIII.

THE SEVEN DAYS' BATTLES BEFORE RICHMOND.

Jackson created a Major-General—McClellan Lands upon the Peninsula —Occupation of Yorktown—Williamsburgh—Hanover Court-House

—Seven Pines—Fair Oaks—Stuart's celebrated Raid—Position and
Number of the Opposing Forces—FIRST DAY: Battle of Oak Grove
—Confederate Council of War—SECOND DAY: Battle of Mechanics-
ville—THIRD DAY: Battle of Gaines's Mill—The Battle-Ground—
Jackson's Attack on the Federal Rear—The River crossed by the
Federal Right Wing—Council of War—FOURTH DAY: Battle of Gar-
nett's Farm—FIFTH DAY: Battle of Peach Orchard—Battle of Sav-
age's Station—SIXTH DAY: Battle of White Oak Swamp—Battle of
Glendale—SEVENTH DAY: Battle of Malvern Hill—Losses of the
Combatants—Importance of Jackson's Services during the Week, . 94

CHAPTER IX.

THE CAMPAIGN AGAINST GENERAL POPE.

Organization of Pope's Army—His Address and Orders to his Troops
—Strength of his Army — Confederate Plan to crush him—Com-
mences to advance — He is opposed by Jackson—Battle of Cedar
Mountain—Narrow Escapes—Jackson's Official Report—Losses in
the Battle—The Field of Operations removes to near Washington—
Pope retires behind the Rappahannock—Stuart's Cavalry Raid—
Pope's Papers captured—Jackson's March upon the Federal Right
Flank—Reaches Manassas Junction—Feast of his Famished Soldiers
—Pope's Project to capture him—Critical Position of Jackson—
Battle of Groveton—Jackson reënforced by Lee and Longstreet—
Second Battle of Bull Run—Federal Defeat—Pope retires to Cen-
treville—Battle at Chantilly—Jackson's Share in the Campaign, . 129

CHAPTER X.

THE INVASION OF MARYLAND.

The Federals retire within the Lines of Washington—Resignation of
Pope—Appointment of McClellan—Jackson leads the Way into Maryland—Enters Frederick—Incidents during its Occupation—Lee's Proclamation—Jackson marches upon Harper's Ferry—Maryland Heights
abandoned—Harper's Ferry bombarded—Its Surrender—Jackson's
Report of the Capture—Federal Inquiry into the Cause of Surrender
—Battle of South-Mountain—Battle of Antietam—The Battle-ground
and Positions of the Combatants—Terrific Contest between Jackson
and Hooker—Change in the Scene of Conflict—The Losses—Jackson
demolishes Thirty Miles of Railroad—Affair at Blackford's Ford, . 154

CHAPTER XI.

THE BATTLE OF FREDERICKSBURGH.

Jackson's Antagonists—Burnside supersedes McClellan—The Army of
the Potomac marches to the Rappahannock—The Battle-Ground—
The Federals cross the River—Positions of the two Commanders—
Advance of Franklin—Heroism of a Confederate Officer—Opening
of the Battle—Sublimity of the Scene—Attack on the Fortifications
—The Field of Death—The Combat described—Reserves brought
into Action—The Losses—Councils of War—The River recrossed, . 177

CHAPTER XII.

THE BATTLE OF CHANCELLORSVILLE.

Jackson created Lieutenant-General—Burnside's proposed Operations—
Hooker placed in Command of the Army of the Potomac—Winter
Quarters—Movements against Fredericksburgh—The Rappahannock
crossed—Hooker reaches Chancellorsville—Description of the Place
—Lee's and Jackson's Movements — Arrival at Chancellorsville —
Jackson's Celebrated Attack upon the Federal Flank—Receives his
Death-Wound—A Federal Officer's Interview with Jackson—Subse-
quent Engagements—Losses in the Battles—Lee's Estimate of Jack-
son's Abilities, ... 193

CHAPTER XIII.

LAST MOMENTS AND OBSEQUIES.

Jackson's Daily Condition after being Wounded—He is attended by
Mrs. Jackson—His Last Remarks—His Death—General Lee's Order
to the Army—Jackson's Successor—The Remains reach Richmond—
Received with Public Honors and lie in State—Arrive in Lexington
—The Funeral, ... 216

CHAPTER XIV.

THE SOLDIER AND THE MAN.

Jackson's Military Career an Episode in the Rebellion—Compared with
the Puritan Leaders of England—Resemblance to Havelock—Northern Appreciation of his Gallantry — Qualities as a Commander —
"Mystery the Secret of Success"—Firmness under Fire—Love of
Truth—Hatred of Flattery — Alleged Unfitness for Separate Com-

mand—Admiration of General Lee—Personal Appearance and Habits —Estimates of Jackson's Character—Viewed from a Northern Standpoint, ... 229

CHAPTER XV.

THE CHRISTIAN HERO.

Jackson's Religious Habits—Returns Public Thanks to God for Victory —Seeks Guidance in Prayer—His Missionary Spirit—Services before the "Stonewall Brigade"—Secret Prayer—Religious Condition of Jackson's Army—A Revival among the Soldiers—Letter of General Jackson on Sabbath Mails and Despatches—Dying Exclamations, . 251

CHAPTER XVI.

INCIDENTS AND ANECDOTES.

Jackson's Peculiarities subject him to Caricature—Military Discipline at Lexington—War Means Fighting—Secrecy—Going to the Commissary — An Inquisitive Friend — A Ruse — Coolness — Sambo's Prisoner—An Irish Rebel—A Watery Wish—Daily Work—Abhorrence of Sectional Hate — Double Rations — "Old Jackson always Moving"—Poking about—Crossing the Potomac—Surrounded—An Incentive to Victory—The Observed of all Observers—"No Great Shakes, after all"—A Federal Captain's Opinion—An Equestrian Compliment—Experiences on Horseback—"Jackson Resigned"— Headquarters and their Attractions—Playing with Children—Visit to Jackson in Camp, ... 261

CHAPTER XVII.

THE FOOT-CAVALRY.

Why called the "Foot Cavalry"—The old "Stonewall" Brigade — Doubts about the Name—A Parting Scene—The Greatest Marcher in the World—No Excuses permitted—Obedience to Orders—A Colored Thermometer—Jackson's Army not to be found by the Federals —A Cause of Reverse—The Army in Repose—Sports and Pastimes of Camp-life — "Old Jack" extremely popular — A Talk with the General—Disaffection of Officers—Discipline—Characteristics of the old "Stonewall" Brigade, ... 281

LIFE OF

LIEUT.-GEN. THOMAS J. JACKSON.

CHAPTER I.

FIRST STEPS TO FAME.

An Anxious Visitor—Obstacles overcome—The Journey of Life commenced—A Dreary March—Perseverance rewarded—Our Hero's Birth and Parentage—His Early Life—He becomes a Student at West-Point—Slow at Study—Futile Attempt to play the Flute—Specimens of Eccentricities—He Graduates—Class-Mates—Enters the Army—Proceeds to Mexico—Promoted for his Bravery—Instances of Gallantry—Retires from the Army—Becomes Professor of Mathematics at Lexington, Va.—Escapes Assassination—Married—Becomes a Widower—Married a Second Time—Religious Teachings and Counsel.

On a terribly wet day in the year 1842, an ambitious youth of nineteen, whose ardor was not to be damped by the cold rain which was streaming from his clothes, rushed in a state of great excitement into the office of a gentleman who resided in one of the villages of Western Virginia.

"What brings you hither, my friend, in such a pitiless storm?" anxiously inquired the gentleman, starting and wondering at the unexpected appearance of his youthful acquaintance.

The young man in breathless haste, immediately explained the nature of his errand. He was flushed with that military ardor which so often betokens a spirit of ambition that will yield to no rebuff, and is capable of battling against every obstacle.

A presentation to the military academy at West-Point had been offered to, but declined by a boy in the neighborhood. Our young aspirant was seized with an eager desire to obtain this presentation. His uncle with whom he resided—for he was an orphan—had fruitlessly attempted to dissuade him from pursuing the application. His friends had in vain pointed out to him the deficiencies of his education, and that he was already three years in advance of the age at which pupils are usually admitted. He was fully alive to these drawbacks, but nothing daunted, he determined to attempt to carry out the project upon which he had set his heart.

With a buoyant spirit he had entered the office of his friend, and he now sought from him a letter of introduction to Mr. Hayes, the member of Congress for the district, who was then in Washington. His friend was intimately acquainted with Mr. Hayes, and it was in the latter's power to obtain the cadetship for the applicant. The difficulties which beset the young man's path were again pointed out to him. His friend regarded his scheme as an utter absurdity, and not only plainly told him that he could never successfully pass the preliminary examination, but added many other discouraging remarks. The ambitious youth had prepared himself for this ordeal, he was hopeful and importunate, and eventually obtained the coveted letter.

Armed with this document, he determined to depart for the National Capital without delay. Procrastination has stood in the way of many a man's advancement in life. Of this slothful habit our youthful hero was innocent. One day's, or even one hour's delay might enable some more fortunate applicant to step in, and obtain the appointment. That night a stage started on its regular eastern journey from the neighboring town of Clarksburgh. To enable the youth to reach that place in time to avail himself of this conveyance, he borrowed a horse, and with a negro boy, who was to bring the steed safely back to its owner, perched behind him, he commenced his travels upon what in after years turned out to be the road to renown.

For many weeks Western Virginia had been visited by heavy rains—by such rains as can fall only in those mountainous regions—and the roads were consequently rendered all but impassable. But little business was then transacted in those regions, and few people travelled in those days, and in such weather. The postmaster of Clarksburgh considered it of little moment whether he dispatched the stage with the mail-bags either an hour before or after the appointed time. When our young traveller arrived in the town he found, much to his discomfiture, that the official had on this occasion adopted the first exception from the proper rule, and the unwieldy stage had commenced its weary journey upon the toilsome roads a full hour before the usual time. We do not know how often this conveyance then left Clarksburgh, but it was most probably only once a week. As the delay, which would occur if he waited until its next time of starting, might be fatal to the young man's prospects, no inducement could tempt him from the endeavor to overtake the vehicle. Therefore, dispatching the negro boy home with the borrowed horse, he set off in pursuit, on foot, over a dreadfully muddy road, and after a toilsome march of thirteen miles on this dark stormy night, he overtook the conveyance.

How far the stage carried him we are unable to state. However, it is evident that he did not indulge in this mode of travelling all the way to Washington, for it is certain that he made the greater part of his long journey on foot, carrying his scanty wardrobe in his hand. Arriving at the Capital, our youthful aspirant, "all muddy as he was," presented his letter to Mr. Hayes, who received him kindly, and in his turn presented him to the Secretary of War, who granted the much coveted presentation, and thus rewarded him for his praiseworthy ambition and perseverance.

The youth whom we have depicted as thus mounting the first step in the ladder of life, was destined many years afterwards to play a very important part in the terrible war which has shaken the country to its foundations, and has fearfully devastated his native State. His name was

Thomas Jonathan, but history will record it as "Stone-wall," Jackson. Why history will thus speak of him, we shall mention hereafter.

He was born on January 21st, 1824, in the town of Clarksburgh, already named, in Harrison County, Virginia. His grandfather, Edward Jackson, had been surveyor of the neighboring county of Lewis, which he for a long time represented in the State Legislature. His father, Jonathan Jackson, moved to Clarksburgh, where he studied and commenced the practice of law with his cousin, Judge John G. Jackson. He acquired considerable reputation in his profession, and married a daughter of Thomas Neale, of Wood County. He died in 1827, leaving four children—two sons and two daughters—of whom our hero, then three years old, was the youngest. Misfortune had overtaken the father before his death, and all his property had been swept away to meet the failures of unfaithful friends. The children were therefore thrown penniless upon the world. Soon after the death of his parents, young Jackson was taken to the home of an uncle in Lewis County, the family homestead of the Jacksons in which his father had been born. During the time of the residence with his uncle, he labored on the farm in summer, and for three months in the winter went to school, where he gained the rudiments of a plain English education, the small stock of learning which he possessed when he was seized with the desire to obtain the cadetship at West-Point. His habits of life, even at this early age, are said to have been grave and serious, his discharge of every duty conscientious and complete. He assisted his uncle in the management of the farm ; and soon secured among the residents of the county a high character for industry, intelligence, and probity. His orphan condition excited great sympathy among the neighbors, who knew and respected the good character of the Jackson family ; and every assistance was rendered him in his struggle to carve out his own pathway in life, and secure an honorable independence. A proof of this sympathy is contained in the fact that at the age of *sixteen*, he was elected constable of the county of Lewis, the duties of which office he discharged with intelligence and credit.

The future hero entered upon his studies at West-Point, three years in advance of his class-mates, but in every other respect far behind them. A shy and bashful youth, he took his place among them, just old enough to feel his own deficiencies in education and social position. In the four years of his study at the Military Academy, he was a plodding, persevering student, systematically mastering the task of yesterday, before he undertook that of to-day ; and slowly but surely working his way by hard application to a respectable, if not a leading position amongst his fellow-students. It is stated that he was so slow in his studies, that it took him three times as long to master his tasks as the average of the other pupils ; but what he did learn he learned thoroughly.

Whilst young Jackson was at the Academy, his disposition was retiring and taciturn, but his face would brighten up with a pleasant smile whenever he entered into conversation. In illustration of the difficulty which he experienced in learning any thing, we may relate an anecdote told by General Seymour. During the time that the latter and Jackson were both young lieutenants, Seymour amused himself by learning to play the flute, which instrument Jackson also felt an inclination to learn. To accomplish this he went to work with his accustomed vigor and perseverance ; but he was never enabled to master even the most simple air, and at last gave up his attentions to the goddess of music, after having for six months unsuccessfully courted her in an attempt to master the first bar of " Love Not." It is evident that he had " no music in himself," and, if Shakspeare is to be believed, he was, in this respect at least, " fit for treasons, stratagems, and spoils."

Many curious anecdotes are related of the peculiarities exhibited by the young student, during his stay at West-Point. It is stated that he used to fancy that he suffered from consumption, and that he should die a painful death. He was also possessed with the notion that he was in danger of having his limbs paralyzed, and he would pump on his arm for many minutes, counting the strokes, and feeling annoyed beyond measure whenever his companions interrupted him in his count. He was accustomed to sit upright at his meals, and had a curious way of holding up his head very straight, whilst his chin would appear as if it were trying to get up to the top of his head. Another of his eccentricities was a remarkable precision as to the time he took his meals, and he was so particular in this respect that he would lay his watch before him on the table at the hour of meal, and if the latter was not ready at the precise moment appointed, he would obstinately refuse to partake of it.

The accustomed period of four years' study at West-Point having terminated, Jackson graduated on June thirtieth, 1846. He was the seventeenth in a class of fifty-nine. Probably at the outset every boy surpassed him, but he had now only sixteen who outstripped him, and a joke prevailed among his comrades that, so great was his perseverance, had he had ten years to study instead of four, he would have become the head of the whole class. His sterling character had gained him the esteem of his masters, his unpretending merit and steady perseverance had won the admiration of his comrades. In spite of his ungainly appearance, his unpolished manners, and his " slow " capacities, he had overcome all prejudices, and had quickly secured the affection and respect of his contemporaries.

The class of 1846 has been considered the most remarkable of any that ever graduated from the Academy. By a strange coïncidence there appear in its list the names of McClellan, Stoneman, Foster, Sturges, Couch, Reno, Seymour, and many others who have become distinguished during the present conflict.

Immediately after young Jackson had graduated at West-Point, he entered the army of the United States as a Brevet

Second Lieutenant of the First artillery, and received his full commission on the succeeding third of March. Among the officers of the First artillery at this period were the following military men who either have taken, or at the present time are taking prominent parts in the present war. On the side of the North, Justin Dimick, W. H. French, J. Hooker, L McDowell, J. B. Ricketts, J. M. Brannan, Seth Williams, Abner Doubleday, E. C. Boynton, T. Seymour, and others; and on the side of the South, J. H. Winder, J. B. Magruder, J. W. Mackall, A. P. Hill, and others.

At the commencement of the campaign in Mexico, Jackson proceeded to that country, as one of the officers of Magruder's battery. He took part in all the battles of that campaign, and was several times rewarded with promotion for his gallant and meritorious conduct therein. For the bravery which he displayed in the battles of Contreras and Cherubusco he was raised to the rank of Lieutenant on August twentieth, 1847, with the additional brevet rank of Captain, which bore the same date, but which was not award-ed until August of the following year. He so much further distinguished himself at the battle of Chepultepec on the thirteenth of September, 1847, that in March, 1849, he received the brevet rank of Major—the commission for which was dated from the day on which the action took place. The *Army Register* and the actual history and facts of the Mexican war do not furnish the name of another person entering that war without position or office who attained the high rank of Major in the brief campaign and series of battles from Vera Cruz to the City of Mexico.

Several instances are recorded of the gallantry which was displayed by Jackson at the battle of Chepultepec. Magruder being a man of remarkably intemperate habits, it almost invariably happened that during the Mexican campaign, the chief command of his battery devolved on Lieutenant Jackson. Upon the eve of this battle Jackson, who then had charge of the battery, was advancing with it toward the scene of the following day's engagement, when, on turning a bend of the road, he found his progress arrested by a battery of four guns which the Mexicans had planted behind a small earth-work. A fight ensued, in which every horse and man in Jackson's command were killed or wounded, he only being left unharmed. The Mexicans rushed upon the battery, but the young officer would not leave his guns, when fortunately his enemies were suddenly outflanked, and compelled to retire in great haste, leaving him in indisputable possession thereof.

It is also related that at the battle of Chepultepec, Jackson was ordered by Pillow, to whose division Magruder's battery was attached, to withdraw his section, as his superior officer considered that it was too much exposed. He gave no heed, however, to the General's order, but rapidly limbered up, and moved his guns a hundred yards nearer the enemy's works, on which he did great execution.

Another anecdote related of Jackson's behavior in this engagement states that, upon the Fourteenth regular infant-

ry being ordered to charge up a road, the men seemed dis-
inclined to advance, in consequence of the heavy fire to
which they were exposed. Jackson, upon perceiving this,
stepped forward amid a shower of missiles and exclaimed,
"You see, my men, there is no danger, follow me!" which
daring act so inspired the troops that they immediately
sprang forward to the charge.

The gallantry displayed by the young soldier throughout
the entire of the battle of Chepultepec was of such a nature
as to gain for him special mention in the official despatches
of the Commander-in-Chief; an honor which was not award-
ed to any other officer. In these despatches General Scott
alluded to him as " the brave Lieutenant Jackson."

The career of a soldier in time of peace is so generally uninteresting and so unmarked by important events, that it is
barren of interest to the public. The proceedings of to-day
are almost a repetition of those of yesterday, and with the
exception of the time occupied in the removal from fort to
fort, the story of a day is but an epitome of a soldier's life
at such a time. For the three or four years that succeeded
the Mexican war, Jackson's life was no exception to this
general rule.

On February twenty-ninth, 1852, Jackson retired from the
army of the United States, having served therein nearly six
years. After his retirement he took up his residence in his
native State of Virginia, and became a Professor of Mathematics in the Military College of Lexington in that State.

Although he had a very fine class of pupils, his services at this establishment were not very conspicuous. Colonel Gilham was considered as the military genius of the school, and Jackson was but little thought of by the small hero-worshippers of Lexington. He was devoutly religious in all his actions, and stern in the performance of his duties; and, as is too often the case with such professors, he was not viewed with much favoritism by his pupils.

During the period of his professorship Jackson had a narrow escape from assassination, the consummation of which he averted by his great coolness and fearlessness of death. The person by whom his life was threatened was a cadet who had been dismissed from the institution. The youth actually went to the extremity of lying in wait for him on the road leading from the Institute to the village. As Jackson, in his accustomed walk toward the village, approached the spot where his enemy awaited him, a bystander called out to him of his danger. "Let the assassin murder if he will," replied the Professor, as he walked in the most unconcerned manner toward the young man, who slunk abashed from his path.

Perhaps none of the acquaintances of Jackson were more surprised at his brilliant exhibition of genius in this war, than were those who knew his blank life at the Institute, and were familiar with the stiff and uninteresting figure that was to be seen every Sunday in a pew of the Presbyterian church at Lexington. But true genius awaits occasion commensurate with its power and aspiration. The spirit of Jackson was trained in another school than that of, West-Point or Lexington, and had it been confined there it never would have illuminated the page of history. How peculiarly appropriate, in such a case, would these oft-quoted lines of Gray's Elegy have applied to him :

> " Full many a gem, of purest ray serene,
> The dark, unfathomed caves of ocean bear ;
> Full many a flower is born to blush unseen,
> And waste its sweetness on the desert air."

During the time of Jackson's residence in Lexington, he became connected with the Presbyterian church of that place. Of this denomination he was an earnest member, and, in fact, throughout his future life he displayed those eminently religious qualities which so elevate man in the estimation of his fellow-beings, but which are so rarely found in the camp or on the battle-field. He held the position of a deacon in the church to which he belonged, and participated in its councils.

Whilst residing in Lexington, he became acquainted with the family of the Rev. George Junkin, D.D., whose daughter he married in the year 1853. But, unfortunately, in the following year, the occurrence of an event which usually adds to the happiness of a married life was to him a source of sorrow, and deprived him not only of his wife, but of the infant offspring she had borne him.

Jackson was married a second time in the year 1857 to a daughter of the Rev. Dr. Morrison, a Presbyterian

minister, and President of Davidson College, North-
Carolina, by whom he had one child, who was about six
months old at the time of its father's death. Another
daughter of this gentleman was married to the Confederate General D. H. Hill; the two chieftains were
therefore nearly related.

Jackson was, during his professorship, not only a regular teacher in the Sabbath-school, but wherever Christian aid and counsel were required, wherever the sick and
sorrowing claimed sympathy, or religious instruction was
necessary, he was at hand. Among the negroes, seldom
was such a patient, zealous friend to be found as "Mass'
Thomas." Every Sabbath he assembled the little darkies
to hear and learn the word of God. Nor was his anxiety for their welfare confined to his own household; for
wherever his influence could be exerted for the spiritual
and moral progress of the negro, his voice was heard.

CHAPTER II.

Jackson resigns his Professorship and joins the Confederate Army—Becomes a Colonel—Joins Johnston's Forces on the Upper Potomac—Rebel Evacuation of Harper's Ferry—Scenes of Devastation—Encounter with Patterson at Falling Waters—Jackson's First Display of Strategetic Ability—Johnston eludes Patterson and joins Beauregard—Jackson made a Brigadier-General.

AT the commencement of the Rebellion, Jackson was busily engaged with his professional duties at Lexington, and it was not until the secession of his State that he resigned his peaceful occupation for the hazards and excitements of a soldier's life. Like his celebrated companion in arms, General Lee, he was a theoretical Unionist up to the very date of Virginia's secession, struggling long in deciding between his duty to his country and his devotion to his State; and it was only when his own State drew the sword that he determined to follow her fortunes. This occurred at the latter end of April, 1861. His first command was a regiment of infantry, which he drilled so quickly, and yet so perfectly, that he was enabled to rely upon it at any moment. He was commissioned Colonel by the Governor of Virginia, and was with his regiment attached to the forces of General Johnston on the Upper Potomac.

2

It will be remembered that on the nineteenth of April, shortly after the commencement of the Rebellion, the Federals evacuated Harper's Ferry, after partially destroying the public works and armory there situated. Around this place—which is of historic interest from its having been the scene of that insurrection, small in itself but great in the influences it created, which in 1859 caused the name of John Brown to become celebrated in song and renowned in story—nature has lavished a wild beauty. On every side are seen the lofty ridges of the Blue Mountains, pierced at one bold point by the Potomac and the Shenandoah, whilst the railroad which here crosses the former stream, acts as a connecting-link between this bold mountain scenery and the great cities of the East and the West. It was in the neighborhood of these scenes that Jackson gathered the first leaves of that laurel-wreath with which his memory is now crowned.

The demonstrations of the Federal army in the Valley of Virginia were of such a nature that it was considered necessary to thwart them by the falling back of the Confederate army from Harper's Ferry to Winchester. General Patterson's approach was expected by the great route into the Valley from Pennsylvania and Maryland, leading through Winchester; and it was an object of the utmost importance to the Confederates that they should prevent any junction between his forces and those of General McClellan, who was already making his way from Western Virginia to the upper portions of the Valley. On the morning of the thirteenth of June, information was received from Winchester that Romney was occupied by two thousand Federal troops, supposed to be the vanguard of McClellan's army. A detachment was therefore despatched by railroad to check the Union advance; and on the morning of the fifteenth, the Confederate army left Harper's Ferry for Winchester.

The Rebels found it necessary the next morning to retire from their possession of the Ferry, and their destruction of the buildings, which had been left unscathed at the time of the evacuation of the place by the Federals, brought one of those wild, fearful scenes which make the desolation that grows out of war. This devastation is thus described: " The splendid railroad-bridge across the Potomac — one of the most superb structures of its kind on the continent — was set on fire at its northern end, while about four hundred feet at its southern extremity was blown up, to prevent the flames from reaching other works which it was necessary to save. Many of the vast buildings were consigned to the flames. Some of them were not only large but very lofty, and crowned with tall towers and spires, and we may be able to fancy the sublimity of the scene, when more than a dozen of these huge fabrics crowded into a small space were blazing at once. So great was the heat and smoke, that many of the troops were forced out of the town, and the necessary labors of the removal were performed with the greatest difficulty."

The Confederates received information on the day after their evacuation of Harper's Ferry, that General Patterson's army had crossed the Potomac at Williamsport; also that the Federal force at Romney had fallen back. The Rebels were therefore ordered to gain the Martinsburgh turnpike by a flank movement to Bunker's Hill, in order to place themselves between Winchester and the expected advance of Patterson. On learning this, the Federals immediately re-crossed the river. Resuming his first direction and plan, General Johnston proceeded to Winchester, so that his army might be in a position to oppose either General McClellan from the west, or Patterson from the north-east, and to form a junction with General Beauregard when necessary.

Intelligence having been received by the Confederates indicating a further movement by General Patterson, Colonel Jackson with a brigade was sent to the neighborhood of Martinsburgh to support Colonel Stuart, who had been placed in observation with his cavalry on the line of the Potomac. On the second of July, Patterson again crossed the river, and Colonel Jackson, pursuant to instructions, fell back before him, but in retiring, he engaged the Federal advance at Falling Waters, with a battalion of the Fifth Virginia regiment and Pendleton's battery of field-artillery. Skilfully taking a position where the smallness of his force was concealed, he engaged the Federals for a considerable time, inflicted a heavy loss, and retired when about to be outflanked, scarcely losing a man, but bringing off forty-five prisoners. In this engagement, which was after all merely a skirmish, Jackson exhibited his ready-witted strategy, and concealed from his opponents the knowledge that they were fighting an insignificant force, skilfully disposed to conceal their weakness, while Johnston was making his dispositions in the rear. The Confederate forces engaged in this action were four regiments of infantry and one regiment of cavalry, together with four pieces of artillery, mostly rifled.

The Northern reports inform us that between three and seven o'clock of the day in question, the Federal troops which had been concentrating at Hagerstown and Williamsport, Maryland, for several days previous, crossed the ford at the latter place. The morning was bright and beautiful, and the soldiers were in high spirits. The advancing force approached the enemy within a distance of seventy-five yards, and a brisk encounter ensued, without much loss on the Northern side. In anticipation of a retreat by the Federal forces, the Confederates had levelled the fences on both sides of the turnpike even with the ground, so as to cut them off in the event of their retiring to the Potomac. The first stand was made at Parkerfield farm, near Haynes ville, where it was necessary to destroy a barn and other outbuildings, so that the Federals could make a charge upon the enemy. Here the conflict was fierce, the Rebels standing well up to their work, and finally, slowly retreating, knapsacks and canteens being hastily thrown aside as incumbrances to a backward march, and blankets and other articles of value left behind.

Upon receipt of the intelligence that Jackson had found it necessary to retire before the advancing forces of General Patterson, the Confederate force at Winchester, strengthened by recent arrivals, were ordered forward to his support. General Johnston took up a position within six miles of Martinsburgh, which town was now invested by the Federals, and for four days waited, with the expectation that he might be there attacked; but after being convinced that Patterson would not approach him, he returned to Winchester. General Johnston having placed Colonel Stuart to watch the Federal General's proceedings, he became enabled by the seventeenth of July to penetrate Patterson's design, and to ascertain that his object was to keep him in check, while General McDowell could attack the forces of Beauregard at Manassas. Our readers will readily recollect the obloquy which fell upon the name of General Patterson for his failure in the execution of that part of the military plan with which he was intrusted. Had he fulfilled his instructions, and prevented Johnston from uniting his forces to those of Beauregard, the story of the battle of Bull Run might perhaps have been told with a termination different to that which is now appended to it in the pages of history.

The marks of active determination which Colonel Jackson displayed and the military skill which he exhibited in the engagement at Falling Waters, and in the short campaign on the Upper Potomac, obtained for him promotion to the position of Brigadier-General.

CHAPTER III.

Jackson's Position at the Opening of the Battle — His Timely Appearance upon the Principal Scene—Origin of the Sobriquet "Stonewall"—Description of the Main Battle-Ground — Desperate Position of the Confederates — Terrible Conflicts between the Opposing Forces — Gallantry of Jackson's Brigade — The Federals finally Repulsed — They become Panic-Stricken — Reasons why they were not Pursued by the Rebels — Beauregard's Official Remarks on Jackson's Heroism — His Appearance on the Field of Battle.

THE affair at Falling Waters was, after all, but the prologue to the great military drama in which the subject of our memoir was to play so important a part. The scene of the first great act was the battle-field of Bull Run, or Manassas, as it is termed by the people of the South. At this battle Jackson had the command of the First Virginia brigade, which consisted of five regiments, and the manner in which he handled this force, in several of the critical periods of the action, is considered by General Beauregard to have contributed largely to the Confederate success.

Jackson's brigade was amongst the first of the forces of General Johnston who, after they had eluded Patterson, hastened to the support of General Beauregard at Manassas.

At the opening of the engagement, shortly after dawn,

on July twenty-first, Jackson was placed as a support to General Bonham, who was detailed to guard Mitchell's Ford. About half-past seven o'clock A.M., his brigade was deployed along with Imboden's, and five pieces of Walton's battery, to take up a position along Bull Run. In the heat of the forenoon's engagement, when the Confederate forces were driven back, and the goddess of victory for the time seemed to smile upon the Union arms, the brigade under General Jackson got separated from Imboden's and Walton's commands; but being afterward reünited, they took up another position below the brim of the plateau, nearly east of the Henry House, and to the left of a ravine and woods occupied by the mingled remnants of other commands. It was here that the battle was to rage so long and so furiously, and where for some time the Rebels had to fight desperately against fearful odds, so that they could hold their own until their reënforcements could reach them.

Jackson's timely arrival at this point, as we shall hereafter show, was considered by General Beauregard to have contributed greatly to the change in the fortune of war, which was shortly to be experienced by the Confederates. It also gave to his troops an opportunity of winning for themselves a renown and an imperishable name. Jackson felt every confidence in the prowess of his force, and the reply which, upon this field, he made to his Commanding General, obtained for him that sobriquet which history will ever connect with his name. Beauregard fancying that his troops were raw, asked Jackson if he thought that they would be likely to stand. "Yes," replied he, "like a stone wall." But Jackson, with his usual modesty, ever after insisted that the name which has now become a type of valor belonged properly to the brigade which he commanded and not to its commander.

The topographical features of the plateau, now the stage of the contending armies, is thus described by General Beauregard, in his Report of the day's proceedings. "A glance at the map will show that it is inclosed on three sides by small water-courses, which empty into Bull Run within a few yards of each other, half a mile to the south of the Stone Bridge. Rising to an elevation of quite one hundred feet above the level of Bull Run at the bridge, it falls off on three sides to the level of the inclosing streams in gentle slopes, but which are furrowed by ravines of irregular direction and length, and studded with clumps and patches of young pines and oaks. The general direction of the crest of the plateau is oblique to the course of Bull Run in that quarter, and on the Brentsville and turnpike roads which intersect each other at right angles. Completely surrounding the two houses before mentioned, (as being situated upon this plateau,) are small open fields of irregular outline, and exceeding one hundred and fifty acres in extent. The houses occupied at the time — the one by Widow Henry, and the other by the free negro Robinson — are small wooden buildings, densely embowered in trees, and environed by a double row of fences on two sides. Around the eastern and southern brim of the plateau, an almost

3*

unbroken fringe of second growth pines gave excellent shelter for our marksmen, who availed themselves of it with the most satisfactory skill. To the west, adjoining the fields, a broad belt of oaks extends directly across the crest on both sides of the Sudley Road, in which, during the battle, regiments of both armies met and contended for the mastery. From the open ground of this plateau, the view embraces a wide expanse of woods and gently undulating, open country of broad grass and grain-fields in all directions."

Such are the general features and the surroundings of the spot for the possession of which, during this eventful day, the contending forces of the Federals and the Confederates disputed with varying success. Though the clangor of arms, the roll of musketry, and the roar of cannon indicated that the battle was raging far and wide, yet it was upon this stage that were enacted the most eventful scenes of the contest, and as it was principally in these scenes that General Jackson played his part in the drama of the day, they naturally form the only ones which come within the scope of our work.

This plateau was, during the morning, occupied by a division of the Confederate army under General Bee, but shortly after mid-day it was dislodged therefrom by the Federals. Overwhelmed by the surging mass of Northern troops, which pressed heavily upon the Rebels, the lines of the latter fell back. As the shattered battalions retired, the slaughter was terrible. They fell back in the direction of the Robinson

House, and were compelled to engage the Federals at several points in their retreat, losing both officers and men, in
order to keep them from closing in around them. It was at
this period of the battle that the telegraphic wires flashed
the news of victory to the people of the North—news which
was, alas, too soon to be followed by sinister intelligence of
a defeat at once complete and disastrous.

The retreat of the Confederates was finally arrested, just
in rear of the Robinson House, by the energy and resolution
of General Bee, assisted by the support of the Hampton Legion and the timely arrival of Jackson's brigade of five regiments. A moment before, General Bee had been well-nigh
overwhelmed by superior numbers. He approached General
Jackson with the pathetic exclamation, "General, they are
beating us back;" to which the latter promptly replied:
"Sir, we'll give them the bayonet." General Bee immediately rallied his overtasked troops with the words: "There
is Jackson standing like a stone wall. Let us determine to
die here, and we will conquer."

The intentions of the Federals now became developed in
the minds of the Commanding Generals, and they were enabled to discern that the conflict which was raging in the
vicinity of Mitchell's Ford was merely a feint, and that the
triumph of the day would have to be decided upon or around
the plateau which has been described. Generals Johnston and Beauregard were four miles distant from this
critical scene of action, having placed themselves upon a
commanding hill to observe the movements. There could

be no mistake now of the Federal intentions, from the violent firing on the left and the immense clouds of dust raised by the march of a large body of troops from their centre.

At this important moment General Beauregard received information that certain instructions, which he had forwarded relative to an attack upon the Federal flank and rear at Centreville, had miscarried. It therefore now became necessary to depend on new combinations, and to meet the National forces upon the field on which they had chosen to give battle. It was plain that nothing but the most rapid combinations, and the most heroic and devoted courage on the part of the Rebel troops, could retrieve the field, which, according to all military conditions, appeared to be positively lost.

About noon, the scene of the battle is described as being utterly sublime. Not until then could one of the present generation, who had never witnessed a grand battle, have imagined such a spectacle. The hill occupied in the morning by Generals Beauregard and Johnston and their respective staffs placed the whole scene before one—a grand, moving diorama. When the firing was at its height, the roar of artillery reached the hill like that of protracted thunder. For one long mile, the whole valley was a boiling crater of dust and smoke. In the distance rose the Blue Ridge, to form the dark background of a most magnificent picture.

The condition of the battle-field was now at least desperate for the Confederates, and their left flank being now over-powered, it became necessary to bring immediately up to their support the reserves not already in motion. Dashing on at headlong gallop, Generals Johnston and Beauregard reached the field of action not a moment too soon. They were instantly occupied with the reörganization of the troops, and the presence of the two commanders upon the field and under fire, had a most salutary effect upon the men, and order was soon restored. To reöccupy the plateau was now the object of the Confederates, and for this purpose they planted their artillery upon an open space of limited extent, behind a low undulation, just at the eastern verge of the plateau, some five hundred or six hundred yards from the Henry House, and upon a level with that held by the batteries of the National army. From the action of these guns, and from the galling fire of musketry placed under cover upon the right and left flank, the Federal force suffered so dreadfully that, according to the reports of its generals, regiment after regiment, which was thrown forward to dislodge the Rebels, was broken, never to recover its entire organization on that field.

In the mean time also two companies of Stuart's Rebel cavalry made a dashing charge down the Brentsville and Sudley road upon the New-York Fire Zouaves — then the Federal right on the plateau — which added to the disorder which the Confederate musketry wrought on their flank. However, the Union forces still pressed the Rebels heavily in that quarter of the field, and threw out fresh troops to

3

outflank them. Some three guns of a battery belonging to the former, in an attempt to obtain here a position apparently to enfilade the batteries of the latter, were thrown so close to a regiment of Jackson's brigade that the soldiers sprang forward and seized them with severe loss, but they were subsequently driven back by an overpowering force of Federal musketry.

At two o'clock in the afternoon, General Beauregard gave orders for the right of his line, except his reserves, to advance to recover the plateau. It was done with uncommon resolution and vigor. At the same time Jackson's brigade pierced the Federal centre with the determination of veterans, but it suffered seriously. With equal spirit the other parts of the Rebel line made the onset, and the Federal lines were broken and swept back at all points from the open ground of the plateau. The latter, however, soon strongly reënforced by fresh regiments, re-commenced the conflict, pressed the Confederate lines back, recovered their ground, and renewed the offensive.

Between half-past two and three o'clock P.M., the Confederates were also strongly reënforced by troops pushed forward from the rear by General Johnston, who had about noon repaired thither for the purpose of despatching the reserves to those positions on the field of battle where they were most required. General Beauregard received these reënforcements just as he had ordered forward to a second effort, for the recovery of the disputed plateau, the whole line, including his reserves. At this crisis of the battle, he felt called upon to lead in person. The attack was general, and was shared in by every Rebel regiment then on the field. The Confederates again swept the whole ground clear of the Union forces, and the plateau around the Henry and Robinson houses remained finally in their possession. But this victory was purchased with the lives of General Bee, Colonel Bartow, and many officers of distinction in the Confederate army.

The Rebels now, rapidly receiving the reënforcements which had been despatched from the rear under the direction of General Johnston, and which included troops that had only arrived at noon by railroad from the Valley of the Shenandoah, commenced to dislodge the Federals from the adjoining woods, in which they swarmed. Having accomplished this task, they commenced the pursuit of the Union army, which had become panic-stricken, and was in retreat. Being encumbered with prisoners which they had captured, a portion of the Confederate forces were compelled to desist from the pursuit, whilst the brigades of Generals Bonham and Longstreet followed the flying army nearly as far as Centreville, until night and darkness came on, when they retired from farther pursuit and returned to Bull Run.

General Beauregard admits that his troops were so exhausted from the laborious operations of the day—operations which had to be performed under cover of a burning July sun, and without water and without food, except a meal hastily snatched at dawn—that a general pursuit upon that evening was physically impossible; whilst on the following day an unusually heavy and unintermitting fall of rain intervened to obstruct his advance with reasonable prospect of fruitful results. Added to this, he states that the want of a cavalry force of sufficient numbers, made an efficient pursuit a military impossibility.

Among the panegyrics which the Confederate Commander passed upon the various officers of his army who specially distinguished themselves upon this eventful day, General Jackson's conduct, he stated to have been that of "an able, fearless soldier and sagacious commander, one fit to lead his brigade." He further said that "his efficient, prompt, timely arrival before the plateau of the Henry House, contributed much to the success of the day. Although painfully wounded in the hand, he remained on the field to the end of the battle, rendering invaluable assistance."

With regard to Jackson's personal appearance at the battle of Manassas, a Southern newspaper contained at the time some paragraphs which expressed great merriment at the first apparition of the future hero on the battle-field. His queer figure on horseback, and his habit of settling his chin in his stock, were also very amusing to some correspondents, who made flippant jests thereat in some of the Southern newspapers. These jests were, however, soon forgotten and forgiven in the tributes of admiration and love which afterward ensued to the popular hero of the war.

CHAPTER IV.

WINTER CAMPAIGN ON THE UPPER POTOMAC.

Lull in Military Proceedings — Jackson placed in Command on the Upper
Potomac—March to Hancock—Severity of the Weather and Suffering of
the Troops—Skirmish at Bath—Engagement at Hancock—Results of the
Expedition—Jackson's Energy as a Commander—His Endurance of Fatigue—Illustrations of his Piety.

BOTH the Federal and Confederate armies that held joint
possession of the sacred soil of Virginia, were so prostrated
by the extraordinary exertions which they had made during the day upon which was fought the memorable battle
of Bull Run, that for many months to come, they felt little
inclined to renew active operations.

The Northern army, now placed under the charge of
General McClellan, had little other occupation than the
daily drill, and for a lengthened period the telegraphic
wires flashed from its camp scarcely any intelligence of its
proceedings beyond the well-worn and stereotyped phrase
of "All quiet on the Potomac." If the military school
masters in the Federal army now busied themselves in
teaching "the young idea how to shoot," the Confederate
preceptors were not the less active in imparting the neces
sary rules of military science. General Jackson took ad-

vantage of this period of abstinence from active operations to raise both officers and men under his command to a state of military discipline which their future actions proved to have been of the highest order.

The energy and abilities displayed by General Jackson at the battle of Bull Run, were sufficiently prominent to mark him out for a separate command. Consequently, during the closing days of 1861, he was despatched with a force of about ten thousand men, from General Johnston's line, to Winchester, for the purpose of watching and impeding the progress of a portion of the Federal army, who were then in possession of the Upper Potomac, and who threatened the Valley of the Shenandoah. It has been considered by a Southern writer, that had the same force been placed at his command in early autumn, " with the view to an expedition to Wheeling, by way of the Winchester and Parkersburgh road, the good effects would, in all probability, have shown themselves in the expulsion of the Federals from North-Western Virginia." Though the people of the North may dispute the accuracy of these presumptions, it is needless at this date to cavil at them.

At the commencement of 1862, portions of several Federal regiments were quartered at Hancock, a small town on a bend of the Upper Potomac, at Bath, a village in Virginia, some six miles south of that place, and at other points contiguous to these two places. General Jackson was desirous of dislodging the Union troops from these positions, which they evidently intended to hold throughout the remainder of the winter. For this purpose, therefore, on the first of January, 1862, his command left Winchester and proceeded on the road toward Romney, a small town to the north-west of that place, when it filed to the right, and marched toward Morgan County. Though the weather on the first day of the march was pleasant, the second was remarkably cold, and the road to be traversed was so bad, that the wagons could not keep up with the troops, which necessitated the men to lie out upon the ground, without covering, and to suffer from the want of food. The wagons, however, came up on the following morning, and the troops, after partaking of breakfast, proceeded on their march, but continued to suffer from the severity of the weather.

Another night was passed but with little rest; after which they proceeded on their journey, their sufferings being augmented by an increase in the coldness, to which was added a heavy snow-storm. When within four miles of the town of Bath, they met and drove back a small Federal force. Shortly after this the Confederates encamped for the night, but it was such a night that few except those accustomed to the hardships of a soldier's life when on active service, have ever the misfortune to experience. Though snow, rain, and hail alternately fell the whole night upon the prostrate troops, who were compelled to endure the same without blankets or covering of any kind, they were so completely exhausted that they fell down before the blazing fires which they had kindled, and slept soundly upon the wet ground. Approaching Bath, on the following morning, they announced their arrival by a discharge of cannon upon that place, in which several Union troops had taken up their winter quarters. The Federals replied to this volley from two batteries, but on some of the Rebel troops being deployed to charge these batteries, the soldiers spiked their guns, and rapidly fell back to the banks of the Potomac, hotly pursued by Ashby's cavalry, followed by infantry and artillery. The Federals having reached the river-bank before the arrival of the Rebel cavalry, they placed themselves in ambush, and fired upon their pursuers, several of whom they seriously wounded. The latter then fell back upon the main body, who brought up their artillery and shelled the woods.

Leaving a picket-guard, the Confederate forces retired to the rear, and encamped for the night. The intensity of the cold had increased so much that the soles of the troops on duty froze to the ground, and their sufferings were truly terrible. On Sunday morning, January fifth, the Confederates advanced to the shores of the Potomac, from which they had been encamped only half a mile distant, and found themselves in front of the pretty little town of Hancock, which was situated upon the Maryland side of the river. In this place the Federals were quartered in considerable force. Upon his arrival, General Jackson sent a flag of truce, by Colonel Ashby, to the authorities of the town, notifying the inhabitants that they should vacate the place, as he intended to bombard it, and he gave them two hours to do so. In accordance with this demand,

General Lander, who was in command of the town, at once removed all the non-combatants therefrom. At the expiration of the time, the Confederate batteries, which had been previously placed in position, opened fire, and the Federals replied thereto, but their shots fell short. The bombardment continued for about an hour, after which time the firing on both sides ceased for the day, little or no damage having been suffered by either party. As General Jackson desired to avoid burning the town, no shells were discharged for that purpose.

On the following (Monday) morning, the Federals reopened fire, their balls falling thickly among the Confederates, but doing little or no damage. The Rebels did not reply to this firing, but occupied themselves in carrying off army stores, clothing, and other property from the Commissary Department of the Federals, which was placed on the Virginia side of the Potomac. While this was in progress a detachment of the Confederates was deployed to make a detour for the purpose of burning the Capon bridge, and tearing up the rails of the Baltimore and Ohio Railroad. On their progress, however, they met and routed some Northern troops who were placed in ambush, after which they proceeded in their work of destruction, in which they were somewhat impeded by the long-range guns of their antagonists.

This expedition to the banks of the Upper Potomac resulted in the capture of several prisoners, the expulsion of the Federals from this part of Virginia, the destruction of a fine railroad bridge, and the possession of guns, clothing, and several wagon-loads of military stores. In it, however, the Rebels suffered less from the bullets of their foes than they did from the inclemency of the weather; and many a stout heart had to succumb to the terrible sufferings caused by exposure and exhaustion in the severest portion of the winter. Of General Jackson's conduct therein, it is stated that the heroic commander, whose courage had been so brilliantly illustrated at Manassas, gave new proofs of his iron will in this expedition, and in the subsequent events of his campaign in the upper portion of the Valley of Virginia. No one would have supposed that a man who, at the opening of the war, had been but a Professor in a State Military Institute, would have shown such active determination and such grim energy in the field.

To Jackson's merit as a commander, writes Mr. Edward A. Pollard, in his History of the first year of the War, "he added the virtues of an active, humble, consistent Christian, restraining profanity in his camp, welcoming army colporteurs, distributing tracts, and anxious to have every regiment in his army supplied with a chaplain. He was vulgarly sneered at as a fatalist; his habits of soliloquy were derided as superstitious conversations with a familiar spirit; but the confidence which he had in his destiny was the unfailing mark of genius, and adorned the Christian faith which made him believe that he had a distinct mission of duty in which he should be spared for the ends of Providence."

Of the habits of his life, the following description is

also given by one who knew him well: "He is as calm in the midst of a hurricane of bullets as he was in the pew of his church at Lexington, when he was Professor of the Institute. He appears to be a man of almost superhuman endurance. Neither heat nor cold makes the slightest impression upon him. He cares nothing for good quarters and dainty fare. Wrapped in his blanket, he throws himself down on the ground anywhere, and sleeps as soundly as though he were in a palace. He lives as the soldiers live, and endures all the fatigue and all the suffering that they endure. His vigilance is something marvellous. He never seems to sleep, and lets nothing pass without his personal scrutiny. He can neither be caught napping nor whipped when he is wide awake. The rapidity of his marches is something portentous. He is heard of by the enemy at one point, and before they can make up their minds to follow him he is off at another. His men have little baggage, and he moves as nearly as he can without incumbrance. He keeps so constantly in motion that he never has a sick-list, and no need of hospitals."

Among the many anecdotes which are current of General Jackson's mode of life, there is one which illustrates the earnestness of his piety, and his never-failing appeal to his Maker to view with favor his every undertaking. He had in his service a negro, who had become so accustomed to his ways that he was enabled to discern whenever he was about to start upon an expedition, without receiving any notice to that effect. When once asked how he was able to ascertain this, as his master never divulged his plans, the negro replied : "Massa Jackson allers prays ebery night and ebery mornin'; but when he go on any expedishun, he pray two, or tree, or four times durin' de night. When I see him pray two, or tree, or four times durin' de night, I pack de baggage, for I know he gwine on an expedishun."

CHAPTER V.

THE BATTLE OF WINCHESTER.

Jackson retires from the Upper Potomac—Skirmish at Blue's Gap—Encounter at Blooming Gap—Death of General Lander—Harper's Ferry reoccupied by the Federals—Advance of General Banks to Winchester—Skirmishes before the Battle—Country around Winchester—Opening of the Engagement—Terrific Conflict near a Stone Wall—The Confederates finally repulsed—Numbers and Losses of the Combatants.

ALTHOUGH Gen. Jackson was enabled, without much difficulty, to drive the small Federal force, which was stationed on the Virginia side of the Upper Potomac, to the northern banks of that river, yet he soon discovered that the ground which he had gained was untenable. He therefore speedily commenced to retrace his steps to the Valley of the Shenandoah, closely followed by the Federals under command of General Lander. On the morning of the seventh of January, 1862, a small force of Rebels, under the leadership of Colonel Blue, who had intrenched themselves at Blue's Gap —a pass strongly fortified by nature, and situated between two hills, a few miles to the east of Romney—were driven therefrom by a party of Union soldiers under Colonel Dunning, with a loss to the former of two guns and several men. On the seventh of February, General Lander occupied

8

Romney, the Confederates having previously evacuated that place and retreated toward Winchester.

On the fourteenth, with four hundred cavalry, he drove from Blooming Gap a considerable force of Confederates, and pursued them for eight miles beyond the Gap on the road toward Winchester, and across the line which divided his department from that of General Banks. This work was only accomplished through the dashing behavior of General Lander, who had to rally his soldiers after they had become panic-stricken. It resulted in the capture of a great number of Rebel officers and men, and a large amount of commissariat stores. It was during this engagement that the popular writer, Lieutenant Fitz-James O'Brien, who was aid-de-camp to the Commanding General, received a bullet-wound in his breast which afterward resulted in his death; and a fortnight after the battle the country had to mourn the loss of General Lander, who died in his camp from congestion of the brain, superinduced by the debilitating effects from the wound he had received near Edward's Ferry, in his reconnoissance the day after the fall of Colonel Baker. He was one of the bravest and most energetic officers, and one who had given the highest promise of valuable service to the Union in this its time of greatest need.

The Rebels had likewise previous to this encounter been routed at New-Creek, forty-five miles south of Romney, by another portion of General Lander's command, under Colonel Dunning. They were now completely driven out of the former's department.

In a previous chapter we have stated that Harper's Ferry, which was evacuated by the Federals at the beginning of the Rebellion, again fell into their hands upon the advance of General Patterson, when just before the battle of Bull Run, that officer was required to prevent a junction between the forces under the command of General Johnston, and those then situated at Manassas. This important position was afterward reöccupied by the Confederates, and was in their possession upon the second appearance of General Jackson in the region of the Upper Potomac. After that General was driven back by General Lander to the Valley of the Shenandoah, it was again deserted by the Rebels, and reöccupied by the National forces on February twenty-fourth. The place was, however, the scene of stirring events about three weeks previous to this date, when the greater part of what was left of it was reduced to ashes by the Federals, as a punishment to the Confederates for their having fired upon a boat of the former, which was sent to meet one of the latter, carrying a flag of truce.

Entering Virginia at the mouth of the Shenandoah, General Banks now commenced to pursue Jackson in his retrograde movement up the valley of that river, and on the last day of February occupied Charlestown, situated eight miles south of the Potomac, upon the line of railroad leading toward Winchester; and on March third he also took unopposed possession of Martinsburgh, on the Baltimore and Ohio Railroad, a few miles west of Harper's Ferry.

By a rearrangement of the Army of the Potomac, the same was now divided into five army corps, the fifth of which included the forces under General Shields, who had succeeded to the command of General Lander, and those of General Banks, the entire force to be under the command of the latter General.

Advancing in the wake of the retreating forces of General Jackson, the Union troops approached Winchester, and, after two skirmishes on the way, entered that town on the twelfth, a strong fort to the north of it having been evacuated by the Rebels on the previous evening. Here they were received with joyful acclamations, the people hailing the coming of the Union army as the harbinger of peace and future prosperity, and cheering the regiments as they passed, which cheers were warmly responded to by both officers and men. On the following afternoon, while a party of Union cavalry were foraging on the Strasburgh road, three miles from Winchester, and while the teams were being loaded with hay, they encountered a small force of Ashby's cavalry, with whom a skirmish took place, the latter advancing as the former returned to Winchester with their loaded teams, in good order and unharmed. General Banks on this day issued an order to his troops, in which he forbade depredations of any kind whatsoever, and deeply regretted that officers, in some cases, from mistaken views, had either tolerated or had encouraged such a course.

The people of the North will well remember how, at this time, like to a will-o'the-wisp, Jackson retreated before the advancing Federals, being driven away in an inglorious retreat, and compelled to abandon the strongholds which he had held some months. He, however, transported his baggage previous to the removal of his forces, which proves that the retreat had been carefully provided for. On the eighteenth and nineteenth of April, General Shields made a reconnoissance in the direction of Mount Jackson, a place situated on the Shenandoah River, at the termination of the Manassas Gap railroad. He there ascertained that the Confederates under Jackson were strongly posted near that place, and in communication with a large force at Luray and Washington to the east thereof. He deemed it important to draw Jackson from his position and supporting force if possible. To effect this, he fell back upon Winchester on the twentieth, giving his movement all the appearance of a hasty retreat. But, as it was scarcely considered likely that Jackson would fall into the trap laid for him, and as it was advisable that the army on the Rappahannock should be reënforced from Banks's *corps d'armee*, the first division of the latter was being removed upon the turnpike which leads directly from Winchester to Alexandria, and the last brigade left for Centreville, by the way of Berryville, on the morning of the twenty-second. Only Shields's division and the Michigan cavalry were now at Winchester.

The Confederate scouts, observing this movement, signalled Jackson, with fires upon the hill-tops, that Winchester was being evacuated by the Federal forces, and about five o'clock P.M., some of Ashby's cavalry drove in the pickets of the latter. The troops immediately sprung to their arms, and two regiments of infantry, accompanied by two batteries of artillery, pushed forward and drove back the Confederates, who retreated, after a short resistance, to a little distance beyond Kernstown, a small village on the Valley turnpike, about three and a half miles southernly from Winchester. During this attack, General Shields, while directing one of the batteries to its position, was struck by a shell which burst near him, broke his arm above the elbow, and for the time entirely paralyzed one side of his body. No one around supposed that he was injured, for the old hero gave no word or sign of having been wounded, but continued to give his orders, through his staff-officers, as coolly and deliberately as if nothing had happened, until every thing had been arranged to his satisfaction. This was the fourth time that the General had received wounds which had endangered his life, the three previous ones having been received during the campaign in Mexico.

The General, divining the attack of the enemy to be only a ruse to make him show his strength, kept the rest of his forces out of sight; and though prostrated by the injuries he had received, set to work to make the requisite disposition of his troops for the ensuing day. These dispositions being made, the General rested as well as his wounds would permit.

A brief description is here necessary of the approaches to Winchester, and of the field which the next day became the

scene of one of the most bloody and desperately fought battles of the war, and the only one in which General Jackson
experienced a severe reverse. Winchester is approached
from the south by three principal roads. These are the
Cedar Creek road on the west, the Valley Turnpike leading
to Strasburgh in the centre, and the Front Royal road on the
east. On the Valley Turnpike, about three and a half miles
from Winchester, is the little village of Kernstown, already
mentioned; about half a mile north of this village and west
of the Valley Turnpike is a ridge of high hills commanding
the approach by the Valley road and a part of the surrounding country.

This ridge was the key-point of the Federal position, and
on this Colonel Kimball, the senior officer in command of
the field, took his station. Along the ridge Lieut.-Colonel
Daum, Chief of Artillery, posted three of his batteries, keeping one battery in reserve some distance in the rear. Part
of the Federal infantry was posted on this ridge, within
supporting distance of the artillery, and sheltered by the
irregularities of the hills.

The main body of the Confederates was posted in order
of battle, about half a mile beyond Kernstown, their line
extending about two miles from the Cedar Creek road on
their left, to a ravine near the Front Royal road on their
right. They had so skilfully selected their ground, that
while it afforded facilities for manœuvring, they were completely masked by high and wooded grounds in front, and
so adroitly did they conceal themselves, that at eight o'clock

A.M., of the twenty-third, nothing was visible but the force which had been repulsed the evening previous.

Being unable, in consequence of his wound, to reconnoitre the point in person, General Shields despatched an officer to perform that duty, who returned about an hour after, reporting that there were no indications of any hostile force, except that of Ashby's cavalry. General Shields and General Banks, after consulting together, came to the conclusion that Jackson was nowhere in the vicinity, and, therefore, General Banks took his departure for Washington. Although the conclusion had been reached that Jackson was not before Winchester, yet General Shields, knowing the ever-vigilant foe he had to deal with, did not neglect a single precaution. About half-past ten o'clock A.M., a Confederate battery opened upon the Federals, which disclosed to the latter indications that a considerable force of the former was planted in the woods. In consequence of this discovery, a brigade was pushed forward, and placed in a position to oppose the advance of the right wing of the Rebels.

The action opened by a fire of artillery on both sides, but at too great a distance to be very effective. The advance was made by the Confederates, who pushed a few more guns to their right, supported by a considerable force of infantry and cavalry, with the apparent intention of enfilading the Federal position and turning Shields's left flank. An active body of skirmishers was immediately thrown forward by the latter to check the advance of the

Rebels. These skirmishers were supported by four pieces of artillery and a brigade of infantry, and this united force repulsed the Confederates at all points. The latter withdrew the greater part of their force on their right, and formed it into a reserve to support their left. They then added their original reserve, and two batteries to their main body, and under shelter of a hill on their left, on which they had posted other batteries, they advanced their formidable column, with the evident intention of turning the Federal right flank, or overwhelming it. The National batteries on the opposite hill were soon found insufficient to check or even retard the Rebels. A message was therefore sent to General Shields informing him of the state of the field. Not a moment was to be lost. "Throw forward all your disposable infantry, carry the enemy's batteries, turn his left flank, and hurl it back on the centre," were his orders, and Colonel Kimball executed them with rapidity and vigor. The movement was intrusted to Tyler's splendid brigade, and following their intrepid leader, they pressed forward with enthusiasm to the performance of this perilous duty. The skirmishers of the Confederates were as chaff before the wind. Steadily onward it went until within a few yards of a high stone wall, behind which Jackson's men were securely posted, when it was met by a fire so fierce and deadly that its ranks melted away like frost before the morning sun. They wavered but for a moment, then rushed forward to the desperate struggle. At this juncture, Colonel Tyler was strongly reënforced; and

3*

with a cheer and a yell from his men that rose high and
loud above the roar of battle, he drove the Rebels from
their shelter, and through the woods, with a fire as destructive as ever fell upon a retreating foe. The Rebels
fought desperately, as their piles of dead attested, and to
their chagrin and mortification, Jackson's " invincible stonewall brigade " and the accompanying brigades were obliged
to fall back upon their reserve in disorder. Here they took
up a new position, and attempted to retrieve the fortunes
of the day. But again rained down upon them the same
close and destructive fire. Again cheer upon cheer rang in
their ears. But a few minutes did they stand against it,
when they turned and fled in dismay, leaving their killed
and wounded on the field. Night alone saved them from
destruction. They retreated about five miles, and then
took up a position for the night. The Federal troops now
threw themselves on the field to rest, and to eat the first
meal they had been able to partake of since the dawning of
the day.

Although the battle had been won, still General Shields
could not believe that Jackson would have hazarded a decisive engagement at such a distance from his main body
without expecting reënforcements. So to be prepared for
any contingency, he brought together all the troops within
his reach, and sent an express for Williams's brigade, now
twenty miles distant on its way to Centreville, to march all
night, and join him in the morning. He also gave positive
orders to the forces in the field to open fire upon the Rebels

as soon as daylight would enable them to point their guns, and to pursue them without respite, and compel them to abandon their guns and baggage, or cut them to pieces.

It appears that General Shields had rightly divined Jackson's intentions, for on the morning of the day of battle a reënforcement of five thousand men from Luray reached Front Royal, on their way to join him. This reënforcement was being followed by another body of ten thousand from Sperryville, but recent rains having rendered the Shenandoah River impassable, they were compelled to fall back without effecting the proposed junction.

At daylight on the twenty-fourth, the Federal artillery again opened on the Rebels, but the latter entered upon their retreat in good order, considering what they had suffered. General Banks, hearing of the engagement on his way to Washington, halted at Harper's Ferry, and ordered back a part of Williams's division. He returned to Winchester, and after making a hasty visit to General Shields, assumed command of the forces in pursuit of the flying Rebels. The pursuit was kept up with vigor until the Federals reached Woodstock, where Jackson's retreat became fright, when it was abandoned, in consequence of the utter exhaustion of the troops.

The Federal loss in this engagement is stated to have been one hundred and three in killed, four hundred and forty-one wounded, and twenty-four missing. Of the Confederate loss we are not able to speak with accuracy. General Shields reports that two hundred and seventy were found dead on the battle-field, and that forty were buried by the inhabitants of the adjacent village. He computes, from a calculation made of the number of graves discovered on both sides of the Valley road, between Winchester and Strasburgh, added to these figures, that Jackson's loss in killed could not have been less than five hundred, and that his wounded must have been double that number. Jackson's official report would no doubt satisfy us upon this head, but as the Confederate government have studiously abstained from making the same public, there can be little reason to imagine otherwise than that his loss was a severe one. In fact there can be no denying that this battle of Winchester terminated most disastrously to him, though perhaps it was the only one which has not been more or less instrumental in adding considerably to his fame.

The Federal force engaged in this battle did not exceed seven thousand in infantry, cavalry, and artillery. General Shields calculates that Jackson must have been supported by a much larger number, whilst Confederate correspondents claim that their force was considerably outnumbered by that of the Federals.

Though the battle of Winchester pales into insignificance when it is compared with many of the other conflicts of the present war — conflicts in which twenty times the number of troops were engaged—yet it has been scarcely surpassed by any in the terrible earnestness of the combatants and in the fierceness of the combat. It was a battle in which many for the first time bathed their swords in blood, but they fought like veterans, and were led by commanders worthy of their valor. Although Jackson on this occasion suffered the mortification of defeat, it might have been that had he been opposed by a less practised and a less gallant general than he found the Federal commander to be, his well-known strategy would have won for him the honors of the day. At one time victory appeared to be almost within his grasp. Fighting behind a veritable stone wall, his renowned "Stonewall" brigade poured forth into the Federal ranks their deadly missiles with such unerring aim, that nothing, but the most dogged courage of the Northern men, could have enabled them to dislodge their enemy from his mural breastwork. So terrible was this part of the engagement that, during its progress, four times was the color-bearer of the Fifth Ohio Volunteers laid prostrate, after which the banner was borne forward to victory by the Lieutenant-Colonel of another regiment, who had caught it from the hands of a dying sergeant.

CHAPTER VI.

CAMPAIGN IN THE VALLEY OF THE SHENANDOAH—RETREAT
OF GENERAL BANKS.

Retreat of Jackson up the Valley—Federal Plans to capture him—Battle
of McDowell—Compels Banks to retreat—Battle of Front Royal—Alarm
of General Banks at Strasburgh—He commences a rapid Retreat—Disasters by the Way—Exciting Scenes in Winchester—Second Battle of Winchester—Safe Arrival of the Federals in Maryland—Estimate of Losses.

AFTER the battle of Winchester, General Jackson retreated toward the upper waters of the Shenandoah, closely followed by the forces under Generals Banks and Shields,
who, however, were never able to come up with their swift-
footed antagonist. During this pursuit, they were several
times impeded in their progress by, and had many encoun-
ters with, Ashby's cavalry, who acted as the rear-guard of
the Rebels. They disputed the passage of the Federals at
nearly every point, burning bridges, and throwing every
obstacle in their progress.

On the fourth of April, the Federal troops in this valley
were detached from the Army of the Potomac, in which they
formed a *corps d'armée*, and the district was created into a sep-
rate Department, under the command of General Banks. It
was at this time also that the troops situated upon the Rap-

pahannock were in like manner detached from General Mc-
Clellan's supreme command and placed under that of Mc-
Dowell. These new arrangements it, is utterly impossible
to deny, considerably interfered with General McClellan's
plan of operations upon the Peninsula, from which point he
was now menacing Richmond.

The Confederates were desirous of collecting all their available strength for the protection of their capital, and orders
were forwarded shortly after this time to General Jackson,
instructing him to rejoin his forces to those of General Johnston; but at the earnest remonstrance of the former General,
who considered that he could better defend Richmond on
the Shenandoah than upon the Chickahominy, he was allowed to remain on the banks of the former river.

To capture Jackson and his entire force was one of the
cherished plans of the Federals. While General Banks was
closely treading in his footsteps in his retreat up the valley,
a strong detachment of the army under General Fremont,
who was in command of the Mountain Department of
the Alleghanies, was deployed under Generals Milroy and
Schenck to enter the Shenandoah Valley at Buffalo Gap,
west of Staunton, and there give Jackson a meeting. It was
anticipated that, being thus placed between two fires, it
would be barely possible the Rebel General could escape. How far the Federals were right in their calculations, the sequel will tell.

In the movements of General Milroy, having for their object the circumvention of the Rebels, he encountered a por-

tion of Jackson's force on April the twenty-first, within a few miles of Buffalo Gap, and had a skirmish with a small force of their cavalry. He then fell back to McDowell, on the Bull Pasture Mountain, where he encamped till May the eighth, on which date he was driven therefrom by a superior force of Confederates.

General Jackson, learning the advance of Milroy, sent a force to meet him from Valley Mills, six miles north of Staunton, with five days' rations and without tents or baggage, save blankets, under the command of General Ed. Johnson. Upon the next day, the advance-guard had a skirmish with the outposts of the Federals at the junction of Jennings's Gap and the Parkersburgh turnpike-road, twenty-one miles from Staunton. At the same time, General Jackson came up with an additional force, and after consultation with General Johnson, the latter proceeded along the road toward Shenandoah Mountain in pursuit of the Federals, closely followed by the force under General Jackson. Arriving at the mountain, they discovered that several Federal regiments, which had been encamped there, had hastily retreated, leaving their tents and stores behind them; and, ascending to the summit, they could see them proceeding upon the east side of Bull Pasture Mountain, about five miles in advance.

At sunrise on the morning of the eighth, the Confederates continued their line of march, and arriving at Bull Pasture Mountain they ascended to its summit, and discovered that Milroy had placed a battery on the road leading into Mc-

Dowell, and commanding a narrow gorge on the west side of the mountain, through which the road passes. It becoming late in the day before the Confederate Generals had completed their survey of the Federal position, they concluded to postpone offensive operations until the following morning. But about five o'clock they were attacked by the National forces, who were reënforced, and after a desperate fight of five hours' duration drove them from the field. During the engagement, General Johnson narrowly escaped being captured. He was rescued from a perilous position by the Richmond Zouaves, who, observing his danger, charged upon the Federals, and by this act disobeyed orders which General Jackson had given them to fall back, the latter at the time not being aware of his brother General's critical position.

The Rebels lost on this occasion about three hundred in killed, wounded, and missing, of which one third were either killed or mortally wounded. The Federal loss is stated to have been thirty killed and two hundred and sixteen wounded. The entire force of the latter in the engagement was two thousand and sixty-five men, and of the former two brigades of three regiments each.

It was quite dark before the engagement terminated, when the Federals at once prepared to fall back, and found it necessary to destroy a quantity of stores. The Confederates expected to renew the fight the following morning, but found that their foe had evacuated his camp, leaving behind him all his equipage, a large quantity of ammunition, a number of cases of Enfield rifles, and about one hundred head of cattle, mostly milch cows.

The Federals made their retreat good to Franklin, west of the Shenandoah Mountains, to which place they were closely followed by the Confederates. General Fremont also reached this place on May the thirteenth, having proceeded thither by forced marches, it being apprehended that an attack would be made by the Rebels upon the Union forces there situated.

General Jackson having compelled the retreat of the forces of General Fremont, who had been sent to oppose his progress, now turned round upon General Banks, and instead of being the pursued became the pursuer. The rapidity with which, from this change in the programme, the latter General was compelled to make good his retreat to the northern banks of the Potomac, exhibited a display of strategetical ability on his part which was only equalled by that still greater strategy which necessitated the retreat.

The suddenness with which this scene in the drama of the war was changed from a bright and glowing prospect to one enveloped in mist and darkness was a cause of great alarm to the people of the North, and led the President not only to call for aid from the militia of the loyal States, but to prevent General McDowell from marching with his forces from the Rappahannock to the assistance of General McClellan in his attack upon Richmond.

The most southerly point which General Banks reached

in the Valley of the Shenandoah was Harrisonburgh, where, on April the twenty-ninth, a National salute was fired and rejoicings took place in honor of recent Union victories.

Shortly after this date, finding that Jackson was pressing upon his front and that the place was becoming untenable, the Federal General retreated down the valley. One of the immediate causes which necessitated this retreat was the removal of General Shields's division, of two thousand men or more, from General Banks's corps. There is reason to believe that urgent, but useless, remonstrance was made by General Banks against this depletion of his force, and that a representation which he had made, that Jackson had been heavily reënforced, was met only by incredulity. The number of men left under General Banks's command was but about seven thousand, who were now pressed by three times that number under Generals Jackson and Ewell.

On the twenty-first of May some of Ashby's cavalry showed themselves in the neighborhood of Strasburgh, from which place they were driven by a small force of Federal cavalry. About this time a considerable portion of Jackson's forces were making a detour to Front Royal—a small village twelve miles east of Strasburgh, and situated on the eastern bank of the Shenandoah River, over which is here carried a large bridge of the Manassas Gap Railroad—and on the twenty-third surprised and captured almost the entire Federal force, which was encamped near that place. This latter consisted of about nine hundred men under the command of Colonel John R. Kenly. They were stationed at Front

Royal, for the purpose of protecting the place and the railroad and bridges between that town and Strasburgh against
the local guerrilla parties who infested that locality. So
small a force could never have been expected to defend themselves against much larger numbers, for Front Royal in itself
is an indefensible position. Two mountain valleys debouch
suddenly upon the town from the south, commanding it by
almost inaccessible hills, and it is at the same time exposed
to flank movements by other mountain valleys *via* Strasburgh on the west, and Chester Gap on the east. The only
practicable defence of this town would seem to be by a force
sufficiently strong to hold these mountain passes some miles
in advance, and such a force General Banks had not at his
disposal.

On the twenty-third of May it was discovered that the
entire Confederate force was in movement down the valley
of the Shenandoah between the Massanutten Mountain and
the Blue Ridge, and in close proximity to the town; and
their cavalry had captured a considerable number of the
Federal pickets, before the alarm was given of their near
approach. The little band found itself instantaneously compelled to choose between an immediate retreat or a contest
with overwhelming numbers. They chose the latter. Driven
at last from the camp and the town, they were compelled
to retreat across the river. Again forming into line and
placing their battery in position upon the opposite shore,
they opened fire upon the Rebels, while the latter were ford-
ing the stream. They again found it necessary to retreat,

and had only proceeded two miles upon the Winchester road, when they were overtaken by the Rebel cavalry. A fearful fight ensued, which ended in a complete destruction of the command, Colonel Kenly falling at the head of his column. A very small number only were enabled to escape, accomplishing the same through the friendly covering of the neighboring woods.

Very early on the following morning, the Confederates marched upon the road to Middletown, a place situated on the turnpike between Strasburgh and Winchester, and about eight miles north of the former place. At Middletown they came upon and attacked a part of General Banks's force as it was retreating along the road. Having cut the same in twain, a brigade of Ewell's division pursued the Strasburgh wing, capturing many prisoners, and demoralizing the rest of the troops, whilst the main body hurried swiftly down the valley after General Banks. Every few hundred yards, they passed one or more Federal wagons, upset, broken, or teamless, and full of baggage or military stores. Upon approaching Newtown, a few miles north of Middletown, the Rebels were for a while checked with artillery, after which the Federal rout and flight became precipitous and exciting beyond degree. The Federals made another stand in the neighborhood of Winchester, but after an engagement of short duration, they were compelled to give up the contest, and continue their retreat.

On the evening of the twenty-third, information was re-

ceived by General Banks at Strasburgh of the critical position in which Colonel Kenly was placed at Front Royal;
but as he viewed with distrust the extravagant statements
which he received of the Confederate strength, he only forwarded a regiment of infantry, a detachment of cavalry, and
a section of artillery to his assistance. He had, however,
scarcely despatched these reënforcements when information
reached him of the utter annihilation of Colonel Kenly's
troops. He therefore recalled them, and sent out numerous reconnoitring parties to ascertain, if possible, the
force, and the position and purpose of this sudden movement
of General Jackson. It was soon found that his pickets were in possession of every road leading from Front
Royal to Strasburgh, Middletown, Newtown, and Winchester, and rumors from every quarter represented him
in movement in rear of his pickets in the direction of the
Federal camp.

General Banks could not now doubt the extraordinary
force of the Confederates by which he was threatened, nor
could he believe otherwise but that they had a more extensive purpose than the capture of the " brave little band at
Front Royal." He at once divined that this purpose could
be nothing less than either the defeat of his own command
or its possible capture by the occupation of Winchester,
through which means the Rebels would be enabled to intercept his supplies and reënforcements, and cut him off from
all possibility of retreat. He also ascertained that he was
menaced by the divisions of Generals Jackson, Ewell, and

Johnson, numbering not less than twenty-five thousand men, under command of the first-named General.

Considering his position a very critical one, General Banks felt that the most expedient course for himself to adopt was to make a rapid movement on Winchester with a view to anticipate the occupation of that town by Jackson. He would thus place his command in communication with its original base of operations in the line of reënforcements by Harper's Ferry and Martinsburgh, and by this means secure a safe retreat in case of disaster.

Calling in all his outposts, he prepared to march at three o'clock on the morning of the twenty-fourth of May. Several hundred disabled men who had been left in his charge by Shields's division, were first put upon the march, and his wagon train was ordered forward to Winchester, under an escort of cavalry and infantry. General Hatch, with nearly the whole force of cavalry and six pieces of artillery, was charged with the protection of the rear of the column, and the destruction of army stores for which transportation was not provided. All the preparations being completed with incredible alacrity, the column was put in motion shortly after nine o'clock. It had not proceeded many miles when information was received from the front that the Rebels had attacked the train, and were in full possession of the road at Middletown. This report was soon confirmed by the return of fugitives, refugees, and wagons, which came tumbling to the rear in dreadful confusion. The immediate danger being now in front, the troops were ordered to the head of the column, and the train transferred to the rear. Cedar Creek Bridge, three miles north of Strasburgh,—over which the entire column had passed, with the exception of the rear-guard, which had been instructed to remain in front of Strasburgh as long as possible, and thus hold the enemy in check in that direction —was also prepared for the flames, in order that its destruction might prevent any pursuit on the part of the Confederates. By the burning of the bridge, Captain Abert and the *Zouaves d'Afrique* were cut off from the column, but after a sharp conflict with a party of Rebel cavalry at Strasburgh, they made their way safely to Williamsport, where they joined their comrades.

The advance-guard encountered the Confederates in force at Middletown, thirteen miles south of Winchester, and after a sharp engagement drove them back. The column had not, however, proceeded much farther, before it was again attacked by a considerable force of infantry, cavalry, and artillery. After repeated attempts to force a passage through the Rebel lines which had possession of the turnpike, a part of the force which had been cut off from the main body made several ineffectual attempts to join it by proceeding upon a parallel road. Failing in this, they returned to Strasburgh, from which place they proceeded by a circuitous route to Winchester, and other places north thereof, where they joined the main body.

The rear of the column was again attacked by an increased force between Newtown and Kernstown, and large bodies of Jackson's cavalry passed upon the Federal right and left, the increased vigor of his movements demonstrating the rapid advance of his main body.

The early and rapid march of the front portion of the train prevented the accomplishment of Jackson's contemplated plan of crushing it between those forces which he had despatched to intercept it, and the troops which pressed upon the rear of the column. It was, therefore, only the end of the column which encountered the main difficulties that beset it on its journey. Those of the front who, after a long and anxious day's march, were enabled to retire to rest in the town of Winchester on the evening of that eventful Saturday, were startled at daybreak on the Sabbath morning by the noise of cannon and the rattle of musketry, and could see the smoke as it rose from the hills three miles distant. Some of the people of Winchester gazed thitherward, as upon an interesting spectacle, and rejoiced that Jackson was again coming to free them from the Northern yoke; whilst others could see nothing in the anticipated change which could give them cause for joy.

Presently, and there were heard the tramping of horses' hoofs upon the road, and the heavy rolling of artillery over the pavement, and then every thing was in commotion. The women sobbed, and the men ran to and fro. The forces which had been quartered for the night in the town were started upon a hasty retreat. Flames rose from burning buildings, and heavy columns of smoke which roll-

4

ed upward, betokened to distant eyes that a scene of destruction was being enacted.

Whilst the Confederates were entering the town at the
southern end, the Federals were rapidly making their exit
through its northern portals. "All the streets were in
commotion," writes an eye-witness to the scene; "Cavalry
were rushing disorderly away, and infantry frightened by
the rapidity of their mounted companions, were in consternation. All were trying to escape faster than their neighbors, dreading most of all to be the last. . . . . Guns,
knapsacks, cartridge-boxes, bayonets, and bayonet-cases,
lay scattered upon the ground in great profusion, thrown
away by the panic-stricken soldiers. . . . . But this
confusion and disorder was not of long duration. General
Banks riding continually among the men, and addressing
them kindly and firmly, shamed them to a consideration of
their unbefitting consternation. At length stationing himself and staff with several others across a field through
which the soldiers were rapidly flying, the men were ordered to stop their flight, were formed into line, and were
made to march on in a more soldier-like manner."

Vehicles of every description, crowded with sick soldiers
and citizens, and bound northwards, passed rapidly through
the streets on this eventful morning. The contrabands
flocked through them, each with his little bundle; and
whole families of negroes, some of them with packs strap-
ped on head and shoulders, little children almost too small
to walk, and lean horses carrying two or three, went fol-

lowing the train. Meantime, the thunder of cannonading
had commenced. Nearer and nearer it came, and the cry
went forth that the Rebels were driving the Federal forces.
As the fugitives retired from the city, they looked back
and beheld flames ascending from many of the buildings, in which military stores and powder had been contained, and to which the torch had been applied to prevent
them falling into the hands of the Rebels. Here was por-
trayed a vivid illustration of the horrors of war. Homes
that once had been the abodes of happiness, now became
desolate, and fell a prey to the ravages of the flames. The
town in which but two months previous the Federals had
entered with joyous hearts, treading to the sound of martial music, and under the shadow of their waving banners,
they now left in despondency, and with the marks of fear
depicted in their faces.

We will now return to the rear. Two hours past midnight on Saturday the two brigades under the command of
Colonels Gordon and Donnelly, upon whom, toward the
close of the day, had devolved the duty of protecting the
end of the column, and who had thus far succeeded in keeping the Confederates at bay, halted for the night in the outskirts of Winchester. The men went into bivouac without fire, with but little food, and completely exhausted.

At Winchester all doubts as to the number of the Confederate forces were set at rest. All classes—secessionists,
Unionists, refugees, fugitives, and prisoners — agreed that

it was overwhelming, and that from twenty-five to thirty thousand men were in close proximity to the place. Rebel officers who came into the Federal camp with entire unconcern, supposing that their own troops occupied the town, confirmed these statements, and added that an attack would be made on the National forces at daybreak. Measures were, therefore, promptly taken to repel the attack; and at early dawn the two brigades in question were under arms. Soon after four o'clock, the artillery opened its fire, which was continued without intermission until the close of the engagement. Colonel Gordon's brigade was placed on the right of the line, and was partly covered from the fire of the enemy by stone walls. Colonel Donnelly's brigade was assigned to the left. The earliest movement of the Rebels was in this direction, but this being intercepted by a detachment of cavalry, it was apparently abandoned.

The main body of the Confederates was hidden during the early part of the action by the crest of a hill, and the woods in the rear. Their force was apparently masked on the Federal right, and their manœuvres indicated a purpose to turn it upon the Berryville road, where it appeared subsequently that they had placed a considerable force with a view of preventing reënforcements arriving from Harper's Ferry. In this, however, they were frustrated until a small portion of the National troops under the erroneous impression that an order had been given to withdraw, made a movement to the rear. No sooner was this observed by the Rebels than their regiments swarmed upon the crest of the hill, and advanced from the woods upon the Federal right, which fell back upon the town, continuing its fire by the way.

The overwhelming force of the Confederates thus suddenly showed itself. It was considered unwise to make further resistance, and orders were given to the entire Federal force to withdraw, which was done in good order. A portion of the troops passed through the town in some confusion, but the column was soon re-formed, and continued its march.

This engagement held the Rebels in check for five hours. The forces were greatly unequal, there being not less than twenty-five thousand of Jackson's troops in position, and capable of being brought into action, whilst the two brigades of Federals consisted of less than four thousand men. The latter were, however, assisted by nine hundred cavalry, ten Parrott guns, and a battery of six-pounders.

This battle took place upon nearly the same spot on which the previous battle of Winchester had been fought; but when we take into consideration, the great disparity in the forces which met in deadly encounter on the occasion of this second engagement, it can scarcely be admitted that the Confederate commander here regained all the laurels which he had here lost.

The Federals now continued their march in three parallel columns, and proceeded in the direction of Martinsburgh.

The Confederates pursued them with promptitude and vigor, but the movements of the retreating party were now rapid and without loss. Halting for two hours and a half at Martinsburgh, they proceeded on their way to the banks of the Potomac, and the rear-guard reached that river at sundown—forty-eight hours after the first news of the attack upon Front Royal. Thus was completed a march of fifty-three miles, thirty-five of which had been performed in one day.

"The scene of the river," says General Banks in his report, "when the rear-guard arrived, was of the most animating and exciting description. A thousand camp-fires were burning on the hill-side, a thousand carriages of every description were crowded upon the banks, and the broad river between the exhausted troops and their coveted rest."

On the following morning, the entire force was moved across the river in safety, and, remarks the Federal Commander "There never were more grateful hearts in the same number of men, than when, at mid-day on the twenty-sixth, we stood on the opposite shore."

The entire number of men lost by this retreat was estimated at about nine hundred, of whom thirty-eight were killed, one hundred and fifty-five wounded, and seven hundred and eleven missing. Of the wagon-train which consisted of nearly five hundred wagons, General Banks states that he only lost fifty-five, and that these with but few exceptions were all burned on the road, and not abandoned to the enemy. He further states that nearly all his supplies were saved with the exception of the stores lost at Front Royal and at Winchester, at which latter place a considerable portion was destroyed by his own troops.

The Confederates consider this expedition of General Jackson to have been a most glorious one, and they find reason to ascribe its results to the zeal, heroism, and genius of its Commander alone. They claim for it a comparison with some of the most famous campaigns in modern history. It was brief but brilliant, only three weeks having passed between the commencement of the aggressive movement, and the expulsion of the Federal army from the valley of Virginia. During this short period it is claimed that Jackson fought four battles and had a number of skirmishes, killed and wounded a considerable number of the Federals, captured four thousand prisoners, secured millions of dollars' worth of stores, destroyed many millions of dollars' worth for the Federals, recovered Winchester, and annihilated the invading army of the valley — and all this with a loss scarcely exceeding one hundred in killed and wounded.

We leave it to the reader to compare these statements with those made by the commander of the National forces, and to draw his own deductions therefrom.

CHAPTER VII.

Excitement in the North—Federal Plan to capture Jackson—Attack on Harper's Ferry—Front Royal recovered—Fremont and Shields pursue Jackson — Death of General Ashby — Battle of Cross Keys — Port Republic — Jackson escapes his Pursuers — Discomforts of Fremont's March — The Valley devastated — Jackson's Devotional Habits.

As we have already stated, the retreat of General Banks led to the wildest excitement in the cities of the North. In Baltimore this excitement culminated in acts of violence, and prominent citizens who were tainted with Secession proclivities were publicly mobbed in the streets, and their lives placed in jeopardy. The Administration not only found itself necessitated to make a call upon the country for additional troops, but it required the Governors of several of the loyal States to forward detachments of their militia for the protection of the National Capital.

It now became a part of the Federal plan to outflank Jackson and to capture him with his entire force, before he could return to his base of operations. For this purpose General Fremont was instructed to advance from Franklin, in the Mountain Department, where his force was now located, and enter the valley, from the west, in the neighborhood of Strasburgh; whilst General Shields was sent from the Rappahannock to reach the same point *via* Manassas Gap on the east.

General Jackson, learning of these movements, hastened from his advanced position on the line of the Potomac, and rapidly retraced his steps up the valley, with the hope of eluding his pursuers, and reaching the upper end thereof before they would be enabled to intercept him. Before doing this, however, he made an attempt to dislodge the National forces at Harper's Ferry, but failed to accomplish his object. For two days he endeavored to draw them out from their stronghold, so that he could give them battle on ground of his own choosing; but General Saxton, who was then in command of the Federal troops there stationed, would not be lured by the wiles of his scheming foe. Foiled in these attempts, Jackson determined to storm the place. This he did about nightfall on Friday, May the thirtieth, amid a terrific storm. The scene at the time was very impressive. The night was intensely dark; the hills around were alive with the signal-lights of the Rebels; the rain descended in torrents; vivid flashes of lightning illuminated, at intervals, the magnificent scenery; while the crash of thunder, echoing among the mountains, drowned into comparative insignificance the roar of the artillery.

After an action of about one hour's duration, the Confederates retired. They made another unsuccessful attack at

4*

midnight, and after a short engagement disappeared. Jackson then retreated. On the following morning the Federals pursued him as far as Charlestown, only to learn that his rear-guard had passed through the place an hour before their arrival.

On the morning of the day that this affair took place at Harper's Ferry, a portion of Jackson's forces stationed at Front Royal were driven from that place by a brigade of National troops. The Rebels were taken as completely by surprise as Colonel Kenly's command had been the week previous, and they had no time left either to save or destroy any thing. Railroad engines and cars filled with stores, along with many prisoners, fell into the hands of the Federals, and several of the Union men who were here captured by the Confederates, on their attacking the place, were recaptured.

General Fremont left Franklin on Sunday, May the twenty-fifth, and his advance-guard entered Strasburgh on the evening of the following Sunday, the troops having halted one day on the road, being compelled to do so from exhaustion. The march was made amid heavy rains, which rendered the roads almost impassable.

With the exception of a small skirmish, which occurred at Wardensville, the advancing party met with no opposition to their progress, until the morning of the day on which they reached Strasburgh. On this morning, however, Colonel Cluseret's brigade, which formed the advance guard of Fremont's army, had a sharp encounter and brisk cannonading with Jackson's rear-guard or flanking column. Although the latter were repulsed, after an engagement of two hours' duration, they had been enabled to gain time for and to protect Jackson's main force, which was then hurriedly retreating over the road from Winchester to Strasburgh.

Jackson had pushed on his forces so swiftly that he succeeded in reaching Strasburgh just in season to pass between Fremont on the one side and Shields on the other. The advance-guard of the former entered Strasburgh on the evening of the day that Jackson passed through the town, whilst Shields's advance-guard reached it the following morning. Shields's advance-guard now joined Fremont's force, whilst his main army passed up the valley to the eastward.

The Federals were now close upon Jackson's heels, and the Confederate rear-guard now found it necessary on many occasions to dispute the progress of the National forces. General Ewell was in the command of this rear-guard, and received able assistance from Ashby's cavalry. During the passage of the Union soldiers, they found strewn along the roads and in the adjoining woods, such relics as a fugitive army is wont to scatter in its trail; and dead, wounded, and exhausted soldiers lay by the side of the road.

Woodstock was reached on Monday night by the Federals, Jackson's army having passed through the town on the same day. The Confederates were so closely pressed that their bridge-burners could but half accomplish the task which was allotted to them, and the Federals were easily able to repair any damage which the bridges sustained at their hands. However, at Mount Jackson, the long bridge which there crosses the Shenandoah, a river too swift and deep to be forded, was so far destroyed as seriously to delay the Federals in their onward progress. Upon reaching this point Jackson was so closely pressed that his rear-guard had but barely passed over one end of the bridge, when the Federal cavalry were about to enter upon the other.

On, on, Jackson sped, much delayed in his progress by the exhaustion of his troops, and the breaking down of his trains, and sorely pressed by the advancing forces of his pursuers. On June the sixth he had another severe encounter with the National troops in a woody district in the southern outskirts of the town of Harrisonburgh. In this engagement he first obtained a slight advantage, owing to the mismanagement of Colonel Windham, who had the command of such of the Federal forces as were brought into action. The ground lost by this repulse to the National troops was, however, speedily regained by General Bayard, who made a vigorous attack upon the Rebels, and ultimately drove them back, and compelled them to renew their retreat. In this engagement the distinguished Rebel General Ashby, who covered the retreat with his whole cavalry force and three regiments of infantry, and who exhibited admirable skill and audacity, was killed.

On June the eighth the two armies came into collision at Cross Keys, seven miles beyond Harrisonburgh. Although Jackson had a much superior force to Fremont, throughout his retreat he had studiously avoided fighting a pitched battle, as he was fearful that the delay which would be caused thereby would prevent him from escaping the large force which was marching to the eastward, under the command of General Shields, to outflank him. General Fremont was consequently the attacking party on this occasion. The battle took place on a Sunday, and the day was one of those bright and glorious ones which, at this period of the year, so intoxicate with their freshness, and so elevate the spirits. It is said that battles commenced on a Sunday are seldom successes for the attacking party, and we fear that we can not claim this battle as any exception to the general rule.

Having upon the previous evening, and upon that morning, caused reconnoissances to be made with a view of ascertaining the position of the Rebels, General Fremont approached them about eleven o'clock, and the advance soon opened that preliminary fire which usually precedes a general engagement. The face of the country in this district is rolling, and covered at various points with woods, generally of oak, from the size of a small sapling to that of a man's body. The ground on which the battle was fought is a succession of hillocks, on which several farms stretch out for two or three miles from north to south, and form a belt of cleared land, which is lowest in the centre and gradually rises as the timber is approached in either direction. To the north, as if standing sentinel and gravely looking down upon the scene, rises a lofty mountain-peak, its top enveloped in a blue haze, and its steep sides bathed in the sunlight of a beautiful morning. Far off to the east, stretching up and down the Shenandoah, the distant peaks of the Blue Ridge form a background of indescribable beauty.

The attack was commenced by General Fremont's right, the line of which extended for nearly a mile and a half. The Rebels were here driven back, and in this quarter the chances of success were strongly in favor of the Federals, until an order was given for this wing to withdraw slowly and in good order from the position it had gained, and proceed to the relief of the left, which had suffered severely from the fire of the Confederates.

On the left General Stahl's German brigade, whilst in the act of ascending a slope as they were about proceeding to the attack, were opposed by a murderous fire from the Rebels, which produced sad havoc and caused their ranks to be terribly thinned. They were consequently compelled to fall back. Some mountain howitzers were then directed upon the Rebels; the cannonading became furious; the deep thunders of the artillery reverberated through the valley; the sharp crash of musketry rang through the woods; shells went screaming on the errand of death; and the cloud of sulphurous smoke which hung like a funeral pall over the advancing and receding waves, told too well the work of carnage and death then going on.

Had Stahl been enabled to advance but a few feet farther, his troops would have had an opportunity to pour into the Rebels a fire which would have driven them before him. This, with the combined movement of the Federal troops on the right, and of those which already had penetrated the centre, would doubtless have swept Jackson's entire line, would have put him to rout, would have captured his guns, and would have gained a most complete victory for the National forces. But this was prevented by the mistake of an order, which had been forwarded to some regiments directing them to relieve the advancing party, having been construed into one to retire.

The misfortune of this misunderstanding can scarcely be estimated. One more effort and the regiments which had forced themselves right up to the Rebel guns would doubtless have gained a splendid triumph. But the opportunity was lost, and General Jackson again slipped through the fingers of the Federals, after Fremont had for fifteen days marched his army through mud and rain to catch him.

There was for a time a lull in the storm—each party seeming satisfied to take a rest. Then in retiring, Jackson sent a few shells which fell in the midst of General Fremont's staff, and caused them to scatter far and wide. These compliments were returned, and a brisk artillery duel was kept up for a short time, and then all again was quiet. Night came on, the clouds of smoke which had obscured the sky disappeared, and the moon smiled down as peacefully upon the scene where carnage had held high carnival as if no ghastly features, pale in death, were there.

On the following morning General Fremont again march ed with his troops in pursuit. They had not proceeded far before they reached Mill Creek Church, which had been used as a hospital by the Rebels, and in which they found several wounded Union soldiers. "Let it be said to the Rebels' credit," writes a gentleman who was present at the time, "that they treated our wounded humanely. Many left upon the field had blankets thrown over them and canteens of water placed by their side, while they nearly all say that they were as well treated as the Rebels themselves."

The Federal loss in the battle of Cross Keys was about one hundred and twenty-five killed, and five hundred wounded. General Fremont states that upward of two hundred of the Confederates were counted dead in one field, and that many others were scattered through the woods. Several more of the dead and the entire of Jackson's wounded had been removed in wagons under cover of the night.

On the same day that the battle of Cross Keys was being fought, a minor action took place at Port Republic between the train-guard of Jackson's army and a small Federal force belonging to General Shields's division, and under the command of Colonel Carroll. This resulted in the repulse of the latter; the forces engaged being more than two to one against him. On the following day occurred the battle of Port Republic.

While General Fremont was closely pressing Jackson in the rear, a portion of General Shields's command, under General Tyler, was moving on the east in advance of the main column, with the intention of reaching Waynesboro, on the Virginia Central Railroad, for the purpose of destroying the railroad, and thus cutting off Jackson's line of communication by that route with Gordonsville and Richmond. The troops under Colonel Carroll formed the advance-guard of this force. Jackson was well aware of this plan to intercept him, and to frustrate it he brought into operation that celerity of movement for which he was so celebrated.

After Colonel Carroll's repulse on the Sunday, he fell back to and joined the troops under General Tyler. It was a part of General Shields's instructions to these officers that they should destroy the long bridge which crosses the Shenandoah at Port Republic, and by this means cut off Jackson's retreat at this point also. This, however, they were prevented from accomplishing.

Jackson, continuing his retreat, reached Port Republic on the morning of the ninth, when he immediately despatched a force to attack General Tyler. This force was repulsed, but on reënforcements being received, the Confederates drove back the Federals and captured their guns, which could not be removed, owing to the horses having been killed or disabled, and the roads being so heavy that it was impossible for the men to drag them through the deep mud.

During this time General Fremont's army moved in the direction of Port Republic without opposition. As it drew near the place a dense volume of smoke was seen rising in the air. The troops pressed on to discover the cause, but reached the river just as the last Rebel had crossed the Shenandoah; arriving, however, in time to observe Jackson's interminable train winding along like a huge snake in the valley beyond. Several Rebel regiments were drawn in line of battle on the opposite side of the Shenandoah. An unfordable river lay between the opposing armies, and the bridge was in flames.

Thus ended the Federal pursuit of the fleet-footed Jackson. General Fremont had left Franklin on Sunday, May the twenty-fifth, taking up his line of march for the Valley of Virginia. At Petersburgh he had left his tents and heavy baggage. With one exception, he had marched sixteen consecutive days. The rains had been heavy and severe, and the soldiers had been compelled to bivouac in water and mud, lying down in their drenched clothes to obtain a few hours' rest, so that they might be enabled to endure the fatigues of the coming day. Transportation had been difficult. Forage and provisions had been scarce, for the country had been swept clear thereof by former armies. Sometimes the soldiers had but a short allowance of bread;

sometimes they had none, whilst some of them had worn out their shoes, and were compelled to march barefooted. However, they endured these trials with great patience. Under circumstances such as these, and after seven days of almost continuous skirmishing, was fought the battle of Cross Keys. It has been argued that if General Fremont had closely followed Jackson after this battle, the latter would have been attacked in both front and rear, and he would thus have been prevented from making good his escape. The prostration of the Federal troops from the causes which we have here related may possibly have been a barrier to this desirable consummation.

It is much to be regretted that, during General Fremont's progress, some of his troops had conducted themselves in a manner that necessitated their commander to issue an order, calling their attention to the many disorders and excesses and the wanton outrages upon property which had marked their line of march from Franklin to Port Republic. He considered that the magnitude of the evil should be summarily and severely checked. He, therefore, threatened severe punishment for any similar offences that might occur in future. The men had entered dwellings and appropriated to themselves property of various kinds which fell in their way. It was stated that the Germans were the greatest offenders, but witnesses to these excesses state that these men were too often made the scapegoats for the offences of their comrades of American birth.

After Jackson had made his escape from his pursuers, he proceeded toward Stewardsville, passed through the Gap of the Blue Ridge mountains, and thence, *via* Gordonsville, to Richmond, there to take his part in the battles which' were to relieve that city from the presence of a besieging army.

The state in which this charming Valley of Virginia was left by the contending armies of the North and the South, after they had trodden and retrodden its fertile fields, and after they had passed through and pillaged its pleasant towns, is thus pictured by one who was an eye-witness to the desolation which war had left behind :

"A more beautiful country than this Valley of the Shenandoah God's sun never smiled on. The scenery is magnificent, but not with sterile peaks and frowning rocks. Green vestured fields and gentle, round-bosomed hills nestle down in the arms of great mountains, and you know they are quick with growing life, even while they slumber. It rather moves me to sympathy to see the trail of devastation that the two armies have left after them. Meadows of clover are trodden into mud ; the tossing plumes of the wheat-fields along the line of march are trodden down, as though a thousand reaping-machines had passed over and through them. Dead horses lie along the road, entirely overpowering the sweet scent of the clover-blossoms, and flinging out upon the air a more villainous stench than could by any possibility ascend from the left wing of the Tartarian pit. Fences are not, landmarks have vanished, and all is one common waste."

Before the war this Valley was dotted with happy homes, but the curtain had not descended upon this, the second act of the bloody drama, before these homes were tenantless, and their former peaceful occupants were scattered like chaff before the piercing blast of the pitiless storm.

Amid the dreadful scenes which were here enacted, Jackson did not omit to appeal to his Maker for support in the trying ordeal through which he had to pass. His secret devotions were on one occasion witnessed by the Colonel of an artillery regiment, who happened to be encamped close to his headquarters, and whose tent was so pitched, that from its rear he commanded a view of a corner of a field, surrounded by a wood, not far from Jackson's own tent. This spot could only be seen by those who were in either of these two tents. The Colonel states that twice a day for weeks, rain or sunshine, he saw Jackson slip away to this secluded place— unseen, as he believed, by no mortal eye. He would seat himself upon a small fence which bounded the field, and there he would remain often for an hour, with his hands clasped and his face turned upward, convulsed with emotion, and the tears streaming down his face, deep in the performance of secret and agonizing prayer. Nothing can be said to increase the value of this evidence to prove the sincerity of the man.

CHAPTER VIII.

THE SEVEN DAYS' BATTLES BEFORE RICHMOND.

Jackson created a Major-General—McClellan Lands upon the Peninsula— Occupation of Yorktown—Williamsburgh—Hanover Court-House—Seven Pines—Fair Oaks—Stuart's celebrated Raid—Position and Number of the Opposing Forces—FIRST DAY: Battle of Oak Grove—Confederate Council of War—SECOND DAY: Battle of Mechanicsville—THIRD DAY: Battle of Gaines's Mill—The Battle-Ground—Jackson's Attack on the Federal Rear—The River Crossed by the Federal Right Wing—Council of War—FOURTH DAY: Battle of Garnett's Farm—FIFTH DAY: Battle of Peach Orchard—Battle of Savage's Station—SIXTH DAY: Battle of White Oak Swamp—Battle of Glendale—SEVENTH DAY: Battle of Malvern Hill— Losses of the Combatants—Importance of Jackson's Services during the Week.

IMMEDIATELY after Jackson had foiled his pursuers in the Valley of Virginia, he hastened to unite his forces with those which were guarding the Confederate capital against the grand attack of General McClellan's army, then daily anticipated. Jackson steps upon this scene in the character of a Major-General, having been advanced to that position in consequence of the great military abilities which he had exhibited during the Valley campaign just terminated.

Before entering into the particulars of the seven days' battles, it is advisable that we should refresh the reader's memory by referring to a few of the leading events which preceded this week—a week so terribly prominent in the calendar of our history.

It having been conceived that Richmond could be more easily reached by the army of the Potomac if it traversed the Peninsula, and took advantage of the communication by water which it possessed, instead of having to cross the numerous rivers which intercept the road by Fredericksburgh, it was resolved to adopt the former route to the Rebel capital. General McClellan having made all his arrangements for the removal of his vast army from the Potomac to the vicinity of Fortress Monroe, in the middle of March issued a spirited and cheerful address to his troops, in which he informed them that the "period for inaction" had passed, and that he was about "to bring them face to face with the Rebels."

At the beginning of April, he had landed his forces upon the eastern point of the Peninsula, and immediately commenced moving upon Yorktown. He found that place strongly fortified, and it was not until the fourth of May that he obtained possession of it, the Rebels having evacuated the town during the preceding night. Before this time, the troops under General McDowell—upon which McClellan depended for assistance, by a flank movement at the head of the York River either encircling the Confederate forces or forcing them to retreat farther up the Peninsula—were removed from his command, to which cause has been attrib-

uted the delay that occurred in the occupation of Yorktown.

Following the retreating Rebels, McClellan came into collision with them on May the fifth, at Williamsburgh, where
they stoutly contested his farther progress. From this place
they were finally expelled, but the action resulted in great
loss to the Federal forces, and at one period thereof it
was decidedly in favor of the Confederates. On the following day, a minor action occurred at the head of the York
River, where a force of Federals who had landed there were
driven back under cover of their gunboats.

The Federal army now advanced toward the banks of the
Chickahominy, being, however, slightly impeded in its progress by repeated skirmishes with the Rebels. On the twenty-seventh of May, a portion of McClellan's right wing, under
command of General Fitz-John Porter, had an engagement
with them at Hanover Court-House, and after a sharp conflict succeeded in accomplishing the object of the mission, which was to cut off railroad communication between
Richmond and the North.

General Casey's division, which formed the left wing,
having crossed the Chickahominy, the Confederates took
advantage of a severe thunder-storm—which they trusted
would cause the river to be much swollen, and Casey's communication with the main body of the army thus cut off—to
attack this force on the thirty-first of May, at the Seven
Pines. The Confederates greatly outnumbered the Federals,
and would doubtless have totally annihilated the division

had it not been strongly reënforced. Some of the ground lost in the early part of the action was eventually regained, but at the close of the day the Rebels remained occupants of a portion of the Federal camp, and were in possession of several guns which they had captured. On the following morning the battle was resumed, when the Rebels were defeated and compelled to fall back upon Richmond. This second day's engagement is called the battle of Fair Oaks.

At this time McClellan was loudly calling for reënforcements, and it was naturally the object of the Confederates to prevent any addition to his forces. For this purpose, the latter planned Jackson's raid into the valley of the Shenandoah, which we have already described, and the successful accomplishment of which, Jackson was informed by his superiors, would be the greatest service he could render to his country.

Very little further of importance occurred until May the thirteenth, when the Confederate General J. E. B. Stuart, with a force of twelve hundred cavalry and a section of artillery, left the Rebel lines near Richmond, and as a feint moved as if he was proceeding to reënforce Jackson, but afterwards wheeled about and passed round the whole of the rear of the Union army, returning to his post on the fifteenth. During this dashing exploit, he took a number of prisoners, and captured stores to a large amount.

A brief reference to the situation of the opposing armies at the commencement of the seven days' contests, will here

be necessary to enable the reader to thoroughly understand
the movements. If he will take a map of Virginia, and run
his eye along the Virginia Central Railroad until it crosses
the Chickahominy at the point designated as the Meadow
Bridge, he will be in the vicinity of the position occupied
by the extreme right of the Federal army. Tracing from
this position a semi-circular line which crosses the Chickahominy in the neighborhood of the New Bridge, and then
the York River Railroad, further on, he arrives at a point
south-east of Richmond, but a comparatively short distance
from the James River, where rests the Federal left. To be
a little more explicit, let the reader spread his fingers so that
their tips will form as near as possible the arc of a circle.
Imagine Richmond as situated on his wrist ; the outer edge
of the thumb as the Central Railroad, the inner edge as the
Mechanicsville turnpike ; the first finger as the Nine-Mile,
or New-Bridge road ; the second as the Williamsburgh turnpike, running nearly parallel with the York River Railroad ;
the third as the Charles City turnpike, (which runs to the
southward of the White Oak Swamp ;) and the fourth as
the Darbytown road. Commanding these several avenues
were the forces of McClellan. The Confederate troops, with
the exception of Jackson's corps, occupied a similar but of
course smaller circle immediately around Richmond ; the
heaviest body being on the centre, south of the York River
Railroad.

It will thus be seen that the Federal troops were situated
on both sides of the Chickahominy, whilst the Confederates

were confined exclusively to the right bank, scarcely a single scout crossing the stream. At the commencement of the siege—which may be considered to have extended from the twenty-second to the twenty-fifth of June — three Federal corps were stationed upon the Richmond side of the river, and two corps with General Stoneman's command on the other. One corps of the latter afterward crossed toward Richmond, making four upon that side, and General McCall's division of Pennsylvania Reserves, which arrived on June the eighteenth, were added to the force which remained on the left bank. The left corps was commanded by General Keyes, and the rest, following in rotation toward the right, by Generals Heintzelman, Sumner, Franklin, and Porter, the latter's corps being that situated upon the left bank of the river, with its extreme right resting upon Meadow Bridge, about four miles north of Richmond, and forming the nearest approach of the Federal force to the Confederate capital.

The Confederate army consisted of eight grand divisions, each of which corresponded to a Federal army corps. These were commanded by Generals Huger, D. H. Hill, Longstreet, Smith, Magruder, A. P. Hill, Rains, and Ewell. Huger was stationed opposite the Federal left wing, and the others along to the right, in the order in which we have given their names. General Jackson, upon his arrival, was assigned to the extreme left of the Confederate army, where Stuart's cavalry was also stationed. He was thus placed in juxtaposition to Franklin's corps on the Federal right.

During the month of June the Confederate army was strongly reënforced from the West and South-west, as well as by Jackson's troops, and their forces in and around Richmond, at the commencement of the seven days' battles, have been variously estimated at from two hundred to two hundred and fifty thousand men, but we conclude that one hundred and fifty thousand will more nearly approach the actual number. To meet this vast force, General McClellan could not at the time muster more than eighty-six thousand men.

FIRST DAY—OAK GROVE.

Though Wednesday, June the twenty-fifth, was the day upon which the seven days' battles before Richmond commenced, the operations on that day, so far as regarded the Confederates, were merely defensive. It was not until Thursday that the latter commenced those offensive proceedings which they anticipated would, and which actually did, remove from the vicinity of their capital the National forces so determinedly bent on its capture.

Information was received on Tuesday that General Jackson, with his own troops, along with those of Ewell and Whiting, was at Frederick's Hall, and that it was his intention to attack the Federal right flank and rear, in order to cut off McClellan's communication with the White House, and to throw the right wing of his army into the Chicka. hominy. The raid made by Stuart had induced the Federal commander to provide against this contingency, and he had consequently ordered to the James River, now relieved from the presence of the fearful Merrimac, a number of transports laden with commissary, quartermaster, and ordnance stores. General Stoneman was at the same time placed in charge of the cavalry on the right, with instructions to keep a vigilant watch over Jackson, and to give immediate information of any advance of the Rebels from that direction.

The right being thus guarded, General Heintzelman was directed to drive in the Confederate pickets in the woods from their front, in order to give the National forces command of cleared fields still farther in advance. This object was gallantly accomplished, although stubbornly resisted, the fighting falling principally on Hooker's division. The engagement took place at Oak Grove, about a mile in advance of the battle-field at Fair Oaks, and continued throughout the entire day of the twenty-fifth, commencing at nine o'clock in the morning and not terminating until ten o'clock at night. Just as the new line was gained, General McClellan was called from the field by intelligence which tended strongly to confirm the belief that Jackson was really approaching. Such, however, was not the case, but these repeated alarms are sufficient to prove with what fear any approach of the irresistless Rebel was viewed.

The Confederates being now in sufficient force to become the attacking party, they resolved upon ridding their capital from the presence of a besieging host. The plan proposed to be adopted having been thoroughly completed, a great council of war was being held at the Rebel headquarters, during the progress of the events which we have just nar-

rated. In it were assembled nearly all that was eminent in
the Rebel army. Johnston had been severely wounded at
the battle of Seven Pines, and the mantle of the commander
had fallen upon the shoulders of General Lee. Gazing cheerfully over the countenances of his comrades, for each of
whom he had a part already assigned, the new commander
stood like a rock. " Thoughtfully his eyes wandered from
one to the other, as though he wished to stamp the features
of each upon his memory, with the feeling that he, perhaps,
should never behold many of them again. Close beside him
towered the knightly form of General Baldwin ; at his left
leaned pensively Stonewall Jackson, the idol of his troops,
impatiently swinging his sabre to and fro, as though the quiet
room were too narrow for him, and he were longing to be
once more at the head of his columns. A little aside, quietly
stood the two Hills, arm in arm, while in front of them old
General Wise was energetically speaking. Further to the
right stood Generals Huger, Longstreet, Branch, Anderson,
Whiting, Ripley, and Magruder, in a group. When all
these generals had assembled, General Lee laid his plans before them, and in a few stirring words pointed out to each
his allotted task. The scheme had already been elaborated.
It was compact, concentrated action, and the result could
not fail to be brilliant. When the conference terminated,
all shook hands and hastened away to their respective army
corps, to enter upon immediate activity." *

The plan of battle developed by the Confederates was,

* Richmond Correspondent of the *Cologne Gazette.*

first, to make a vigorous flank movement upon the Federal extreme right, which was within a mile or two of the Central Railroad; secondly, as soon as they fell back to the next road below, the Rebel divisions there posted were to advance across the Chickahominy, charge front, and in cooperation with Jackson, who was to make a detour, and attack the Federals in flank and rear, drive them still further on; and finally, when they had reached a certain point known as "The Triangle," embraced between the Charles City, New Market, and Quaker Roads, all of which intersect, these several approaches were to be possessed by the Confederates; the National forces were to be thus hemmed in and compelled either to starve, capitulate, or fight their way out with tremendous odds and topographical advantages against them. How this plan happened to fail, at least partially, in the execution, will appear in the course of our narrative.

Looking at the position of the two armies, it will be seen that the vantage ground lay with the Southern army, for General McClellan had his forces necessarily on both sides of the Chickahominy, and, owing to the many ravines in the neighborhood, he could not, without great difficulty and much loss of time, execute his military movements. His front line reached over a distance of more than twenty miles in the form of a semi-circle, extending from the vicincinity of the James River toward Richmond and Ashland. The heights on the banks of the Chickahominy were, however, so fortified that his army, notwithstanding the great length of its line, had excellent defensive cover. The Confederate army occupied the inner side of the semi-circle, and the various divisions thereof being more contiguous to each other than those of the Federal army necessarily could be, they were more readily able to assist each other, whenever, from force of circumstances, any assistance should be required.

SECOND DAY—MECHANICSVILLE.

Thursday dawned, and the morning was clear but warm. Jackson was in motion as early as three o'clock. His *corps d'armée*, strengthened by the addition of Whiting's division, now consisted of about thirty thousand men. He moved by a forced march from Ashland, twenty miles distant from Richmond, for the purpose of commencing his outflanking operations.

At Hanover Court-House he threw forward General Branch's brigades between the Chickahominy and Pamunkey Rivers, to establish a junction with General A. P. Hill, who had to cross the stream at Meadow Bridge. Jackson then bore away from the Chickahominy, so as to gain ground toward the Pamunkey, marching to the left of Mechanicsville and toward Coal Harbor, while Hill, keeping well to the Chickahominy, approached Mechanicsville, and there engaged the National forces. This was shortly after mid-day. The fight was opened with artillery at long-range, but the Rebels discovering the Federal superiority in this arm, foreshortened the range and came into closer conflict. Previous to this, however whilst the shells of the

Confederates were not destructive in the intrenchments of the Federals, the gunners of the latter played upon the exposed ranks of the former with fearful effect. The fight increased in fury as it progressed, and it finally became the most terrible artillery combat that the war had thus far witnessed. The uproar was incessant and deafening for hours. No language can describe its awful grandeur. The Rebels at last essayed a combined movement. Powerful bodies of troops rushed forward to charge the Federal lines, but they were ruthlessly swept away. Again and again the desperate fellows were pushed at the breastworks only to be more cruelly slaughtered than before.

General McCall, whose division of Porter's corps was here engaged, in the mean time had his force strengthened by the brigades of Martindale and Griffin, of Morell's division. The volume of infantry firing was thus increased, and at dark, the Rebels retired from the contest, resigning the honor of the day to the Federals.

While the battle of Mechanicsville was in progress, another action took place at Ellyson's Mills, to the right or south-east of that place, and about a mile and a half distant therefrom; but the two engagements occurred so near to each other that they may be considered as part of the same battle. At this latter place, the Federals had a battery of sixteen guns situated on elevated ground, and defended by epaulements, supported by rifle-pits. Beaver Creek, about twelve feet wide and waist-deep, ran along the front and left flank of this position, while abattis occupied the space

5*

between the creek and the battery. General Lee ordered this battery to be charged, but his troops were unable to advance any nearer than the opposite side of the creek. The Rebels suffered very severely, during the engagement, and retired from the conflict about ten o'clock at night.

Another occurrence also took place on the twenty-sixth of June which is worthy of being recorded. Colonel Lansing was ordered to proceed with the Seventeenth New-York and Eighteenth Massachusetts regiments to Old Church, about six miles east of Mechanicsville, there to intercept General Jackson, who was on his way to cut off the Federal communications with the White House. Jackson succeeded in separating Lansing's communication with the right wing of the Federal army, at that time fighting on the banks of Beaver Creek. The latter, however, was ulti mately enabled to make his way to Tunstall's Station upon the railroad, and from thence to the York River, where he was taken up by the transports.

Whenever General Branch acted directly under General Jackson's command, he implicitly obeyed his instructions, and acted with energy and courage; but when he was out of his commander's sight, he became nervous and unresolved how to act. On the present occasion he failed to carry out the orders which Jackson had distinctly given to him, and instead of advancing boldly he hesitated, and delayed his march from hour to hour. General Hill sent his Aid-de-Camp during the battle to order up Branch's brigade, but the latter was not to be found, and he did not make his appearance on the battle-field until night had put an end to the contest.

It being now evident to General McClellan that Jackson was proceeding toward the Pamunkey, he considered that the position of his right wing was no longer tenable. He therefore determined to concentrate his forces, and withdrew Porter's command to a position near Gaines's Mill, where he could rest both his flanks on the Chickahominy, and cover the most important bridges over that stream. As it was also evident that Jackson was intent upon seizing the public property on the banks of the Pamunkey, and cutting off the Federal retreat in that direction, Stoneman's command was moved swiftly down to finish operations there, and orders were issued for the removal or destruction of all public stores at White House. Meantime all trains and equipages of the right wing were withdrawn during the night to Trent's Bluff on the right bank of the Chickahominy, and the wounded were conveyed to the hospital at Savage's Station — alas! there to be deserted to the enemy they had beaten. These movements indicated that there was danger in the distance.

THIRD DAY—GAINES'S MILL.

By daylight on Friday morning, General McCall had fallen back in the rear of Gaines's Mill, and in front of Woodbury's bridge, where he was posted, his left joining the right of Butterfield's brigade, which rested on the woods and near to the swamps of the Chickahominy. Morell was on his right in the centre, and General Sykes's command, five thousand regulars, and Duryea's Zouaves, held the extreme right. The line occupied crests of hills, near the New Kent road, some distance east by south of Gaines's Mill. In addition to these changes, General Slocum's division, about eight thousand strong, was moved across the river to support Porter, as it was assumed that the Rebels would reappear in that quarter in stronger force than they had been on the previous day. General McClellan having received intelligence, in the course of the morning, that Longstreet's corps was at Mechanicsville, ready to move down on either bank of the Chickahominy, according to circumstances, this, with other threatening movements of the Rebels on various parts of the centre and left, placed a limit to the number of reënforcements for the support of Porter. Under these circumstances it was likewise impossible to withdraw him to the right bank of the river by daylight, especially as the enemy was so close upon him that the attempt could not have been made without severe loss, and would have placed the right flank and rear of the army at their mercy. It was consequently necessary to give battle upon and hold the position now occupied at any cost, and in the mean time perfect arrangements for the change of base to the James River.

Let us now impart to the reader a knowledge of the ground in the vicinity of Gaines's Mill. For this purpose we will approach the scene from the Confederate lines. Emerging from the woods, the road leads to the left and then to the right round Gaines's house, where the whole ground, for the area of about two miles, is an open, unbroken succession of undulating hills. Standing at the north door of the house, the whole country to the right, for the distance of one mile, is a gradual slope toward a creek, through which the main road runs up an open hill and then winds to the right. In front, to the left, are orchards and gulleys running gradually to a deep creek. Directly in front, for the distance of a mile, the ground is almost tableland, suddenly dipping to the deep creek mentioned above, and faced by a timber-covered hill which fronts the tableland. Beyond this timber-covered hill the country is again open and is a perfect plateau, with a farm-house and outhouses in the centre, and the main road winding to the right and through all the Federal camps. To the south-east of Gaines's house is a large tract of timber, commanding all advances upon the main road. In this timber a strong body of Federal skirmishers were posted with artillery, to annoy the Confederate flank and rear, should they advance upon the Federal camps by the main road or over the table-lands to the north.

Early in the morning a portion of Longstreet's corps drove back such of the Federals as had been left in the vicinity of Mechanicsville, the latter retiring upon their new defensive line. The Confederates shortly after advanced along the entire line in the following order of battle: Longstreet on the right, resting on the Chickahominy swamp; A. P. Hill on his left; then Whiting; then Ewell and Jackson's corps, under command of the latter general;

then D. H. Hill on the extreme left of the line, which extended in the form of a crescent beyond New Coal Harbor, on the north, and toward Baker's Mills on the south. The battle commenced about mid-day by the batteries of D. H Hill opening a vigorous fire on the Federal right. He however, soon found it impossible to hold his position, and his guns were soon silenced. Reënforced, he renewed the attack, but only to meet with a second repulse and considerable loss. A third attack met with no better success. The object, however, of the Confederates in this attempted flank movement on the right of the Federals was mainly intended to draw the attention of the latter from Longstreet's contemplated attack on their left.

The din of battle now veered round to the centre and the left. At about half-past three o'clock P.M., Longstreet commenced to drive the Federals down the Chickahominy. At four o'clock the battle raged with intense fury in the vicinity of Gaines's Mill, and upon the ground which we have described. Here the conflict lasted for nearly two hours. The columns surged backward and forward, first one yielding and then the other. The Federal centre made a desperate stand, but it was not until it had hurled its last fresh brigade against the Rebels that they were beaten back. The Confederates finding that they could not force the Federal centre, now threw their columns against its left. Here the roar of musketry increased in volume, and the conflict became more terrific as time sped on. The Confederates had suffered severely from the raking fire which the Federals had poured upon them from the plateau. The latter swept the whole face of the country with their artillery, and would have annihilated the Rebel force if it had not been screened by the inequalities of the land. The Rebels descended into the deep creek and passed up the hill beyond, but so terrific was the hail-storm of lead which fell thick and fast around them, that it was with great difficulty their regiments could be induced to withstand it. In fact, in one instance, one of their generals, sword in hand, threatened to behead the first man that hesitated to advance. The Federals were now compelled to withdraw their guns and take up a fresh position wherefrom to assail the foe, which was advancing from the woods and toward the plateau. Forward pushed the Confederates. Officers had no horses—all were shot. Brigadiers marched on foot, regiments were commanded by captains, and companies by sergeants; yet onward they rushed, with yells and colors flying, and backward, still backward fell the Federals. When the plateau was reached, the Confederates found in their front the Federal camps stretching far away to the north-east. Drawn up in line of battle were the commands of McCall and Porter and others. Banners darkened the air, and artillery vomited forth incessant volleys of grape, canister, and shell. Brigade after brigade of the Confederates was hurled against the Northern heroes. In vain did the brave Butterfield, with hat in hand, rally, cheer, and lead his men forward again and again. In vain did he cry, "Once more, my gallant men!" as a last rallying order. The opposing hosts were too strong to be withstood. They assailed him in front, flank, and rear, and compelled him to fall back.

The Federals now moved with the evident intention of flanking the Rebel force engaged on its left, but the latter pressed onward to the heart of the Federal position, and when the National troops had almost succeeded in carrying out their flanking operations, great commotion was heard in the woods. Volley after volley was repeated in rapid succession. These welcome sounds were recognized and cheered by the Rebels. "It is Jackson," they shouted, "on their right and rear!" Yes, two or three brigades of Jackson's corps had approached from Coal Harbor and flanked the National forces. The fighting now increased in its severity. Worked up to madness, the Confederates dashed forward at a run, and drove the Federals back with irresistible fury.

Wheeling their artillery from the front, the Federals turned part of it to break the Rebel left and save their own retreat. The earth trembled at the roar. Not one Confederate piece had as yet opened fire; all had thus far been done by the bullet and the bayonet. Onward pressed the Rebel troops, through camps upon camps, capturing guns, stores, arms, and clothing. They swept every thing before them. Presenting an unbroken, solid front, and closing in upon the Federals, they kept up an incessant succession of volleys upon their confused masses. There was but one "charge!" and from the moment that the word of command was given, " Fix bayonets! forward!" the Rebel advance was never stopped, despite the awful reception which it met.

" But where is Jackson?" was the universal inquiry. He had travelled fast and was heading the flying foe. As night closed in, all was anxiety for intelligence from him. At seven o'clock, just as the victory was complete, the distant and rapid discharges of cannon told that Jackson had fallen on the retreating columns. Far into the night his troops hung upon and harassed the hard-pressed National forces.

General Jackson had accomplished his flanking march without encountering any serious resistance. Hardly had he arrived at the position marked out for him, ere he sent his columns to the charge. Notwithstanding the difficulties and exertions of the march which his troops had executed on short allowance, he flung them at once upon the Federals. In vain was all the courage, all the bold manœuvring of the latter. Like a tempest, General Stuart and his cavalry swept down upon them, and hurled every thing to the earth that stood in their way. Although the Federals had at first made obstinate resistance, they ultimately lost ground and fell back, throwing away arms, knapsacks, blankets—in fine, every thing that would impede their flight. Jackson could with a clear conscience issue the order : " Enough for the day." None of the other generals had performed their task with such rapidity and such success as he, and therefore the fruits of his victory were unusually large. The booty was immense; but in a strategetic point of view, Jackson's success was of far greater importance, since it completely cut off General McClellan from his original base on the York River. When, therefore, the triumph of his arms became known at the Confederate headquarters, the rejoicings bordered on frenzy, and all counted with perfect certainty upon the destruction or capture of the entire Federal force.

With the close of the day terminated the terrible scene of strife.

The army of the Potomac now occupied a very singular position. One portion of it was situated on the south side of the Chickahominy, fronting Richmond, and confronted by General Magruder. The other portion was on the north side of the river, and had turned its back upon Richmond, and fronted destruction in the persons of Lee, Longstreet, Jackson, and the two Hills.

By this engagement, General Stoneman's command had been separated from the rest of the army. Upon the previous day he had been scouting near Hanover Court-House, and after doing all that he could in the contests of both days to harass the Rebel flank and rear, he retired to the White House, whence he proceeded down the Peninsula to Fortress Monroe.

During the night the final withdrawal of the Federal right wing across the Chickahominy was completed, without difficulty or confusion, a portion of the regular troops only remaining on the left bank until early on the follow ing morning, when the bridges were burned, and the whole army concentrated on the right bank of the river.

During the evening of the twenty-seventh, General McClellan's determination to change his base to the James River was for the first time whispered abroad. The plan was naturally very much canvassed, and the movement was considered a most critical one, especially as it had to be taken under compulsion. The tents of General McClellan's headquarters, which had been pitched in Doctor Trent's field, near the bank of the river, were moved at dusk to Savage's Station, on the railroad. "At night, as the several brigades came over the bridge, and clustered on the borders of the swamp, one single tent stood on the hillside, and that was General McClellan's. At eleven o'clock a council of war was held in front of this tent, in which the General commanding, corps commanders, with their aids, among them the French Princes and the General of Engineers, took part. A large fire had been lighted just beyond the arbor in front, and its blaze lighted up the faces of the generals as they sat in the arbor, which formed a pavilion for the tent. The conference was long and seemingly earnest. This was the first council called by General McClellan since he took the field, and here he disclosed his plans of reaching the James River." *

Keyes's line, which was on the extreme left, resting on

* "Leaves from the Diary of an Army Surgeon," by Thomas T. Ellis, M.D.

White Oak Swamp, was extended during the night, and the Federal artillery and transportation trains were ordered to prepare to move forward. That night General Casey was also directed to destroy all public property at the White House which could not be removed; to transport the sick and wounded to a place of safety, and to retire himself and rejoin the army on the James River. Friday night was thus actively and mournfully passed. The troops were ignorant of the true position, and it was desirable to conceal the truth from them. It was feared that the Rebels would renew their attack on the following morning, and every preparation was made to resist them successfully. The defensive right of the Federals was disposed on Trent's Bluffs, where it was supposed that the crossing of the Rebels might be successfully opposed. The night of Friday, June the twenty-seventh, was gloomy, but it was felicity itself when compared with those of the following Saturday, Sunday, Monday, and Tuesday.

FOURTH DAY—GARNETT'S FARM.

Saturday dawned hot and cheerless to the National forces. No sound of a hostile gun disturbed the dread stillness until nine o'clock. The profound quiet of the morning became almost oppressive, so great was the contrast between its calmness and the fiery storm of the previous day. Shortly after that hour, however, the ominous silence which prevailed was broken by an awful cannonade, which opened from two forts in Garnett's field—a battery at General Porter's old position, and another below it—on the left bank of the Chick-ahominy. The fire was terrible, and compelled the forces upon which it was launched to abandon the strongest natu-ral position on the whole Federal line. The troops attacked fell back a few hundred yards to the woods and threw up breastworks out of range. The Rebels, content with their success, ceased firing, and quiet was not again disturbed that day. The silence of the Confederates was explained that night by a negro slave who had escaped from his mas-ter at headquarters in Richmond. He said a despatch had been sent by Jackson to Magruder, who remained in com-mand in front of Richmond, expressed thus : " Be quiet. Every thing is working as well as we could desire." Omi-nous words !

Saturday was also marked by the capture of the Fourth New-Jersey (Stockton's) regiment, the Eleventh Pennsylva-nia, and the famous "Bucktails," with their regimental standards. Also by rapid and successful movements of Jackson and Stuart, between the Chickahominy and the Pamunkey, in which they took the York River Railroad, cut off McClellan's communication with his transports, and des-troyed his line of telegraph. Meanwhile, measures were tak-en by the Federals to increase the number of bridges across the White Oak Swamp. The trains were set in motion early in the day, and they continued moving along the swamp day and night until all had passed. Endless streams of artillery trains, wagons, and funereal ambulances, poured down the roads from all the camps, and plunged into the narrow fun-

nel which was now the only hope of escape. It was absolutely necessary for the salvation of the army and the cause,
that the wounded and mangled heroes who lay moaning in
physical agony in the hospitals, should be deserted and left
in the hands of those against whom they had so bravely
fought.

Another fearful night was spent, but it was without catastrophe. Officers were on horseback throughout the greater
part of the night, ordering on the great caravan and its
escorts. There was again no wink of sleep, nor peace of
mind, for any who realized the peril of his country in those
dread hours.

FIFTH DAY—PEACH ORCHARD; SAVAGE'S STATION.

At daylight, General McClellan was on the road. Thousands of cattle and wagons, and immense trains of artillery,
intermingled with infantry and cavalry, choked up the narrow road. Generals Sumner's, Heintzelman's, and Franklin's corps, under command of the first named, were left to
guard the rear, with orders to fall back at daylight, and
hold the enemy in check until night. At no point along the
line were the Federals more than three fourths of a mile
from the Confederates, whilst in front of Sedgwick's line,
the latter were not over six hundred yards distant. It was
therefore necessary to move with the greatest caution, so as
to conceal from the enemy the nature of their movements.
Fortunately, however, by skilful secresy, column after column was marched to the rear—Franklin first, Sedgwick

next, then Richardson and Hooker, and lastly the knightly Kearny.

A mile had been swiftly traversed when these splendid columns quickly turned at bay. The Confederates, keen-scented and watchful, had discovered the retrograde move-ment, and quick as thought were swarming and yelling at their heels. They were quickly met by fearful volleys of musketry and artillery, and all who were left of the slaugh-tered Rebel column fled howling back. Fresh troops step-ped forth, and they, too, were sent surging back, until finally the Confederates retreated, content to watch and wait a hap-pier moment to assail that desperate front. This engage-ment, which lasted for four hours, took place at Peach Or-chard. The Federal troops which were engaged in it, hav-ing held the position as long as was necessary, marched on to Savage's Station in order to concentrate with other corps.

Toward noon the line had retired several miles, and rested behind Savage's Station to destroy the public pro-perty which had accumulated there. A locomotive and a train of cars were started and sent plunging madly into the Chickahominy. Ammunition was exploded, and the match was applied to stores of every description, until nothing was left to welcome the Confederates, who were closely treading in the Federal footsteps.

The advancing column and all its mighty train was in due course of time swallowed up in the maw of the dreary for-est. It swept onward, onward, fast and furious, like an avalanche. But the march was as orderly as on any ordinary occasion, only swifter. It seemed marvellous that such caravans of wagons, artillery, horsemen, soldiers, camp-followers, and other *impedimenta* of an army should press through the narrow road with so little confusion.

The Confederates, under Magruder, pressed closely on the Federal rear. After the latter retired from Peach Orchard, the former entered the camping-ground to find almost every thing of value either removed or destroyed. The Rebels then followed on to Savage's Station, guided thither by the dense volume of smoke which was seen to issue from the woods, and betokened the destruction which was in progress. Arriving at the station about four o'clock P.M., the Rebels made a furious onslaught on the Federal rear, commanded by General Heintzelman, which engagement raged hotly for about three hours. The Federals held the Confederates in check, fighting and retiring until they reached White Oak Swamp. Here the fight continued until darkness put an end to the contest. This battle in the forests was a fearful one. Long lines of musketry vomited forth their liquid fire, while nature, as if emulous of man's fury, flashed its lightnings and rolled its grand thunder over the distant domes of Richmond. So mingled were the flash and roar of heaven's artillery with the fire and din of battle, that it was at times difficult to decide which was the power of God, and which the conflict of man. No combination of the dreadful in art and the magnificent in nature was ever more solemnly impressive. It was a Sunday battle.

The Federal rear crossed the swamp under cover of night, whilst the Confederates lay on their arms with the design of renewing the battle on the return of daylight. Whilst Magruder was busily engaged pressing the National forces on the south side of the Chickahominy, the ever-active Jackson and the redoubtable Stuart were not less active on the north. Dashing down to the White House, the latter succeeded in capturing an immense quantity of supplies, ammunition, ordnance, a balloon, the rolling-stock of the railroad, and fifteen hundred prisoners, besides burning several large transports at the wharves. It was during this day (Sunday) that the Confederates became alive to the fact that General McClellan had succeeded in eluding them, and that he had stolen a march of twelve hours on General Huger, who had been placed in a position on his flank to watch his movements. So confidently had the Rebels calculated upon capturing the Federal army, that they were greatly mortified at the discovery of the fact that they had been out-generalled.

SIXTH DAY—WHITE OAK SWAMP ; GLENDALE.

About midnight on Sunday the lights were still blazing at the Federal headquarters. The commander was yet working with unyielding devotion; aids were still riding fast, but all else was silent. Presently, and the prostrate soldiers were startled from their slumbers by what appeared to be the terrific uproar of battle. Again and again the thundering sound was heard. It rolled sublimely away

6

off on the borders of the Chickahominy. The Rebels have crossed the river and are destroying the Federal right wing in the darkness. Such was the general impression, but the illusion—a natural one when the sounds of cannon and of musketry are dinning in every ear—was speedily dispelled. A dark cloud appeared in the horizon, and approached nearer and nearer, until at last it hung like a canopy over the black forest, and above the weary warriors.

Monday morning beamed like its predecessor, brilliantly and hotly. Until this day the Confederates evidently had proceeded upon the supposition that General McClellan was intending to retire to the Pamunkey, and the appearance in the north of the Federal cavalry and infantry—which we have already alluded to as having been severed from the rest of the army whilst watching the movements of Jackson—served to impress the Rebels with this idea. It was plain by this time, however, that the Federal intentions had become apparent to the Rebels, but the trains had been hurried on so rapidly that they had now nearly passed the point at which the latter could make any flank movement upon them.

At daybreak the Rebels resumed the pursuit of their flying foes. The troops of Generals D. H. Hill, Whiting, Ewell, and Jackson, under the command of General Jackson, crossed the Chickahominy and followed the Federals on their track by the Williamsburgh road and Savage's Station. Generals Longstreet, A. P. Hill, Huger, and Magruder at the same time proceeded by the Charles City road on the south, with the intention of cutting them off. Jackson came up with the Federal rear about eleven o'clock, at White Oak Swamp. The Federals had crossed the swamp and the bridge had been destroyed, and their artillery was posted so as to command the road and the crossing. Jackson ordered his artillery to be brought forward, under cover of a hill on the north bank of the swamp, and then to be thrown rapidly upon its crest and suddenly open fire upon the Federal batteries. This was about noon. The artillery duel which then commenced and continued with great spirit and determination until night closed the scene, was probably the most severe fight of field artillery which has taken place during the war. Jackson made some desperate efforts to cross the creek, but he was repulsed and kept back by General Smith's brigade, while the main body of Heintzelman's corps passed on toward the James River.

General A. P. Hill, who in the absence of Longstreet commanded the troops moving upon the Charles City road, came up with the Federals about five o'clock in the afternoon, at the Cross-roads, or Glendale, where he attacked Heintzelman's corps on the flank with much fierceness. During the evening the gunboats Aroostook and Galena, on the James River, got in range of the Confederate masses advancing from Richmond, and opened upon them with fearful havoc, the direction in which they should fire having been indicated by the signal corps. The Rebels were finally repulsed by a vigorous charge led by

General Heintzleman in person. The loss on both sides of this engagement was very great. Portions of nearly all the Federal corps were engaged, and Generals McCall and Reynolds were taken prisoners. The Confederate forces in action were A. P. Hill's and Longstreet's, commanded by the former. Magruder did not arrive until the battle was over, when he moved upon and occupied the battle-field, General Hill's troops being almost prostrated from their long and toilsome fight, and from their tremendous losses.

The Confederate President was on the field during the day, and had a narrow escape. He had taken a position in a house near the scene, when he was advised by General Lee to leave it at once, as it was threatened with danger. He had scarcely complied with the advice before the house was literally riddled with shell from the Federal batteries.

SEVENTH DAY—MALVERN HILL.

By an early hour on Tuesday morning General McClellan had concentrated the entire of his forces at Malvern Hill, and in close proximity to the James River. The troops were placed in position to offer battle to the Rebels should they renew the attack, the left of the line resting on the admirable position of Malvern Hill, with a brigade in the low ground to the left, watching the road to Richmond. The line then followed a line of heights nearly parallel to the river, and bent back through the woods nearly to the James River on the right. General McClellan relied on the left for the natural advantages of the position. On the right, where the natural strength was less, some little cutting of timber was done, and the roads blocked. Although the Federal force was small for so extensive a position, its commander considered it necessary to hold it at any cost.

Tuesday, the first of July, was not a cheerful day for the Federals. The prospect was not a pleasant one. The Prince de Joinville, always gay and active as a lad, and always where there was battle, had gone. The Count de Paris, heir to the Bourbon throne, and the Duke de Chartres, his brother—the two chivalric and devoted aids to General McClellan, on whose courage, fidelity, intelligence, and activity he safely relied, and who served with him to learn the art of war—suddenly, without previous warning, took passage on a gunboat, and fluttered softly down the river. Two officers of the English army, who had also accompanied the Federal commander, and who had intended to remain with the army until Richmond was captured, announced their intention to leave in the first boat. These departures were at least ominous. The paymasters were advised to deposit their treasure on a gunboat. People looked gloomy. It had been stated that by the time the army reached Malvern Hill, the river at that point would be full of transports. On Monday, at noon, there was not one there, excepting a schooner laden with hay. By Tuesday evening, however, several steamers and a few forage-boats had arrived.

On Tuesday morning the Confederates renewed their pursuit. The divisions of D. II. Hill, Whiting, Ewell, and Jackson—the three latter under the command of Jackson—crossed the White Oak Bridge, Hill's division being to the right and Jackson's to the left. About three o'clock in the afternoon, they took their position to the left of the Rebel line, Longstreet, A. P. Hill, Magruder, and Huger, forming the right. In this order they advanced toward the lines of the Federals under the fire of artillery from land and water. Shortly after four o'clock, the rage of battle commenced. For an hour and a half battery after battery and regiment after regiment were advanced to the front, to be in turn driven back by the iron hail of the Federal artillery and the tremendous projectiles showered forth by the National gunboats. During this time, the indomitable Jackson assailed the Federals with that energy which he was ever wont to display.

Great was the slaughter in the Rebel ranks, and fruitless was their attempt to dislodge the Federals from the position they held, and where they had chosen to turn at bay and give battle to their eager pursuers. The sun of the first of July set upon the retiring columns of the Confederate host, and when night came on the final battle of the Peninsular campaign had become a matter of history.

Let us picture to the reader the appearance of this battle-field, as it met the eye a few days after the termination of the strife. The entire district appeared as if the lightnings of heaven had scathed and blasted it. The forests showed, in the splintered branches of a thousand trees, the fearful havoc of the artillery. The houses were riddled, the fences utterly demolished, the earth itself ploughed up in many cases for yards. Here stood a dismantled cannon, there a broken gun-carriage. Thick and many were the graves, the sods over which bore the marks of the blood of their occupants. On the plateau, across whose surface for hours the utmost fury of the battle raged, the tender corn that had grown up as high as the knee betrayed no sign of having ever laughed and sung in the breeze of early summer. Every thing, in short, but the blue heavens above, spoke of the carnival of death which had been there so frightfully celebrated.

It is needless to state that the losses on both sides in the seven days' battles were very great. The Federal loss in killed, wounded, and missing, has been officially given at about fifteen thousand. There is no official announcement of the Confederate loss, but, in consequence of the superiority of the artillery which the Federals brought into action, it must have exceeded that sustained by the latter.

It is impossible to peruse the narrative of the memorable events which occurred in the vicinity of Richmond during this historic week, without being convinced that General Jackson was in no small degree instrumental in compelling the Federal forces to raise their siege of the city. Before the Confederates commenced their offensive operations, we find his name a tower of strength to them, and a source of continual disquietude to the Federal army. It is easy to observe how the approach of this ubiquitous general was feared by the latter. Rumor followed rumor that he was drawing nigh to the Federal right, each succeeding rumor only tending to intensify the terror which the previous rumors had originated.

At the battle of Gaines's Mill—the only one of the series which can be claimed as a Confederate victory—it is evident that the decisive blow was struck by Jackson when he outflanked his foes and attacked them so mercilessly on their rear. In the future operations consequent on the Federal retreat, we find him ever active. Placed in prominent command, he harassed the rear of the retreating army until it was considered necessary that the pursuit should be abandoned. General Lee was well aware of the unsurpassed energy and the unweariness of his companion in arms, and if he gave to him a lion's work, he knew that it would be performed in a manner befitting its importance. It was long before dawn on the first day of the Confederate attack, that Jackson moved from Ashland to take up the position which had been allotted to him ; as day succeeded day in this week of carnage, he was unwearied in his activity ; and it was not until the last shot had been fired in the last battle, that he sheathed his sword and retired from the conflict.

CHAPTER IX.

Organization of Pope's Army—His Address and Orders to his Troops—
Strength of his Army—Confederate Plan to Crush him—Commences to
Advance—He is opposed by Jackson—Battle of Cedar Mountain—Narrow Escapes—Jackson's Official Report—Losses in the Battle—The Field
of Operations removes to near Washington—Pope retires behind the
Rappahannock—Stuart's Cavalry Raid—Pope's Papers Captured—Jackson's March upon the Federal Right Flank—Reaches Manassas Junction—
Feast of his Famished Soldiers—Pope's Project to capture him—Critical
Position of Jackson—Battle of Groveton—Jackson reënforced by Lee
and Longstreet—Second Battle of Bull Run—Federal Defeat—Pope retires to Centreville—Battle at Chantilly—Jackson's Share in the Campaign.

On the twenty-sixth of June, the National forces, under
Generals Fremont, Banks, and McDowell, were consolidated
into one army under the name of the Army of Virginia, and
General Pope was assigned by the President to the chief
command. General Fremont objected to be thus placed in
a subordinate command, and at his own request he was relieved from duty, and the corps which he would have com
manded in the new army was placed under General Sigel.

It was against this army that General Jackson was called
upon to act, after he had reörganized his forces at the close
of the battles before Richmond, in which they had suffered

6*

severely, and were considerably lessened in numbers. General Pope was beginning to threaten Richmond from the North, and the new aspect of affairs drew the attention of the Confederates from General McClellan's forces who were resting at Harrison's Landing, preparatory to their evacuation of the Peninsula.

On the eleventh of July, General Halleck was assigned to the command of the whole land forces of the United States, as General-in-Chief.

Shortly after General Pope entering upon his new command, he issued an address to the officers and soldiers of his army which was particularly remarkable for the pretentious language in which it was clothed. He also issued several orders in which he declared that his troops " should subsist upon the country in which their operations are carried on;" and pointed out the manner in which celerity of movement could be best secured by his army. He notified the people of his department that they should be held responsible for any injury done to railroad-trains, bridges, and telegraph-lines, or for any attacks upon trains of straggling soldiers by guerrilla bands ; and stated that residents within five miles of any place where any such outrage occurred should be compelled to repair the damage done, or be assessed therefor ; and that individuals detected in any outrages against property or persons should be shot without waiting for civil process. He also directed that disloyal male citizens within the lines of his army should be arrested and sent beyond the lines unless they took the oath of allegiance to the United States and gave security for their good behavior; and notified that persons violating such oath would be shot. A retaliatory order issued by the Confederate President, declared that in consequence of General Pope's threatened arrest of disloyal citizens, that general and all commissioned officers serving under him should not be considered as soldiers, and therefore should not be entitled to the benefit of the cartel for the parole of prisoners of war; and that in the event of their being captured they should be held in close confinement as long as General Pope's order should remain in force.

The effective strength of General Pope's army at the commencement of his campaign was thirty-eight thousand infantry and artillery, and about five thousand cavalry. These forces were scattered over a wide district of country not within supporting distance of each other; and General Pope states that he found many of the brigades and divisions badly organized and in a demoralized condition, and that the cavalry was badly mounted and armed, and in poor condition for service. He took an early opportunity not only to reörganize his army, but to concentrate as far as possible all the movable forces under his command; consequently Sigel and Banks's forces were ordered from the valley of the Shenandoah to Sperryville on the east side of the Blue Ridge, and part of McDowell's force to Waterloo Bridge, a point between Warrenton and Sperryville. The remainder of McDowell's corps was left at Falmouth, opposite Fredericksburgh, to cover the crossing of the Rappahannock at that point, and to protect the railroad between it and Acquia

Creek, until the arrival of General Burnside's forces, who were on their way from North-Carolina to Fredericksburgh. These movements were in progress during the time the battles near Richmond were being fought. Their object had been to draw off a portion of the Confederate forces from McClellan's front; but the retreat of the latter commander now enabled General Lee to oppose the greater part of his army to General Pope. General Pope was now called upon to resist at all hazards any advance of the Confederates toward Washington, and to delay and embarrass their movements so as to gain time for the removal of the Army of the Potomac to the banks of the Rappahannock.

In pursuance of this plan, several cavalry expeditions were despatched from Fredericksburgh to destroy the railroad communication between Richmond and the North and the North-west, the latter point leading to the valley of the Shenandoah. These expeditions were completely successful. At the same time General Banks sent all his cavalry and a brigade of infantry on a forced march to Culpeper Court-House, which place was taken possession of, and the cavalry pushed forward to Orange Court-House, where they destroyed the railroad and Confederate stores and munitions of war, and burned the bridge which crossed the Rapidan. After this was accomplished, a force was despatched to Gordonsville with instructions to destroy the railroad east and west of that place, but on the sixteenth of July, before they were enabled to reach it, the town was entered by the advance of Jackson's forces under Ewell,

and the proposed movement was thereby rendered impracticable.

General Lee had despatched Jackson with a *corps d'armée*
of about twenty-five thousand men to check Pope's advance
This corps consisted of the old Stonewall division, now
under the command of General Taliaferro, and the divisions of Ewell and A. P. Hill. Lee then left a small force to
watch General McClellan, and proceeded with the main
body of his army as rapidly as possible to join General
Jackson; but the movement was not accomplished as
speedily as was desirable, in consequence of deficiency in
the means of transportation. Lee had hoped, with his
united forces, to crush Pope's army before McClellan could
come to his relief, but a sudden rain-storm so swelled the
Rapidan River, rendering it necessary to wait some time
before it could be crossed, that the plan was prevented in
being carried out, and gave Pope, who took the alarm,
time to retire rapidly behind the Rappahannock.

On July the twenty-ninth, General Pope left Washington
with his staff for the headquarters of his army in the field.
All the preparations having been completed, on the seventh
of August he instructed General Banks to move forward
from the vicinity of Little Washington to a point midway
between Sperryville and Culpeper, McDowell having been
ordered on the previous day to advance Rickett's division
to Culpeper Court-House. He had thus on that day twen-
ty-eight thousand infantry and artillery assembled along the
turnpike from Sperryville to Culpeper. Sigel's corps was

stationed at Sperryville, Buford's cavalry at Madison Court-House, and Bayard's cavalry near Rapidan Station, the point where the Orange and Alexandia Railroad crosses the Rapidan River. On the eighth, General Bayard was compelled to fall back slowly from his advanced position on the Rapidan, in the direction of Culpeper Court-House, in consequence of the advance of Jackson's forces, who were reported to be marching not only upon Culpeper, but on Madison Court-House.

In consequence of these movements of the Rebels, General Pope considered it advisable to concentrate his entire force near Culpeper, and to push forward Crawford's brigade of Banks's corps in the direction of Cedar Mountain,* as a support to General Bayard, who was falling back in that direction. At the same time a force was so placed that, if necessary, it could protect Madison Court-House.

Owing to a misunderstanding of the order he received, General Sigel did not arrive at Culpeper Court-House until several hours after the time that he should have reached that point. Consequently, on the morning of the ninth, General Pope was compelled to direct Banks to move forward to Cedar Mountain with his whole corps, and there join Crawford's brigade, instead of ordering Sigel's corps to the front, as he had intended.

General Jackson moved forward from Gordonsville shortly before dawn on the morning of Friday, the eighth. About

---

* This mountain, which is a "sugar-loaf" eminence, is sometimes called Slaughter Mountain, it being the property of the Rev. D. F. Slaughter.

noon his cavalry came into contact with those of General Bayard, and after a short engagement drove them back. The Confederate troops encamped for the night at a place called Garnett's Farm. Early on the morning of the ninth, they again took up their line of march, and during the morning found the Federal cavalry drawn up in line of battle to receive them. After waiting some time to find out their intentions, General Ewell ordered his artillery to fire upon them, which had the effect of compelling them to seek the cover of the woods. Jackson's infantry then advanced, and during the afternoon his force took up a strong position upon the side of Cedar Mountain.

In the mean time, General Banks's corps moved steadily forward, under a blazing sun and over dusty roads which led toward the mountain. Four or five miles south of Culpeper this mountain was seen rising directly in front of the advancing army, although it was still about five miles distant. The road led almost up to the left of the mountain, and then took a sudden curve and wound around to its right. General Banks formed his troops in line of battle in an open meadow lying between the mountain and the road. This was accomplished at half-past four P.M., when General Banks sent word to his superior officer that he hardly expected an engagement to take place that day. His courier had, however, but just started when firing was heard upon the left of his line, and in a few moments a perfect stream of flame belched forth from the mountain, extending from the extreme left to the right wing. The engagement commenced about five o'clock, and the firing did not finally terminate until past midnight.

On Jackson's side a part of Ewell's division led in the attack, and was afterward reënforced by a portion of A. P. Hill's division, the whole numbering about fifteen thousand. Banks's corps, which comprised the entire of the Federal force brought into action, did not number more than eight thousand. Early in the battle, Ewell's troops were in danger of being flanked, and were compelled to fall back, disputing every inch of ground and losing a number of prisoners. They were, however, immediately reënforced, when a most desperate hand-to-hand encounter took place. Jackson's troops charged upon the Federals with great valor, and were bravely met. Bayonets locked and sabres crossed, and each man fought as if the fortunes of the field depended on himself alone. And when the bayonet failed to do its work, or was broken or lost, the contest was continued with clubbed guns, until the Federals were compelled to seek refuge in flight. Here the loss on both sides was terrible, and here fell some of the best and bravest officers of the Southern army. But their comrades pressed forward over their dead bodies, and finally gained a complete but a dear-bought victory, in which they not only released their companions who had been captured in the early part of the fight, but captured a number of the Federals in return.

The losses which many of the Federal regiments sustained in this engagement were extremely severe, some of them retiring from the field of battle with barely half their numbers, whilst others, at the termination of the encounter, had almost ceased to have an existence. The manner in which General Banks handled the small force at his command is worthy of the highest commendation. There can be little doubt but that had he been properly supported, and promptly reënforced by even a portion of the large number of troops who were within a short distance of the battle-field, the tide of victory would have been turned. There was evidently great culpability in some quarter, but it is difficult to define on whose shoulders the blame must rest. The division of General Ricketts remained three hours within sound of the battle, but did not move an inch; not, however, because that General did not desire to take part in the engagement, but because he was under the curb of a superior officer, and that officer still awaiting the orders of his superior. General Ricketts, as well as other Generals within call, would gladly have been in the thickest of the fight, but having been officers in the regular army they were too much accustomed to its regular discipline to march to the relief of General Banks without orders. General Pope eventually led Ricketts's division to Banks's assistance, and also pushed Sigel's corps, which had begun to arrive, to the front, but when these movements took place the evening was so far advanced that they failed to regain the ground which had been lost and to change the fortunes of the day

During the engagement, General Banks had a narrow escape with his life, from a shell which exploded in the midst of his body-guard and killed six of them. Generals Pope and McDowell had also at a later period an equally narrow escape of being either killed or captured. Shortly after mid-night they had dismounted in the front to rest a few minutes from the saddle, when Jackson's cavalry made so sudden a dash upon them that they had barely time to mount and ride rapidly away. In so doing they were mistaken by a company of their own men for charging rebel cavalry, and received their fire, which fortunately only killed some of their horses.

General Jackson's official report of the battle of Cedar Mountain is here given, as it illustrates the character of the man. It is remarkable for its brevity. He had invariably little to say in reference to his own achievements, and pre-ferred to be judged by his actions rather than by his words.

HEADQUARTERS VALLEY DISTRICT,
August 12—6½ P.M.

COLONEL: On the evening of the ninth instant, God blessed our arms with another victory. The battle was near Cedar Run, about six miles from Culpeper Court-House. The enemy, according to the statement of prisoners, con-sisted of Banks's, McDowell's, and Sigel's commands. We have over four hundred prisoners, including Brig.-General Prince. While our list of killed is less than that of the ene-my, yet we have to mourn the loss of some of our best officers and men. Brig.-General Charles S. Winder was mortally wounded while ably discharging his duty at the head of his command, which was the advance of the left wing of the army. We have collected about one thousand five hundred small arms, and other ordnance-stores.

I am, Colonel, your obedient servant,

T. J. JACKSON, Major-General.

Col. R. H. CHILTON, A.A.G.

The Federal loss in the battle was about one thousand eight hundred in killed, wounded, and prisoners, besides which fully one thousand men straggled back to Culpeper Court-House and beyond, and never entirely returned to their commands. The Confederates, according to their own reports, did not suffer a loss of much over seven hundred in killed and wounded. The advantageous position which the latter occupied during the battle naturally sheltered them from the Federal fire.

At daybreak on the morning of the tenth, Jackson's sharp-shooters were found to occupy the same spot which had been their front at the close of the battle. Several skirmishes and slight engagements took place in the course of the morning, but the battle was not renewed, and in the afternoon Jackson retired from the position which he held. Early on the following morning he retired to the south of the Rapidan, to which river he was followed by a cavalry and artillery force under General Buford. Though Jackson had only fifteen thousand engaged in the action, the entire force he had then under his command, and the remainder of whom came up during the night, was from fifty to sixty thousand.

The seat of war in Virginia was now to revert to the old field of operations in the vicinity of Washington. Not only was General McClellan's army transported, in the middle of August, from the James River to Alexandria and Acquia Creek on the banks of the Potomac, but General Burnside had earlier in the month.reached Falmouth on the Rappahannock with a considerable force, with which he had been successfully operating in North-Carolina. These changes naturally relieved the main Confederate army from the necessity of closely watching over and protecting the Confederate capital. Consequently, Lee and Longstreet, and other rebel leaders, moved northward to assist Jackson, and Ewell, and Hill, in their proceedings against General Pope. And Gen. Pope, on the other hand, had his army increased by considerable detachments from the commands of McClellan and Burnside.

After the battle of Cedar Mountain, Jackson fell back to the south of the Rapidan, with the view of moving westward and outflanking Pope on his right; whilst he resigned the front to Generals Lee and Longstreet, who were rapidly approaching from Richmond. Pope being reënforced by a portion of Burnside's forces under General Reno, again moved forward to the Rapidan, and took up a strong position on that river. He, however, became convinced by the eighteenth of August that he was about to be confronted by the main Confederate army, and feared that he might be attacked by overwhelming numbers before he could be reënforced by any portion of the army of the Potomac. He therefore retired from the line of the Rapidan, and fell back to the Rappahannock, the entire army safely crossing the latter river on the eighteenth and nineteenth. The troops of Jackson, followed by those of Lee and Longstreet, advanced in close proximity to the Federals, as the latter retired. On the twentieth, and two following days, the Rebels made efforts to cross the river at various points, but were unable to effect their purpose from the rapid and continuous artillery fire with which they were opposed. The Rebels now moved slowly up the river for the purpose of turning Pope's right, whilst the latter being required to keep himself in communication with Fredericksburgh, was unable to extend his lines farther westward. During the night of the twenty-second, a dashing raid was made by a large force of Stuart's cavalry upon Catlett's Station, in the rear of the Federal army. They captured General Pope's private baggage, letters, official papers, and plans of his campaign, along with several prisoners, attacked a railroad train, and destroyed a number of army wagons filled with supplies.

General Pope determined on the twenty-second that on the following day he would recross the river, near Rappahannock Station, and fall furiously with his whole force upon the flank and rear of Lee's army, then moving toward his right. A heavy storm occurring that night, carried away all the bridges, and destroyed all the fords, and thus rendered the proposed attack impracticable.

The Confederate forces who at this time confronted General Pope on the Rappahannock, were those of Lee and Longstreet. To Jackson had been assigned another duty, and it was one for which he was especially fitted, from the rapidity with which he was ever able to move large masses of troops between distant points. The task which had been allotted to him was to move to the west of the Bull Run Mountains, and then crossing that range at Thoroughfare

Gap, march upon the rear of the Federal right, and fall upon their flank. Let us follow Jackson in this detour.

On the evening of the twenty-second, he bivouacked opposite Sulphur Springs, and threw over the river two brigades of Ewell's division. These brigades met with opposition from the Federals, and were withdrawn on the following night, after some sharp fighting.

On Monday morning, the twenty-fifth, Jackson was confronted at the same place by a heavy Federal force, and some firing took place, but without much loss having been sustained therefrom. That evening Jackson's whole force moved up to Jefferson, in Culpeper County, whence it marched through Amosville, in Rappahannock County, and then still farther up the river. The Federals appeared to have been unaware of this movement, as Longstreet remained for some time on the Rappahannock, in the neighborhood of Sulphur Springs, and covered the commencement of Jackson's march. The latter crossed the river within ten miles of the Blue Ridge, and then marched across open fields, by strange country paths and comfortable homesteads, passed the little town of Orleans, and reached Salem, on the Manassas Gap Railroad, about midnight. By day-dawn of Tuesday, his troops were again on the march, and proceeded along the Manassas Gap road to Thoroughfare Gap, in the Bull Run Mountains; thence to Gainesville, and on to Bristow Station, on the Orange and Alexandria Railroad, four miles south of Manassas Junction; thus accomplishing the march from Amosville, of about forty-eight miles, in the

same number of hours.   At Bristow he captured a railroad
train and several prisoners, and tore up the track.

On the twenty-seventh, Jackson moved up to Manassas
Junction, where he found an immense amount of stores of
every description, to which his troops freely helped themselves.   "It was a curious sight," writes one of his
soldiers, "to see our ragged and famished men helping
themselves to every imaginable article of luxury or necessity, whether of clothing, food, or what not.   For my part,
I got a tooth-brush, a box of candles, a quantity of lobster-
salad, a barrel of coffee, and other things which I forget.
. . . Our men had been living on roasted corn since
crossing the Rappahannock, and we had brought no wagons, so we could carry little away of the riches before us.
But the men could eat, for one meal at least.   So they were
marched up, and as much of every thing eatable served out
as they could carry.   To see a starving man eating lobster-
salad and drinking Rhine wine, bare-footed and in tatters,
was curious; the whole thing was incredible."

Jackson's situation was certainly now a very critical one,
for he had placed himself and his eighteen thousand jaded
men, who here comprised the entire number of his corps,
between Alexandria and Warrenton—between the forces of
McClellan at the former place and those of Pope at the
latter.

When General Pope learned that Jackson was approaching his rear by Thoroughfare Gap, he felt satisfied, from the
promise of reënforcements which he had received, that he

would be in a position to give battle to and defeat him before he could be joined by Longstreet, who was also making his way by the same route. General Pope assigned to his corps commanders certain positions which they should occupy to enable him to carry out his plan. The non-arrival of the reënforcements at the time promised, seriously interfered with the Federal General's arrangements, and the non-compliance of certain of his corps commanders with his instructions, he states, frustrated his plans, and enabled Jackson to reach Manassas without encountering any serious obstacle, beyond an engagement which took place between Ewell's division and that of General Hooker, at Kettle Run, upon the approach of the former toward Bristow Station.

Jackson being now separated from the main body of the Rebel army, General Pope was naturally anxious to prevent any junction of Longstreet's forces with his, and for this purpose he despatched Generals McDowell, Kearny, and Reno, to Gainesville and Greenwich, east of Thoroughfare Gap. These officers reached those points on the night of the twenty-seventh, and completely cut off Jackson from the main body of the Rebel army, that was still west of the Bull Run range. To enable General Pope to more thoroughly cover Washington, he found it necessary to break off his communication with Fredericksburgh, so that he could mass his forces in greater numbers in the district where danger was most imminent.

We have stated that General Jackson had placed himself

in a critical position, but if he had been aware of the weakness of the Federal line to the south of Manassas Junction, —a mistake which the commanding general has since sought to conceal by sacrificing General Porter—he might have inflicted a severe blow on the Federals in that quarter. General Pope, in his report, thus explains the position : " There were but two courses left open to Jackson, in consequence of this sudden and unexpected movement of the army. He could not retrace his steps through Gainesville, as it was occupied by McDowell, having at command a force equal, if not superior, to his own. He was either obliged, therefore, to retreat through Centreville, which would carry him still farther from the main body of Lee's army, or to mass his force, assault us at Bristow Station, and turn our right. He pursued the former course, and retired through Centreville. This mistake of Jackson's alone saved us from the serious consequences which would have followed this disobedience of orders on the part of General Porter."

During the early part of the night of the twenty-seventh, General Pope being satisfied of Jackson's position, sent orders to McDowell, Kearny, and Reno, to advance from Gainesville and Greenwich to Manassas Junction and Bristow. Kearny reached Bristow at eight o'clock the following morning, and was immediately pushed forward in pursuit of Jackson toward Manassas, followed by Hooker. Reno was at the time on the left, marching direct upon the Junction, but McDowell being delayed in his movement from Gainesville, enabled Jackson to retreat toward Cen-

7

treville, a performance which he hardly would have been able to accomplish, had McDowell arrived in time to intercept his crossing at Bull Run.

At night-fall on the twenty-seventh, Jackson set fire to the dépôt, store-houses, loaded trains, and other Government property at Manassas Junction, and as the conflagration had begun to subside, the Stonewall, or First division of his corps, moved off toward the battle-field of Manassas, and the other two divisions to Centreville, six miles distant. General Pope reached Manassas Junction, with Kearny's and Reno's troops, about mid-day of the twenty-eighth, less than an hour after Jackson in person had retired. These forces, along with those of Hooker, were sent in pursuit, and orders were forwarded to McDowell to change his march to the direction of Centreville. Late in the day, Jackson's rear-guard was driven out of Centreville, and the place occupied by Kearny. One part of Jackson's force now moved by Sudley Springs, and the other pursued the turnpike road toward Gainesville. King's division of McDowell's corps encountered the advance of Jackson's force about six o'clock in the evening, as it was making for Thoroughfare Gap. A severe action took place, which terminated at dark, each party maintaining his ground. Jackson had returned to within six miles of the Gap through which Longstreet must come, and whose arrival he anxiously longed for. General Pope now so arranged his forces that he felt satisfied there was no room left for Jackson's escape. McDowell, Sigel, and Reynolds, with twenty-five thousand men, were to the west, situated between him and his reënforcements; whilst twenty-five thousand more, under Kearny and other generals, approached him from the opposite side. With these forces, General Pope felt satisfied that he could crush Jackson before the latter could receive any aid from Longstreet. Unfortunately, however, General King, from some misapprehension, fell back to Manassas Junction, and left open the line of communication between the Rebel forces, which rendered new combinations of troops necessary on the part of the Federal commander.

The Federal plan now consisted in massing the entire force upon Jackson, and compelling him to fight. General Sigel commenced the attack about daylight on the morning of the twenty-ninth, a mile or two east of Groveton, near Bull Run, where he was soon joined by the divisions of Hooker and Kearny. Jackson fell back several miles, but was so closely pressed by these forces that he was compelled to make a stand and to offer the best defence possible. He accordingly took up a position with his left in the neighborhood of Sudley Springs, his right a little to the south of Warrenton turnpike, and his line covered by an old railroad grade which leads from Gainesville in the direction of Leesburgh. His batteries, which were numerous, and some of them of heavy calibre, were posted behind the ridges in the open ground on both sides of Warrenton turnpike, while the mass of his troops were sheltered in dense woods behind the railroad embankments.

The battle continued without intermission until mid-day, when both armies were considerably cut up from the sharp action in which they had been engaged. From twelve until four o'clock, severe skirmishing occurred constantly at various points of the line.

Heintzelman and Reno recommenced the attack about half-past five, as at that time information was received that McDowell was advancing to join the main body of the Federal army by the Sudley Springs road, and orders had been sent to Porter to push forward at once into action on the enemy's right. By this attack, the whole of Jackson's left was doubled back toward his centre, and the National troops, after a sharp conflict for an hour and a half, occupied the field of battle, with Jackson's dead and wounded in their hands. McDowell now arriving on the field, was immediately pushed to the front, along the Warrenton turnpike, with orders to fall upon Jackson, who was retreating toward the turnpike from the direction of Sudley Springs. This attack was made by King's division, about sunset; but by that time the advance of the main body of the Confederate army, under Longstreet, had begun to reach the field, and King encountered a stubborn and determined resistance at a point three quarters of a mile in front of the Federal line of battle. In the mean time, Heintzelman and Reno continued to push back Jackson's left in the direction of the turnpike, so that about eight o'clock they occupied the greater portion of the field of battle. General Pope remarks in his report that nothing was heard of Porter up to this time, and that his force took no part whatever in the action. He also gives it as his opinion that had he received Porter's assistance before the arrival of Longstreet, the larger portion of Jackson's force would have been utterly crushed or captured before sufficient reënforcements could have been received by him wherewith to make an effective resistance possible. The losses this day were extremely heavy on both sides.

During the night of the twenty-ninth, and up to ten o'clock on the morning of the thirtieth, there were numerous indications that the Confederates were retreating from the Federal front, and reconnoissances ascertained that they were retiring in the direction of Gainesville. The National troops were so exhausted from long fasting and hard fighting that their commander considered it indispensable that they should be reënforced; but the required reënforcements not being forthcoming, he determined that he would again give battle to the Rebels, and, if possible, so cripple them that they could make no farther advance toward the National capital. The force which General Pope had available for action upon this day was about forty thousand men, which number included seven thousand of Porter's corps. The remainder (five thousand) of the latter, had been despatched at daylight to Centreville, and were thus rendered unavailable for operations on that day. Banks's corps was at Bristow Station, guarding the railroad and wagon trains of the army.

The point at which our narrative now arrives is the com-

mencement of the second battle of Bull Run, which took
place close to the far-famed battle-field of that name. The
Confederates were posted with Longstreet on the right, and
Jackson on the left, and formed an obtuse angle. It was
presumed by this arrangement that if the Federals forced
either of the Confederate Generals back, their flank would
be exposed to the direct attack of the other. The Federal
left rested upon that portion of the Bull-Run battle-field,
which on the previous year was occupied by the main body
of the Rebel army. The line extended in the direction of
Manassas Junction. Though there were skirmishing and
some slight cannonading during the morning, the battle
did not begin until about one o'clock.

The Federals made the attack. General Pope found it
necessary to act promptly, as Jackson was continuing to be
rapidly reënforced by the main Rebel army, portions of
which had been arriving during the whole of the previous
night and throughout that morning. Pope was already confronted by greatly superior forces, and these forces were
every moment being largely increased by fresh arrivals.

Porter's corps and King's division were moved forward
to the attack upon the turnpike, and Heintzelman and Reno
were pushed to the right to attack Jackson's left in flank.
The Confederates massed their troops as fast as they arrived
on the field on their right, and quickly moved forward from
that direction to turn the Federal left. Ricketts's division
was immediately posted so that it could resist this movement. Porter's troops soon retired in considerable confu-

sion, but later in the day regained their lost laurels. This retrograde movement led the Rebels to advance to the assault, and the whole Federal line was soon furiously engaged. The main attack was on the left, but it was stubbornly resisted by Schenck, Milroy, Reynolds, and Ricketts. The battle raged furiously for several hours, the Confederates bringing up their heavy reserves, pouring mass after mass of troops upon the Federal left, and while overpowering it, assaulting the right with superior forces. Porter's troops were again sent into action on the left, where they rendered distinguished service, especially the brigade of regulars under Colonel Buchanan; but notwithstanding the utmost firmness and obstinacy of the National forces, the odds were too great for successful resistance, and they were ultimately compelled to retire.

At sunset the wings of the Confederate army swept round in pursuit—Jackson swinging his left on the right as a pivot, and Longstreet swinging his right on his left. But the Federals were enabled to retire in perfect order. Night closed the contest, and put a stop to the slaughter, which, as in the battle of the previous day, had been great in the extreme.

General Pope felt that he was no longer able to maintain his position so far to the front against such overwhelming numbers, and with such weakened and fatigued forces as those he commanded. He therefore determined to retire to Centreville, and the movement was made without any difficulty and without any pursuit being attempted by the

Rebels. General Banks was also ordered to retire from Bristow to Centreville, and to destroy such trains and stores as he could not carry with him.

The thirty-first of August was comparatively a quiet day. On the following morning, the Confederates moved heavy columns toward the Federal right, in the direction of Fairfax Court-House. In consequence of the great exhaustion of his men, General Pope desired to delay an engagement until the following day, but the Rebel movement became so developed by the afternoon of September the first, that it was evident it was made with a view of turning the Federal right, and cutting off the line of communications with Washington. This had to be resisted at all hazards. The necessary dispositions of troops were made to stop the Rebel progress, and a very severe action occurred at Chantilly, a place north of Centreville, and north-west of Fairfax Court-House, and about six miles distant from each. The engagement took place in the midst of a terrific thunder-storm. It was not terminated until after dark, when the Confederates were entirely driven back from the Federal front. This battle was especially unfortunate to the North, as it deprived it of the life of General Kearny, whose services on many fields had rendered his name distinguished.

The engagement at Chantilly closed the Confederate campaign against General Pope. It will be observed that throughout it General Jackson was given the most prominent place. The campaign was commenced by him alone ; and after he was joined by Lee and Longstreet, we find him invariably pushed forward as the pioneer during the remainder of its progress. The battle of Cedar Mountain was fought by him alone. In the battle of Groveton he had, unaided, to contend against a much superior force, and if it had not been for the fortunate arrival of Longstreet with fresh troops, there can be little doubt but that he would there have suffered a severe defeat. In the closing actions of the campaign he was joined by the main body of the Confederate army, and though the honor of the victory could not in them be entirely awarded to him, it is evident that no inconsiderable share thereof can be claimed on his behalf.

7

CHAPTER X.

THE INVASION OF MARYLAND.

The Federals retire within the Lines of Washington—Resignation of Pope —Appointment of McClellan — Jackson leads the Way into Maryland— Enters Frederick—Incidents during its Occupation—Lee's Proclamation —Jackson marches upon Harper's Ferry—Maryland Heights abandoned —Harper's Ferry bombarded—Its Surrender—Jackson's Report of the Capture—Federal Inquiry into the Cause of Surrender—Battle of South-Mountain—Battle of Antietam—The Battle-ground and Positions of the Combatants—Terrific Contest between Jackson and Hooker—Change in the Scene of Conflict—The Losses—Jackson demolishes Thirty Miles of Railroad—Affair at Blackford's Ford.

AFTER the battle of Chantilly, great changes again took place in the movements of the contending armies, and the Federal forces on the Potomac were again destined to be placed under the command of General McClellan.

On the second of September, the remnant of General Pope's army retired from Centreville, and moved within the lines of Washington, but not without suffering early on the morning of that day the loss of one hundred wagons filled with commissary stores, which were captured by the Rebels between Centreville and Fairfax Court-House, at that time the rear of the Federal army. On the same day General Pope desired to be relieved from his command. His resignation was accepted by the President, and General McClellan was at once appointed to the "command of the fortifications at Washington, and of all the troops for the defence of the capital."

The events of the past week rendered it advisable to concentrate the National forces as much as possible. Consequently, on the day after the second battle of Bull Run, General Burnside removed his stores from Fredericksburgh, evacuated the place, destroyed the bridges crossing the river, and retired with his forces to Acquia Creek, where he placed himself under the protection of the gunboats. Two days later, the Federal forces under General Julius White evacuated Winchester, and retired to Harper's Ferry.

Every preparation was made to resist a direct attack should it be made upon Washington by the Confederates, which it was naturally feared would result from the defeat of the Federal forces in front. The various garrisons were strengthened and put in order, and the troops were so disposed that they covered all the approaches to the city, and could be readily thrown upon threatened points. But it was no part of the plan of the Confederate General to hurl his forces against fortifications. He rather preferred to initiate a new era in the history of the war. The Confederate theory had thus far been that in battling against the Northern soldiers, who had marched in measured tread over Southern soil, they were acting strictly on the defensive, and merely desired to expel the "invader" from their land. This assumed defensive action was now to be changed into one of offence, and

for the first time during the Rebellion a Confederate army
was to plant its standard over Northern soil.

It was anticipated that if a strong Confederate force was
present in Maryland, there would be found in that State
"an uprising of the people" in favor of the South, which
would result in the secession of that State, and the severance of Washington from the loyal North.

The Confederates, having driven the Federal army under
cover of the guns which bristled on the hill-tops around
Washington, had no desire to spend their time in inactivity,
and the smoke which curled upward from the last hostile
gun was scarcely more rapidly cleared away from the sky
than were the numerous troops under the command of Lee
and his brother generals removed from the vicinage of the
National Capital. Jackson was again the pioneer and moved
forward on the march to Maryland on September the third.
He passed that night at Drainesville, and on the following
day reached Leesburgh, where he was joined by the corps
commanded by General D. H. Hill, and other troops. On
the fifth the Potomac was crossed by both Jackson's and
D. H. Hill's commands in the vicinity of the Point of Rocks,
and that day's march continued until past midnight, when
the troops bivouacked in the neighborhood of Buckeyestown.
At Monocacy Junction, near that place, the telegraph operator, who had failed to receive any notice of the rebel approach, was discovered by General Hill busily occupied in
despatching messages on the business of the railroad. The
General informed him that he was a prisoner, and desired

him to telegraph in his own name for a large train of cars to be sent immediately from Baltimore. On the operator stating that the wires had just been cut, he was desired, as a test, to despatch information that the Rebels had arrived, and had taken him prisoner. He repeated his statement, when one of Hill's men tried the instrument, and found it, as reported to be, not in working order.

The Rebel troops, after about two or three hours' rest, renewed their march before daybreak, and about ten o'clock Jackson's advance force entered Frederick, the capital of Maryland, their music, such as it was, playing "My Maryland" and "Dixie." This advance force consisted of about five thousand men, and their appearance was of so motley a nature that it was hardly likely to impress the people of Frederick in their favor. Their clothes, instead of being uniform were multiform, and as might naturally be expected from the rough usage their habiliments had been subject to, they were neither spotless nor perfect.

The reception was lacking that hearty welcome which they had calculated upon receiving. Though in some few instances outrages were committed against property, it must be admitted that every precaution was taken to prevent them. Guards were placed at the stores, and only a few men allowed to enter at a time. They usually paid for what they took away with such money as they possessed; but to use the expression of one of the citizens, the "notes depreciated the paper on which they were printed." It is true that in some of the most crowded stores, especially shoe-stores, articles would be smuggled away without payment, but these were exceptional cases. An attack was made by some of the soldiers on the *Examiner* printing-office, and the contents of the office thrown into the street. The Provost-Marshal, however, not only suppressed the riot and put the rioters in the guard-house, but he compelled them to return every thing belonging to the office.

On Sunday, the seventh, all the churches were opened as usual, and General Jackson attended the Presbyterian and German Reformed churches. At the latter place the minister, Dr. Zacharias, prayed for the President of the United States in a firm voice.

Confederate troops continued to arrive in Frederick, and enrollment offices were opened for the purpose of obtaining recruits for the Southern army. On Monday, General Lee issued a proclamation to the people of Maryland, in which he announced to them that he had entered that State for the purpose of restoring her to freedom, and of rescuing her citizens from the thraldom under which they had been placed by Northern bayonets, and giving them an opportunity freely to decide for themselves whether they would join the Southern Confederacy or not.

On Wednesday, the tenth, the Rebel army commenced to move away from Frederick, Jackson, as usual, leading the van. The object which was now to be attained was the capture of Harper's Ferry, with all the Federal forces and munitions of war there situated. It was most important to the Confederates that they should obtain possession of this stronghold. It was the key to the valley of the Shenandoah, and its occupancy would not only enable them to obtain their supplies by that direction, but it would open to them a road for retreat in the event of a retrograde movement becoming necessary.

It was considered advisable that the place should be approached and attacked from various points. General Walker's division proceeded by the Point of Rocks (destroying on its way the canal aqueduct at the mouth of the Monocacy) to Loudon Heights, separated from Harper's Ferry by the Shenandoah River. At the same time, the divisions of General McLaws and R. H. Anderson moved for Maryland Heights, which overlooked the place from the northern side of the Potomac. Whilst these Generals were marching to their respective positions, General Jackson made a detour for the purpose of attacking the stronghold from the south-west. He re-crossed the Potomac at Williamsport, and then marched upon Martinsburgh, twenty miles above Harper's Ferry. Upon his approach, three or four thousand Federal soldiers who were stationed at the last-named place, fell back and united with the forces at Harper's Ferry. Jackson pursued them, and on the morning of Saturday, the thirteenth, reached Halltown, four miles south-west of the Ferry. From this point he communicated with General Walker, who was already in possession of Loudon Heights, and with Generals McLaws and Anderson, to whom the heights on the Maryland side had been most unaccountably surrendered by the Federal officer in command, and directed them to open fire on the following (Sunday) morning, by which time he would have his guns in position. Maryland Heights had been attacked on that morning, and the position had been stoutly defended, but, about four o'clock in the afternoon, the Federal regiments retreated down the mountain in good order, having first spiked their guns, and then crossed the river to Harper's Ferry. No sooner had they retired than the Confederates occupied the heights above the guns, and deliberately commenced a musketry-fire upon the village below. However, a shell from one of the Federal batteries posted near the bridge soon dislodged them from this position. Colonel Ford, who commanded the Heights, was afterwards dismissed the Federal service for military incapacity and abandoning this position without sufficient cause.

Every thing was quiet within Harper's Ferry on Sunday morning. There was no enemy in sight, with the exception of Jackson's forces, who were in front. Every person expected to be awakened with the booming of artillery from the evacuated Heights, and the silence which reigned was not ominous of good. About noon, two companies of the Garibaldi Guard bravely ascended the Maryland Heights and secured some of their camp equipage, and brought down four of the pieces of artillery which had been left spiked the previous day. Hour after hour passed by, and no signs of the Rebels appearing on the heights, it began to be imagined that they had been foiled in their plans, and **that the** only force to contend with would be that in front.

Preparations, however, had been made to resist any assault, although it was evident that resistance would be useless, unless reënforcements could be received.

About two o'clock in the afternoon, the silence was broken by a furious fire which burst forth simultaneously on every side. Shot and shell flew in every direction, and the soldiers and citizens were compelled to seek refuge behind rocks and houses, and in every nook and corner which offered a friendly shelter against the unwelcome visitors. The Federal artillery replied with much spirit. Heavy cannonading was brought to bear upon them from five different points, yet they held their own manfully. However, before night closed the struggle, they had been compelled to contract their lines, and Jackson's forces occupied some intrenchments which the Federals had been compelled to desert on the hills of Bolivar. That night General Jackson sent a message to General Walker that his forces were in possession of the first line of the Federal intrenchments, and that, with God's blessing, he would have Harper's Ferry and the National forces early the next morning.

The fight was renewed the following (Monday) morning at five o'clock. The attack was obstinately resisted until about eight o'clock, when the ammunition of the Federals gave out, and it was deemed impossible for them to hold out any longer. A council of war was immediately held, when it was decided, but not unanimously, that the place should be surrendered. White flags were run up in every direction, and a flag of truce was sent to inquire on what conditions a surrender would be accepted. General Jackson demanded an unconditional surrender; but he eventually agreed that the officers should be allowed to go out with their side arms and private effects and the rank and file with every thing except arms and equipments.

A murmur of disapprobation ran along the entire Federal line, when it became known that the place had been surrendered. Officers exhibited strong demonstrations of grief, while the soldiers were equally demonstrative in their manifestations of rage.

As soon as the terms of surrender were completed, Generals Jackson and A. P. Hill rode into the town, accompanied by their respective staffs. General Hill immediately selected his headquarters, whilst General Jackson rode down to the river, and then returned to Bolivar Heights, the observed of all observers. He was dressed in the coarsest description of homespun, which bore every mark of having seen much service. An old hat which covered his head harmonized with the rest of his attire—in fact, in his general appearance he was hardly to be distinguished from the rough-looking but hardy fellows who called him their commander.

As soon as Jackson returned from the village the entire Federal force was mustered on Bolivar Heights, preparatory to stacking arms and completing the surrender. All the cavalry, about two thousand, under the command of Colonel Davis, had cut their way out on Sunday night, and had proceeded along the road to Sharpsburgh, capturing an ammunition train, belonging to General Longstreet, and several Rebel prisoners by the way. The number of men, guns, stores, wagons, etc., captured are given in General Jackson's Report, which we here append:

HEADQUARTERS VALLEY DISTRICT,
September 16, 1862.

COLONEL: Yesterday God crowned our arms with another brilliant success on the surrender at Harper's Ferry of Brigadier-General White and eleven thousand troops, an equal number of small arms, seventy-three pieces of artillery, and about two hundred wagons. In addition to other stores, there is a large amount of camp and garrison equipage. Our loss was very small. The meritorious conduct of both officers and men will be mentioned in a more extended report.

I am, Colonel, your obedient servant,

T. J. JACKSON, Major-General.

Colonel R. H. CHILTON, Assistant Adjutant-General.

The officer in command of Harper's Ferry, at the time of its surrender, was Colonel D. S. Miles, and the surrender was the subject of a court of inquiry. General Julius White, who was present at the time, had merely taken refuge there on the retirement of his forces from Winchester and Martinsburgh. Throughout the attack he acted with decided capability and courage, and on Sunday led his troops against Jackson on Bolivar Heights. During the siege he assumed a subordinate position, and at the close of the engagement he was sent by Colonel Miles to arrange terms for a surrender. The Confederates did not cease firing for more than half an hour after the white flag had been raised, during which time Colonel Miles was mortally wounded.

The court of inquiry, in pronouncing judgment upon Colonel Miles in reference to this surrender, says: "An officer who cannot appear before any earthly tribunal to answer or explain charges gravely affecting his character, who has met his death at the hands of the enemy, even upon the spot he disgracefully surrenders, is entitled to the tenderest care and most careful investigation. This the commission has accorded Colonel Miles, and, in giving a decision, only repeats what runs through over nine hundred pages of testimony, entirely unanimous upon the fact that Colonel Miles's incapacity, amounting almost to imbecility, led to the shameful surrender of this important post." Re-enforcements were but a few miles distant at the time of the surrender, but the Court was of opinion that sufficient alacrity had not been displayed in forwarding them to the relief of the beleaguered place. It remarked *inter alia:* "Had the garrison been slower to surrender, or the army of the Potomac swifter to march, the enemy would have been forced to raise the siege, or would have been taken in detail, with the Potomac dividing his force."

During the occurrence of the events which we have thus far narrated in this chapter, there was great activity in the Federal camp. The disappearance of Lee's army from the front at Washington, and its passage into Maryland, enlarged the sphere of McClellan's operations, and made an active campaign necessary to cover Baltimore, prevent the invasion of Pennsylvania, and drive the Rebels out of Maryland.

The advance of the Federal army under General Burnside entered Frederick on September the twelfth. While at Frederick, on the following day, General McClellan considered it was necessary to force the passage of the South-Mountain range, and by that route afford relief to Harper's Ferry, the siege of which he had been already made acquainted with. The two armies came into collision, at Crampton's and Turner's Passes, on the South-Mountain range, on Sunday, the day upon which the bombardment of Harper's Ferry was commenced. The action resulted in the two Passes being carried, and in important military positions being gained by the Federal army.

On the day after this engagement General Lee's army fell back toward Antietam Creek, situated from six to eight miles west of the South-Mountain range, and running for some distance almost parallel thereto. This creek, from which the battle we are now about to chronicle derives its name, rises in Central Pennsylvania, and after running in a southerly direction, mingles its waters with those of the Potomac, about five miles above Harper's Ferry. This battle is called by the Confederates Sharpsburgh, such being the name of the town in the vicinity of which it was fought. In this new position Lee was enabled to resist any attack upon him, and to cover the Shepherdstown Ford on the

Potomac, by which he would be enabled to form a junction with Jackson at Harper's Ferry.

On the fifteenth McClellan pushed his army forward to Antietam Creek, in the hopes of coming up with Lee during the day in sufficient force to beat him again and drive him into the river. But the day was too far advanced before he had an opportunity of making an attack. On the following morning he found that the Confederates had slightly changed their line, and were posted on the heights near Antietam Creek.

Before the prisoners taken by Jackson at Harper's Ferry could be paroled, that General found it necessary to leave suddenly with twenty thousand troops for the reënforcement of Lee, leaving A. P. Hill with his division in command of the captured city. General Ewell having been severely wounded at the battle of Groveton, and amputation of the leg rendered necessary, his division was commanded by General Lawton. The Stonewall division was commanded by General Stark, its previous chief, General Taliaferro, having also been severely wounded in the same battle.

Let us describe the field upon which the approaching battle was to be fought, and the positions of the combatants at the commencement of the struggle.

The Confederate line was drawn up upon the right or western bank of Antietam Creek, upon a small peninsula formed by the waters of that creek and the Potomac, which river is the western and southern boundary. Their left and centre were upon and in front of the road from Sharpsburgh to Hagerstown, and were protected by woods and irregularities of the ground. Their extreme left rested upon a wooded eminence near the cross-roads to the north of Miller's farm, the distance at this point between the road and the Potomac, which makes here a great bend to the east, being about three fourths of a mile. Their right rested on the hills to the right of Sharpsburgh, near Snavely's farm, covering the crossing of the Antietam and the approaches to the town from the south-east. The ground from their immediate front to the Antietam is undulating. Hills intervene, whose crests in general are commanded by the crests of others in their rear. The position was favorably located for both offensive and defensive operations, and occupied a range of hills forming a semi-circle, with the concave toward the National army. The arrangement of the line was as follows: General Jackson on the extreme left, General Longstreet in the centre, and General D. H. Hill on the extreme right.

The Federals occupied a position on the opposite or eastern bank of Antietam Creek, in close proximity to the road leading from Boonsboro to Sharpsburgh, having the creek in front, and the Elk Mountain range in their rear. The position was much less commanding than that held by the Confederates; the extreme right, however, rested upon a height commanding the extreme Confederate left. The forces on the extreme right were commanded by General Hooker, (supported by General Mansfield,) and those on the

extreme left by General Burnside.   The centre was occupied
by the corps of Generals Sumner, Franklin, and Fitz-John
Porter whose forces were held in reserve, so that, if necessary, they could render assistance to either the right or left
wing, on whichever the force of battle might fall.   Unsupported, attack in front was impossible.   McClellan's forces
lay behind low, disconnected ridges, in front of the Rebel
summits, all or nearly all being unwooded.   They gave,
however, some cover for artillery, and guns were therefore
massed on the centre.   The lines stretched four miles from
right to left.

It will thus be seen that Jackson and Hooker were placed
in antagonistic positions to each other at one end of the
lines, and Burnside and D. H. Hill confronted each other at
the other end.   In the centre, Longstreet faced Sumner,
Franklin, and Porter.

The numbers of the men actually brought into action with
each other were about one hundred thousand in each army,
and one hundred guns on each side belched forth their deadly
missiles.

The battle commenced on the afternoon of the sixteenth
by Hooker's corps, consisting of Ricketts's and Doubleday's
divisions, and the Pennsylvania reserves, under General
Meade.   They were sent across the creek by a ford and
bridge to the right of Kedysville, with orders to attack, and
if possible to turn the Rebel left.   General Mansfield's corps
was sent in the evening to support Hooker.   Placed in position, Meade's division, the Pennsylvania reserves, which

was at the head of Hooker's corps, became engaged in a sharp contest with the enemy, which lasted until after dark, at which time it had succeeded in driving in a portion of the opposing line, and held the ground.

The sun of September the seventeenth rose upon a bright, but a blood-stained day. With its earliest light, the contest was opened between Hooker and Jackson. Between six and seven o'clock the Federals advanced a large body of skirmishers, and shortly after the main body of Hooker's corps was hurled against the division of General Lawton. When we consider that Jackson and Hooker were the two Generals who in this portion of the battle-field were pitted against each other, it is almost useless to say that the contest was severe, and that the fortunes of the day were varying. Now an advance, and then a repulse. Then again another advance, to be followed by another repulse. Words like these, with the addition of phrases referring to the receipt of reënforcements, are almost sufficient with which to write the history of this encounter. If one was for a time driven back, it was but for a time. With increased energy, he not only gained his lost ground, but drove back his foe in return.

Hooker's attack was successful for a time, but masses of Rebels having been thrown upon him, his progress was checked. So severe was the clash of arms at one time, that upon his troops closing up their shattered lines, there was a regiment where a brigade had been, and hardly a brigade where a whole division had been victorious. When Mans-

8

field brought up his corps to Hooker's support, the two corps drove the Confederates back—the gallant and distinguished veteran Mansfield losing his life in the effort. About the same time, General Hooker was wounded and had to leave the field. The command devolved on Sumner, whose corps had come up to the Federal relief. The firing was now fearful and incessant. At one period when the Federals had obtained a position which enabled them to pour a flanking fire upon their foes, General Stark, who commanded the Stonewall division, galloped to the front of his brigade, and seizing the standard, rallied his men. This gallant act cost him his life, for, as he threw himself in the van, four bullets pierced his body, and he fell dead upon the field. The effect, instead of discouraging the soldiers, fired them with determination and revenge, and caused them to dash forward, drive back the Federals, and regain a position which they kept during the rest of the day.

Two divisions of Franklin's corps were, during the afternoon, added to the strength of the Federal right, where the condition of things was not particularly promising, notwithstanding the success which had been wrested from the Rebels by the stubborn bravery of the troops. Sumner's, Hooker's, and Mansfield's corps had lost heavily, and several general officers had been carried from the field. Some of the best of the Federal troops had been concentrated upon the single effort to turn Jackson's forces on the Rebel left, with whom, as we have stated, the tide of battle ebbed and flowed alternately. His men fought desperately—perhaps as they never fought before. Whole brigades were swept away before the fiery storm, and the ground was covered with the wounded and the dead. At one time, Ewell's old division, overpowered by superior numbers, fell back. Being supported by other troops, who rushed into the gap and retrieved the loss, Ewell's men returned to the fight, added their weight to that of their enthusiastic comrades, and in turn drove back the Federals. About the time when General Stark was killed, Lee ordered to the support of Jackson, McLaws's division, which had been held in reserve. It came most opportunely. Jackson's men had fought until not they alone, but their ammunition also, was well nigh exhausted, and discomfiture stared them in the face. Encouraged by the assistance of fresh troops, every man rallied and fought with redoubled vigor. They swept on like a wave—its billows rolling thick and fast upon the columns that had so stubbornly forced their way to the position on which the Rebels had originally commenced the battle—and regained the greater part of the ground which they had originally lost.

The fighting in this part of the field had been for many hours so excessive that the combatants were too exhausted to continue the strife. The contest here closed with scarcely any advantage being derived by either side. Some corn-fields and woods, the occupation of which had been hotly contested during the day, were at its close held by the Federals, who took possession of the ghastly harvest which had been reaped, and which was strewn upon the ground.

The brunt of battle was now transferred to the opposite wings, commanded respectively by Burnside and D. H. Hill. As Jackson took no part therein, we will only briefly describe this section of the battle. To Burnside had been intrusted the difficult task of carrying the bridge near Rohrback's farm and assaulting the Rebel right. He received his instructions at ten o'clock in the morning, but up to three o'clock he had made little progress, beyond having successfully carried the bridge. At the last-named hour he advanced, and drove the Rebels before him nearly as far as Sharpsburgh. At this point the latter were reënforced by A. P. Hill, who opportunely arrived with the force that Jackson had left behind at Harper's Ferry, and Burnside was compelled to fall back. The fighting in this part of the field was almost entirely between artillery.

As the day was drawing to a close, McClellan was hastening from the centre to the left. He was met by a courier from Burnside, with the message : "I want troops and guns. If you do not send them I cannot hold my position for half an hour." Porter's corps was the only one in reserve left to the army, and it would have been dangerous to have sent it to Burnside's relief. McClellan glanced at the western sky, and then said slowly : "Tell General Burnside this is the battle of the war. He must hold his ground till dark at any cost. I will send him Miller's battery. I can do nothing more. I have no infantry." When the messenger was riding away, he called him back. " Tell him if he *cannot* hold his ground, then the bridge to the last man! always the bridge! If the bridge is lost, all is lost."

As the light faded the cannonade died away, and before it was quite dark the battle was over. After fourteen hours of hard fighting, all that the Federals had been enabled to accomplish was to turn the Rebel line on one flank, and secure a footing within it on the other. Both armies slept on their arms. Both commanders expected that the battle would be renewed on the following day, but neither was willing to commence the attack. So exhausted were their troops, that both felt glad to be able to escape a continuance of the contest. Upon the eighteenth General McClellan gave orders for a renewal of the attack at daylight on the following morning, but during that night the Confederate army was moved to the Virginia shore of the Potomac, and morning found a wide river separating the contending forces.

The Federal loss in the battle of South-Mountain was four hundred and forty-three killed, and one thousand eight hundred and six wounded; and in the battle of Antietam two thousand and ten killed, nine thousand four hundred and sixteen wounded, and one thousand and forty-three missing; making a total loss, in the two battles, of fourteen thousand seven hundred and ninety-four. We have no data from which to state the actual Confederate loss, but from the number of their dead who were left upon the field and were buried by the Federals, it was without doubt considerably greater than that of the National army.

Thirteen guns and thirty-nine colors, more than fifteen thousand stand of small arms, and upward of six thousand prisoners, were the trophies obtained by the Federals.

The battle of Antietam was an unfinished one, consequently it was not a decisive one. It can hardly be claimed as a great victory if we are to judge of it by the results. It is true, however, that the Federals gained a little in the matter of space, and held at the close some important positions, which the Rebels had occupied at the beginning of the day. The losses which took place were of more serious import to the Rebels than they were to the Federals, as any reënforcements which the former could receive were too far away to be immediately available, whilst those of the latter were within reach. This doubtless led Lee to avoid risking another engagement, and to adopt the only course left open to him to ward it off—remove his army beyond the borders of Maryland.

To throw every obstacle in the way of the Federal army was naturally the desire of the Confederates. In this Jackson was remarkably prominent. Almost within gun-shot of McClellan's army, with a force not exceeding seven thousand, he destroyed thirty miles of the Baltimore and Ohio Railroad track, from seven miles west of Harper's Ferry to the North Mountain. He actually obliterated the road, so that when the road-masters with their gangs went to work to restore it, it was only by the charred and twisted *debris* that the track could be traced. Every tie was burned, every rail bent—nothing remained to be done but to cart off the bare ballast. The General took off his coat, and, with a cross-tie for a fulcrum and a rail for a lever, helped to demolish the " permanent way," and with his own hands he assisted in bending the heated rails around the trunks of trees. When all this rail-stripping and burning and twisting was done, Jackson walked over the whole thirty miles of his work to see that it was done thoroughly. He looked upon that road with the eye of a military genius, well aware of its great importance as a military thorough-fare. The prominent part it must play in the warlike machinery of the Government was plain to him; therefore he took the greater pains to destroy it totally.

A week after the battle of Antietam, General McClellan caused a reconnoissance to be made on the Virginia side of the Potomac, in the neighborhood of Shepherdstown, so that information might be obtained of the Rebel position and force in that vicinity. The troops, consisting of a brigade, with a portion of three regiments, and a battery, had their crossing at Blackford's Ford disputed by a few field-pieces. These were soon silenced, and the gunners took to flight, after which no enemy was visible. When the Federals were fairly landed, Jackson suddenly appeared in large force from ambush in the adjoining woods and opened upon them with shot and shell. The numbers were so unequal that although the Federals at first stood their ground, they were eventually compelled to retreat hastily, and recross the river under the Rebel fire. In this unfortunate affair the Federal killed, wounded, and missing numbered three hundred and twenty-six out of a force of about seventeen hundred.

The Confederates did not tarry many days upon the banks of the Potomac. After holding Harper's Ferry for less than a week they evacuated it, having first removed much of the property which they had captured, and destroyed some of the public buildings. They then retreated up the valley of the Shenandoah, from which they proceeded by the mountain passes into Eastern Virginia, where they once more took up their position on the banks of the Rappahannock.

CHAPTER XI.

THE BATTLE OF FREDERICKSBURGH.

Jackson's Antagonists—Burnside supersedes McClellan—The Army of the Potomac marches to the Rappahannock—The Battle-Ground—The Federals cross the River—Positions of the two Commanders—Advance of Franklin—Heroism of a Confederate Officer—Opening of the Battle—Sublimity of the Scene—Attack on the Fortifications—The Field of Death—The Combat described—Reserves brought into Action—The Losses—Councils of War—The River recrossed.

It was Jackson's fortune, during his short but brilliant military career, to have crossed swords with some of the best and bravest of the Federal Generals. Thus far in our narrative we have found him opposed by Lander, on the Upper Potomac; by McDowell at Bull Run; by Shields, and Banks, and Fremont in the Virginian Valley; by Porter and Heintzelman, with McClellan as their chief, in the eventful conflicts near Richmond; by Pope, from the Rapidan to the lines of Washington; and by Hooker and Sumner, with McClellan again as chief, at the battle of Antietam. The remainder of his career we shall find passed upon a still different field, on which his might and military genius were resisted by still different Generals.

On the fifth of November the army of the Potomac was subject to a change of commanders. It was on that day

8*

ordered, by direction of the President, "that Major-General McClellan be relieved from the command of the army of the Potomac, and that Major-General Burnside take the command of that army."

This army had remained in the neighborhood of Harper's Ferry until near the end of October, when it commenced its march by the upper gaps of the Blue Ridge to Warrenton. After Burnside took command, it removed from the latter place to Falmouth, on the northern bank of the Rappahannock, by which river it is separated from the town of Fredericksburgh. On the twenty-first of November, General Sumner, who commanded the advance, demanded the surrender of the last-named town, but his request was not complied with.

It was General Burnside's intention to have crossed the Rappahannock at once, and taken possession of the heights above Fredericksburgh before General Lee was able either to concentrate his forces there or to fortify the position. The delay in the arrival of pontoon-bridges beyond the time anticipated compelled General Burnside to postpone active operations, and gave the Confederates sufficient time to gather together their army and erect fortifications.

After nearly a month of preparation, the Federal commander felt himself in a position to cross the river on the eleventh of December. At this date, General Lee, being deceived in the point where the river would be crossed, had rapidly despatched Jackson with a large portion of the army to a spot fifteen or twenty miles down the river, and D. H.

Hill with another portion of it in the opposite direction, in anticipation of the Federals crossing at one or other of those neighborhoods. Finding the Confederate forces thus divided, General Burnside hoped that by rapidly throwing over the whole of his command close to Fredericksburgh he would be enabled to fight the enemy in detail, and gain possession of the heights commanding the town. That this plan did not succeed is probably owing to the delay of a whole day in moving the army across the river, which delay was caused by the stubborn resistance of a brigade of Mississippi riflemen under General Barksdale, who thrice by their deadly fire compelled the Federals to abandon the attempt. This delay enabled Jackson and Hill to rapidly countermarch their forces and join the main army.

The battle of Fredericksburgh may be conveniently divided into two parts, in each of which the scene of action and the actors were distinct. It will render our narrative more intelligible to the reader if we lay before him separate descriptions of these two scenes of action, and of the combatants who met upon them.

The opposing armies that were to meet in deadly encounter were thus divided : General Burnside's army was divided into three grand divisions, under the respective commands of Generals Sumner, Franklin, and Hooker. General Lee's army was divided into two large *corps d'armée*, commanded respectively by Generals Longstreet and Jackson.

The theatre of operations extended from the town of

Fredericksburgh on the west, and along the south side of the Rappahannock for two miles to the east.

The stage on which the western battle was fought was immediately behind the town. Here the land forms a plateau, or smooth field, running back for about a third of a mile. It then rises for forty or fifty yards, forming a ridge of ground, which runs along to the east for about a quarter of a mile, where it abuts at Hazel Dell, a ravine formed by the Hazel River, which empties into the Rappahannock east of the town. At the foot of the ridge runs the telegraph-road, flanked by a stone wall. This eminence was studded with Rebel batteries. To the west, along up the river, the ridge prolongs itself to opposite Falmouth, and beyond ; and here, too, batteries were planted on every advantageous position. Back of the first ridge is another plateau, and then a second terrace of wooded hills, where a second line of fortifications were placed. Between the rear of the town and the first ridge a canal runs right and left, and empties into the river some distance above Falmouth. The plain between the suburbs of the city and the first ridge of hills was the scene of encounter between General Sumner's forces and those of General Longstreet. General Hooker's division, which had been held in reserve on the northern side of the river, reënforced Sumner toward the close of the day.

The eastern battle-field was a short distance down the river. The ridge upon which the town is built slopes abruptly in this direction to a comparatively level or undulating country, which stretches for some miles down the Rappahannock. This plain is bordered on the south by thickly wooded heights, situated about two miles from the river Upon these heights Rebel batteries were placed. The battle-ground, though very marshy in some places, presented a fine field for military evolutions. The turnpike leading to Fredericksburgh runs about half a mile from and nearly parallel to the river. Beyond is the railroad, and still farther beyond the woody range of hills in which the Rebels were strongly intrenched. On this battle-ground General Franklin was met by General Jackson. The latter's forces were thus placed: A. P. Hill on the left, and next to Longstreet's command; behind A. P. Hill, D. H. Hill was held in reserve. Ewell's division, now commanded by General Early, held the woody heights, with Walker's artillery in his front, and Stuart's cavalry and horse-artillery on his extreme right.

The Federal army had for some days been coiling itself up into a small space, and on the morning of Thursday, the eleventh of December, lay closely huddled together opposite to Fredericksburgh. Before daylight tents were struck and knapsacks packed, and the troops prepared to cross the river. The Rebels opened their fire upon the pontooners, and stoutly resisted the laying of the bridges. The firing was replied to by the Federals, who shelled the town for several hours. The Seventh Michigan regiment, who volunteered for the purpose, were sent across the river in boats to dislodge the Rebel sharp-shooters, who were picking off the bridge-builders. After several ineffectual attempts, the bridges were completed, and during Thursday night and throughout Friday the river was crossed by the Federal troops. The right grand division, under Sumner, crossed upon three pontoon-bridges, placed opposite the city, and the left grand division, under Franklin, upon two pontoon-bridges, placed about two miles down the stream. The centre grand division, under Hooker, comprising forty thousand men, was held in reserve upon the north bank of the river.

But little firing took place on Friday. Either General Lee wished to avoid damaging the town, which was at the time in possession of the Federals, or he was desirous of offering no further obstacle to the crossing, in the hopes that when he had got the Federal army between himself and the river, he would be enabled either to crush it or drive it into the stream. The Federals occupied the day in massing their troops, and in preparing for the coming struggle. Their siege-guns on the north side of the river at times fired upon the intrenchments of the Rebels, with the view of learning their position, but General Lee did not feel inclined to reply to the fiery interrogatories.

General Burnside's proposed plan of attack was that the battle should be opened by Franklin, who should advance and take possession of a road in the rear of the line of heights, which road formed a connecting link between Jackson's and Longstreet's commands. This position being gained, it was supposed that the Rebels would be so much confounded that Sumner could successfully storm and capture their intrenchments in the rear of Fredericksburgh. That this plan did not succeed, it is stated, is owing to Franklin having misunderstood his instructions, and having made the attack with an insufficient force.

Saturday the thirteenth dawned hazily, the fog being such as at that time of the year generally prefaces a genial Indian summer's day. The day was to become an eventful one in American history. The two great actors in the drama placed themselves in conspicuous positions to watch its progress. General Burnside took his stand at the Phillips House, situated on an eminence a little to the north of the town. General Lee took up his position upon a hill south-east of the heights which command Fredericksburgh, and which hill, from its having been his usual station, bore his name.

At half-past eight General Lee, accompanied by his full staff, rode slowly along the front of the Confederate lines, from left to right, and then took up his station for a time in the rear of Jackson's extreme right. As soon as Franklin's advance could be seen through the fog, General Stuart moved up a section of his horse-artillery in front of the position occupied by Lee, and opened with effect upon the Federal flank. Stuart ordered Major John Pelham, his chief of artillery, to advance one gun considerably nearer to Franklin, and to open upon him. Major Pelham obeyed, and opened the fire of a twelve-pounder Napoleon gun with great precision and deadly effect upon the Federal flank. The galling discharges of this gun quickly drew upon it the

fire of three of Franklin's field-batteries, while from across
the river two other heavy batteries joined in the strife, and
made Major Pelham and his gun their target. For hours
not less than thirty Federal cannon strove to silence Pelham's pop-gun, but strove in vain. Pelham's unyielding and
undemonstrative courage, and his composure under the deadliest fire, had long made him conspicuous, but never were
his daring qualities the subject of more glowing eulogy than
upon this occasion. General Lee exclaimed: "It is inspir-
iting to see such glorious courage in one so young." Major
Pelham was not more than twenty-two. General Jackson
remarked: "With a Pelham upon either flank, I could van-
quish the world."

At a subsequent period of the day, General Lee assumed
his station on the hill which bears his name, and there, in
company with General Longstreet, calmly watched the repulse of the Federal efforts against the heights near which
he stood. Occasionally General Jackson rode up to the
spot and mingled in conversation with the other two leading
Generals. Once General Longstreet exclaimed to him, "Are
you not scared by that file of Yankees you have before you
down there?" to which Jackson replied: "Wait till they
come a little nearer, and they shall either scare me or I'll
scare them."

The battle opened when the sun had let in enough light
through the mist to disclose the near proximity of the Federal lines and field-batteries. The first shot was fired shortly before ten o'clock from the batteries in the Federal centre,

and was directed against General Hood's division of Longstreet's corps, which division was drawn up immediately on
Jackson's left, and was next to the large division commanded by General A. P. Hill. The Pennsylvania reserves, commanded by General Meade, advanced boldly under a heavy
fire against the Confederates, who occupied one of the copse-
wood spurs, and were for a time permitted to hold it; but
presently the Confederate batteries opened on them, and a
determined charge of infantry drove the Federals out of the
wood in confusion, from which nothing could subsequently
rally them. Simultaneously a heavy fire issued from the
batteries of A. P. Hill and Early's divisions, which was
vigorously replied to by the Federal field-batteries. The
only advantage momentarily gained by Franklin in this
quarter, was on the occasion of the collapse of a regiment
of North-Carolina conscripts, who broke and ran, but whose
place was rapidly taken by more intrepid successors. The
cannonading then became general along the entire line.

A spectator of this part of the battle thus graphically
describes the conflict: "Such a scene, at once terrific and
sublime, mortal eye never rested on before, unless the bombardment of Sebastopol, by the combined batteries of
France and England, revealed a more fearful manifestation
of the hate and fury of man. The thundering, bellowing
roar of hundreds of pieces of artillery, the bright jets of
issuing flame, the screaming, hissing, whistling, shrieking
projectiles, the wreaths of smoke, as shell after shell burst
into the still air, the savage crash of round-shot among the

trees of the shattered forest, formed a scene likely to sink forever into the memory of all who witnessed it, but utterly defying verbal delineation. A direct and enfilading fire swept each battery upon either side, as it was unmasked; volley replied to volley, crash succeeded crash, until the eye lost all power of distinguishing the lines of combatants, and the plain seemed a lake of fire, a seething lake of molten lava, coursed over by incarnate fiends, drunk with fury and revenge."

Twice the Federals, gallantly led and handled by their officers, dashed against the forces of Generals A. P. Hill and Early, and twice they recoiled, broken and discomfited, and incapable of being again rallied to the fray. The Confederates drove them with horrid carnage across the plain, and only desisted from their work when they came under the fire of the Federal batteries across the river. Upon the extreme Confederate right, General Stuart's horse-artillery drove hotly upon the fugitives, and kept up the pursuit until after dark.

Upon the Confederate right, where the antagonists fought upon more equal terms than they did upon their left, the loss sustained by the Rebels was the greatest; but still it was not so great as that of their Federal assailants.

Meanwhile, the battle which had raged so furiously between the forces of Franklin and Jackson, was little more than child's play as compared with the onslaught made by Sumner and Hooker against Longstreet in the rear of Fredericksburgh.

During the first two hours of the conflict between Jackson and Franklin, Sumner's skirmishers had. been briskly engaged. The force in Fredericksburgh had driven the Rebels out of the suburbs of the town, and rested their columns on the canal. The time had now come, in accordance with the Federal plan, to attempt an advance on the Rebel position. It was mid-day. The orders were to move rapidly, charge up the hill, and take the batteries at the point of the bayonet. Orders easy to give, but ah! how hard of execution!

Here is a picture of the position which had to be stormed. A bare plateau of a third of a mile in width is required to be crossed by the storming party. In doing this they would be exposed to the fire of the enemy's sharp-shooters, posted behind a stone wall running along the base of the ridge; to the fire of a double row of rifle-pits on the rise of the crest; to the fire of the heavy batteries placed behind earthworks on the top of the hill; to the fire of a powerful infantry force lying concealed behind these batteries; to a plunging fire from the batteries on the lower range; and to a double enfilading fire from

"Cannon to the right of them, cannon to the left of them."

The distance to be traversed was short, but how many obstacles there were in the way of its being passed scathless!

To French's division of Couch's corps was assigned the duty of making the first attempt to cross this fiery plain. This division was composed of the brigades of Kimball,

Morris, and Weber. It was supported by Hancock's division, consisting of the brigades of Caldwell, Zook, and Meagher. The men were formed under cover of a small knoll in the rear of the town, and skirmishers were deployed to the left toward Hazel Dell. At the same time, General Sturgis supported and moved up and rested on a point on the railroad.

The scene which was witnessed when French's troops rushed upon this plateau was truly fearful. "The moment they exposed themselves upon the railroad," writes one who viewed the same, "forth burst the deadly hail. From the rifle-pits came the murderously-aimed missiles; from the batteries, tier above tier, on the terraces, shot planes of fire; from the enfilading cannon, distributed on the arc of a circle two miles in extent, came cross-showers of shot and shell.

"Imagine, if you can, for my resources are unequal to the task of telling you, the situation of that gallant but doomed division.

"Across the plain for a while they swept under this fatal fire. They were literally mowed down. The bursting shells make great gaps in their ranks; but these are presently filled by the 'closing up' of the line. For fifteen immortal minutes at least, they remain under this fiery surge. Onward they press, though their ranks grow fearfully thin. They have passed over a greater part of the interval, and have almost reached the base of the hill, when brigade after brigade of Rebels rise up on the crest and pour in fresh volleys of musketry at short-range. To those who, through the glass looked on, it was a perilous sight indeed. Flesh and blood could not endure it. They fell back shattered and broken, amid shouts and yells from the enemy.

"General French's division went into the fight six thousand strong; late at night he told me he could count but fifteen hundred!"

Again and again the Rebel battlements were attempted to be stormed, but each time with the same terrible result. "Where is Franklin?" began to be the eager inquiry. "Every thing depends on Franklin coming up on the flank." Sumner sent a message begging Burnside that Franklin be directed to advance. But Franklin could not advance. He had enough to do at the time to hold his own, for Jackson had thrown in reënforcements, and was pushing hard to turn his left.

At four o'clock the reserves had not been sent into action. Hooker's central grand division, comprising forty thousand men, were still on the north bank of the river. At Sumner's request, General Burnside directed them to cross, which they immediately did, notwithstanding the Rebel fire directed upon the pontoons. Half an hour afterwards, and prodigious volleys of musketry announced that Hooker with the reserves was engaged, but the last assaulting column had hardly got into action before the sun went down, and night closed around the clamorous wrath of the combatants.

The last assaulting column consisted of the divisions of Humphrey, Monk, Howard, Getty, and Sykes. The last assault is thus described by the writer from whom we last quoted : " Creeping up on the flank by the left, Getty's troops succeeded in gaining the stone wall which we had been unable all day to wrench from the Rebels. The other forces rushed for the crest. Our field-batteries, which, owing to the restricted space, had been of but little use all day, were brought vigorously into play. It was the fierce, passionate climax of the battle. From both sides two miles of batteries belched forth their fiery missiles athwart the dark background of the night. Volleys of musketry were poured forth such as we have no parallel of in all our experiences of the war, and which seemed as though all the demons of earth and air were contending together. Rushing up the crest, our troops had got within a stone's throw of the batteries, when the hill-top swarmed forth in new reënforcements of Rebel infantry, who, rushing upon our men, drove them back. The turn of a die decides such situations. The day was lost ! Our men retired. Immediately cannon and musketry ceased their roar, and in a moment the silence of death succeeded the stormy fury of ten hours' battle."

The morning had opened with a general want of confidence, and gloomy forebodings that the plan of battle was fraught with danger. It was difficult to comprehend that the Confederate fortifications could be successfully assailed from the front, and there were grave doubts as to whether the operations on the right and on the left could be made to harmonize. That these surmisings and these forebodings were not fallacious was evidenced by the result of the day's engagement. That the Federals suffered a severe defeat there need be no denial, and this too after they had brought the entire of their vast force into action, whilst their antagonists, from the impregnable position which they held, were enabled to repel their assault with half the number.

The Federal loss in the day's battles amounted to one thousand one hundred and fifty-two killed, between six and seven thousand wounded, and about seven hundred prisoners, which latter were paroled and exchanged for about the same number taken from the Confederates. The Confederate killed and wounded amounted to about eighteen hundred.

After the close of the engagement, councils of war were held at the headquarters of each army. At that called by General Burnside, and which was attended by Sumner, Hooker, and Franklin, the Commanding General proposed to renew the attack on the following morning, but he was induced to abandon his intentions at the earnest solicitations of his brother Generals. It is reported that during General Lee's council General Jackson slept throughout the proceedings, and that upon his being awakened and asked for his opinion, he curtly exclaimed: "Drive 'em in the river! drive 'em in the river!"

On the two days succeeding the battle (Sunday and Monday) the time was principally occupied in burying the dead and caring for the wounded. There was little to disturb the quiet of these bright and breezy days, beyond the sounds of musketry from some skirmishing parties, and a little artillery firing.

It now became palpable to the Federal Generals, in consequence of the little opposition which Lee had offered to the crossing of the river, that he had been desirous of getting them between his intrenchments and the Rappahannock, so that he could eventually crush them. It was now advisable to get out of the trap into which they had fallen; consequently, at a council of war held on Monday, it was unanimously agreed upon that the river be recrossed that night. This decision was not made known to the troops until after they had arranged their bivouacs in the evening. It was necessary that the withdrawal should be accomplished silently and rapidly, and that every precaution should be taken to avoid observation, and thus escape drawing the Confederate fire. Intense darkness and a heavy storm favored the Federal retreat. Earth was strewn on the pontoon-bridges, to deaden the sound of the artillery as it passed over; but this expedient was barely necessary, as a gale of wind, blowing all night from the direction of the Rebel camp toward the Federal lines, rendered it impossible for any sound to reach the former from the river.

When some time after midnight, the stars had made their appearance in the sky, and the moon had risen to shed her pale light on the earth, the army of the Potomac had crossed the river and was rescued from the annihilation which the Rebel Generals had prepared and predicted for it. General Lee was compelled to admit that the masterly retreat of his army across the Potomac, after the battle of Antietam, had been surpassed by this successful passage of the Federal force across the Rappahannock.

CHAPTER XII.

THE BATTLE OF CHANCELLORSVILLE.

Jackson created Lieutenant-General — Burnside's proposed Operations — Hooker placed in Command of the Army of the Potomac—Winter Quarters—Movements against Fredericksburgh—The Rappahannock crossed—Hooker reaches Chancellorsville — Description of the Place — Lee's and Jackson's Movements—Arrival at Chancellorsville—Jackson's Celebrated Attack upon the Federal Flank—Receives his Death-Wound—A Federal Officer's Interview with Jackson—Subsequent Engagements—Losses in the Battles—Lee's Estimate of Jackson's Abilities.

In every army promotion is sure to follow upon every successful display of military ability, unless the soldier who proves his claim to an increase of honor has already arrived at the highest rank in the service. In the Confederate army there were two degrees of rank superior to that which Jackson held at the battle of Fredericksburgh—Lieutenant-General and General. That battle gained him the first, death alone prevented him from obtaining the second. It was, therefore, under the dignified title of a Lieutenant-General that Jackson was known in the few remaining months of his short military career. It took but a year and a half for the man who, at the beginning of the rebellion was the Colonel of a Virginia regiment, to rise to the second rank in the army in which he served. But if promotion had been made

9

to keep pace with his increase of renown, we have no hesitation in stating that the highest rank was that to which he
was justly entitled.   We fancy that the reason why he did
not obtain the highest military title is attributable to the
misfortune of birth.   Had it been Jackson's lot to have been
a scion of one of the proud Virginian families, instead of a
humble son of the Old Dominion, there can be little doubt
but that the case would have been far different.   At any
rate, he had the proud satisfaction of knowing that what
honors he did receive were fairly earned by him, and that
the Government under which he served owed him more for
his services than he owed it for its honors.

Immediately after the battle of Fredericksburgh, General
Sigel hastened to reënforce Burnside with the corps under
his command, but no farther active operations were attempted until the close of the month.   General Burnside then
prepared for another aggressive movement which embraced
an attack in front of Fredericksburgh, and a formidable raid
of cavalry and light artillery, which was to threaten the
communications of the Confederates, and divert their attention from the main attack.   The execution of the movement
was fixed for the last day of the year.   The column destined to make the raid was actually in motion, when President Lincoln sent a despatch forbidding the movement, having been induced to do so in consequence of the protest of
some of General Burnside's subordinate officers.

By Wednesday the twenty-first of January, the Federal
commander was again prepared to move on Fredericks-

burgh. Every thing having been arranged, and the Rebels having been completely deceived by feints, as to the point at which the river was to be crossed, the army was put in motion on Tuesday, with the intention of commencing active operations early on Wednesday morning. However, a heavy rain-storm and a tempest of wind occurred during the night, and so moistened the roads as to render it impossible to move either pontoons or artillery with the celerity demand ed. This, added to the evident intentional delay of some of the superior officers in the marching of their troops, gave time to enable the Confederates to discover the Federal movement, and rally their forces to avert it. The moment for the surprise having thus passed, the movement was abandoned.

General Burnside having thus found himself thwarted in his operations by officers under his command, and feeling himself not properly supported by the Government, tendered his resignation, which was accepted, and on the twenty-sixth of January the command of the Army of the Potomac was transferred to General Hooker.

The snows and storms of winter were a barrier to any military operations during the next three months. The opposing armies took up their winter-quarters on opposite banks of the Rappahannock, and within sound of each other's bugles. At the close of April, when the snow had disappeared from the ground, and the winds of spring had somewhat hardened the roads, the bristling bayonet and the booming cannon were called on for more active duty than that which for the past few months they had been accustomed to perform.

General Hooker having massed what he termed "the finest army on the planet," commenced the offensive operations of the year by a flank movement upon Fredericksburgh, for which a portion of his army crossed the Rappahannock above that place, and gained a position in its rear distant ten miles west by south, whilst another portion crossed a short distance below the town, and menaced it from that quarter. But in this grand game of strategy he had to play with a formidable antagonist. If General Lee was at first nonplussed by Hooker's manœuvres, he was soon able to grasp the situation on the military chess-board, and make the move which was most likely to checkmate his opponent. He abandoned his position in Fredericksburgh and the line for twenty miles down the Rappahannock, which he had held for months, changed his front, and presented his face instead of his back to the Federal commander.

General Hooker had adjusted his plan of procedure by the middle of April, but the unsettled weather, which is not uncommon to that month, prevented its being put into operation until Sunday the twenty-sixth. He had, however, kept his own council, and even his corps commanders were unacquainted with the nature of the duties which they would be called on to perform. By Monday morning the entire army was in motion; the vast area which it covered for miles and miles in extent was an animated scene. Tents were struck, camps broken up, log huts abandoned, and their recent occupants moved away on a dozen different roads, carefully concealing themselves from the Confederate view by marching through woods and behind the knolls and ridges of the broken ground along the Rappahannock. Long trains of artillery, packed mules, and ambulances, intermingled with the moving throng, and added to the picturesqueness of the scene.

Shortly after Hooker took command, he abandoned the disposition of his army into grand divisions, and introduced the corps organization instead, and his army was now composed of seven *corps d'armée.*

By Tuesday morning some idea of his plan was discernible. Three of the seven *corps d'armée*—Reynolds's, Sickles's, and Sedgwick's—had left their camps the night before, and taken up their positions two miles below Fredericksburgh, at the point where Franklin crossed in December. The corps of Meade, Slocum, and Howard (formerly Sigel's) had already moved up the river, and on Tuesday were in the neighborhood of Banks's and United States Fords, respectively eight and eleven miles above Fredericksburgh. It seemed probable that operations would be inaugurated at the points above and below Fredericksburgh, though it was doubtful where the main attack would be made. By these movements Hooker had divided his army, and placed a space of a dozen miles between the two parts, which caused them to be out of supporting distance of each other. He doubtless intended to make a demonstration at one point, and the real attack at the other. He was ultimately compelled to enter the lists with his antagonist at both points.

Before dawn of Tuesday, and under cover of a very heavy fog, the pontoons were laid across the river at the point below Fredericksburgh, with but little opposition from the Rebel rifle-pits. An effort to lay pontoons at a later hour, and lower down the river, was not so successful, and it was not until forty guns had been brought to bear upon the Rebel sharp-shooters that the pontoons could be successfully placed. One division of each of the army corps, commanded by Sedgwick and Reynolds, were sent across the river. The remaining four divisions left the cover of the fringe of hills which had sheltered them from the view of the Rebels, and by marching and countermarching round the crests, magnified their number to their enemy. This ruse had the effect of causing the Confederates to move their columns from down the river to the vicinity of Fredericksburgh. These consisted of Jackson's entire corps, which had been posted there as an army of observation. Jackson was now upon the field where he had given battle to Franklin the previous December, but in this case history was not to repeat itself, and he was not here to fight a second battle on the same ground.

Let us now turn our attention to the three corps which had moved up the river. On the night of Tuesday, between ten P.M. and two A.M., Howard's entire corps crossed the Rappahannock on the pontoon bridge at Kelly's Ford, twenty-seven miles above Fredericksburgh. At daylight

Slocum's corps followed, and during the forenoon Meade's corps was thrown across. The movable column then struck direct for Germania Ford on the Rapidan River, distant twelve miles. General Meade, however, instead of taking this direction, on passing the river struck a road diverging eastward, and made Ely's Ford on the Rapidan, eight miles nearer than Germania Ford to the *embouchure* of that stream into the Rappahannock. Both columns having crossed the respective fords, moved on Chancellorsville, at the junction of the Gordonsville turnpike with the plank-road leading to Orange Court-House. Communication was kept up between the two movable columns by a squadron of Pleasanton's cavalry, while another part of the same horsemen moved on the right flank of the outer column to protect it from Rebel cavalry attacks. This manœuvre having uncovered United States Ford, (which lies between Kelly's Ford and Fredericksburgh—twelve miles from the latter,) Couch's corps, which had for three days been lying at that point, was passed over the Rappahannock by a pontoon bridge on Thursday, without any opposition or indeed any demonstration more formidable than a brass band playing "Hail Columbia." This force also converged toward Chancellorsville, and on Thursday night four army corps — namely, Howard's, Stevens's, Meade's, and Couch's—were massed at that point. The same night General Hooker with his staff reached Chancellorsville, and established his headquarters in the only house there.

The military movement had thus far been executed with

celerity and success, and it was certainly a signal achievement to have marched a column of seventy-five thousand men, each laden with sixty pounds of baggage, together with artillery and trains, thirty-six miles in two days ; and to have bridged and crossed two streams, along a line which a vigilant enemy undertook to observe and defend, with a loss of perhaps half a dozen men, one wagon, and two mules.

That General Hooker was himself satisfied with his past proceedings is evidenced in an order which he issued upon reaching Chancellorsville. In it he stated : "It is with heartfelt satisfaction that the General Commanding announces to the army that the operations of the last three days have determined that our enemy must ingloriously fly, or come out from behind their defences and give us battle on our own ground, where certain destruction awaits him."

On Friday morning General Hooker began the strate-getic disposition of his force. It was formed in a line of battle of a triangular or redan shape, resting with its wings respectively on the Rappahannock, between Banks and United States Fords, and Hart's Creek, and having its apex at Chancellorsville.

The day was occupied with operations along the skirmish line and reconnoissances for the purpose of feeling the enemy.

The situation of Chancellorsville is in the middle of a clearing in the woods, which takes the form of an irregular ellipse, about a mile in length and half a mile in width.

The solitary house that makes up Chancellorsville stands almost in the middle of this opening. The ground in the region between here and Fredericksburgh is broken and wooded, there being occasional clearings in the forests. It rises as it nears Fredericksburgh, when it develops into bold heights. Its strategetic importance is derived from the fact that it covers the Gordonsville turnpike and the Orange Court-House plank-road, and threatens the line of Gordonsville.

This wild, dreary region is called the Wilderness, which name the Confederates have given to the battle which here took place.

Working parties of the Federals were employed during the whole of Friday night in throwing up breastworks, and the woods resounded with the strokes of a thousand axe-men felling trees for the purpose of constructing abattis. Similar working parties of the Rebels were engaged in like manner not half a mile distant. On Saturday morning both armies were well intrenched, and it became the question which of the two should come out and give battle.

Having followed General Hooker to the place where he was compelled to encounter the Confederates, we will now enter the camp of General Lee, and narrate his march to the scene of strife.

On Wednesday, the twenty-ninth of April, the Con-federates discovered that General Hooker had broken up his camp at Falmouth, and that his troops had crossed the

Rappahannock at the places we have already named. The discovery was not a satisfactory one, as General Lee was at the time not only deprived of his "old war horse," General Longstreet, but his force was less in numbers than it had been for some time. But the Rebels were relieved when they witnessed the unruffled calmness of their Commanding General, who, without bustle or agitation, made the necessary disposition of his forces for the purpose of warding off the blow with which he was threatened. General Early was left with his division to guard Fredericksburgh and its vicinity, whilst Lee and Jackson slowly marched westward along the turnpike and plank-roads in the direction of Chancellorsville.

From the evidence which General Hooker had given at the court of inquiry, relative to the defeat at Fredericksburgh the previous December, General Lee was in a measure somewhat enabled to define the Federal plan. He consequently held all his troops, except Early's division, closely in hand, and on Thursday threw up earthworks midway between Fredericksburgh and Chancellorsville, and there arrested the advance of Hooker's force.

On Thursday, however, General Stuart had somewhat delayed the advance of the Federals near Kelly's Ford by cutting the head of one of their columns. The Confederate General Anderson, who was stationed with his division at United States Ford, was on the same day compelled to fall back, recoiling before the immense Federal host which was approaching.

Hooker did not press Lee hotly, but in his turn fell slowly back toward Chancellorsville, followed still more slowly by the Confederates. On Thursday evening, Stuart attacked a small force of the Federals on the Spotsylvania road, and caused them to retire with some loss.

On Friday, the first of May, General Lee continued to advance, and General Hooker to fall back. But as the opposing forces neared Chancellorsville, the former penetrated the latter's purpose in retreating, when he discovered that about five hundred yards in front of that place, in the midst of a dense thicket of scrub-oak or black-jack, the Federal pioneers had thrown up very strong intrenchments at right angles to the turnpike and plank-roads, with an abattis of felled trees bristling outward in front, and seemingly defying the passage of any living and walking animal. Running southward for about a mile from the plank-road, the Federal works turned short to the west, until they again met the plank-road between Chancellorsville and Orange Court-House, toward the latter of which points the plank-road deflects in a south-westerly direction after leaving Chancellorsville. Within these works the Federals stood thickly and savagely at bay, their powerful artillery massed on some high ground a little in the rear. Their position was fearfully formidable—repulse, if the works were attacked solely from the front, seemed inevitable—the loss of life to the assailants anyhow must have been ghastly. Under these circumstances, General Lee resolved to outflank the flanker,

In the early part of Saturday several small engagements

took place at different parts of the lines, and toward the close of the day commenced the battle of Chancellorsville, which did not terminate until mid-day on Sunday. It was on Saturday evening that the subject of our memoir received those wounds which resulted in his death, and deprived the Confederate army of its most brilliant commander.

The movements of the Rebels seemed to indicate to the Federals that they were retreating, and as the main line of the retreat was occupied by the latter's forces, an attack to recover that line was confidently expected. The surprise of the Federals was consequently very great when, on Saturday afternoon, they found Jackson upon their extreme right and rear, between Chancellorsville and Germania Mills.

The particulars of this battle have been so graphically narrated by the Special Correspondent of *The* (London) *Times* in the Confederate States, who was present at the battle, that we have no hesitation in transferring them to these pages. He says:

"If ever man was adapted for the execution of a plan daring and hazardous in the extreme, but depending for its safety upon the celerity and audacity of its execution, assuredly that man was 'Stonewall' Jackson. With the first break of dawn he plunged with his three famous divisions— the first commanded by A. P. Hill; the second, in the absence of Trimble, by Coulson; the third, lately under D. H. Hill, by Rhodes—into the country-road which leads to the Furnace.* At the Furnace he ascended a hill, and was viewed

* A road which diverges from the plank-road two miles east of Chancel-

by the enemy from an adjoining hill, called Fairview, and heavily though harmlessly shelled.   With his usual temerity he sent back word to General Lee that the Furnace hill must be held by one regiment until his artillery and wagons had got by.   A South-Carolina regiment was accordingly sent there, but was, I believe, shortly carried forward in company with the cavalry, and in its place three or four companies of a Georgia regiment were left to guard the critical spot.   The enemy discovering the weakness of the guard, attacked and took the Georgians prisoners.   The last of Jackson's batteries was passing as the Georgians were captured, whereupon Captain Brown unlimbered his guns, opened on the Federals, and drove them back.   He then passed on after Jackson, whose wagons had to fall back and pursue their General by a more circuitous route.   Marvellous to say, it never seems to have suggested itself to General Hooker, although this large body of Confederates passed under his nose, that his rear was in danger, or that General Lee, greatly weakened, was lying within a few hundred yards of the mighty Federal host of eighty thousand men.

"At four in the afternoon General Lee, knowing that Jackson could not be far from his destination, opened fire steadily along his whole line, feeling the gigantic masses of his intrenched foe.   For two hours and a half a heavy fire was interchanged between the hostile batteries, each party holding its own line.   Suddenly, about half-past six in the

lorsville, and enters it again five miles to the west of that place.   In this road is situated a foundry called the Catherine Furnace.

evening, the rattle of musketry was heard in the distance,
followed by the loud boom of artillery, and instantly General
Lee passed word along his lines · 'Jackson at work; press
them heavily everywhere.' Swift and sudden as the falcon
swooping on her prey, Jackson had burst on his enemy's
rear, and crushed him before resistance could be attempted.
Passing right over the plank-road, and extending almost up
to the Ely's Ford road, getting behind Chancellorsville, the
three noble divisions raced gallantly forward, drunk with
the animal joy and inebriation of battle. Not a trench had
been dug, not a tree felled, not a stick raised to resist them.
The unconscious Federals, engaged in cooking their supper—
one regiment on dress-parade—heard in the sudden volley
of Jackson's long line the knell of their doom. An intelli-
gent Virginia farmer, Mr. Green, taken prisoner by 'the
Federals, heard one of their Generals say to his men about
six o'clock : 'Jackson and his rebels don't dare face us to-
night. Get your supper ready, boys, and enjoy yourselves.'
With faces turning eastward, secured, as they fancied, by
the dense masses of their friends within the intrenchments
in front, without a thought of their rear, the Federals rum-
maged their knapsacks for all the luxuries with which Boston, New-York, and Philadelphia pamper and recruit their
Sybarite soldiers. Before that supper could be eaten, the un-
washed, unkempt, starving ragamuffins of the South had burst
on them from the west, and scattered them, nerveless, panic-
stricken, helpless, like chaff before the blast. Major Reyton,
of General Lee's staff, found a coffee-pot, with cups round it,

standing in the wood. He poured the liquid out, but it was so hot he could not drink it. What might have been the result but for one casualty, which alone almost counterveiled the victories of a week, who shall say? Formation or order the Federals had none; reserves, tactics, organization, disposition, plan, all went down before the whirlwind suddenness of the surprise. The loss of the Confederates was ludicrously small; their advance like that of a white squall in the bay of Naples.

" Night had fallen. About eight o'clock General Jackson rode forward with two or three of his staff along the plankroad, and advanced one hundred and fifty yards in front of his foremost skirmishers, peering with those keen eyes which you might fancy could be seen through the densest gloom forward into the night. He turned to ride back—a heavy fire from one of his own regiments, hailing from South-Carolina, but whose number I will in mercy withhold, saluted him. One bullet struck his left arm four inches below the shoulder, shattering the bone down to the elbow. The wound was intensely painful; he half fell, half was lifted from his horse. An aid galloped back to A. P. Hill to report that Stonewall Jackson was wounded and lying in the road. General Hill galloped hastily up, flung himself from the saddle, began, choked with emotion, to cut the cloth of Jackson's sleeve, when suddenly four of the Federal videttes appeared on horseback, and were fired on by the staff-officers. The videttes fell back upon a strong and swiftly advancing line of Federal skirmishers. General Hill and all

the officers and couriers of both staffs had no alternative but
to mount and ride for their lives, leaving Jackson where he
lay. Right over the ground where was stretched the wounded lion the Federals advanced. Within their grasp lay the
mightiest prize, the most precious jewel in the Confederate
crown; but it was not destined that Stonewall Jackson
should be struck by a Federal bullet, or yield himself prisoner
to a Federal soldier. As General Hill and his companions
galloped back they also became the target of the same luckless South-Carolinians. General Hill's boot was cut by a
bullet, but his leg uninjured; Colonel Crutchfield, Chief of
Artillery to Jackson, was seriously if not mortally wounded;
Boswell, of Jackson's staff, killed; Howard, Engineer to A.
P. Hill, knocked from his horse, but whether killed, or
wounded, or a prisoner, is not known; two or three couriers
killed. Without losing a moment, General Hill threw his
own skirmishers forward, backed by heavy supports, and
the ground on which lay General Jackson was again occupied by the Confederates. But in the mean time two more
bullets, both from his own men, had struck him as he lay on
the ground, one passing through the wrist of his shattered
arm, the other entering the palm of his right hand and coming out through its back. He was at once carried to the
rear and his arm instantly amputated under chloroform.

"Never was it more apparent than this evening what
Jackson's presence and influence are to his men. With his
wound ceased the fiery desperation of their onslaught; tidings of it flew like wildfire through the ranks; the routed

Federals found themselves no longer closely pressed, and took heart of grace as they poured grape and canister down the plank-road. Between nine and ten General A. P. Hill was struck by a bit of shell on the calf of his leg, which caused a painful contusion, and forced him reluctantly from the field. At ten P.M., General J. E. B. Stuart was by General Lee withdrawn from his cavalry command, and put temporarily at the head of General Jackson's corps, stripped as it was of the two leading Generals who have hitherto partaken its dangers and glories without being arrested by disease or stricken by bullet."

The same writer thus describes the appearance of the field upon which Jackson received his death-wound, as viewed by him after the termination of the battle:

"With astonishing accuracy Stuart's enfilading fire had torn through their ranks. In every variety of attitude of death, torn, rent, and shivered into scarcely distinguishable humanity, lay what so lately had breathed and moved. Still more terrible and strangely appalling was the road from Chancellorsville toward Orange Court-House, along which and on either side of which Jackson had descended to the harvest of death. Tumbrlls overthrown, caissons exploded, horses dead and dying, sometimes with broken legs, sometimes with ghastly wounds; human bodies in every guise of suffering and death, tortured and riven trees, and, most fearful of all, a crackling fire, running swiftly through the grass and black-jack brushwood, and suggesting dreadful thoughts of wounded and helpless men perishing by the most agonizing death known to humanity, froze the blood with horror, as the spectator in agony turned his eyes to heaven, to gain a moment's relief from the unutterable and woeful anguish of earth."

A quarter of an hour previous to the discharge of the fatal shots which deprived Jackson of his life, a Federal officer, who was wounded and taken prisoner, appeared before him. This officer was Captain Wilkins, of the staff of General A. S. Williams, who commanded a division of the National Army. The particulars of the interview between that officer and General Jackson are here given, as we find them narrated in a Northern journal :

" When captured, Captain Wilkins was placed in charge of a guard, who took him a short distance to the rear, where he met General Jackson and staff. Jackson was sitting on his horse at the head of the column, surrounded by his staff. He wore a new suit of gray uniform, and was a spare man with a weather-beaten face and a bright, grayish-blue eye. He had a peculiarly sad and gloomy expression of countenance, as though he already saw a premonition of his fate. It was but fifteen minutes later that he was mortally wounded. As they came into his presence the guard announced : 'A captured Yankee officer.' Captain Wilkins asked if it was Major-General Thomas J. Jackson. On being answered in the affirmative, he raised his hat. General Jackson said : 'A regular army officer, I suppose—your officers do not usually salute ours.' Captain Wilkins replied : 'No, I am not; I salute you out of respect to you as a gallant officer.'

He then asked his name and rank. On being told, he further inquired what corps and commanders were opposed in front. Captain Wilkins replied that, as an officer, he could not return a truthful answer to such questions. Jackson then turned to the guard and ordered them to search him. He then had in the breast-pocket of his coat Hooker's confidential orders to corps commanders, giving a plan in part of the campaign; the countersigns of the field for a week in advance, and the field returns, giving the effective strength of the Twelfth corps (Slocum's) on the preceding day. These were all exceedingly important papers.

"Fortunately, before the guard could carry the orders into execution, a terrific raking fire was opened on Jackson's column by twenty pieces of artillery, from an eminence on the plank-road. The first eight or ten shots flew over the heads of the column. The men and gunners dismounted, leaving horses and guns. Our artillery soon got the range with more precision, and the shell and round shot ricochetted and ploughed through this dense mass of the enemy with terrific effect. Shells were continually bursting, and the screams and groans of the wounded and dying could be heard on every side. As an instance of the terrible effect of this fire, one of the guard was struck by a solid shot just below the hips, sweeping off both his legs. A battery came dashing up, but when they got into the vortex of the fire the gunners fled, deserting their guns, and could not be made to man them. An officer, splendidly mounted and equipped, attempted, in a most gallant manner, to rally them. A ball struck him on the neck, completely severing his head from his body and leaving his spinal column standing. His body rolled to the ground, and the horse galloped to the rear. One of the shells struck a caisson full of artillery ammunition, which, exploding, ascended in a crater of various colored flame, and showered down on the heads of the men below a mass of fragments of shot and shell. The loss inflicted by this fire must have been terrible, placing considerable over one thousand men *hors du combat* and effectually breaking up the contemplated attack of the column.

" While Captain Wilkins was being taken to the rear he devoted his attention to disposing of the important papers which he had on his person. He dare not take them from his pocket to attempt to tear them up, but continuously placed his hand in his pocket and worked the papers into a ball, and as they were passing along, got them into his bosom, and finally into the arm-pit under his arm, where he carried them all that night. The next morning the guard halted to get their breakfasts, and a soldier was trying to kindle a fire to cook some coffee which they had taken from our men. The wood was damp and the fire refused to burn. The soldier swore at it until his patience gave out, when Captain Wilkins asked him if he would not like some kindlings, and handed him the important papers. The soldier took them, and, not dreaming of their importance, used them to kindle the fire."

Our narrative is drawing to a close. The military career

of Thomas Jonathan Jackson has terminated. But we have
yet to be silent watchers by the bedside of the dying soldier, and to accompany his remains to the tomb. However,
before we enter upon a description of the mournful scenes
which are left to us to narrate, it is necessary that we
should briefly sum up the remaining events which occurred
between the opposing armies, before the series of conflicts
which were initiated by the engagement of the first of May
were brought to an end.

The portion of Hooker's army which was broken by Jackson's onslaught, and which so ingloriously fled from the
battle-field, was Howard's corps, formerly commanded by
General Sigel. These troops have been subject to much
censure for their conduct on this occasion, but they claim
that if they had not been deceived in the position of the
enemy, and had not been deprived of their cavalry, by which
they could have learned the true position of the Rebels in
their front, the disaster would not have taken place.

Fighting took place during the greater part of the night
that Jackson fell, and continued with increased fury during
Sunday morning, when the Federals were driven within
their breastworks. On that day General Sedgwick's troops
captured the heights in the rear of Fredericksburgh, and
emboldened by their success over Early's division, followed
it on the road for a short distance toward Chancellorsville.
On Monday, General Lee being satisfied that Hooker would
not further give him battle, repaired to Fredericksburgh,
and, in person, marshalled the brigades of the three divi-

sions in that part of the field. That evening he drove Sedgwick back with great slaughter, when the latter repaired to
Banks's Ford and crossed the river. The day had been a
quiet one at Chancellorsville, and on the following morning
General Hooker, being satisfied that his attempt to capture
the Confederate army was a failure, retired from his position, and sought refuge on the northern bank of the Rappahannock.

In connection with these military proceedings, a dashing
cavalry raid was made by General Stoneman, who approached within a few miles of Richmond, and severed
Lee's communications by railway with that place.

The Federal losses in the engagements which took place
in these early days of May were extremely heavy, and numbered about twenty-five thousand in killed, wounded, and
missing. The Confederates estimated their loss at one
thousand killed, four thousand wounded, and one thousand
prisoners. They claim to have captured from the Federals
seven thousand six hundred and fifty prisoners. On the
other hand, General Hooker stated in a general order,
issued after the battles: "We have taken from the enemy
five thousand prisoners and fifteen colors, captured and
brought off seven pieces of artillery, and placed *hors du
combat* eighteen thousand of his chosen troops."

But the Confederates suffered one loss which was to them
irretrievable. We need not say that that was the loss of
General Jackson. General Lee considered the deprivation
of his services so great that, before he was aware that the

accident would result in death, he exclaimed to a friend: " Had I been able to dictate events, most gladly would I have been disabled in my own person if he had been spared. Such an executive officer the sun never shone on. I have but to show him my design, and I know that if it can be done it will be done. No need for me to send and watch him. Straight as the needle to the pole he advances to the execution of my purpose. Pure, high-minded, unselfish, he has no earthly thought of himself or his own advancement. The sole aim and object of his life is the good of his country."

CHAPTER XIII.

LAST MOMENTS AND OBSEQUIES.

Jackson's Daily Condition after being Wounded—He is attended by Mrs, Jackson—His Last Remarks—His Death—General Lee's Order to tne Army—Jackson's Successor—The Remains reach Richmond—Received with Public Honors and lie in State—Arrive in Lexington- The Funeral.

WHILE General Jackson was being carried on a litter to the rear of the battle-field at Chancellorsville, one of the bearers was shot down, and the wounded soldier fell from the shoulders of the men. This fall caused him to receive a severe contusion, which, added to the injury of his arm, created severe pain in his side. The General was left on the ground for five minutes, until the fire under which they were situated slackened. He was then placed in an ambulance and carried to the field-hospital at Wilderness Run On being conveyed thither, frequent inquiries were made by the soldiers : " Who have you there ?" He said to the doctor : " Do not tell the soldiers that I am wounded."

From the large amount of blood which he lost, he fancied that he was dying, and stated so to Dr. McGuire. It was feared that he would have bled to death, consequently a tourniquet was immediately applied to stop the further effusion of blood. The shock which he had received rendered

ROBERT E. LEE

him nearly pulseless for the space of two hours. After the reäction, a consultation was held between the surgeons present, and it was decided that amputation of the arm was necessary. Jackson was asked: "If we find amputation necessary, shall it be done at once?" He replied: "Yes, certainly, Dr. McGuire; do for me whatever you think is right." He bore the operation, which was performed while he was under the influence of chloroform, extremely well.

On Sunday morning, after a good sleep, the wounded soldier was cheerful, and in every way was doing well. He desired that his wife should be sent for, and asked minutely about the battle. He spoke cheerfully of its result, and said smilingly: "If I had not been wounded, or had had an hour more of daylight, I would have cut off the enemy from the road to the United States Ford, and we would have had them entirely surrounded, and they would have been obliged to surrender, or cut their way out. They had no other alternative. My troops sometimes may fail in driving the enemy from a position, but the enemy always fail to drive my men from a position."

His chaplain left him during the morning to go and perform service before the troops. The text was suggested by General Jackson, and was taken from Romans viii. 28: "We know that all things work together for good to them that love God." It was one of the General's favorite texts, and furnishes a key to the character of his religious belief.

Not for one moment did he question or murmur when struck down at the zenith of his fame. "I consider these

10

wounds a blessing. They were given me for some good and wise purpose. I would not part with them if I could." Such was substantially the language he used during the last few days of his life.

He complained on Sunday of the effects of the fall from the litter on the previous day, but no contusion or abrasion was apparent as the result thereof. However, he did not complain of his wounds, and never spoke of them unless when they were alluded to.

Jackson slept well on Sunday night, and on Monday was carried to Chancellor's house near Gurness's dépôt. He was cheerful during the day, conversed about the battle, and inquired after all his officers. During his removal, he complained greatly of the heat, and begged that a wet cloth be applied to his stomach, which was done and added greatly to his relief. He slept well that night, and relished his food the following morning.

On Monday he received the following note from General Lee, expressive of the regret the latter felt upon receiving intelligence of the accident that had befallen him:

CHANCELLORSVILLE, VA., May 4, 1863.

To Lieutenant-General T. J. JACKSON:

GENERAL: I have just received your note, informing me that you were wounded. I cannot express my regret at the occurrence. Could I have directed events, I should have chosen for the good of the country to have been disabled in your stead. I congratulate you upon the victory which is due to your skill and energy.

Most truly yours, R. E. LEE, General.

On Tuesday, his wounds were proceeding very well. He asked: "Can you tell me, from the appearance of the wounds, how long I will be kept from the field?" He seemed much satisfied when he was told that they were doing remarkably well. During the day he did not complain of any pain in his side, and expressed a desire to see the members of his staff; but he was informed that such an interview would not be advisable.

As Jackson's wounds were progressing so favorably, it was intended to have removed him on Wednesday to Richmond, but the removal was prevented by a fall of rain. That night, while his attending surgeon, who had been deprived of rest for three nights, was asleep, the patient complained of nausea, and ordered his boy to place a wet towel over his stomach, which was done. The surgeon was awakened about daylight by the boy exclaiming: "The General is in great pain." The pain was in the right side, and resulted from incipient pneumonia and a slight degree of nervousness, which Jackson attributed to his fall from the litter.

On Thursday Mrs. Jackson arrived, greatly to the joy and satisfaction of the wounded hero, whom she faithfully nursed during the few remaining days of his life. By that evening all pain had ceased, but the patient suffered greatly from prostration. This prostration increased on the following day, but no pain was experienced. On Sunday morning it was apparent that Jackson was rapidly sinking, when it became necessary to intimate the same to his wife.

Mrs. Jackson was then allowed full and free converse with her husband. She told him that he was going to die, upon which he replied: "Very good, very good. It is all right."

The closing scene of Jackson's life bore a striking resemblance to that of the first Napoleon. While in the case of the great European Captain "the ruling passion was strong in death," it was none the less so in that of the Southern soldier. The battle-field, with all "the pomp and circumstances of war," was all before him, while what remained of life was ebbing fast. His mind wandered back, in the delirium of approaching dissolution, to the scenes of the battle. He gave the word of command, uttered words of encouragement to regiments staggering under fire, ordered his commissary to hasten on with needful food to exhausted troops. Almost the last sentence was the order he had so often given in life : "A. P. Hill, prepare for action."

Sunday, the tenth day of May, 1863, will ever be a day of mournful memory to the people of the sunny South. On that day set the most resplendent star in their galaxy of Generals. He, who had forsaken the quietude of the Professor's life to place himself at the head of charging columns, on that day breathed his last. He, who, amid the blaze of cannon, the rattle of musketry, and the clash of steel, had won honor and renown, died a soldier's death, and died as he had lived—strong in his religious faith. His years numbered only thirty-nine, but he had gained during the two closing years of his life more of military glory than is won by many whose lives are permitted to be extended to three-score years and ten.

General Jackson's death was officially announced to the army in which he served by the following order, which was issued by the Commanding General:

GENERAL ORDERS—NO. 61.
HEADQUARTERS, NORTHERN VIRGINIA, May 11, 1863.

With deep grief the Commanding General announces to the army the death of Lieutenant-General T. J. Jackson, who expired on the tenth instant, at a quarter-past three P.M. The daring, skill, and energy of this great and good soldier, by an all-wise Providence, are now lost to us. But while we mourn his death, we feel that his spirit still lives, and will inspire the whole army with his indomitable courage and unshaken confidence in God as our hope and strength. Let his name be a watchword to his corps, who have followed him to victory on so many fields. Let the officers and soldiers imitate his invincible determination to do every thing in the defence of our beloved country.

R. E. LEE, General.

When Jackson felt that death was approaching, and that his corps would soon be deprived of its commander, he frequently expressed to his aids his desire that General Ewell, in whom he had great confidence, might be appointed his successor. In accordance with this desire, General Ewell received the appointment.

In no city of the South was General Jackson more greatly respected than in the Confederate capital. So anxious were the people of Richmond to be informed of the daily condition of the illustrious chieftain, that on the Sunday upon which he died, his critical position was announced from the pulpits of many churches. This announcement prepared the people for the mournful intelligence which was so soon to follow; but it was for a time hard for them to believe in the correctness of such unwelcome news. It was to this city that Jackson's remains were removed after he had breathed his last.

Richmond clothed herself in mourning, and cast off the cares of business, so that she might fittingly receive the body of the departed hero. On Monday afternoon, a large concourse of ladies and gentlemen attended at the railway station to receive the corpse. It arrived about four o'clock, in charge of the following officers:

Of Lieutenant-General Jackson's staff:

Major S. Pendleton, Adjutant-General in charge; Dr. Hunter McGuire, Medical Director; Major W. J. Hawks, Lieutenants Morrison and Smith, Aids.

On the part of the army:

Major D. B. Bridgford, Captain H. K. Douglas.

On the part of the Commonwealth of Virginia:

Dr. John Mayo, Aid to the Governor, Colonel John C. Shields.

The coffin was covered with wreaths, which had been placed upon it by the ladies of Ashland as the remains passed that place. With as little delay as possible, the body was removed under military escort to the Governor's mansion, to which place it was followed by perhaps the largest assemblage of persons ever collected in Richmond.

On Tuesday, the last offices of honor to the dead soldier were performed by the citizens of Richmond with fitting magnificence. We give the particulars of the proceedings, as we find them narrated in the Richmond *Enquirer* of the following day:

"In no public ceremony, not even the grand display which attended the inauguration of the monument to Washington some years ago, has Richmond been rendered more memorable than upon this occasion, when every branch of the Confederate and State Governments, with an army of bronzed and hardy heroes, and the whole city pouring forth its living tribute, aged and young of both sexes, joined in the pageant, and gave it all the imposing grandeur which sympathy, sorrow, love and admiration united, could bestow.

"In accordance with arrangements made upon Monday, the procession was formed upon Capitol Square at ten o'clock, stretching along Monument Avenue from the Governor's mansion, out upon Grace street, and consisted of the following civil and military bodies:

Public guard, with armory band, followed by the Nineteenth and Fifty-sixth Virginia Infantry, Major Wren's battalion of cavalry, and the Richmond Lafayette artillery, all preceded by a full band.

Hearse drawn by four white horses, appropriately caparisoned, the hearse draped and plumed, and the coffin wrapped and decorated with flowers.

Pall-bearers, consisting of the staff of the lamented hero,
and several other officers of high rank, wearing
the insignia of mourning.

Carriages, containing—first, His Excellency the President,
and the family of the deceased, followed by personal
friends and distinguished admirers; various chiefs
of Departments, State and Confederate; civil,
military, and judicial; the Mayor of the
city and members of the Council.

"On either side, and in the rear, an immense throng of
ladies and gentlemen, children, servants and soldiers, mingled ready to move along with the procession. The banners were draped with crape, and the swords of the military
officials were draped at the hilt. The artillery bore the sad
insignia; the arms of the infantry were reversed; the
drums were muffled, and at the given hour a gun stationed
beneath the monument boomed forth the signal for motion.

"General George W. Randolph, Chief Marshal of the
ceremony, proceeded to the front, and the cavalcade moved
slowly out upon Governor street, through the Mansion Gate.
The bells of the city commenced tolling, and soon a melancholy dirge swelled forth in moving tones from the leading
corps of musicians. The procession passed down Governor
to Main street, turning up the latter, and proceeding as far
as Second street. The streets were crowded with people;
stores were closed, as the pageant moved along, and from
many windows floated flags draped in mourning. The flags
upon the public buildings remained as on Monday, at half-

mast. The scene on Main street was beyond adequate description, so impressive, so beautiful, so full of stirring associations, blending with the martial dirges of the bands, the gleam of musket, rifle, and sabre drawn, the sheen of black cannon, thousands of throbbing hearts, and the soul of sorrow that mantled over all. From Second street, through which the procession partly passed, it wheeled into Grace street, down which it returned to Capitol Square, entering by Monument Gate. At different stages of the obsequies the cannon, which remained stationed at the foot of the monument, pealed out in tones of thunder, which heightened the effect of the tolling bells, the solemn music, and the grand display.

"The hearse being drawn up in front of the Capitol, the coffin was removed to the hall of the House of Representatives, where it was laid in state in front of the Speaker's seat. Thousands crowded into the building, many bearing splendid bouquets with which to adorn the coffin, and at night hundreds were turned away, after hours of fruitless efforts, without seeing the face of the beloved departed warrior. All the courts in Richmond passed resolutions of respect to the memory of Jackson, and adjourned to attend the ceremonies."

Jackson had never seen his home since the war broke out; nor would he, he declared, until it was over, "unless the war itself should take him thither." The war *did* take him thither, but alas! it was not for him to *see* the place he loved so well. Richmond would fain have found a fitting

10*

resting-place for the remains of one she so much honored, but all that she was enabled to do was merely to pay them a passing tribute as they were being conveyed to their final home. Says the Richmond *Examiner:*

"All the poor honors that Virginia, sorely troubled and pressed hard, could afford her most glorious and beloved son, having been offered to his mortal part in this capital, the funeral *cortége* of the famous Jackson left it yesterday (Wednesday) morning, on the long road to 'Lexington, in the Valley of Virginia.' It was the last wish of the dead man to be buried there, amid the scenes familiar to his eyes through the years of his manhood, obscure and unrecorded, but perhaps filled with recollections to him not less affecting than those connected with the brief but crowded period passed upon a grander stage. This desire, expressed at such a time, demanded and has received unhesitating compliance. Yet many regret that his remains will not rest in another spot. Near this city is a hill crowned by secular oaks, washed by the waters of the river identified with what is great in the State's history from the days of Elizabeth to the present hour, which has been well selected as the place of national honor for the illustrious dead of Virginia. There sleep Monroe and Tyler. We have neither a Westminster nor a Pantheon, but all would wish to see the best that we could give conferred on Jackson. Hereafter, Virginia will build for him a stately tomb, and strike a medal to secure the memory of his name beyond the reach of accident, if accident were possible. But it is not possible; nor is a monument necessary to cause the story of this man's life to last when bronze shall have corroded and marble crumbled."

Jackson's remains reached Lexington on Thursday afternoon, having been escorted thither by a portion of his staff, the Governor of the State, and a committee from Lynchburgh. "They were received," says the Lynchburgh *Virginian*, "at the boat-landing by the corps of cadets, under General F. H. Smith, the professors of the Institute, and a large number of citizens, and were escorted in solemn procession to the Institute barracks, where they were deposited in the old lecture-room of the illustrious deceased. The room was just as he left it two years before, save that it was heavily draped in mourning—not having been occupied during his absence. The hall which so often echoed the voice of the modest and unknown professor, received back the laurel-crowned hero with the applause of the world and the benedictions of a nation resting upon him. It was a touching scene, and brought tears to many eyes, when the body was deposited just in front of the favorite chair from which his lectures were delivered. Professors, students, visitors, all were deeply moved by the sad and solemn occasion, and gazed in mute sorrow on the affecting spectacle of the dead hero lying in his familiar lecture-room. Guns were fired every half-hour during the day in honor of the departed chieftain, and an air of gloom was visible on every face."

The funeral took place on the next day, Friday, the fifteenth of May. The coffin was enveloped in the Confederate flag, and covered with flowers. It was borne on a caisson of the cadet battery, draped in mourning. The procession consisted of such officers and soldiers of the old Stonewall brigade as happened at the time to be in the county. It awakened thrilling associations to see the shattered fragments of this famous brigade assembled under the flag which for some time was the regimental standard of Jackson's old Fourth regiment, and which that regiment carried in triumph over the bloody field of Manassas on the ever memorable twenty-first day of July.

An interesting part of the ceremonies of the day were the religious services. These took place in the church in which the great chieftain had delighted to worship God for ten years before the beginning of his late brilliant career. They were conducted by the Rev. Dr. White, a pastor whom he tenderly loved, and whose religious counsels he modestly sought, even in the midst of the most absorbing scenes through which, during the last two years, he had passed.

The body was deposited in the cemetery connected with the church, where his first wife and child are buried.

There, within the borders of that quiet town in which had been spent the happiest and most peaceful moments of his life; there, under the shadow of that institution in which he had worked so assiduously, lie the remains of one that Lexington may well be proud to own. There, under the green Virginian sward, lies all that remains of one of Virginia's noblest sons.

CHAPTER XIV.

THE SOLDIER AND THE MAN.

Jackson's Military Career an Episode in the Rebellion—Compared with the Puritan Leaders of England—Resemblance to Havelock—Northern Appreciation of his Gallantry—Qualities as a Commander—"Mystery the Secret of Success"—Firmness under Fire—Love of Truth—Hatred of Flattery — Alleged Unfitness for Separate Command — Admiration of General Lee—Personal Appearance and Habits—Estimates of Jackson's Character—Viewed from a Northern Stand-point.

OF all the names which the surges of the Rebellion have thrown upon the dry sands of history, there is none stands more prominent than does that of THOMAS JONATHAN JACKSON. His military career was brief, but it was crowded with startling incidents. It was the career of an enthusiastic, chivalrous, and religious soldier. The story of that career is an episode in the history of the Rebellion, which we have thought worthy of being separated from the general narrative of the events with which the last few years have been so prolific. We have therefore woven together such of the threads of this hero's life as we were enabled to gather, and have placed them before our readers in as perfect a fabric as possible.

There are many points in Jackson's character which

strongly remind us of Cromwell, and Hampden, and Pym, and other sturdy and God-fearing Puritans of the time of England's great Rebellion; but we have cause to regret that the resemblance is not perfect. These patriotic Puritans unsheathed the sword to fight the battle of freedom and of the people against the powerful autocratic element which in their days ruled the destinies of the British nation; whilst, on the contrary, Jackson, in a misguided moment, was induced to bare his blade for the purpose of wielding it on the side of a Southern slave-ruling oligarchy, and against the free people of his own country.

There is much, too, in Jackson's character, that resembles the pictures which have been drawn of Havelock, who, a few years ago, rendered his name famous by the brilliancy of his military performances in India. Added to a strong religious feeling which was predominant in the character of both these Generals, they alike possessed great activity of mind and fertility of resource, and each exercised over those under his command such a parental sway, that his entire force was ever ready to move almost as one man at the beck of its commander. This is plainly shown in the celerity of movements and in the long and rapid marches which so mainly tended to the greatness of their successes. Each considered that he had a duty to perform—his duty to his country — a duty, however, which in one case was directed to a sectional part thereof, and against the best interests of the entire nation; and the singleness of purpose of each was so great, that he removed every obstacle out of the way which interfered with the proper performance of this duty—never omitting that greater duty of all men, the duty to his Maker; never undertaking any enterprise without first invoking the Deity to guide his steps and to bless his endeavors with success.

The death of a brave soldier is ever mourned by friend and foe, and it is honorable to the loyal people of America that they did not hear of Jackson's death without a thrill of emotion passing through their hearts. Though they viewed him as one of the most dangerous and most resolute of their antagonists, they ever considered him one of the most conscientious and most chivalrous. Though they had reeled under the blows which he had inflicted upon them, and though they had felt the full force of the lightnings of battle which he had launched against them, they knew that the blows had been struck by a valorous hand, and that it was a noble spirit that had directed those fearful lightnings.

"War," writes one of our Northern journalists, referring to Jackson's death, "is never so hateful as when it kills in men the supremely manlike quality of justice to our enemies; and the spontaneous, irrepressible tribute which rose to all men's lips when they heard that the bravest of the rebel brave had died a soldier's death, was a victory won by the heart and temper of the Northern people, on which the muse of history will linger, perhaps, with something like relief from her sad chronicle of men arrayed for mutual slaughter."

" The Northern people," also says the same writer, " honored in Jackson qualities which the worst cause cannot obscure. They respected the sincerity of the man as much as they admired the daring of the soldier. They believed him misled, but they felt that he was no misleader. They lamented in his victories only this, that feats which reflected such renown upon American gallantry should have been performed in a cause so fatal to American hopes; and not even the sense of gain we all must feel in the loss to the rebel hosts of such a captain, can make us stand otherwise than with uncovered heads before the early grave of a heroic chieftain, the example of whose high qualities the truest and most loyal soldier of the Union and the Right may honorably lay to heart."

We here collect together, from a variety of sources, the opinions of many people upon Jackson's characteristics as a man and as a soldier. It is scarcely to be expected that our civil strife will mould for the pages of history another hero in the sounding of whose praises friend and foe will be equally unanimous.

Jackson was undoubtedly a man of very extraordinary military genius. His unconquerable will seemed to defy all opposing forces, and to wring victory from the very jaws of fate. His qualities as a commander are summed up by a Southern writer in the following terms:

" He knew what was necessary to insure victory—was fertile in resource — of unfailing prudence in guarding against disaster, never leaving unstrengthened that fatal weak point in the dam, through which the flood will slowly but surely work its way, sweeping every thing eventually before it. With him there were no trifles—nothing was too small or unimportant to guard against. Like the painter, who, when criticised for his multitudinous touches, replied, 'These may seem trifles, but they secure perfection, and perfection is no trifle,' he never rested until he had seen in person that all things were attended to, down to the minutest details ; rightly thinking that the grand result was worth any amount of trouble. He never failed to keep his line of retreat open, and left nothing to good fortune. All was calculation of forces, time, and material.

"His dispositions for attack were always perfect, thorough, and the very best that the time and place would admit of. He uniformly proceeded on the hypothesis that the assailing force possessed from that circumstance an enormous advantage; and, once in motion, he advanced with the utmost rapidity, and struck with all his strength. If one blow failed, another was delivered; if that was unsuccessful, every available force he could control was concentrated for another and another. It was only when the overpowering numbers of the enemy made the encounter hopeless, that he retired with dogged, sullen deliberation— as dangerous when retreating as when advancing.

"His tenacity of purpose was invincible. Never has a soul of more stubborn nerve been born into the world. He refused to recognize the possibility of defeat, and never knew when he was whipped. At Kernstown he was firmly convinced that if daylight had continued, his little handful of weary troops, worn down by exhausting marches, and shattered by a day of terrible conflict, would have put to rout the fourfold forces of Federals in front of them. At Manassas, he believed that with ten thousand men he could have captured Washington. In Charles City he was confident that if McClellan was attacked in his defences near Harrison's Landing, his army would be forced to surrender. At Fredericksburgh he projected and nearly executed an audacious assault, with the bayonet, upon Burnside's entire force in front of our position at nightfall. Who shall say that on any of these occasions Jackson miscalculated his strength, or over-estimated his ability? History has recorded the battles which he won. Who shall say that those which he declared his ability to win would have resulted in defeat?

"He struck boldly, but formed his plans in secret. Mystery is the favorite resort of charlatans; but with Jackson it was the herald of victory. He talked little, and measured his words when speaking of military affairs. No one knew whither he was going—what he designed. He proceeded upon the sound and excellent maxim that a secret is always guarded from indiscretion when confined to a single person; and the person whom he selected as the sole repository of his plans was himself. He even put himself to great trouble to mask his designs—camping often when he arrived at cross-roads, and leaving thus that body of quidnuncs, which are found in every army, profoundly puzzled as to what direction he would take with his command upon the morrow. On one occasion he reprimanded an officer on the march for engaging dinner for head-quarters at a house a few miles in advance, upon the highway which the troops were pursuing; it afforded information of his line of march to that extent, and so was reprehensible. A favorite device with him was to institute inquiries in the presence of the crowd around him as to roads and water-courses in a direction which he did *not* intend to take; even to order maps to be prepared, and roads laid down, as though for instant use. Having thus set every gossip talking and predicting his intentions, he would calmly march directly in the opposite direction.

" 'Mystery, mystery, is the secret of success!'

"He was just to his officers and men, taking up prejudices rarely for or against persons, and measuring out equal justice to all. No man could say that he had treated him with conscious unfairness; and if a calm examination of those cases wherein he is said to have acted from personal dislike, be instituted, it will be found that he proceeded upon grounds which appeared to him incontrovertible, and not from haste and ill-temper. Ill-tempered, in the proper meaning of the phrase, he never was. He was stern, abrupt, harsh at times, but the occasion always demanded plain speech; and his object of reprimand, correction, or repulse of ill-advised interference once attained, the offence was entirely forgotten, and the offender restored completely to his former position.

" He had the faculty of calculating forces, rarely developed. He always knew his strength and his weakness. When he attacked, it was because he knew that victory was, humanly speaking, in his grasp. He based his calculations not upon numbers only, but upon position, material, the morale of his troops, and the effect of the situation upon the morale of the enemy. He estimated to their full extent the decisive character of a sudden, bold, and obstinate attack. He trusted most to the bayonet, but had a marked fondness for artillery. He did not overestimate its value in inflicting injury upon the enemy, but he trusted greatly to its influence upon the morale of his opponents. To 'demoralize' the enemy was a large part of his military philosophy, and he rightly thought that a foe disheartened is a foe half beaten.

" In summing up, briefly and generally, the peculiarities of Jackson's military genius, it may be said, without unmeaning panegyric, or the least disposition to over-estimate his faculties as a leader, that he was profound and comprehensive in his plans—as rapid and mortal as a thunderbolt in execution ; that he possessed a courage in the face of danger which no peril could affect, no possible reverse, however sudden, unexpected, and disheartening, deprive him of; that he was cautious, prudent, judicious in all his dispositions ; lastly, that he possessed the native faculty of penetrating the intentions of the enemy, of guarding himself wholly from surprise, of delivering his blows upon the weakest point, and of making war on all occasions and against the most dangerous opponents, with the mastery, precision, and success of the greatest leaders which the world has yet produced."

Jackson's firmness when under fire is also thus alluded to by the same writer:

" What marked him as one of the ' men of fate' was his astonishing equanimity in the face of perils which would have overwhelmed other men; his cool determination not to ' give up;' his refusing to entertain the idea that he could be defeated. At Manassas he surveyed with utter calmness the terrible spectacle of the Confederate lines reeling back before the Federal hosts, pressing down with their enormous reserves of infantry and artillery; and when General Bee, with uncontrollable anguish in his voice, told Jackson that the day was going against them, his cold reply was: ' Sir, we will give them the bayonet.' The last words of the brave South-Carolinian tell how he fought his old brigade. He stood ' like a stone wall'—as stern, stubborn, and immovable. At Kernstown, when a portion of his line gave back before the overwhelming numbers assailing it, he took his stand close to the enemy, amid a storm of bullets— called to a drummer-boy—and placing his hand firmly upon the boy's shoulder, said, in his brief, curt tones: '*Beat the rally!*' The rally was beaten; Jackson remained by the drummer's side, holding him to his work with the inexorable hand upon the shoulder—the rally continued to roll, and the line was speedily re-formed."

Another incident in this connection is related by one of Jackson's intimate acquaintances. He says:

"In the midst of the terrible cannonade at the battle of Fredericksburgh, when I counted the number of shot and shell, during fifteen minutes, that fell within a hundred yards of the position that he and I occupied, and estimated them at five hundred *during the action*, he was seen calmly sitting on his horse with his hand raised, as if in prayer."

During the few months which separated the battle of Fredericksburgh from that of Chancellorsville, General Jackson was situated with his troops in winter-quarters at a place called Moss Neck, some ten miles below Fredericksburgh. He employed himself during these moments of leisure in preparing the official reports of his battles. Of the mode of their preparation we quote the following from the pen of a partisan, as it illustrates Jackson's extreme love of truth:

"The embodiment of the facts, as given in the reports of officers engaged, was intrusted to Lieutenant-Colonel Faulkner, A. A. G., but General Jackson carefully revised and corrected the statements before his official signature was appended. He was exceedingly careful not to have any thing placed thus upon formal record which was not established by irrefutable proof. *Truth* was with him the jewel beyond all price, and nothing discomposed him more than the bare suspicion that accuracy was sacrificed to effect. He disliked all glowing adjectives in the narratives of his battles; and presented to the members of his staff and all around him, a noble example of modesty and love of truth. He seemed, indeed, to have a horror of any thing like ostentation, boasting, or self-laudation, expressed or implied. Nothing was more disagreeable to him than the excessive praises which reached his ears through the newspapers of the day; and he shrunk from the attempts made to elevate him above his brother commanders with a repugnance which was obvious to every one. His dislike for all popular ovations was extreme. He did not wish his portrait to be taken, or his actions to be made the subject of laudatory comment in the journals of the day. When the publishers of an illustrated periodical wrote to him requesting his daguerreotype and some notes of his battles for an engraving and a biographical sketch, he wrote in reply that he had no picture of himself and *had never done any thing*.

" So carefully did he guard all the statements in his reports from error, and such was the rigid censorship which he established in relation to the most minute portions of these narratives, that the official reports revised and signed by him, may be relied upon as the very quintessence of truth, and historians may quote them through all coming time, as the sworn statements of a man who would have laid down his very life before he would have attached his name to what was partial, unfair, or aught but the simple, absolute truth."

It has been pretty generally stated that Jackson was more fitted to carry into effect the plans of others than to direct the movements of a large army. It is true that whilst he was a co-laborer with General Lee, his executive abilities were severely tested, and were not found wanting; but the directing power which he displayed in the Valley campaign was equally prominent and proved equally successful. General Joseph Johnston, in conversation with an English officer, gave it as his opinion that Jackson "did not possess any great qualifications as a strategist, and was, perhaps, unfit for the independent command of a large army; yet he was gifted with wonderful courage and determination, and had a perfect faith in Providence that he was destined to destroy his enemy. He was much indebted to General Ewell in the Valley campaigns." Johnston also said that Jackson was most fortunate in commanding the flower of the Virginian troops, and in being opposed by some of the most incapable Federal commanders.

Generals Lee and Jackson met for the first time in the war at the commencement of the seven days' contest near Richmond. They had an opportunity during that contest of seeing each other at work; and there sprung up at once between them that profound respect, confidence, and regard which thenceforth knew no diminution, no shadow of turning. Jackson said of Lee: "He is a phenomenon. I would follow him blindfolded." When Jackson was struck down by the fatal bullet, General Lee, who knew his incomparable value more than all other men, exclaimed, with tears in his eyes: "He is better off than I am. *He* lost his *left* arm, but *I* have lost my right!"

Jackson's estimate of General Lee is further exhibited in the following:

"The love and admiration he at all times evinced for Lee resembled the devotion with which Turner Ashby had followed *him*. Replying to the remarks of a friend about his own peculiar military ideas and habits, and his proneness 'to do his marching and fighting his own way,' he said: 'We are blessed with at least one General whom I would cheerfully follow blindfold, whose most dubious strategy I would execute without question or hesitation, and that General is Robert E. Lee.' The anecdote is authentic. But Jackson had the sagacity to perceive very early that his military genius was essentially local and partisan—that it was as an executive officer exclusively that he was remarkable—and that kaleidoscopic conceptions and subtle combinations must be left to the Lees and Johnstons of the Rebel army."

Speaking of Jackson as "the great controlling mind," the "sledge-hammer of the war," a Federal officer declared: "Every time we have been beaten it has been his doing, and that of no one else. The first time I saw his face, my heart sank within me." "His moral brain is grand," said another. "He appears to act under a solemn sense of obligation to his Maker, who, he believed, had appointed him his work."

The critics began in time to understand that war reveal-
11

ed men ; falsifying all estimates previously made of them in the quiet days of peace. Jackson had been regarded as a commonplace, somewhat eccentric "professor," who, by some singular chance, at an early period in his life, had blundered into the arena of arms. A command was intrusted to him by those who knew him better, and the result is before the world.

"How does he look?" is invariably asked of every popular favorite. We must, therefore, not fail to impart to our readers some particulars of General Jackson's personal appearance. This we give in the words of a Confederate officer who first saw him shortly after the battle of Port Republic:

"The outward appearance of the famous leader was not imposing. The popular idea of a great general is an individual of stiff and stately bearing, clad in splendid costume, all covered with gold lace and decorations, who prances by upon a mettled charger, and moves on, before admiring crowds, accompanied by his glittering staff, and grand in all the magnificence of high command. The figure of General Stonewall Jackson was singularly different from this popular fancy. He wore an old sun-embrowned coat of gray cloth, originally a very plain one, and now almost out at elbows. To call it sun-embrowned, however, is scarcely to convey an adequate idea of the extent of its discoloration. It had that dingy hue, the result of exposure to rain and snow and scorching sunshine, which is so unmistakable. It was plain that the General had often stretched his weary form upon the bare ground, and slept in the old coat; and it seemed to have brought away with it no little of the dust of the Valley. A holiday soldier would have disdained to wear such a garb; but the men of the Old Stonewall Brigade, with their brave comrades of the corps, loved that coat, and admired it and its owner more than all the holiday uniforms and holiday warriors in the world. The remainder of the General's costume was as much discolored as the coat—he wore cavalry boots reaching to the knee, and his head was surmounted by an old cap, more faded than all: the sun had turned it quite yellow indeed, and it tilted forward so far over the wearer's forehead, that he was compelled to raise his chin in the air, in order to look under the rim. His horse was not a 'fiery steed' pawing, and ready to dart forward at 'the thunder of the captains and the shouting,' but an old raw-boned sorrel, gaunt and grim—a horse of astonishing equanimity, who seemed to give himself no concern on any subject, and calmly moved about, like his master, careless of cannon-ball or bullet, in the hottest moments of battle.

"The General rode in a peculiar fashion, leaning forward somewhat, and apparently unconscious that he was in the saddle. His air was singularly abstracted; and, unless aware of his identity, no beholder would have dreamed that this plainly clad and absent-looking soldier was the idolized leader of a great army corps, at that very instant hurling themselves, column after column, upon the foe.

"The glittering eye beneath the yellow cap would have

altered somewhat the impression that this man was a 'nobody'—that wonderful eye, in whose blaze was the evidence of a slumbering volcano beneath ; but beyond this, there was absolutely nothing in the appearance of General Jackson to indicate his great rank or genius as a soldier."

A different estimate, however, of the peculiarities of expression which indicate the warrior is given by another gentleman, who is stated to be a rare and quick judge of character. When asked for a description of Jackson, whom he had met but for a few moments on the battle-field, he replied : " He is a fighting man, rough mouth, iron jaw, and nostrils big as a horse's." This description has doubtless much force in it, although blunt and homely in its expression.

Another picture of our hero is given by the correspondent of a Southern journal. He says :

" There you see self-command, perseverance, indomitable will, that seem neither to know nor think of any earthly obstacle, and all this without the least admixture of vanity, assumption, pride, foolhardiness, or any thing of the kind. There seems a disposition to assert it pretensions, but from the quiet sense of conviction of his relative position, which sets the vexed question of self-importance at rest—a peculiarity, I would remark, of great minds. It is only the little and frivolous who are forever obtruding their petty vanities before the world. His face also expresses courage in the highest degree, and his phrenological developments indicate a vast amount of energy and activity. His forehead

is broad and prominent, the occipital and sincipital regions
are both large and well balanced; eyes expressing a singular union of mildness, energy, and concentration; cheek
and nose both long and well formed. His dress is a common gray suit of faded cassimere—coat, pants, and hat—
the coat slightly braided on the sleeve, just enough to be
perceptible, the collar displaying the mark of a Major-Gen
eral. Of his gait, it is sufficient to say that he just goes
along—not a particle of the strut, the military swagger,
turkey-gobbler parade, so common among officers of small
rank and smaller minds. It would be a profitable study
for some of our military swells to devote one hour each
day to the contemplation of the magnificent plainness of
' Stonewall.' To military fame which they can never hope
to attain he unites the simplicity of a child and the straight-
forwardness of a Western farmer. There may be those
who would be less struck with his appearance as thus ac-
coutred than if bedizened with lace and holding the reins
of a magnificent barb caparisoned and harnessed for glorious war; but to one who had seen him, as I had, at Coal
Harbor and Malvern Hill, in the rain of shell and the blaze
of the death-lights of the battle-field, when nothing less
than a mountain would serve as a breastwork against the
thirty-six inch shells which howled and shrieked through
the sickly air, General Jackson in tatters would be the
same hero as General Jackson in gilded uniform. In my
simple view he is a nonpareil—he is without a peer. He
has enough energy to supply a whole manufacturing dis-

trict, enough military genius to stock two or three military schools of the size of West-Point."

The Hon. F. Lawley, special correspondent of the London *Times* with the Southern army, portrays the great Confederate general in the following terms :

"The interest excited by this strange man is as curious as it is unprecedented. A classmate of McClellan at West-Point, and there considered slow and heavy, unfavorably known in Washington as a hypochondriac and *malade imaginaire*, he has exhibited for the last ten months qualities which were little supposed to reside in his rugged and unsoldierlike frame, but which will hand his name down for many a generation in the company of those great captains whom men will not willingly let die. More apt for the execution than conception of great movements, leaning upon General Lee as the directing brain, and furnishing the promptest hand, the most dauntless heart, the most ascetic and rigorous self-denial, the greatest rapidity and versatility of movement, as his contributions towards the execution of General Lee's strategy, his recent operations in turning General Pope's right, and passing with a force believed not to exceed thirty thousand men to the rear of such an army, massed close to its base of operations, and in the act of receiving daily large reënforcements, command universal wonder and admiration. It is said that, like Hannibal, he is accustomed to live among his men without distinction of dress, without greater delicacy of fare, and that it is almost impossible, on this account, for a stranger to recognize or distinguish him among them. Every despatch from his hand has, as its exordium : 'By the blessing of God.' Continual are the prayer-meetings which he holds among his men, invoking a blessing upon his arms before the battle and returning thanks for preservation, and (as it has rarely failed to happen) for victory after it is over. In fact, they who have seen and heard him uplift his voice in prayer, and then have witnessed his vigor and prompt energy in the strife, say that once again Cromwell is walking the earth and leading his trusting and enraptured hosts to assured victory. It is not necessary to add that Jackson's men idolize and trust their leader enthusiastically, and have the most implicit faith in his conduct, otherwise the bold and daring steps which he has frequently taken, and from which he has never failed to come off triumphantly, would have been utter impossibilities."

In this connection, the *Saturday Review* (London) says: "General Jackson's powers of endurance were certainly equalled by his dash and daring. Less than two years fill up his public life, and not much more than twelve months complete the cycle of his leading victories ; but he compressed into the narrow space of two campaigns as many triumphs as have distinguished the long military life of several famous captains. Although not the general-in-chief of an army, not a few of his successes were won in an independent command, and as many as six great victories are attributed to Jackson. . . . His religion, though it may not be our religion, was not inconsistent with charity, gentleness, and courtesy; and the victorious general who is a high-minded gentleman, a consistent Christian, and whose popularity is universal among his men, is not, after all, a very common character. The military profession wants such bright and rare reliefs; and we will venture to say that throughout England, and even among the better spirits of the Federals, there is a general share in that 'deep grief' with which the South may well mourn the death of Lieutenant-General Jackson. There is something of a national sympathy with those simple and touching words with which General Lee records 'the daring, skill, and energy of this great and good soldier,' and asks his comrades, 'while they mourn his death, to feel that his spirit lives, and will inspire the whole army with his indomitable courage and unshaken confidence in God as their hope and strength.'"

The New-York *Independent* criticises Jackson's character and career from a Northern stand-point, as follows :

"We are in some respects better judges of his military talents than Southern men, since we felt the blows which they only saw dealt. It is certain that no other man has impressed the imagination of our soldiers and the whole community so much as he. An unknown name at the beginning of the war, save to his brother officers, and to his classes in the military school at Lexington, Virginia, his footsteps were earliest in the field from which now death has withdrawn them. But in two years he has made his name familiar in every civilized land on the globe as a general of rare skill, resource, and energy.

THE SOLDIER AND THE MAN.

"No other general of the South could develop so much power out of slender and precarious means, by the fervid inspiration of his own mind, as Jackson. He had absolute control of his men, seeming almost to fascinate them. He drove them through marches long and difficult, without resources, feeding them as best he could; he delivered battles as a thunder-cloud discharged bolts, and, if the fortunes were against him, then, with even more remarkable skill than in advancing, he held his men together in retreat; and with extraordinary address and courage eluded pursuit, sometimes fighting, sometimes fleeing, till he brought off his forces safely. Then, almost before the dust was laid upon the war-path, his face was again toward his enemies, and he was ready for renewed conflict. His whole soul was in his work. He had no doubts nor parleyings within himself. He put the whole force of his being into his blows for the worst cause man ever fought for, as few of our generals have ever learned to do for the best cause for which trumpet ever sounded. Henceforth we know him no more after the flesh. He is no longer a foe. We think of him now as a noble-minded gentleman, a rare and eminent Christian! For years he has been an active member of the Presbyterian Church, of which he was a ruling elder. He never, in all the occupations of the camp, or temptation of campaigns, lost the fervor of his piety, or remitted his Christian duties.

"We know that before every important move he spent much time in prayer. He had so put his soul in the keeping of his Master, that he was relieved from all thought of

11*

self, and had the whole power of his life ready for his work. Officers of Fremont's army, who pursued him in his famous retreat from the Shenandoah Valley, found him to be greatly beloved by the common people, among whom, in former times, he had labored, in prayer-meetings, in temperance meetings, and in every Christian word and work. No wonder he fought well along a region whose topography he had mapped down with prayers, exhortations, and Christian labor!

"He was unselfish. He fought neither for reputation now, nor for future personal advancement. . . . He incessantly struck on the right and on the left, and kept alive the fire in the hearts of ill-clad, poorly-fed, and over-worked men by the excitement of enterprise and the constant relish of victories, small in detail, but whose sum was all-important. Let no man suppose that the North will triumph over a fallen son with insulting gratulations! Nowhere else will the name of Jackson be more honored."

CHAPTER XV.

THE CHRISTIAN HERO.

Jackson's Religious Habits—Returns Public Thanks to God for Victory—Seeks Guidance in Prayer—His Missionary Spirit—Services before the "Stonewall Brigade"—Secret Prayer—Religious Condition of Jackson's Army—A Revival among the Soldiers—Letter of General Jackson on Sabbath Mails and Despatches—Dying Exclamations.

In the previous chapter, and incidentally in the body of our narrative, allusions have been made to the religious spirit which influenced General Jackson's every action. In his official reports he attributed every victory which he gained to the blessing of God; and at the termination of an engagement, he assembled his troops to render thanks to God for the victory they had achieved, and to implore his continual favor in the future. An example of the latter will be found in the following extract from a letter of a Southern correspondent, written shortly after the battle of McDowell:

"A significant illustration of the elevated virtues and principles which governed Jackson's public acts was given on Monday last, three miles north of Franklin, in Pendleton county. On the morning of that day, he addressed his troops in a few terse and pointed remarks, thanking them for the courage, endurance, and soldierly conduct displayed at the battle of McDowell, on Thursday, the eighth instant, and closed by appointing ten o'clock of that day, as an occasion of prayer and thanksgiving throughout the army, for the victory which followed that bloody engagement. There, in the beautiful little valley of the South Branch, with the blue and towering mountains covered with the verdure of spring, the green sward smiling a welcome to the season of flowers, and the bright sun, unclouded, lending a genial refreshing warmth, that army, equipped for the stern conflict of war, bent in humble praise and thanksgiving to the God of battles for the success vouchsafed to our arms in the recent sanguinary encounter of the two armies. While this solemn ceremony was progressing in every regiment, the minds of the soldiery drawn off from the bayonet and sabre, the enemy's artillery was occasionally belching forth its leaden death, yet all unmoved stood that worshipping army, acknowledging the supremacy of the will of Him who controls the destinies of men and nations, and chooses the weaker things of earth to confound the mighty."

The Reverend Moses Hoge, D.D., pastor of one of the principal churches in Richmond, Virginia, and one of Jackson's personal friends, speaks of him in the following terms :

" No pressure of military duties caused him to neglect the necessary offices of religion. Prayer was mingled with all his plans and acts. A distinguished officer, who ascribes his own religious impressions to his association with General Jackson, told me that on one occasion he went with a comrade to the General's tent to consult him about the plan of a battle, soon to be fought. After some interchange of views, the officer said: 'General, what is your decision?' 'Call to-morrow morning,' was the reply, 'and I will inform you.' On leaving the tent, his comrade said to the officer: 'Do you know why the General said he would give his decision to-morrow?' 'No; I suppose he wants to think it over,' was the answer. 'Not exactly that,' rejoined the other, 'he wants to pray it over.' In about half an hour the officer had occasion to return to the tent, on some other errand, and on thoughtlessly entering, without being announced, was struck with awe at seeing the General on his knees engaged in prayer."

"This was the man," continues the narrator, "who knew how to stand up like a stone wall against the enemies of his country, bowing humbly before his God, begging his guidance and powerful aid."

In writing of the missionary spirit displayed by Jackson, Dr. Hoge assures us that—

"In every possible way he labored to elevate the moral and spiritual character of the soldiers. He gave to chaplains, to colporteurs, and to the clergymen who occasionally visited his camp, all the encouragement and coöperation in his power. When the Holy Sacrament was administered, he assisted in the distribution of the elements. And when revivals of religion occurred among the troops under his command, he rejoiced with a joy which even victory did not inspire. In the last conversation I ever had with him, he said he intended to make every effort to increase the number and efficiency of chaplains in the army.

"When he suddenly came in view of a body of troops, and the men began to cheer, as they always did when they caught sight of him, he would spur his horse into a rapid gallop, as if anxious to escape the clamorous homage so joyously accorded to him."

An extract from another private letter which further illustrates Jackson's devout character has been permitted to be published. It is addressed to Dr. Hoge by his brother, who says:

"I have just returned from a visit to General Jackson's headquarters, at Moss Neck, the grand mansion of Mr. ——, some ten miles from Fredericksburgh. The General modestly occupies the lower room of one of the offices in the yard. As soon as I arrived, General Jackson claimed me as his guest, and I gladly spent what time I could with him. I found Mr. —— regularly ensconced in his office, as a sort of chaplain-general, not officially, of course, but virtually. His work is partly to increase the number of chaplains, placing them where most needed, and partly to preach himself wherever there is need of it in the corps. His position is very important, and his residence with General Jackson not only furthers his influence, but is personally profitable to him. Indeed, it seems hardly possible to be long in the society of that noble and honored general, that simple-hearted, straightforward, laborious man of God, without catching something of his spirit—the spirit of toil, of patience, of modesty, of careful conscientiousness, of child-like dependence on God, of fervent, believing prayer. While in camp I preached five times in the Stonewall Brigade. How the men crowded into their log church, how they listened, how they seemed to hang upon the word, you, of all men, need least to be told, for you have seen so much of them from the beginning of the war. On Sunday night, after preaching, the General, Mr. ——, and myself had a long talk, as we sat drying our boots in front of the open fire. When it was near eleven o'clock, the General asked me to conduct worship; and afterward, before retiring, he set us the example of kneeling again for secret prayer. He then shared his bed upon the floor with me, and we talked till long after midnight. Though usually taciturn, he led the conversation. How anxious he was for his army! how anxious for himself! How manifest it was that he is a man whose great desire is to be right in all things, and especially to be right before God! In our whole intercourse I could not detect the slightest trace of self-importance, ostentation, or seeking after vainglory. To glorify God possessed all his thoughts. 'I have been thinking a great deal about our chief end lately,' said he, 'and I believe the first answer in our catechism tells us it is to glorify God, and to enjoy him for ever; and I think,' he added, 'we need not trouble ourselves much about the second part, if we only attend well to the first. I find my life in camp a very happy one when I am enabled to keep this aim steadily before me—to live for the glory of God.' I found him very earnest also in his views as to our duties to the negroes. He used to teach a Sunday-school for colored children in Lexington, and all the pressure of his great duties and cares does not divert his thoughts from the spiritual interests of our servants."

Another illustration of the religious condition of Jackson's troops is given in the following extract from a letter written by the Rev. Dr. Stiles, who was, at the time of writing, laboring as an evangelist in the Confederate army of the Potomac :

"At his earnest request, I preached to General Pryor's brigade last Sabbath. Upon one hour's notice he marched up twelve or fifteen hundred men, who listened with so much interest to a long sermon, that I was not surprised to hear of such a beginning of religious interest in various regiments of the brigade as issued in a half-way promise on my part to fall in with the proposal of the General to preach very early to his soldiers for a succession of nights. In General's Lawton's brigade there is a more decided state of religious excitement. The great body of the soldiers in some of the regiments meet for prayer and exhortation every night, exhibit the deepest solemnity, and present themselves numerously for the prayers of the chaplains and the Church. Quite a pleasant number express hope in Christ. In all other portions of General Early's division, (formerly General Ewell's,) a similar religious sensibility prevails.

" In General Trimble's, and the immediately neighboring brigades, there is in progress, at this hour, one of the most glorious revivals I ever witnessed. Some days ago a young chaplain of the Baptist Church — as a representative of three others of the same denomination—took a long ride to solicit my coöperation, stating that a promising seriousness had sprung up within their diocese. I have now been with him three days and nights, preaching and laboring constantly with the soldiers when not on drill. The audiences and the interest have grown to glorious dimensions. It would rejoice you over-deeply to glance for one instant on our night-meeting in the wild woods, under a full moon, aided by the light of our side-stands. You would behold a mass of men seated on the earth all around you, (I was going to say for the space of half an acre,) fringed in all its circumference by a line of standing officers and soldiers, two or three deep, all exhibiting the most solemn and respectful earnestness that an assembly ever displayed. An officer said to me, last night, on returning from worship, he never had witnessed such a scene, though a Presbyterian elder, especially such an abiding solemnity and delight in the services as prevented all whispering in the outskirts, leaving of the congregation, or restless change of position. I suppose, at the close of the services, we had some sixty or seventy men and officers come forward and publicly solicit an interest in our prayers, and there may have been as many more who from the press could not reach the stand. I have already conversed with quite a number, who seem to give pleasant evidence of a return to God, and all things seem to be rapidly developing for the best.

"The officers, especially Generals Jackson and Early, have modified military rules for our accommodation. I have just learned that General A. P. Hill's division enjoys as rich a dispensation of God's Spirit as General Early's. Ask all the brethren and sisters to pray for us and the army at large."

The following letter, written by General Jackson three days before the battle of Fredericksburgh, is here given, as it so plainly corroborates the previous assertions:

To Colonel A. R. Boteler, Member of the Confederate Congress.

. . . "I have read with great interest the report of the Congressional Committee, recommending the repeal of the law requiring the mails to be carried on the Sabbath, and hope you will feel it a duty, as well as a pleasure, to urge its repeal. I do not see how a nation that thus arrays itself, by such a law, against God's holy day, can expect to escape his wrath. The punishment of national sins must be confined to this world, as there is no nationality beyond the grave. For fifteen years I have refused to mail letters on Sunday, or take them out of the office on that day, except since I came into the field. And so far from having to regret my course, it has been a source of true enjoyment. I have never sustained loss in observing what God enjoins, and I am well satisfied that the law should be repealed at the earliest practicable moment. My rule is to let the Sabbath mail remain unopened until Monday, unless it contains a despatch, but despatches are generally sent by couriers, or telegraph or some other special method. I do not recollect a single instance of any pressing despatch having reached me since the commencement of the war through the mail. . . .

"If you desire the repeal of the law, I trust you will bring all your influence to bear upon its accomplishment. Now is the time, it appears to me, to effect so desirable an object. I understand that not only our President, but also most of our colonels, and a majority of our congressmen are professing Christians. God has greatly blessed us, and I trust that he will make us 'that people whose God is the Lord.' Let us look to God for an illustration in our history that 'Righteousness exalteth a nation, but sin is a reproach to any people.' . . .

"Very truly, your friend,

"T. J. JACKSON."

Living and dying, a strong religious sentiment ever pervaded Jackson's thoughts. "My trust is in God," said he to one of his aids, with whom, a night or two before Chancellorsville, he had been discussing the probability and issue of a battle. He talked over the matter fully, became unusually excited, then paused, and with deep humility and reverence uttered the words which we have quoted. He immediately after displayed that remarkable energy which seemed to be so closely connected with his devotional spirit. As if the sound of battle was in his ear, he raised himself to his tallest stature, and with flashing eyes, and a face all blazoned with the fire of the conflict, he exclaimed : "I wish they would come." When Lee wrote to him condoling with him for his accident, on hearing the note read, Jackson exclaimed to his attendants : " General Lee should give the glory to God." It was an expression of his modesty and his reverence.

A religious friend and companion of Jackson's remarks that the General, during his dying moments, endeavored to cheer those who were around him. Noticing the sadness of his beloved wife, he said to her tenderly : " I know you would gladly give your life for me, but I am perfectly resigned. Do not be sad—I hope I shall recover. Pray for me, but always remember in your prayer to use the petition, Thy will be done." Those who were present noticed a remarkable development of tenderness in his manner and feelings during his illness, that was a beautiful mellowing of that iron sternness and imperturbable calm that characterized him in his military operations. Advising his wife, in the event of his death, to return to her father's house, he remarked : " You have a kind and good father ; but there is no one so kind and good as your heavenly Father." When she told him that the doctors did not think he could live two hours, although he did not himself expect to die, he replied : " It will be infinite gain to be translated to heaven, and be with Jesus." He then said he had much to say to her, but was too weak.

Jackson had always desired to die, if it were God's will, on the Sabbath. God granted him that wish. He seemed to greet the light of the day on which he breathed his last with peculiar pleasure, and exclaimed with evident delight : " It is the Lord's day "

CHAPTER XVI.

INCIDENTS AND ANECDOTES.

Jackson's Peculiarities subject him to Caricature — Military Discipline at Lexington—War Means Fighting—Secrecy—Going to the Commissary — An Inquisitive Friend — A Ruse — Coolness — Sambo's Prisoner — An Irish Rebel—A Watery Wish — Daily Work—Abhorrence of Sectional Hate—Double Rations—"Old Jackson always Moving"—Poking about —Crossing the Potomac—Surrounded—An Incentive to Victory—The Observed of all Observers—"No Great Shakes, after all"—A Federal Captain's Opinion—An Equestrian Compliment—Experiences on Horseback—"Jackson Resigned"—Headquarters and their Attractions—Playing with Children—Visit to Jackson in Camp.

AMONG the numerous anecdotes which have been related of our hero, there are many that are well worth preserving. These, together with the particulars of several incidents in his career, which if inserted in the body of our work would have somewhat interfered with the line of narrative, are collected into this chapter:

Before the outbreak of the Rebellion, Jackson was almost unknown beyond the limits of Lexington. In the Institute he was as much a soldier as he had been before, or proved himself to be after, his professional career. He was then as strict in the performance of duty, and as exact in regard to others as if he were in the field. It is stated of him that "he was scarcely known beyond the walls of the Institute in which he continued to perform his official duties with military regularity, and if the outer world heard of him at all, it was only through jests or witticisms directed against his peculiarities of character and demeanor by some of the students who, with the love of fun proverbial in their class, had much to say of the eccentricities and odd ways of 'Old Tom Jackson.' The universal tendency to caricature the peculiarities of a man of original genius is well known—to make fun of those very great traits which separate such men from the commonplace mass of human beings—and Jackson received more than a fair share of this undesirable attention on the part of his students. He was a martinet in the performance of his duties—administered things in his department 'on a war footing,' and no doubt caused the volatile young men whom he taught, to regard him a most unreasonable and exacting stickler for useless military etiquette and ceremony. But he was conscientious in this extreme attention to little things, and he was clearly right. The Institute was a *military* school—its chief value consisted in the habits of military obedience which it impressed upon the ductile characters of the youth of the Commonwealth—and Jackson no doubt regarded any relaxation of the rules of the establishment as tending directly to strike at the intentions of its founders, and destroy its usefulness. We have heard that he once continued to wear a thick woollen uniform late in the summer, and when asked by one of the professors why he did so, replied that he had seen an order prescribing that dress, but none had been exhibited to him directing it to be changed. This was the source of some amusement to the young gentlemen who had no idea of military 'orders,' and the implicit obedience which a good soldier considers it his bounden duty to pay to them."

At one time the Richmond newspapers, which had shown the most eagerness for the "aggressive action" of the Confederate Government, filled their columns with anecdotes of Jackson; and the *Whig* became extremely facetious in satirizing what it chose to term the "slow movements of the Government." There was a long advertisement from a supposed superintendent of a lunatic asylum, offering a liberal reward for the capture of "one calling himself Thomas J. Jackson, who was attempting to make his way to Washington; the entire efforts of the United States and the Confederate authorities having failed to arrest him," . . . and that if he were not "stopped without delay, he would succeed in establishing the independence of the Southern Confederacy; as he had evidently taken it into his head that war meant fighting."

It was about this time that the hero himself became somewhat irascible, and sent the following terse telegram to the War Department at Richmond: "Send me more men, and fewer questions."

Jackson's words, "Mystery, mystery is the secret of success!" have already been quoted. The author of *Battle-*

Fields of the South, who took part in Jackson's campaign against Pope, says :

" Secrecy has been the characteristic of all our movements ; civilians are seldom allowed admission to our camps under any pretence ; strong guards always encircle our lines, so that it is almost an impossibility to gain entrance. Thus, until the latest moment, none know the destination of troops, or the object in view, and even the brigadiers are frequently no better informed than the humblest patriot in the ranks. If this is true of movements generally, it is peculiarly so in regard to the rapid marches of ' Stonewall ;' for a person might as reasonably ' whistle jigs to a milestone' as attempt to glean information from the sharp-eyed, tart, sarcastic, crabbed-spoken Jackson. When his corps received orders to move, some imagined merely ' a change of camps,' or some such indifferent movement; yet when Richmond was left far to the south, and the column proceeded rapidly in a north-western direction, many old campaigners began to whistle ominously, and with a mysterious wink in the direction of the Shenandoah Valley, would sarcastically observe, ' Lee's short of rations again ! Jackson's detailed to go to the commissary !' in allusion to the immense supplies more than once captured by Jackson from the unfortunate Banks." -

Another illustration of Jackson's reticence is here given :

" He firmly declined the luxury of 'hospitable mansions ' along the line of his march ; nor, after his occupation of Winchester, could he, without much difficulty, be induced to

pass a night in the house of any old friend in Frederick, Clarke, or Jefferson. He preferred to sleep among his men. It was one of these valley friends of his who miscarried so absurdly in an attempt to cajole him out of his imperturbable reticence. The gentleman, at whose house Jackson had been induced to make a brief visit in passing, was eagerly curious to learn what the next movement of the ubiquitous rebel would be; so he boldly claimed his confidence on the score of ancient friendship. After a few minutes of well-affected concern and reflection, the grim joker button-holed his bore. 'My staunch old friend,' said he, with mysterious deliberation, ' can—you—keep—a secret?' 'Ah! General.' 'So can I.' "

Some of the incidents of the Valley campaign are extremely amusing. We will give a few examples. The first relates to the coolness of the commander.

"In one of his late flights, 'Old Stonewall' got into a tight place. He found himself surrounded, with only one way of escape, which was over a bridge raked by a battery of the Federals. The old hero saw, in a moment, his strait. With his cape over his uniform, he rode up to the battery, and said, 'Boys, you have this battery in the wrong place; move it to that eminence,' pointing to a hill a short distance up. 'Limber up and be in a hurry.' The order was obeyed, and, as the artillery was taking the new position, ' *Stonewall* ' rode safely across the bridge."*

* Another version of the story is this:

" Jackson, finding that this gun commanded the bridge which it was

12

Next we have an account of the manner in which a "contraband" treated a "Yankee:"

"A negro entered the quartermaster's office in Staunton, tipped his wool, and said:

"'Mar's 'Arman—here a prisoner.'

"'Where did you get him?'

"'Massa sent him, and tole me to see him shot up safe, and de key turned on him.'

"'Well, Sambo—as you have brought him safely so far —take him over to the jail and see him locked up.'

"'Thank'e Massa—come along, Yankee;' and he proudly marched off his prisoner to the jail."

An Irish Rebel's wit sparkles forth in the following:

"What army do you belong to, Pat?" inquired a gentleman of a son of Erin.

"Faith, thin," replied Pat, "it's meself that's a part of the ould *Stone*wall, and be jabers! ivery man in that same is a *brick*, shure."

Here is the opinion of a native Virginian. On the re-

necessary for him to pass, for once in his life played the Yankee, and riding briskly forward, stood erect in his stirrups, exclaiming, 'Bring that gun over here,' designating the place. The ruse succeeded. The Yankee captain limbered up and commenced moving his piece, when Old Stonewall, putting spurs to his horse, dashed across the bridge. The Yankee discovered the ruse, and let fly with his gun, but it was too late. It was not in the book of fate that the glorious chieftain should fall in that way. The Federal soldier in charge of the gun was a Captain Robinson, who, on relating the incident, exclaimed: 'I might have known that I could not hit him.'"

treat of Banks, one of the Stonewall Brigade, who was in the van, wearied with tramping over the bad roads, said to a comrade:

"I'm tired of pulling my legs out of the mud; I wish all the Yankees were at the bottom of the sea."

"No, no," said his friend; "if that were the case, ' Old Stonewall' would be within stone's throw, and the first brigade would be in the lead."

Captain Cooper Nisbet, whose company of the Twenty-first Georgia Regiment had been with Jackson in his battles, thus wrote to a friend:

" Marching, fighting, and skirmishing, have been our daily business since the middle of May. Without tents, and often with short rations, we cheerfully move wherever our glorious leader orders. General Jackson, like old Frederick the Great, fights to win, and will win or die. At the same time, he is very considerate of the lives and comfort of his men. He shares our fate, and never says, 'Go in, boys, and fight;' but 'Come, boys, let us whip the Yankees.' And when he says the word, we are ready, for we all feel that what he does is right. His men all love the old Gamecock of the Valley, and if the humblest soldier gives him a salutation, his hat is lifted in return. Now that he has whipped out Banks, Shields, and Fremont, he will soon be in Maryland, and thundering at the gates of Washington City, if our authorities will only send him men."

Sectional hate formed no part of our hero's character, which fact is illustrated in the subjoined anecdote:

"When the question of Secession, Union, or 'Armed Neutrality' went before the people of Virginia, Stonewall Jackson voted the Union ticket; but when the State went out he went with her. From first to last he had no patience (if such a phrase can be true of such a man) with the intemperate expressions of bitter sectional hate that continually affronted his ear; and he was blunt in his admonition to the women of Winchester—when he again left the checkered fortunes of that town to our advancing troops—'not to forget themselves.' 'My child,' he would say to some immoderate rebel in crinoline, 'you and I have no right to our hates; personal rancor is the lowest expression of patriotism, and a sin beside. We must leave these things to God.'"

Jackson's native shyness clung to him through life. Public demonstrations in the form of cheers were exceedingly embarrassing to him. It is said that, after the two days' bombardment of Harper's Ferry, when at last the garrison capitulated, the Federal soldiers, in due appreciation of the gallantry of their captors, surrendered with hearty cheers; and that Jackson was so confused and astonished at the unexpected compliment, that wholly incapable of making an appropriate "speech," he could think of no other acknowledgment than to order *double rations* to his prisoners.

An "English combatant" in the Confederate service narrates an incident, which occurred upon one of the nights of the eventful week which terminated the siege of Richmond. He says.

"More asleep than awake, duties called me in various directions, and the universal bustle indicated that a general engagement was anticipated. Infantry were busy cleaning arms, field officers stood aloof in groups, conversing; generals and staff moved to and fro, while couriers were everywhere inquiring for Jackson, Longstreet, Hill, Magruder, and all the generals in the army. None could tell where these officers were. A few moments before, such an one was seen passing up the road, another down, but where they were at any particular time the best informed could not pretend to tell. In and out of the woods they were moving incessantly. 'Where *is* old Jackson, I wonder?' petulantly inquired a dusty courier, with his horse in a foam; 'I wish to heaven these generals would have some fixed spot where they might be found; but the devil of it is, old Jackson is *always* moving about. I think he even walks in his sleep, or never sleeps at all, for here have I been hunting him for the past hour.' Every body in the group laughed, except one seedy, oldish-looking officer, intently listening to the picket-firing in front, whom nobody thought to be more than some old major or other. 'Here is Jackson, young man,' said the officer, turning quietly, without a muscle moving. 'Return to your post, sir,' said he; 'this paper requires no answer.' And he put it in his pocket, and trotted off as unconcerned as if nothing had happened. 'Who would have thought *that* was he?' we all exclaimed. 'Oh! 'tis just like him,' said one; 'I have known him to dismount and help artillery out of the mud for half an hour at the time, and ride off again without being discovered. He is always poking about in out-of-the-way places : not unfrequently he rides unattended to distant outposts at night, and converses with the pickets about the movements of the enemy, and without more ceremony than you just now saw exhibited. It is his continual industry and sleeplessness that have routed Banks, Shields, and others in the Valley. He is continually moving himself, and expects all under him to be animated by the same solicitude and watchfulness.' "

From the commencement of the Rebellion, Jackson had looked forward to an invasion of the enemy's territory, as the only certain means of bringing the war to an end. Long before the invasion of Maryland he wrote to a friend, who was the recipient of his most private feelings : "I am cordially with you in favor of carrying the war north of the Potomac." After the defeat of Pope, Jackson, according to custom, inquired with great interest what roads led to one district, and ordered maps of it to be prepared for his use, and then put his troops into motion in a contrary direction. This latter led him on his road to Maryland. An incident which occurred on the passage of the Potomac is worth relating. A correspondent says :

"When our army reached the middle of the river, which they were wading, the troops were halted, General Jackson pulled off his hat, and the splendid bands of music struck up the inspiring air of 'Maryland, my Maryland,' which was responded to and sung with ' the spirit and with the understanding' by all who could sing, and the name of all who could then and there sing was legion."

Whilst in Maryland Jackson occasioned much curiosity. Upon one occasion, when the ladies crowded around him, he is represented as saying:

"Ladies, this is the first time I was ever surrounded," in spite of which, says a letter-writer, "they cut every button off his coat, commenced on his pants, and at one time threatened to leave him in the uniform of a Georgia colonel—shirt-collar and spurs." Another incident was related of him by Colonel Ford, a Federal officer, who conversed with the General at Harper's Ferry:

"While we were in conversation," says the Colonel, "an orderly rode rapidly across the bridge, and said to General Jackson: 'I am ordered by General McLaws to report to you that General McClellan is within six miles with an immense army.' Jackson took no notice of the orderly apparently, and continued his conversation; but when the orderly had turned away, Jackson called after him, with the question: 'Has McClellan any baggage-train or drove of cattle?' The reply was that he had. Jackson remarked, that *he could whip any army that was followed by a drove of cattle*, alluding to the hungry condition of his men."

"Jackson was the observed of all observers during our stay in Maryland," writes the author of *Battle-Fields of the South*, "and hundreds travelled many score miles to see the great original 'Stonewall,' against which the Federal generals had so often broken their heads. Crowds were continually hanging round his headquarters, and peeping through the windows, as if anxious to catch him at his 'in-cantations,' for many believed he was in league with the Old Boy, and had constant intercourse with him. Others, again, actually thought that he was continually praying, and imagined that angelic spirits were his companions and counsellors; and it was not until the great man had mounted his old horse, and frequently aired himself in the streets, that many began to think him less than superna-tural. His shabby attire and unpretending deportment quite disappointed the many who expected to see a great display of gold lace and feathers; and when he ordered his guards to clear his quarters of idle crowds, many went away muttering: 'Oh! he's no great shakes after all!'"

This redoubtable chieftain was no less a subject of in-terest to his enemies than to his friends. In every Federal account is apparent the intense anxiety his presence and movements created. During the battles before Richmond, a Federal captain, who had been taken prisoner, was re-clining under a tree, when General Lee and staff rode by. The captain, struck with the dignified and soldierly appear-ance of the General, languidly inquired who he was, and expressed unfeigned admiration at his fine figure on horse-back. Soon after General Jackson rode by, and the weary prisoner again proffered his inquiries. "That's glorious old Stonewall!" exclaimed the guard, cheering lustily as his eye followed the hero. Up sprang the recumbent prisoner, and, gazing curiously until the General was out of sight, lay down again, with an expression of disappointment, mut-tering: " Well, he ain't much for looks, anyhow!"

The awkward figure of Jackson upon horseback has been the subject of frequent merriment. He usually rode in a loose, shambling attitude, and was very indifferent about his dress and appearance. On one occasion he approached a squad of soldiers at dusk, his horse floundering along through the mire, and himself reeling in the saddle, like a drunken man; so that one of the soldiers, not recognizing him, shouted, as he passed: "I say, old fellow, you look as if you knew where to help yourself to liquor; I wish you would hand me some." Judge of the man's embarrassment when his comrades hastily silenced him by the information that the awkward cavalier was no other than their idolized hero, Stonewall Jackson.

"General Jackson was never known to put his horse out of a trot," wrote a Southern soldier, "except when desirous of escaping the cheering of his men, on which occasions he would raise his cap, discovering a high, bald forehead, and force his old 'sorrel' into a gallop. This old 'sorrel' war-horse is well known throughout the army; with head down, it seldom attempts more than a trot, but stands fire well, and that may be the reason why the General prefers and always rides him. Many gentlemen, imagining that the hero would appear to better advantage on a blood animal, have presented several to him, but they are seldom used. When our army entered Maryland, in September, 1862, in order to get in the rear of General Miles at Harper's Ferry, and secure the fourteen thousand men under his command, Jackson's corps was stationed east of Fred

12*

erick, and an influential citizen, in token of admiration, gave the commander a very valuable horse, that he might appear to advantage. Jackson mounted in the public street, and was immediately thrown into the mud! The old 'sorrel' was again brought forth, and the General ambled off, very good humoredly, never assaying to mount 'fine' horses again."

The old 'sorrel,' however, unfortunately came to an untimely end. A correspondent of the New-York *Tribune*, in describing Jackson's equestrianism, says:

" On horseback he by no means looked the hero of a tableau. On his earlier fields and marches he had been blessed with a 'charger' that happily resembled its rider—'a plain horse, that went straight ahead, and minded his own business;' but one day it got shot under him, and then his friends presented him with a more ornamental beast, a mare that took on airs, and threw him; so he exchanged her, in disgust, for a less visionary and artistic quadruped —still a horse, but never such a congenial spirit as that original 'Ole Virginny' of his, that never tired, and whose everlasting long-legged, swinging walk was the very thing to make forced marches with. 'He's in the saddle now,' sang those limber Rebels, from the song of their corps:

> 'He's in the saddle now! Fall in!
> Steady the whole brigade!
> Hill's at the Ford, cut off! we'll win
> His way out, ball and blade.

What matter if our shoes are worn?
What matter if our feet are torn?
Quick-step! We're with him before morn!
That's Stonewall Jackson's way.' "

That Jackson was not at all times indifferent to personal appearance we gather from one correspondent, who was "agreeably surprised" to behold him "sweeping along one day on a large, handsome bay horse, showily attired in full general's uniform, with a jaunty cap upon his head, and a full black beard; presenting altogether quite a dazzling sight to *us*, accustomed to our usually slovenly headquarters."

During the time that the opposing armies were lying close to each other on the Rappahannock, previous to the battle of Fredericksburgh, amusing conversations frequently occurred between the outposts on the river-banks.

"How are you, rebels?" asked a Federal soldier, one cold morning, blowing his fingers.

"Oh! not very good, to-day," was the reply. "We have suffered an awful loss! Jackson has resigned!"

" 'Jackson resigned!" was the astonished exclamation in rejoinder. "Why, how was that?" asked the Federals, who greatly feared the very name of old Stonewall.

"Oh! he resigned because they removed his commissary-general, and he wouldn't stand it."

"His commissary-general, eh? Then who was he?" they inquired in much surprise.

"Banks!" was the significant reply.

It was said: " General Jackson's headquarters are often
under a tree, and his couch is a fence corner; his equipage
is little more than a frying-pan and a blanket. He sees personally to the execution of his own orders. The effect of
this industry is evident in the efficiency of his men. The activity of a perpetual ' forward' seems to pervade his army;
they never get out of ammunition—they never lose baggage
or stores; whether drawn from the government, or captured from the enemy, no matter, they are always ready to
move at the right time."

But the quarters which Jackson occupied shortly after
the battle of Fredericksburgh were an exception to the
above rule. We have already stated that he was engaged
at this time in the preparation of his reports. The four
winter months which elapsed before the battle of Chancellorsville were, however, not entirely passed in laborious occupations connected with his official position. "Many pleasant incidents," says a Virginian, "are related of him at
this period, which we could dwell upon at length did time
and space permit. Those who visited Moss Neck during
those days, gave a humorous description of the surroundings of the famous General Stonewall. Before his tent was
pitched, he established his headquarters in a small out-
building of the Corbin House; and all who came to trans-
act business with Lieutenant-General Jackson, were struck
by a series of headquarter ornaments of the most unique
and surprising description. On the walls of the apartment
were pictures of race-horses, well known and dear in former

days to the planters of the neighboring region. Then there was a portrait of some celebrated game-cock, ready-trimmed and gaffed for conflict to the death. A companion-piece of these, was the picture of a terrier engaged in furious onslaught upon an army of rats, which he was seizing, tearing, and shaking to death as fast as they came. These decorations of headquarters excited the merriment of the General's associates; and one of them suggested to him that a drawing of the apartment should be made, with the race-horses, game-cocks, and terrier in bold relief, the picture to be labelled, 'View of the winter-quarters of General Stonewall Jackson, presenting an insight into the tastes and character of the individual.'

"Hearty laughter on the part of General Jackson greeted this jest from the distinguished brother soldier who had stood beside him upon so many bloody fields — whom he loved and opened his whole heart to — and to whom, when struck down by the fatal ball at Chancellorsvile, his mind first turned as his successor.

"The children of the house, and in the neighborhood, will long remember the kind voice and smile of the great soldier—his caresses and affectionate ways. A new military cap had been sent him just before the battle of Fredericksburgh, which was resplendent with gold braid and all manner of decorations. General Jackson did not admire this fine substitute for that old, sun-scorched head-covering which had so long served him; and when, one day, a little girl was standing at his knee, looking up from her clustering curls at the kindly General, whose hand was caressing her hair, he found a better use for the fine gold braid around the cap. He called for a pair of scissors, ripped it off, and joining the ends, placed it like a coronet upon her head, with smiles and evident admiration of the pretty picture thus presented.

"Another little girl, in one of the hospitable houses of that region, told the present writer that when she expressed to a gentleman her wish to kiss General Jackson, and the gentleman repeated her words, the General blushed very much, and turned away with a slight laugh, as if he were confused.

"These are trifles, let us agree, good reader; but is it not a pleasant spectacle to see the great soldier amid these kindly simple scenes—to watch the stern and indomitable leader, whose soul has never shrunk in the hour of deadliest peril, passing happy moments in the society of laughing children?

"At the first battle of Manassas, while Jackson's wound was being dressed, some one said : ' Here comes the President.' He threw aside the surgeons, rose suddenly to his feet, and whirling his old cap around his head, cried, with the fire of battle in his eyes :

"'Hurrah for the President! Give me ten thousand men, and I'll be in Washington to-night!'

"It was the same man who blushed when a child expressed her wish to kiss him."

An Englishman who had brought a box from Nassau to

General Jackson, received an invitation to visit him in his camp. He did so in March, 1863, and on his way thither experienced a drenching rain. He gives the following particulars of his visit:

"Wet to the skin, I stumbled through mud, I waded through creeks, I passed through pine-woods, and at last I got into camp about two o'clock. I then made my way to a small house occupied by the General as his headquarters. I wrote down my name and gave it to the orderly, and I was immediately told to walk in. The General rose and greeted me warmly. I expected to see an old untidy man, and was most agreeably surprised and pleased with his appearance. He is tall, handsome, and powerfully built, but thin. He has brown hair and a brown beard. His mouth expresses great determination. The lips are thin and compressed firmly together; his eyes are blue and dark, with a keen and searching expression. I was told that his age was thirty-eight, and he looks about forty. The General, who is indescribably simple and unaffected in all his ways, took off my wet overcoat with his own hands, made the fire, brought wood for me to put my feet on to keep them warm while my boots were drying, and then began to ask me questions on various subjects. At the dinner-hour we went out and joined the members of his staff. At this meal the General said grace in a fervent, quiet manner, which struck me much. After dinner I returned to his room, and he again talked to me for a long time. The servant came in and took his mattress out of a cupboard and laid it on the floor.

As I rose to retire, the General said : 'Captain, there is plenty of room on my bed ; I hope you will share it with me.' I thanked him very much for his courtesy, but said, 'Good night,' and slept in a tent, sharing the blankets of one of his aids-de-camp. In the morning, at breakfast-time, I noticed that the General said grace before the meal with the same fervor I had remarked before. An hour or two afterward it was time for me to return to the station ; on this occasion, however, I had a horse, and I turned up to the General's quarters to bid him adieu. His room was vacant, so I stepped in and stood before the fire. I then noticed my great-coat stretched before it on a chair. Shortly afterward the General entered the room. He said : 'Captain, I have been trying to dry your great-coat, but I am afraid I have not succeeded very well.' That little act illustrates the man's character. With the cares and responsibilities of a vast army on his shoulders, he finds time to do little acts of kindness and thoughtfulness which make him the darling of his men, who never seem to tire talking of him. Jackson is a man of great endurance; he drinks nothing stronger than water, and never uses tobacco or any stimulant. He has been known to ride for three days and three nights at a time, and if there is any labor to be undergone, he never fails to take his share of it."

CHAPTER XVII.

THE FOOT-CAVALRY.

Why called the "Foot Cavalry"—The old "Stonewall" Brigade—Doubts about the Name—A Parting Scene—The Greatest Marcher in the World—No Excuses permitted—Obedience to Orders—A Colored Thermometer—Jackson's Army not to be found by the Federals—A Cause of Reverse—The Army in Repose—Sports and Pastimes of Camp-life—"Old Jack" extremely popular—A Talk with the General—Disaffection of Officers—Discipline—Characteristics of the old "Stonewall" Brigade.

"WHERE is Jackson?"

How often, how very often was this question asked but a short time ago by both Federal and Confederate. The movements of his army were so rapid that friend and foe alike knew not where to find him. His brave soldiers could only be sure of the present. In vain were their calculations for the future. Just now they are quietly reposing in their camps—an hour hence they may be upon the march—a day hence thirty miles, ay, fifty miles may have been trodden. A confidential messenger was once intrusted with a despatch addressed "General T. J. Jackson, somewhere," which was ofttimes the only address that could be given of the rapidly-moving and reticent commander. To find out where that "somewhere" was, has many times puzzled aching heads at Washington.

It is not, therefore, to be wondered that Jackson's forces, from the rapidity of their movements, obtained the peculiar appellation of "*Foot-Cavalry*." This was the title given to the entire of Jackson's army. There was one portion of it, however, which was more particularly identified with its commander—that was the "*Stonewall* Brigade." It was with this brigade that Jackson fought on the upper Potomac in the early days of the rebellion. It was with this brigade that Jackson gained his imperishable name of "Stonewall" at the battle of Bull Run, on the plains of Manassas. Jackson, however, on several occasions, and especially on his death-bed, insisted that the term belonged to his soldiers, and not to himself. Among his latest expressions he said: "Men who live through this war will be proud to say to their children: 'I was one of the Stonewall Brigade.'" It does seem somewhat curious that it has never been satisfactorily decided whether the name of "Stonewall" was obtained by the leader from the brigade, or was acquired by the soldiers from their leader. It has been mooted that the brigade, composed chiefly of natives of the Shenandoah Valley, where abundance of rocks have brought stone walls into general use, was called by themselves the "Stonewall Brigade" from the commencement of the war. Jackson's death-bed declaration would seem to refer to this fact.*

* There is a village called Stonewall at the junction of a creek, bearing the same name, with the James River, a few miles below Lynchburgh, in Virginia. It has mills known as the Stonewall Mills.

Stonewall Jackson and the Stonewall Brigade were, however, for a time doomed to be separated from each other. This was upon the occasion of Jackson's being assigned, shortly after the battle of Bull Run, to the command of the troops in and around Winchester, then threatened by a large Federal army under General Banks.

"To his great sorrow," writes a Confederate officer, "the old First Brigade, which he had so long commanded, was to stay behind with the main army; and there took place, at the camp of the brigade, near Centreville, on the fourth of October, one of those scenes which irresistibly excite the deepest emotions of the heart, and light up the page of history which records them.

"On that day Jackson took leave of his old 'First Brigade.' The officers and men were drawn up as though in line of battle, and their commander appeared in front, as he had so often appeared before, when about to give the order for a charge upon the enemy. But now, no enthusiasm, no cheers awaited him. All knew for what purpose he came, and the sorrow which filled every heart, betrayed itself in the deep silence which greeted his approach. Not a sound along the line—not a hand raised in greeting—not a murmur even going to show that they recognized their beloved captain. The bronzed faces were full of the deepest dejection, and the stern fighters of the old brigade were like children about to be separated from their father.

"Jackson approached, and mastering his emotion by an effort, said, in the short abrupt tones with which all were so familiar:

"'I am not here to make a speech, but simply to say farewell. I first met you at Harper's Ferry in the commencement of this war, and I cannot take leave of you without giving expression to my admiration of your conduct from that day to this—whether on the march, the bivouac, the tented field, or on the bloody plains of Manassas, where you gained the well-deserved reputation of having decided the fate of the battle. Throughout the broad extent of country over which you have marched, by your respect for the rights and the property of citizens, you have shown that you were soldiers, not only to defend, but able and willing both to defend and protect. You have already gained a brilliant and deservedly high reputation throughout the army of the whole Confederacy, and I trust in the future, by your deeds on the field, and by the assistance of the same kind Providence who has heretofore favored our cause, you will gain more victories, and add additional lustre to the reputation you now enjoy. You have already gained a proud position in the future history of this our second war of independence. I shall look with great anxiety to your future movements, and I trust, whenever I shall hear of the *First Brigade* on the field of battle, it will be of still nobler deeds achieved, and higher reputation won!'

"Having uttered these words, Jackson paused for an instant, and his eye passed slowly along the line, as though he wished thus to bid farewell individually to every old familiar face, so often seen in the heat of battle, and so dear to him. The thoughts which crowded upon him seemed more than he could bear—he could not leave them with such formal words only—and that iron lip, which had never trembled in the hour of deadliest peril, now quivered. Mastered by an uncontrollable impulse, the great soldier rose in his stirrups, threw the reins on the neck of his horse with an emphasis which sent a thrill through every heart, and extending his arm, added, in tones of the deepest feeling :

" ' In the army of the Shenandoah you were the *First Brigade!* In the army of the Potomac you were the *First Brigade!* In the second corps of the army you are the *First Brigade!* You are the *First Brigade* in the affections of your General; and I hope by your future deeds and bearing you will be handed down to posterity as the *First Brigade* in this our second war of independence. Farewell ! '

"As the last words echoed in their ears, and Jackson turned to leave them, the long pent-up feeling burst forth. Three prolonged and deafening cheers rolled along the line of the old brigade ; and no sooner had they died away, than they were renewed, and again renewed. The calm face of the great leader flushed as he listened to that sound, but he did not speak. Waving his hand in token of farewell, he galloped away, and the old brigade, deprived of its beloved chief, returned slowly and sorrowfully to camp."

The separation was, however, fortunately but for a short time, as the " old brigade " soon after hastened to join their old General upon the banks of the Shenandoah.

The arduous duties which Jackson required his officers to perform did not always render him a favorite with them. They found that "active service" with him did not allow them much time for repose; in fact, they considered him the "greatest marcher in the world." One of these officers, writing at the commencement of the Valley campaign, says:

"When we moved up here, our first orders were for a march to Charlestown; next day we moved back to Winchester, in a few days again back to Charlestown, and thence from one place to another, until at last I began to imagine we were commanded by some peripatetic philosophical madman, whose forte was pedestrianism. With little or no baggage, we are a roving, hungry, hardy lot of fellows, and are not patronized at all by parsons or doctors; the latter have a perfect sinecure amongst us.

"'Stonewall' may be a very fine old gentleman, and an honest, good-tempered, industrious man, but I should admire him much more in a state of rest than continually seeing him moving in the front. . . . And don't he keep his aides moving about! Thirty miles' ride at night through the mud is nothing of a job; and if they don't come up to time, I'd as soon face the devil, for Jackson takes no excuses when duty is on hand. . . . From what he says there is no appeal, for he seems to know every hole and corner of this Valley as if he made it, or, at least, as if it had been designed for his own use. He knows all the distances, all the roads, even to cow-paths through the woods, and goat-tracks along the hills. He sits his horse very awkwardly, although, generally speaking, all Virginians are fine horsemen, and has a fashion of holding his head very high, and chin up, as if searching for something skywards; yet although you can never see his eyes for the cap-peak drawn down over them, nothing escapes *his* observation.

" His movements are sudden and unaccountable; his staff don't pretend to keep up with him, and, consequently, he is frequently seen alone, poking about in all sorts of holes and corners, at all times of night and day. I have frequently seen him approach in the dead of night and enter into conversation with sentinels, and ride off through the darkness without saying, ' God bless you,' or any thing civil to the officers. The consequence is, that the officers are scared, and the men love him."

Jackson faithfully obeyed all orders given to him. " No man in the army," writes the officer from whom we have just quoted, " is half so obedient as ' old Stonewall,' or so determined to be obeyed; the result is, that no army has shown greater endurance, marched farther, fought more frequently, suffered less, or done half the work that has fallen to our lot. Our men seem to know intuitively the designs of their commanders, and they second them without a murmur."

The proceedings of the negro servant, to whom allusion is made in a previous chapter, were continually being watched, so that some knowledge might be gained of intended movements.

" When last I put pen to paper," remarks the same officer, " I did not seriously imagine that old ' Stonewall ' intended moving in such fearful weather ; but when it was known the General's servant had packed up, I knew we were all bound for a tramp somewhere. ' Whenever I misses massa a little while in de day, I allers knows he's prayin' a spell ; whenever he's out all night, I knows we's goin' to move next day ; but when he stays out and comes back to have a long spell of prayin', I knows dare's goin' to be a fought somewhar, mighty quick, and dis chile packs up de walibles and gets out ob de way like a sensible colored pusson ! ' This colored thermometer was ' packin' up de walibles '— pots and pans ; so there was nothing to be done but ' grin and bear it.' Sure enough we *had* a long trip : our leader marched us nearly blind ; but as he was always in front himself, cheering on the men, all bore it patiently."

" Where is Jackson ? "

This question was never more difficult to answer than just previous to the seven days' conflict. General McClellan having been informed by a deserter that the ubiquitous commander was approaching Richmond with the intention of attacking the Federal rear, he telegraphed to the Secretary of War at Washington for information as to Jackson's position and movements, so that he might compare such information with that which he had received. The reply of the Secretary of War is so illustrative of Jackson's success in deceiving his foe, that we append it in full :

" We have no definite information as to the numbers or

position of Jackson's force. General King yesterday reported a deserter's statement that Jackson's force was, nine days ago, forty thousand men. Some reports place ten thousand rebels under Jackson at Gordonsville; others that his force is at Port Republic, Harrisonburgh, and Luray. Fremont yesterday reported rumors that Western Virginia was threatened, and General Kelly that Ewell was advancing to New-Creek, where Fremont has his dépôts. The last telegram from Fremont contradicts this rumor. The last telegram from Banks says the enemy's pickets are strong in advance at Luray. The people decline to give any information of his whereabouts. Within the last two days, the evidence is strong that, for some purpose, the enemy is circulating rumors of Jackson's advance in various directions, with a view to conceal the real point of attack. Neither McDowell, who is at Manassas, nor Banks and Fremont, who are at Middletown, appear to have any accurate knowledge of the subject. A letter transmitted to the department yesterday, purporting to be dated Gordonsville, on the fourteenth instant, stated that the actual attack was designed for Washington and Baltimore, as soon as you attacked Richmond; but that the report was to be circulated that Jackson had gone to Richmond, in order to mislead. This letter looked very much like a blind, and induces me to suspect that Jackson's real movement now is toward Richmond. It came from Alexandria, and is certainly designed, like the numerous rumors put afloat, to mislead. I think, therefore, that while the warning of the deserter to

13

you may also be a blind, that it could not safely be disregarded. I will transmit to you any further information on this subject that may be received here."

There can be little doubt but that the rapid march of Jackson and his " Foot-Cavalry " from the Shenandoah to the Chickahominy was mainly instrumental in changing the fortunes of war in front of the Confederate capital. After the battles which immediately succeeded this march had terminated, a Northern journalist wrote:

" It is very easy, now that the affair is over, to perceive the cause of McClellan's recent reverse. At the last moment, when least expected, and equally to the surprise, we have no doubt, of President Lincoln, Secretary Stanton, and General McClellan himself, Stonewall Jackson rushed from the Valley of the Shenandoah, attacked our right wing, forced it back, and got in rear of our whole army. without weakening the rebel force massed in front of it by a single man. No general on earth could make head against such a *coup de guerre*. If McClellan had stood his ground and fought in such a position, nothing in the world could have prevented the utter annihilation of the army of the Potomac."

It has more particularly been the object of this work to depict the doings of Jackson's army, whilst employed in the more active operations of warfare. Let us now give a picture of it in repose. In the beautiful month of October which succeeded the battle of Antietam, Jackson's corps rested in the picturesque valley of the Shenandoah, to recover its strength and spirits amid the scenes which its leader had already made so famous. There, on the banks of the Opequon, which murmurs under its tall trees, as it lapses gently toward the Potomac, did the weary soldiers of the Stonewall Corps find rest and refreshment; and the bracing air made them boys again, filling every pulse with health and joy. The jest, the practical joke, the ready laugh passed around; and for a time the whole army of Northern Virginia was in extravagant spirits, cheering upon the least provocation like a party of boys, and permitting no occasion for indulging in laughter to escape them. A letter written by one of the corps, about this time, conveys a very accurate idea of the manner in which Jackson's men amused themselves; and its careless style and homely details may serve to interest the stay-at-home reader, who is not familiar with the " goings on " of an army. We therefore transfer it to our pages :

" ' Cock-a-doodle-doo-oo !' sounded the 'shrill clarion ' of a neighboring hen-roost *before* day this morning; a wakeful soldier caught up the strain, and he and a hundred others forthwith repeated bogus cock-a-doodle-doos, until they had effectually ' murdered sleep ' throughout the entire regiment. To pass the time till breakfast (!) that is, till some 'solid-shot biscuit' and leather steaks of lean kind be cooked—I will 'retaliate' on you and your readers.

" The campaign having apparently ended, there are no moving accidents by flood or field of interest, and, therefore, nothing left to record but the routine of daily camp life; this shall be true to history, however, to let the old folks at home know how we live 'sure enough' while here. At this particular season though it is particularly dull—

'No mail, no post,
No news from any foreign coast;
No warmth, no cheerfulness, no healthful ease,
No comfortable feel in any member,
No shade, no sunshine, no butterflies, no bees,
November!'

" Our camp not being regulated by military rule for want of material in tents, etc., is left to illustrate the variegated architectural and domestic tastes of the thousand different individuals concerned. Hence, although a wall tent or Sibley graces an occasional locality, the most of the men ensconce themselves in bush-built shelters of various shapes, in fence-corners, under gum-blankets eked out by cedarboughs, or burrow semi-subterraneously, like Esquimaux. If, as is said, the several styles of architecture took their origin from natural circumstances and climate, etc., as the curving Oriental roofs, from the long reeds originally in use —the slanting Egyptian, from the necessity of baking their unburnt bricks in the hot sun—the Corinthian, from its own flowery clime, etc., etc.—an architectural genius might find enough original designs in this camp to supply a century to come.

"The only 'useful occupation' of this brigade for some time past has been to destroy all the railroads in reach; apparently, too, for no better reason than the fellow had for killing the splendid Anaconda in the museum, because it was his 'rule to kill snakes wherever found.' A soldier just said: 'Old Jack intends us to tear up all the railroads in the State, and with no tools but our pocket-knives.' They have so far destroyed the Baltimore and Ohio from Hedgesville to near Harper's Ferry, the Winchester and Potomac almost entirely, and now the Manassas Gap from Piedmont to Strasburgh.

"It is when idle in camp that the soldier is a great institution, yet one that must be seen to be appreciated. Pen cannot fully paint the air of cheerful content, care-hilarity, irresponsible loungings, and practical spirit of jesting that 'obtains,' ready to seize on any odd circumstance in its licensed levity. A 'cavalryman' comes rejoicing in immense top-boots, for which in fond pride he had invested full forty dollars of pay; at once the cry from a hundred voices follows him along the line: 'Come up out o' them boots!—come out!—too soon to go into winter quarters! I know you're in thar!—see your arms stickin' out!' A bumpkin rides by in an uncommonly big hat, and is frightened at the shout: 'Come down out o' that hat! Come down! 'Tan't no use to say you an't up there; I see your legs hanging out!' A fancy staff officer was horrified at the irreverent reception of his nicely-twisted moustache—as he heard from behind innumerable trees: 'Take them mice out o' yer mouth!—take 'em out!—no use to say they an't thar —see their tails hanging out!' Another, sporting immense whiskers, was urged to 'Come out of that bunch of har!

I know your in thar! I see your ears a working!' Sometimes a rousing cheer is heard in the distance, it is explained: 'Boys, look out!—here comes old Stonewall, or an old
hare, one or t'other'—they being about the only individuals
who invariably bring down the house.

"And yet there are no better specimens of the earnest,
true soldier, than the men of this brigade. It is known in
the army, if not in print, as the 'fighting brigade.' It is
now constituted of the Thirteenth, Twenty-fifth, Thirty-first,
Forty-fourth, Forty-seventh, Fifty-second, and Fifty-eighth
Virginia regiments—the Twelfth Georgia, one of the most
gallant regiments in the service, having, to the regret of all
their old comrades of 'the mountain brigade,' been transferred. The brigade has been represented, by some of its regiments, in nearly every battle-field in Virginia—in North-west
Virginia, in the Valley, on the Peninsula, around Richmond,
from Cedar Hills to Manassas plains, at Harper's Ferry, and
when reduced to scarce five hundred men, and surrounded
by overwhelming numbers, it fought a bloody way clear out
through the Yankee lines at Sharpsburgh. Four of its brigadiers have been wounded in the service. Generals Ed.
Johnson, Elzey, Stuart, and Early. Five of the regiments
above named were united in one command under General
Ed. Johnson, whose conspicuous bravery at Greenbrier, Al-
leghany, and McDowell, has never lost its example upon his
men. The Thirteenth and Forty-ninth Virginia have been
since united with it. It is at present commanded by Colonel J. A. Walker, of the Thirteenth, a gallant officer and

courteous gentleman, who has well deserved a brigadier's commission.

"But the whole day of camp-life is not yet described; the night remains, and latterly it is no unusual scene, as the gloaming gathers, to see a group quietly collect beneath the dusky shadows of the forest trees—'God's first temples'—whence soon arise the notes of some familiar hymn, awaking memories of childhood and of home. The youthful chaplain in earnest tones tells his holy mission; another hymn is heard, and by the waning light of the pine torches, the weird-like figures of the grouped soldiers are seen reverently moving to the night's repose. The deep bass-drum beats taps—the sounds die out in all the camps, save at times the sweet strains from the band of the Fifth Stonewall regiment in a neighboring grove, till they, too, fade away into the stilly night, and soon

> 'The soldiers lie peacefully dreaming,
>   Their tents in the rays of the clear autumn moon,
>   Or the light of the watchfires are gleaming;
>   A tremulous sigh as the gentle night wind
>   Through the forest leaves slowly is creeping,
>   While the stars up above with their glittering eyes
>   Keep guard, for the army is sleeping.'"

During these days, General Jackson had his headquarters near Bunker's Hill, and was often seen moving to and fro among his troops, on his old sorrel horse, and with his old uniform. He was always greeted with cheers by his men, and "Old Jack"—a name by which he had now become

universally known—was immensely popular. Nothing delighted the soldiers so much as being distinguished by
the General's notice.

" I say," cried one of the " boys " to his comrade, " I've
seen the General this morning."

" Well, what of that ?　So did I, when he rode out from
headquarters."

" Ah ! but he spoke to *me*—stopped and talked to me as
he passed our camp."

" Oh! yes; you think you'll get me to believe that mighty
quick."

" I'll swear he did; stopped and had quite a talk with
me."

" Now, then, what did the General have to say to *you*,
I'd like to know ? " said the half-doubtful and half-jealous
comrade."

" Why, he asked me what I was doing in that orchard
over yonder."

" A-ha ! now you're caught; and what did Old Stonewall
say then ? "

" Said he expected his men to have respect to their neigh-
bor's property, and told me to march right out."

The reserved and uncommunicative habits of Jackson
were not at first very popular among his officers, and some
disaffection was known to prevail in consequence.　Discipline had been carried so far, that a prominent officer is said
to have been put under arrest on one occasion, and to have
had his sword taken from him, because he had permitted

his men to halt for refreshment, when Jackson had ordered them on a march; which indignity could not for a long time be forgiven. His own example overcame this evil; if he called on his men for self-denial, he was the first to practise it. If he was taciturn regarding his plans, he was ready in sympathy, prompt in execution, and his success soon won for him unlimited confidence. It was said that the activity of his army insured less sickness among his men than any other army of the South. "Wrapped in his blanket, he throws himself down on the leaves to catch a few minutes' repose. He cares nothing for good quarters and dainty fare, and if hungry, will stop and ask permission to share the homely meal his men are cooking, and he is as calm in the midst of a hurricane of bullets, as when in the pew of his church at Lexington. On one occasion, in the midst of an engagement, while writing an order, a shell struck and shattered the tree beneath which he sat, without arresting the movement of his pencil, or seeming to attract his attention.'

During the pursuit of General Banks down the Valley, the Stonewall Brigade passed through their native counties without either asking or receiving the privilege of halting to shake hands with their dear ones at home, though most of them had been absent for about a year from the time of their first enlistment. The strictness of their discipline was a thorough barrier to all such indulgence.

The old Stonewall Brigade, the toils which the hardy fellows who composed it had to undergo, the trials which

13*

they had to overcome, and the glories which they achieved, are characteristically depicted in the following remarks from the pen of a writer in a Southern journal:

"The laws of the human body seemed to have been reversed for these men. They marched, and fought, and triumphed, like war-machines, which felt no need of rest, or food, or sleep. In one day they marched from Harper's Ferry to Strasburgh, nearly fifty miles. On the advance to Romney they walked—many without shoes—over roads so slippery with ice that men were falling and their guns going off all along the column—and at night lay down, without blankets, on the snow, with no camp-fires and no food.

"At the first great battle of Manassas they were nearly starved, but fought with desperation. At the last battles there I saw them by the road-side, where they had halted, and one of my friends, a brave young officer of the command, thanked me for a biscuit.

"The very rapidity of their marches separates them from all soldier-comforts—often from their very blankets, however cold the weather; and any other troops but these and their Southern comrades would long since have mutinied and demanded bread and rest. But the shadow of disaffection never flitted over forehead in that command. Whatever discontent may be felt at times at the want of attention on the part of subordinate officers to their necessities, the 'long roll' has only to be beaten—they have only to see the man in the old faded uniform appear, and hunger, cold, fatigue, are forgotten. The Old Brigade is ready—

'Here!' is the answer to the roll-call, all along the line—and though the eye is dull from want of food and rest, the arm is strong and the bayonet is sharp and bright. Before those bayonets no foe shall stand—to pass them is to advance over the bodies of dead heroes, grasping still the trusty musket, even in death.

"The campaigns of the Valley; the great flank movement of the Chickahominy; the masterly advance upon Manassas in the rear of Pope—these are the fadeless glories of the Old Brigade. Their path has been strewed all over with battles. Incredible have been their marches; countless their combats—almost always against overpowering numbers. The scythe of death has mowed down whole ranks of them; but the Old Brigade still marches on and fights and conquers. The war-worn veterans still confront the foe, though the thinned ranks tell the tale of their glories and their losses. Many brave souls have poured out their blood and fallen; but they are conquerors and more than conquerors, in the world's great eye. The comrades of these heroes hold their memory sacred, and have offered bloody sacrifices to their manes. 'Steady! Close up!' were the last words echoed in the dying ears—and the aim of the survivors was only more steady, the charge with the bayonet more deadly.

"Those survivors may be pardoned if they tell their children, when the war is ended, that they fought under Jackson, in the 'Old Stonewall Brigade.' They may be pardoned even if they boast of their exploits — their wonderful marches—their constant and desperate combats—the skui and nerve which snatched victory from the jaws of defeat, and, even when they were retiring before overwhelming numbers, made it truly better that the foe had 'ne'er been born,' than meet their bayonet charge.

"In speaking of this veteran legion, 'praise is virtue.' Their history is blazoned all over with glory. They are 'happy names, beloved children'—the favorites of fame, if not of fortune. In their dingy uniforms, lying stretched beneath the pines, or by the road-side, they are the mark of many eyes which see them not—the absorbing thought in the breast of beauty, and the idols of the popular heart. In line before the enemy, with their bristling bayonets, they are the terror of the foe, and the life-guard of their dear old mother, Virginia."

www.ingramcontent.com/pod-product-compliance
Lightning Source LLC
Chambersburg PA
CBHW030944110726
47900CB00004B/1129